FALLEN CREED

Prairie Wind Publishing
Omaha, Nebraska

FALLEN CREED

Attention: Permissions Coordinator
Prairie Wind Publishing
15418 Weir Street
Box 207
Omaha, NE 68137

Ordering Information:
Quantity sales. Special discounts are available on quantity purchases by corporations, associations, and libraries. For information, please email the Sales Department at sales@pwindpub.com

Interior design and formatting: Prairie Wind Publishing
Book cover design: Prairie Wind Publishing & Shae Marcu
Jacket photograph: Robsonphoto (ShutterStock)

First Edition

ISBN: 978-1-7320064-3-0 Hardcover
ISBN: 978-1-7320064-4-7 eBook
ISBN: 978-1-7320064-8-5 Paperback

Printed in the United States of America
10   9   8   7   6   5   4   3   2

DEDICATION:

In Memory of my sweet boys:

Duncan
August 2005 — October 2020
and
Boomer
October 2008 — December 2021

Rescue best friends, now eternal buddies.

Also
In Memory of **my boy, Scout**
(March 1998 — May 2014)
who is the *true inspiration* for this series.

ALSO BY ALEX KAVA

RYDER CREED SERIES

Breaking Creed
Silent Creed
Reckless Creed
Lost Creed
Desperate Creed
Hidden Creed

MAGGIE O'DELL SERIES

A Perfect Evil
Split Second
The Soul Catcher
At The Stroke of Madness
A Necessary Evil
Exposed
Black Friday
Damaged
Hotwire
Fireproof
Stranded
Before Evil

THE STAND-ALONE NOVELS

Whitewash
One False Move

NOVELLA ORIGINALS WITH
ERICA SPINDLER AND J. T. ELLISON

Slices of Night
Storm Season

SHORT STORY COLLECTION

Off the Grid

FALLEN CREED

ALEX KAVA

"Fall down seven times,
Stand up eight."
—*Japanese Proverb*

1

Monday, October 4
Central Nebraska

"You need to get out of the house!"

"Who is this?" Libby Homes didn't recognize the high-pitched voice. It was a woman, possibly a girl. No caller ID registered. She pulled the phone away for a quick recheck. UNKNOWN CALLER.

"You need to leave. Now!"

The panic and urgency were contagious. Libby shivered before realizing her hands were shaking, too.

"How did you get this number?"

"It doesn't matter."

"Who are you?" She tried again.

"There's no time for that. You might have only an hour. Go. Now!"

"I don't understand."

"I'm trying to help you." Before Libby could ask anything else, the woman added, in almost a whisper, "He knows where you are."

The caller didn't need to explain who "he" was. An ice-water chill slid down Libby's back.

"I know because I'm running away from him, too."

Then the line went dead.

Libby spun around, eyes darting everywhere, almost as if she expected him to be standing behind her. Panic surged through her veins. She paced the living room, staying back from the windows, all the while straining to see out of them. Instinctively, she rushed from room to room, craning her neck, crouching and stealing glimpses without moving a curtain. Without getting too close.

How could she be so stupid to let her guard down? Deep down, she knew it was only a matter of time before he came for her.

She needed to see as many views as possible. The driveway stretched forever. The tool shed and barn created long shadows. Behind the house, the woods were usually too thick to reveal anything except the leaves had been falling, and if she used her binoculars, she knew she could see all the way across the river.

To the west, the sinking sun lit up the vast expanse of the cornfields, setting it ablaze in an orange glow. The stalks stood too tall and too close to see over or between, yellowish brown row after row. They could easily conceal a person.

Suddenly, Libby realized she was racing through the house on tiptoes as if someone might hear her. She tried to catch her breath, only to find that she was holding it.

Breathe! Think! Settle down.

She gulped air, hiccupped and stopped in her tracks. She could not afford to hyperventilate. Couldn't allow the panic to consume her.

She checked the time. Out of habit, she wondered if she should call Kristin to cover her shift. Except Kristin had covered for her last Thursday, and Libby hadn't heard from her since. Libby believed in repaying her favors before asking for another.

What was she thinking? There wasn't any time for texting.

You need to leave. Now! The urgency in the woman's voice had been genuine. The fear was palpable.

Just then, something in the woods caught her eye. There was a streak of red that didn't belong. As quickly as it appeared, it disappeared.

She needed to get out. The panic triggered so many emotions, many of them she thought she had carefully locked away. And here they were, driving her, propelling her all over again. All her hard work and nothing had changed. She still wasn't prepared. She was still vulnerable, a sitting duck in the middle of a wide-open expanse where no one would even hear her scream.

"Guess you're not so smart after all, Libby," she admonished herself. Yet another old habit seeped to the surface. It wouldn't take long for the other destructive tendencies to rear their ugly heads.

She sneaked down the hallway to her bedroom. Staying away from the windows, she slid along the wall then flung open her closet door. She dove to her knees, pushing and shoving shoes and boxes. She had forgotten how deep the space was. Her stomach flipped with a fresh surge of panic.

Was it gone? Had Nora found it?

She wouldn't have taken it. She wouldn't do that. If she found it, she'd be disappointed in Libby, but Nora would never confiscate it.

And then her fingers found a canvas strap. She tugged until the backpack came free, out from underneath the stack of folded blankets and pillows that hid it.

Libby dragged it into the middle of her bedroom floor, still on her hands and knees, crawling alongside it. Her fingers shook as she yanked zippers back. Her hands dived in, feeling around and taking stock. She couldn't trust her eyes alone to do the inventory, especially since they kept darting up to the windows.

Her chest already ached, and she felt lightheaded. Sitting back on her haunches, she tried to slow her breathing. She closed her eyes and listened, straining to hear over her pounding heart, listening for sounds that didn't belong.

Slow down, she told herself.

"You might have only an hour," the woman had told her.

Libby made a mental checklist then stood on wobbly knees. She hated that after this much time he could still make her physically terrified just by mentioning him.

Stop it! He'll win if you're weak and unprepared. That's exactly what he's hoping to find.

Before she left the bedroom, she changed clothes and shoes. The sun would be down soon. Despite her body slick with sweat, she added another layer and stashed a few more items into the backpack. She took what she needed from her bathroom.

A brief pause in front of the door across the hall took precious moments. She admonished herself again. There was no time to worry about respect and privacy. No second-guessing about stealing something that didn't belong to her.

She went into the master bedroom. She knew exactly which drawer to open and where to dig beneath the stack of T-shirts. Her fingers found the metal, curled around the grip and pulled out the gun, folding back and smoothing the clothes.

Satisfied, she headed to the kitchen, stopping at cupboards and drawers to gather the rest of her list. Her eyes surveyed every window, every sliver between blinds and curtains. Already she was assessing from which direction he'd come. The driveway would be too easy, but she checked the road, stretching to see as far as she could in both directions.

She slipped by a bookcase, and her eyes caught on a framed photo. There was no time to be sentimental, and yet she stopped. She grabbed the frame, worked the back and slipped the photo out gently, tucking it into a side pocket of her backpack. She returned the frame to its spot, leaving its glass down.

At the side door, she took one last look around at the one place that had truly felt like home. She tightened the backpack across her shoulders and swept a long, measured glance over the back property.

Then she took in a deep breath and left.

2

Ryder Creed had grown used to driving by yellow cornfields and green pastures. There was something very soothing about this landscape. Geese filled the big blue sky. Tall cranes feasted between the rows of the few harvested fields.

The paved two-lane needed repair. The white-line edges crumbled away with the broken asphalt. Gold and rust-colored grasses filled deep ditches. It was mesmerizing how the tall grass moved, almost as if something hidden inside was alive and raced alongside his Jeep.

"We're definitely not in Florida anymore," Creed said, glancing into the rearview mirror.

The Jack Russell terrier's ears flapped in the breeze. Grace sat on the center of the bench behind him so she could see between the front captain's seats. She loved the half-rolled windows. Her nose poked at the scents flooding the Jeep's interior. The Nebraska air was cool, crisp and dry. Yesterday morning, when they left the Florida Panhandle, it had been a sultry eighty-five degrees.

Creed recognized the farm a quarter mile away. It wasn't difficult. A variety of law enforcement vehicles filled the front yard. Ten feet in, a sheriff's department SUV blocked the driveway's entrance.

He glanced at the rearview mirror again. Grace already recognized that they were close to their designation. Her eyes focused forward, and she sniffed the air with purpose.

"Almost there, girl," he told her.

Creed and his friend, Hannah Washington, owned a fifty-acre facility where they rescued, housed and trained scent dogs. Grace had become more than Creed's favorite. She was his partner, eager to learn and excited to work. Together, they tracked the missing and the dead. She sniffed out hidden explosives and drugs. She could detect C. diff and the bird flu. Whatever Creed asked, Grace searched and found. Today would be a first for both.

The deputy wore mirrored aviator sunglasses and moved his hands to his hips when he noticed Creed's Jeep slow down. By the time Creed pulled into the driveway, the man had pushed his shoulders back. His right hand inched closer to his holster. He waved at Creed to back out and move on. Creed shifted into park and rolled down his window, but he knew better than to get out of the vehicle.

The deputy approached. He wasn't happy.

"You need to move along," he told Creed. "Nothing to see here."

Creed held his ID wallet out the window, keeping his other hand on the top of the steering wheel.

"I'm a K9 handler. Your guys are expecting me."

The deputy cocked his head to the side, not to get a look at the ID but to examine the front of the Jeep. The state of Florida required only a back license plate. Creed was used to the blank front, but sometimes it threw off law enforcement in other states.

Finally, the man came in closer, bending enough to get a glimpse of Grace sitting on the back bench. That probably didn't help. Creed could see his skepticism even without getting a look at the deputy's eyes. Most people still expected a big dog: German shepherd, Labrador or Golden retriever. Typically, Jack Russell terriers weren't viewed as scent dogs.

Hardly any of Creed's dogs fit the standard description, so he was used to the scrutiny.

Up close, the deputy looked young, clean-shaven, with pockmarks from a recent bout of acne. His hair was military short, his uniform pressed and clean.

"Who did you say you are?" he asked, now taking the ID wallet from Creed's extended hand.

"Ryder Creed. I'm with K9 CrimeScents." He pulled the bill of his ball cap down in case the deputy hadn't noticed the logo imprinted across the front.

"Hey Archie, he's good." A deep voice yelled from the front yard, and the deputy's head jerked in its direction. A guy in a black ball cap, black T-shirt, blue jeans and shoulder holster waved a "come on" gesture. "He's with me. We're waiting for him."

"Oh sure. Yes, sir." He handed Creed back his ID wallet without a word or a glance and headed to his SUV. He gave Creed a liberal berth, edging his own vehicle into the tall grass that lined the driveway.

Creed couldn't help smiling. Tommy Pakula had an air of confidence and authority even before he was promoted from Omaha homicide detective to special investigator for Nebraska's Human Trafficking Task Force. It was almost a year ago that Creed met Pakula. If it hadn't been for the man's gut instinct and dogged tactics, they might have never found Creed's sister, Brodie.

Pakula met him as he parked the Jeep under one of the huge cottonwoods. As Creed opened the tailgate and started getting his gear, Pakula greeted Grace.

"You drive all night?"

"We stopped in Omaha. Got a room, some rest, some breakfast."

"Next time, let me know," Pakula told him. "You can crash at my house, if you don't mind a houseful of women."

He remembered Pakula had three or four daughters.

"Already used to that," Creed assured him. At home, women usually outnumbered him.

"How's Brodie doing?"

"She's good."

"She's a tough young woman."

"That's what *she* keeps telling me," Creed said.

He opened his daypack and found a handful of yellow-wrapped candies scattered on top. He swiped a hand over his jaw.

Brodie.

Recently, she'd learned how to order from the Internet. The Butterscotch candy was one of their grandmother's favorites. Every visit they'd find her crystal candy dishes filled with something different: lemon drops, Bit-o-Honey, brightly colored jelly beans, and assorted flavors of taffy. He imagined he'd find others at the bottom of his bag.

Two months ago, Brodie had earned a paid position at their training facility. Hannah insisted, and Creed agreed. Brodie had taken on not only helping with the kennel chores but was now doing water training exercises with their working dogs. Hannah was teaching her how to manage her new bank account, but it was interesting to see the items she chose to spend money on. Socks, books, dog and cat treats and most recently, Butterscotch candy because they reminded her of their grandmother.

Creed wasn't used to reminiscing. Of course, he wasn't. He'd spent his teenage years on the road with his mother, searching for Brodie, going from city to city following a sighting or a tip and always hoping to find her. In later years, he hoped only to find answers.

But it made him smile when Brodie helped him remember good memories, shoving the horrible ones to the back of his mind. Slowly, she was teaching him that not all of their past, their family history, had to be mired in pain and regret.

This operation, and returning to Nebraska, was something Creed insisted he be a part of. It was his way of giving back, donating his time and Grace's expertise. Last year, this operation and Tommy Pakula helped find his sister. This time, maybe he could help another family find a missing loved one.

"I'm hoping your girl can do her magic," Pakula said with a tilt of his chin to the clapboard farmhouse. "Name's Freddie Mason. Seems like an ordinary guy. Nice place. Never ceases to amaze me how they can blend into a community and hide in plain sight."

"What have you found so far?" Creed asked. It helped to know what devices had already been recovered and from where, in case Grace could still pick up their scent.

"His laptop was on the kitchen counter. Cell phone was in his back pocket. Neither have diddly squat on them. Of course, our cyber guys will dig deeper into them. Right now, he's in the backyard, out of our way. O'Dell's been sweet-talking him, playing good cop to my bad cop, but so far, we can't seem to crack him."

"O'Dell" was FBI agent Maggie O'Dell. She and Pakula had worked together before. Actually, the three of them had been a part of the same operation that ultimately saved Brodie.

Creed and Maggie went back almost three years. They had worked together enough times that the two of them had developed a friendship. No, that wasn't even close. It was more than a friendship. It was complicated, sometimes frustrating, but lately he realized he couldn't imagine not having her in his life, no matter the limitations.

They talked and texted frequently these days, but he hadn't seen her since June. That was the part he didn't like. She lived in Virginia. Creed had a home and a successful business in the Florida Panhandle.

"So let me get this straight," Pakula said, interrupting Creed's thoughts. "Grace might be able to sniff out any external hard drives, jump drives, SIM cards? We've already searched through drawers, cabinets and boxes. You name it. And we've found zilch. These things are so small it's literally like looking for a needle in a haystack."

"This is a first for her. For both of us, but she's done great in our training sessions."

She stood before him on the open tailgate, wagging. She knew they were talking about her, but she waited patiently for him to put on her working vest. Dogs were creatures of habit, so Creed tried to take advantage of that. For a multi-scent dog like Grace, he used a particular vest or collar for each scent.

He also made sure he had a specific name or command for each scent he wanted her to find. He used "fish" for drugs, because it was less likely to cause dealers to run in a crowded airport or through a border stop if they believed the dog was only searching for agricultural contraband instead of drugs.

But sometimes, because Grace was a multi-scent dog, she couldn't help but alert to other scents present at the scene. Other scents she'd been trained for, even if it wasn't the one Creed had asked her to find. Last time he was in Nebraska, she was supposed to lead them to a body buried in a pasture. Instead, she had tried to alert them to the explosives planted over a grave of roadkill. A deputy lost his hand. Creed was lucky, with only a few broken ribs.

"O'Dell's sources believe this guy has a catalog," Pakula was telling him.

Creed glanced over his shoulder. Pakula's eyes looked off toward the back of the house where cornfields stretched as far as you could see. Did he expect the suspect to bolt? How easy would it be to get lost inside the row after row of tall corn?

"And you think he has it stored on an electronic device?"

"Nobody keeps something like that in the Cloud."

Weeks ago, when Maggie talked to Creed about being a part of this operation, she was already calling it Operation Fallen Stars. Before she explained, he knew she meant "fallen stars" represented the missing, some of them children. They hoped to recover as many as possible before all leads burned out. But when Pakula mentioned a "catalog," Creed immediately felt a knot tightening in his gut. What the hell was wrong with people?

Times like this he tried to be grateful that Brodie hadn't fallen into a human trafficking ring, though she had come close. Her captor, a woman named Iris Malone, had grown tired of Brodie constantly trying to escape. Just days before they found her, Brodie had been exiled. He didn't like to think about how close she had come to being lost forever in that hidden world. Not that what she had endured for sixteen years wasn't bad enough.

"You okay?" Pakula asked.

Grace licked Creed's hand, and only then did he realize he'd stopped. "Hard to imagine someone puts together a catalog."

"People think human trafficking is about the border and coyotes smuggling women and children over. They don't realize how many locals go missing. Teenage runaways, drug addicts, kids trying to escape abusive home lives only to find themselves trapped in a worse nightmare. If that isn't bad enough, we've got parents selling their own kids. There certainly are some messed up people."

Pakula paused, and Creed followed his eyes. Maggie came from around the back of the house with a short, thick-chested man walking a pace in front of her.

Grace's tail wagged right at the same time Creed noticed the uptick in his pulse. Maggie looked their way and lifted her chin, a subtle gesture acknowledging their presence but serious and focused, not daring to take her attention off of the man. He was as tall as Maggie, but stocky with bowed legs that made his walk look more like a wobble from side to side. He was barefooted, causing him to step gingerly through the patchy landscape that took the place of his lawn. It made Creed check the ground around the Jeep. Sure enough, some of the yellow-brown tufts had sandburs.

"These scumbags all know each other. They look out for one another," Pakula said. "But that's changing. Lately, there appears to be a turf war brewing. We hit a place outside of North Platte yesterday. A car dealership. By day, the owner is an upstanding guy in the community. By night, he's just another one of these scumbags. Delivering used cars for Johns to test drive, and sometimes—surprise, surprise—there's a girl along for the ride."

Creed shook his head.

"Anyway, that guy led us here. Gave up his buddy pretty easily." Pakula rubbed his jaw. "This one feels too easy."

"You think you're being set up?" Creed asked.

"We were here early." He glanced at his watch. "If something was going to happen, I think it would have by now. Maybe they're looking at ways to knock each other out of business. One more reason we can't afford to screw up. I'm glad you and Grace are here."

"We'll check the house."

Creed finished packing his daypack. Grace was getting antsy. She wanted to greet Maggie and was pacing along the Jeep's windows for a better view. He realized he was anxious to see Maggie, too. She looked good. She always looked good. Her FBI ball cap was pulled down low over her brow. He could see the flash of auburn ponytail. She wore a black T-shirt like Pakula, hiking boots, and blue jeans. And yes, she looked good in blue jeans.

Suddenly, Freddie Mason became agitated as Creed lifted Grace from the Jeep to the ground.

"Get that frickin' dog out of here," he yelled, his arm swinging up, his finger punctuating the air.

The wobble became a trot, ignoring his bare feet. He hurried across the yard. Maggie caught up to him quickly. She grabbed his arm, and he shoved her off.

Big mistake.

The next time she grabbed his arm, she twisted it up behind him, and the man instantly dropped to the ground. She placed a knee in his back then looked up at Pakula and Creed. She lifted her chin at them again, but this time, she was smiling.

3

In Afghanistan, Creed and his fellow Marine K9 handlers often called their dogs truth detectors. He remembered one incident in particular, a dusty, sunbaked afternoon. They were searching a village for an informant who had mysteriously disappeared.

They told Creed they had shown a photograph of the man, but the villagers shook their heads without taking a glance. The unit had been there for almost an hour before Creed and Rufus arrived. The presence of the big Labrador stopped people in their tracks, widened their eyes, and refreshed their memories. It was as if the dog were a magic talisman that could read their minds.

So Creed wasn't surprised that Freddie Mason didn't want Grace inside his house. He hadn't resisted law enforcement officers from the county sheriff's department, state patrol and FBI. He figured he had fooled all of them. But a dog, even a small Jack Russell terrier like Grace, Freddie knew enough to be worried.

"You can't bring that dirty mutt into my house," the man still protested, grunting the words out. His face had gone red and twisted in pain as Maggie kept his arm behind him. Creed noticed Freddie didn't challenge or resist the vice-grip as much as he was resisting Grace.

"We have a search warrant," Pakula reminded the man.

"It doesn't give you a right to bring a mangy dog into my house."

"You're forgetting, Freddie. I've already been inside your house. You can't be worried about this clean, well-behaved dog messing it up. We've already done that. If anything, I might need to be worried the dog doesn't catch something being exposed to your filth."

"I don't want that dog in my house."

Pakula gestured to a deputy who had come out the front door when he heard the ruckus.

"Deputy Trent's going to help you calm down," Pakula told Freddie as he nodded to the deputy then pointed to the handcuffs on his utility belt.

Freddie was still yelling and arguing with Pakula about calling a lawyer as Maggie led Creed and Grace into the house, letting the screen door slam behind them.

"How was your drive?" she asked with a touch of her hand on his arm.

The entrance was small, boxed in, and secluded. Up close, he could see she had hardly broken a sweat from the ruckus with Freddie, but Creed got a distracting whiff of her coconut shampoo. Before he could answer, Maggie squatted down to pet Grace.

"It was a good trip. I forgot how nice and cool the weather is up here."

She stood back up, facing him now and smiling. "Don't get used to it. There's a cold front moving in."

He wanted to kiss her. Something in her eyes told him she was thinking the same thing. It had been too long since he had stood this close to her.

"And snow," a man said as he came around the corner.

"Snow?" Creed asked, pretending the guy hadn't just interrupted an intimate moment. He and Maggie had never really discussed it, but both of them had been careful to keep their professional lives separate from whatever it was they were feeling for each other. "I haven't seen snow since I was a teenager."

"You haven't missed much," the man told him. He pushed his fingers through a thick mop of silver hair. He wore a crisp navy blue shirt with the shirtsleeves rolled up, blue jeans and worn leather work boots. "It's white and cold and can make a mess of things. You must be the K9 handler."

He thumbed over his shoulder as two uniformed deputies came around the corner, excusing themselves without introduction as they headed out the front door.

"They're clearing out," the man said. Creed moved Grace into the arched doorway of the room the deputies had just exited. Still, the entrance was tight enough they had to squeeze past with their equipment, evidence bags and collection kits.

When the screen door slapped behind them, Maggie made the official introduction. "Ted, this is Ryder Creed and Grace. Ryder, this is Ted Spencer. He's the Clay County Sheriff. He's part of Pakula's team."

"Hey there, Grace," Spencer said as he offered his hand. "Agent O'Dell's been telling us a lot about you." Then to Creed he said, "We've tossed the place. Flipped ceiling tiles. Checked heating vents. Pipes under the sink. Toilet tank. Even ran an electronic gizmo. Battery died after three false readings."

"The one thing about Grace," Creed said as he glanced down at her impatiently shuffling, "her battery never seems to die."

"Hold on a minute," Spencer raised his hand and grabbed for his back pocket. He glanced at the cell phone. "I need to take this." He walked a few steps down the hall as he tapped the screen.

"Are you doing collection?" Creed asked Maggie, wanting to get started but not wanting her to leave.

"I think Pakula will insist on bagging anything you find," Maggie said. "I'll go change places with him. Besides, Freddie was just warming up to me before he saw Grace." She said this last part with an uncharacteristic grin. With her back now to Spencer, she put her hand on his arm again and said, "It's really good to see you."

"Sorry about that," Spencer said, marching back while he slipped the phone in his pocket. "My wife."

"I'll go get Pakula," Maggie told Spencer, and she headed out the door.

Creed thought maybe Spencer would follow her. Maggie knew he liked to work a scene without an audience.

"My wife worries too much," Spencer said, still referring to the phone call. "We took in a young woman about six months ago. Apparently, she didn't come home last night after work. I keep telling Nora she's not a kid, you know. But my wife worries."

Creed nodded, glanced out the door after Maggie. He never understood how some people shared their private lives with complete strangers. He had a difficult enough time sharing details of his life with those closest to him.

Spencer rubbed a hand over his face like maybe he recognized Creed's sudden discomfort. But he didn't make a move to leave.

"So, I've seen how cadaver dogs work," he said instead as he crossed his arms and took a good look at Grace. "I know it's the decomposition smells that they're trained to find. But I don't quite understand how they can sniff out electronic devices. Agent O'Dell said your dog might be able to find something as small as a microSD card? Those things are less than a millimeter thick. Smaller than a postage stamp."

"All electronic devices that have memory storage capacity have a chemical coating," Creed told him. "It's called triphenylphosphine oxide. That's a mouthful, so we call it TPPO. The coating prevents overheating. The chemical is cheap. It's effective and all companies use it for everything: microSD cards, thumb drives, smartphones, computers, external hard drives and even smart watches. It's the smell of that chemical that Grace has been trained to sniff out."

"And it's strong enough to smell even on those tiny cards?"

"Dogs can detect odors in the parts-per-trillion range. We know they can smell thresholds of chemicals that different technologies can't even measure."

"Do you mind if I watch?"

Creed did mind. But Grace didn't, and she was getting antsy. There was something about Ted Spencer that Creed liked, even if he was a bit too willing to share how much his wife worries.

"As long as you stay back and stay quiet."

"Sure, sure. No problem. It's just that we spent the last three hours searching. I really can't imagine her finding anything."

Creed leaned down and snapped the leash off Grace's vest. Her nose was already up, sampling the air. To Creed the house smelled with a mixture of fried bacon and the scent of stale marijuana smoke. But Grace's nose could go beyond those.

"Grace, show me Tippo." It was a lot easier to say than garbling the acronym TPPO.

She raced across the living room, zigzagging around shoes left where they were taken off and a coffee table littered with takeout containers.

"I'm surprised she—" Spencer stopped himself before Creed shot a warning glance.

Without being distracted by any of the clutter, Grace went directly to a floor-to-ceiling bookcase. It was built into the wall, real hardwood, maybe walnut. At one time, it probably matched the crown molding that had been painted over several times and removed in some spots.

Freddie Mason didn't look like a reader to Creed, but he had an eclectic library that included blockbuster bestsellers along with the classics and some old textbooks. On closer inspection, Creed could see the markings on the spine. They looked like old library books.

He glanced back at Spencer, who only shrugged, trying to abide by the rules of keeping quiet.

Grace sat at Creed's feet. Her nose poked the air. Her eyes met his.

Ordinarily, he'd never train his dog to alert by touching the target scent. But this was different, and Grace understood that this was an exception.

He picked her up in his arms. A few inches over six feet tall, he could lift her to the top shelf. That wasn't where her nose was going. She was straining to the right and focused down. He leaned her to the place she wanted, and almost immediately, she tapped her nose to the spine of a thick blue cover.

Creed put Grace back on the floor. He tugged a pair of latex gloves from his daypack. Without looking, he could feel Spencer had edged closer to this side of the room and now stood just feet away. With a gloved hand, Creed pulled the book carefully from where it was squeezed in. He held it up for Spencer to see.

"Did I already miss something?" Pakula asked from behind them as he came in the front door.

"Shakespeare," Creed told him.

He waited for Pakula to join them. Then he let the book fall open in his hands. He flipped a few pages to where he could see a slight bulge. Two microSD cards were tucked deep into the middle of the book.

"Well, I'll be damned," Spencer said.

Pakula glanced at the other books still on the shelves. "Do we need to go through all of these?"

Creed was already reaching into his daypack for Grace's reward. She had alerted specifically to just the one volume, but it wouldn't hurt to lift her up again.

"Let me ask Grace," he told Pakula.

When Creed looked down, Grace was gone. He could hear her toenails clicking against tiles in another room.

4

Inside the kitchen, the scent of bacon was strong enough to make Creed's stomach growl. Pakula's team had obviously interrupted Freddie's breakfast. Butter pooled in the middle of the toast. Scrambled eggs coated the cast-iron skillet. And on a paper towel, slices of crispy bacon were left untouched.

But none of these smells distracted Grace.

It was one reason Creed didn't use food as a reward for any of his scent detection dogs. Most handlers didn't. When he decided to add electronic storage devices to Grace's repertoire, he was surprised to find many ESD K9s were trained with food as their reward. Some recommended that the dog didn't get to eat unless it found the requisite hidden device each day. Creed questioned the method, but was told it encouraged the handlers, as well as the dogs, to keep training every day.

That made sense. But to Creed, it seemed cruel. Many of the dogs that found their way to K9 CrimeScents had been discarded or abandoned by their previous owners. Some, like Grace, had been on their own for long enough that they were skin and bones, scraping for what food they could find. To make their daily meal a reward for work rendered was something Creed would not even consider. Every dog in his kennel, whether working or not, deserved to be fed.

Still, it surprised him when Grace could ignore and put aside the heavenly scent of bacon. Instead, she sniffed around the closed doors of cabinets until she came to one at the end of the counter. She stopped and looked up at him over her shoulder.

Creed felt Pakula and Spencer close behind him. He still had his latex gloves on and reached for the cabinet doorknob.

"Hold on," Pakula told him. "Let me check that out first."

Creed stood and backed away. He gestured for Grace to do the same while Pakula dug in a small duffle bag his team had left on the far counter. He pulled out a handheld monitor and squeezed past Creed and Grace. As Pakula swept the tool over the edges of the cabinet door, Creed recognized the gadget. It was an ion mobility spectrometer, a detection device that could identify residues associated with explosives. He watched Pakula hesitate at the hinges, and instinctively, Creed scooped up Grace and moved to the other room.

One of the scents Grace was trained to sniff out was explosive material. It took little to remind him of that last trip to Nebraska. The scavenger hunt for dead bodies had ended in an explosion. It was Creed's fault that he didn't read his dog. Grace had done everything she could to warn him.

"We're safe," Pakula said from around the corner.

Even now, Creed fought the knot in his stomach. He needed to be more careful. He should have been the one to think of the possibility. His partner, Hannah, had been nagging him to take some time off. Maybe he needed to consider it before he got someone hurt again…or killed.

Pakula was watching him. From what he knew about the man, nothing much got past him. His eyes caught Creed's, and he only nodded. Spencer didn't notice the exchange. His attention focused on the contents displayed inside the cabinet.

Two shelves were stacked with different boxes of cereal. Creed couldn't help thinking these looked similar to the books in the living room bookcase.

He put Grace on the floor, and she wiggle-hurried to the opened cabinet. She swiped her nose back and forth, then without hesitating she tapped her nose to a box of Cheerios.

"Is that the one, Grace?"

This time she nudged it, deliberately touching only the Cheerios' box and not the Fruit Loops or Corn Flakes on either side. Then she sat down and stared up at him.

Creed glanced back at Pakula.

"My favorite," Pakula said. "Although I like the honey nut ones better than the plain."

The investigator leaned over and grabbed the box with gloved fingers. He opened upper cabinet doors until he found a big plastic bowl. Then he slipped the tab free at the top of the box and gently separated the bag inside from the cardboard outside. There was nothing between the two. Nothing could be seen inside the translucent bag, either.

Taking his time, Pakula parted the opening at the top of the bag and started spilling cereal into the bowl. It didn't take long for a square object to thump free. The cell phone was wrapped tightly in saran wrap.

Pakula said with a smile, "Grace, I owe you a box of kibble."

But Creed already had her dancing for her pink elephant. He tossed it to her. She caught it in mid-air and immediately began squeaking it.

5

Clay County, Nebraska

Anne Brown had finished her rural postal route and decided to take a shortcut back. She had a late afternoon hair appointment at The Strand in Lincoln. It wasn't just a haircut. Dan Macke, the owner, made the thirty minutes feel like a therapy and spa retreat. And boy, did she need it today.

Snow was forecasted, but the morning had been warm and sunny. The leaves had just started to turn colors, and the ditches were filled with tall red and gold grasses. Football season had barely started.

Snow wasn't unusual in October, but as Anne liked to say, "This is Nebraska. If you don't like the weather today, stick around for tomorrow's."

But she hoped the weather forecasters were wrong, not just because it was a bear to drive in and took her twice as long to do her route. Snow this early didn't just mess up the roads. Farmers, including her brother, Ed Rief, hadn't started harvesting yet.

With leaves still on the trees, snow could gather and stack up, causing enough extra weight to crack branches. She still remembered a Halloween storm from years ago that snapped huge branches off one hundred-year-old cottonwoods and river maples. Many of those branches also brought down power lines, snapping them like rubber bands. Electricity had been out for over a week.

Gravel pinged against the undercarriage of her brand new, charcoal colored Jeep. She slowed down. Anne was one of the last given the allowance to buy and use her own vehicle, and it pained her to hear the new Jeep get battered.

The shortcut was rougher than the last time she had taken it. On either side, the cornfields grew tall enough to block her view. If she hadn't slowed down, she probably would have never seen the patch of white in the red grass.

There weren't any driveways or houses for almost a mile, maybe two, but Anne's first thought was that it could be a package or mail that may have gotten blown into the ditch.

She stopped and backed up. Too far. She couldn't see it anymore. There was no other traffic, but she still pulled to the side. She left the engine running as she got out to take a look.

These back road ditches could fool you. The tall grasses betrayed how deep they were. But there had been no rain, so at least she wouldn't end up with mud and water in her shoes.

She backtracked, keeping her eyes focused on the ditch. Now she wondered if it could have been an animal. White or gray, possibly a possum. The grasses waved and rolled back and forth. Just when Anne convinced herself she was wasting time, she saw it.

Something white with black plastic bunched up and flapping around it. The white moved, too. It looked like a piece of clothing. Maybe a bag of garbage someone had thrown from their car.

She turned around and headed back to her vehicle.

What if it wasn't just a bag of garbage?

Her brother, Ed, and her husband, Keith, read a lot of mysteries and thrillers. Keith would probably give her a hard time later that she didn't take a closer look. Interstate 80 was only twenty miles away and ran parallel with this old gravel road. Maybe some drug runner threw out his stash. There had been bank robberies in the state before. Though she would have already heard about it.

Anne stopped and shook her head. Okay, now the curiosity would drive her crazy.

She went back. The slope into the ditch wasn't as steep as she first expected, but she watched her feet and took baby steps, one after another. Without warning, she found herself standing over the bag. This close, she could see a white shirt or jacket had come loose from the black plastic garbage bag.

Something else had fallen out, too. At first glance, it looked like... No, that wasn't possible. She bent down to get a better look, then jerked backwards. She slipped and skidded, losing her balance and sitting against the ditch's incline in the middle of the tall grass. And now she was close enough, there was no denying what she saw.

Fingers! Someone's hand was reaching out of the bag.

It had to be an early Halloween prank, and yet, at the same time she knew it wasn't. Her stomach retched. She gasped and pushed herself away, digging her heels and elbows into the dirt to climb up the ditch. Still, she couldn't peel her eyes away.

The hand wasn't reaching out of the bag. Instead, it had fallen out. Cut at the wrist, it was clearly no longer attached to a body.

6

David Ruben sat behind the steering wheel of the piece of crap SUV. His girls were getting sloppy or lazy. Neither was acceptable. But the junk vehicle was minor to the big frickin' mistake they'd made last week. Perhaps he should take comfort in the fact that they wanted to make up for it.

Before he could mention a fitting punishment, they had started plotting and planning their redemption. He liked that. He had taught them well. They just needed a bit more experience. Deep down in their souls, Ruben knew the darkness existed. The trick was how to trigger it. And he had become a wizard at triggering darkness.

He pulled the bill of the Huskers' ball cap lower until it tapped his Ray-Ban sunglasses. The sunglasses were a nice surprise. He'd always wanted a pair. Finding these in the glove compartment made up for the crappy SUV. With another glance in the rearview mirror, he had to admit; he looked pretty cool in them. The cap was stupid, but it made him fit in with the locals.

The passenger door opened almost exactly at the same time as the back door on the same side. Two young women slid into the vehicle. He didn't bother to look at either of them. His sunglasses stayed straight ahead. It was always a good idea to make them think he was still disappointed.

"We're taking care of things," the woman beside him said.

He gave a curt nod. She smelled good, but different from when she'd left the vehicle. Those big purses came in handy. He was always interested to see what she had lifted this time. She could afford anything she wanted in the Walmart store. Ruben had made sure of that. But the stealing was an instinct. One of his first lessons—survive or die. It was also one of the best ways for him to find new recruits. He'd walk the aisles watching. He knew how to be invisible. When he'd see a young girl lift something, he'd follow her all the way outside to the parking lot. They never noticed him until he was there, right beside their car.

"I saw what you did."

Their reactions were almost always the same. "Oh my God! Are you a cop?"

In the flood of their relief he'd reel them in, flatter them about their technique.

"How would you like to get paid for what you just did?"

"For real?"

"For real."

It helped that he would have one or two girls with him that looked like them. Funny, they seemed to think that made it safer. It never occurred to them that maybe they should be more afraid of someone who looked like them. More afraid of them than the ordinary, fifty-something-year-old guy who was a little overweight and balding.

He actually liked that they didn't think he looked menacing. They didn't fear him. Instead, they wanted to please him. Sometimes they even asked for their punishment if they knew they'd disappointed him. But Ruben admitted, these two were exceptional students. Some of his finest.

Now inside the cheap-ass SUV, he waited, pretending to watch the assortment of shoppers coming and going. Many of them had their carts piled with bags.

The girl sitting in the back leaned against the front seat. She extended her hand over and jangled a clump of keys. Without moving his head, Ruben slid his hidden eyes up to the mirror. She was grinning as she kept the keys hanging to his side.

"We just need to drive around and find it," she told him.

He glanced at the key fob between her fingers. There were four or five other keys attached to the key chain. She squeezed the "open" button and from somewhere close by Ruben heard the "beep-beep" of a vehicle unlocking its doors.

She did it again, and this time he could see the rear lights blink along with the "beep-beep." The SUV was parked on the end, one aisle across from them. He couldn't tell what model or make, but it looked fairly new, a glossy maroon with chrome bumpers washed clean. It was definitely an upgrade.

They'd need to drive it somewhere else to replace its license plates. They still had a spare set from a vehicle in the long-term parking lot of Lincoln's airport. It was best to stick with plates that matched the state. Less of a reason to stand out. Little things mattered. Made a huge difference. It paid out in the long run, and he'd been getting away with stuff like this for a long time.

He allowed a hint of a smile, a one-side upturn of his mouth that his girls recognized. He was feeling better already. Maybe even a little proud, so he rewarded them with, "Good job."

7

Clay County, Nebraska

Creed opened the windows of his Jeep while Grace had a snack and lapped up water. She knew she was finished for the day, but she still glanced out the windows before she settled down.

She had found one more microSD card upstairs in Freddie Mason's closet. It was in plain sight, too, stuffed into the toe of a brand new pair of hiking boots. The shoes were still in their box. The price tag was hanging from the undone shoestrings.

Grace's finds had given Pakula's team enough to take Freddie in. He kept his distance and Grace away from the man. If Mason had been upset about a dog in his house before, he was now enraged that she had discovered his stashes.

It seemed like a long way to come for only a few hours of work. For Grace, it didn't matter. She loved the game of search and find in exchange for her reward toy. Actually, Creed knew she'd do it just to please him. Grace didn't place different values on the scents she found. Creed praised her with the same level of excitement as any of her other alerts, but he had to admit, these ESD discoveries fell flat with him. They were certainly anti-climatic compared to finding a missing person or recovering a body. Still, he hoped that maybe one device or a memory card would contain the catalog Pakula mentioned.

Catalog.

Creed shook his head. This trafficking stuff was hard to wrap his mind around.

Pakula had handed him directions and a confirmation code for a room at the same hotel the rest of the team was staying. He warned him that there might be some downtime. Pakula's experts needed to review the information they had confiscated from the car dealer and Mason's residence before they decided if, when, and where they did another raid.

Sitting back and waiting was definitely not in Creed's DNA, but he reminded himself that this trip was all about paying back a favor.

Maggie and Pakula waved to the rest of the team as, one by one, they turned their vehicles around and headed out. Spencer was the only one left, pacing the dirt-patched lawn while talking on his cell phone.

"She did real good," Pakula told Creed as he and Maggie joined him at the side of his Jeep. "Did I understand this was her first electronic device search?"

"That's right. But she's a special dog. I think she could learn to detect and find just about anything I asked of her."

Maggie went around back to the open tailgate and petted Grace. "Can I take her for a short walk?" she asked.

Creed saw Grace had her leash in her mouth.

"Sure," he said and smiled. He waited until they were out of earshot before he turned to Pakula. "I owe you an apology for not checking first for explosives."

"Oh, hell no you don't. You brought an ESD dog to the scene. It was our job to make sure everyone was safe. We did a preliminary search. They may have even wanded the cabinets, but it's better to be safe than... Well, you know."

"I do. Thanks."

"We've got a couple of hours," Pakula said, looking at his watch. "Get settled into your room. How about we meet in the lobby around six?

O'Dell and I found a great restaurant last night. I wouldn't mind an encore."

"Tommy," Spencer called out, interrupting.

Creed and Pakula turned at the same time to see the sheriff jogging over. The man's silver hair was plastered to the sides of his head and forehead from sweat. His face was red. He held his cell phone up and kept checking it as he made his way to them.

"What's going on?"

"A postal carrier," he said, almost out of breath. "She called in a suspicious garbage bag in a ditch. One of my deputies is on his way."

"Suspicious how?" Pakula asked.

"It's not far from here," Spencer continued. His jaw twitched, and Creed noticed his eyes darted back and forth. "Off on one of the rural gravel roads. She thinks she saw a human hand."

"Inside the bag?"

"What's going on?" Maggie and Grace came up from behind them.

"Someone may have found a body in a ditch," Pakula said.

"A hand. It spilled out of the bag," Spencer told them. "It wasn't attached."

"What makes her think it's real?" Pakula asked. He yanked off his ball cap and rubbed a hand over his shaved head. Then he pulled the cap back on.

"She got a close look. It might be worse," Spencer said. There was a panic in his voice that Creed didn't like. Only hours ago, the man seemed cool and calm. "The young woman staying with my wife and me since Easter didn't come home last night. She didn't show up at her job yesterday afternoon either. Nora just checked and her car's still in the shed. That girl doesn't go anywhere without her car."

8

Maggie O'Dell was surprised at how close the site was. They hadn't traveled over three miles when Spencer's truck pulled aside and stopped. Then his arm came out, gestured for Creed and Pakula to pull around him.

Spencer swung his vehicle around, bumper to ditch, the length of his big truck blocking access. Maggie could see one of his deputies about a quarter of a mile down, blocking the road from the other direction.

"You think this could be a trafficker thing?" Creed asked.

"Could be a coincidence."

"Except you don't believe in coincidences."

Maggie had slid inside Ryder's Jeep at Freddie Mason's place. Earlier, she had ridden with Pakula, leaving her rental back at the hotel. He simply nodded at her when her natural inclination turned her towards Ryder's vehicle. Pakula was a seasoned investigator, and they'd worked together several times over the last decade. Though she tried to keep her personal and professional lives separate, she figured she wouldn't be able to hide much from Pakula.

"We've noticed some turf wars," she said.

"You mean like the drug cartels?"

"Sort of. Not as sophisticated. They look like ordinary guys," she told him. "Blend in with the community. Some of them even grew up around here. But they can be ruthless."

Maggie glanced back. Grace stared out over the console from her perch on the backseat bench.

"Like Eli Dunn," Creed said.

"Exactly like Eli Dunn."

Maggie looked over, trying to be casual as she checked on him. Dunn was the killer who had taken them on a scavenger hunt across Nebraska pastures to find the bodies he'd buried. At the time, they believed Creed's sister was one of Dunn's victims. But Eli Dunn had been only one guy on the fringes of a network of traffickers that Maggie and Pakula were still hunting down. She suspected Freddie Mason was one of them. But the parallel networks were like tentacles of a hydra monster. As soon as they cut off one head, two grew in its place.

In a strange turn of events, that crazy scavenger hunt had led them to find Brodie. That's why Creed was here. He'd told her he wanted to give back to the team and the project that had given him back his sister. Maggie understood. His dedication and sense of obligation were just two of the things she loved about him.

Yes, that's right. Loved about him. She was saying it more and more these days, though only to herself, never to him. Even while she was taking Mason down to his knees earlier, she couldn't help thinking how good it was to see Ryder. She found it harder and harder to be away from him. Her psychiatrist friend, Gwen Patterson, would have something to say about that. That is, if Maggie ever told Gwen.

"Would they dump a body this close when they know you're actually making arrests?" Creed asked.

"It wouldn't surprise me," she said while her eyes searched out her side window. "But then I don't get surprised too often anymore."

"Spencer seems convinced it's the woman his wife took in."

Now, the sheriff backed almost into the ditch to allow two more vehicles to pass through. The first pulled in directly behind Creed's Jeep.

Maggie watched in the side mirror. Then she smiled. She recognized the driver.

"It really is starting to feel like a reunion from last year," she said.

"Why do you say that?"

"Lucy Coy just arrived."

9

Maggie had first met Lucy Coy years ago when the woman was the coroner of a county in western Nebraska. The county sheriff had prefaced that meeting by calling Lucy "that crazy, old Indian woman." But Maggie found Lucy looked and acted ageless and far from crazy with a grace, spirituality and intellect that soared above most of the people she worked around.

"Maggie O'Dell," Lucy said as she came around her vehicle and hugged her. "I heard a rumor you were back this way."

"And you still haven't retired."

"Not even close."

Pakula and Creed joined them, exchanging greetings. Maggie was taken back how casual they all were with each other. Like a group of old friends getting together.

"And Mr. Creed," Lucy said. "It's good to see you again. How is your sister doing?"

Lucy reached out her hand, holding it flat and parallel to the Jeep's back window, without touching the glass. Her greeting received a wag and sniff from Grace.

"Brodie is doing good. Every week she continues to surprise me."

"She's a remarkable young woman."

"Lucy's with the Nebraska State Patrol now," Pakula said. "I knew she was close by."

"Oh, hell no!" Sheriff Spencer yelled, kicking up gravel.

All of them turned to watch him jog in the other direction. In the distance, Maggie could see a vehicle racing toward them. A plume of dust grew behind it. Spencer waved his arms at his deputy and called out to him.

Pakula hurried to catch up with Spencer. Maggie looked at Creed and Lucy, then she took off after Pakula.

"What's going on?" she asked once they came up beside Spencer.

He stood with his hands on his hips, not on his gun. The car was still coming fast, driving down the middle of the gravel road.

"It's my wife," Spencer said.

"How did she find out so quickly?" Pakula asked, and he was watching Spencer's face now. Not the car.

"I know, I know." Then Spencer looked at him and his eyebrows shot up. "I didn't tell her. You think I told her?"

Pakula just shrugged.

"News travels fast out here," Spencer said. "She's been frantic all morning about Libby. Calling people. She thinks we found her."

"Ted, this is a crime scene," Pakula reminded him.

"Damn it, Tommy! I know that."

He bunched up his fists and slapped them against the sides of his legs, reminding Maggie of a toddler staving off a tantrum. His lips pressed thin, as if keeping him from saying anything more. Without another word, he left them, hurrying around his deputy's SUV.

"Stand down," Spencer yelled at his deputy as he ran down the middle of the road to meet the car head on. Thirty feet away, he began cartwheeling his arms to bring it to a stop.

"I've been working the city streets too long," Pakula said without looking at Maggie. "Out here, every single crime is like a ripple in the water."

Pakula the Poet. His allegories still surprised her, made her smile. They betrayed his gruff exterior. With all the horrible images he'd seen and witnessed in his decades as an Omaha homicide detective, she always expected the jaded skeptic he casually portrayed.

"Actually, her coming here might not be such a bad idea," Maggie told him.

This time, he glanced over, one eyebrow raised.

"It could save a lot of time if she's able to identify the body." She let that sink in before she added, "Or body parts."

10

Grace was restless. She poked her nose out the Jeep's window.

Creed helped the medical examiner unload and carry her equipment to the edge of the ditch. Both of them were distracted by the scene playing out in the middle of the gravel road. Even from fifty feet away, the argument between Spencer and his wife carried on the breeze.

The woman wore the blue scrubs of a health care professional. She was almost a head shorter than Spencer. Her long hair was swept back and tied in a ponytail. Strands broke free and danced around her face. She constantly swiped at them while shouting up at her husband.

Having family members at the scene of a crime always made Creed uncomfortable. Their emotions couldn't help but permeate the air. He immediately wondered if that was what made Grace fidgety.

To Grace, death was a pink, squeaky elephant.

In her mind, her alert equaled her reward. It didn't matter whether the object she alerted to was an SD card, a bag of cocaine, the tripwires to an explosive device or a decomposed body. Dogs didn't bring emotion to their searches, but they could sense it in the people who surrounded them.

Emotion runs down the leash. Creed's handlers grew tired of him drilling that phrase into their training sessions, but it was one thing that determined an expert handler. And in the end, a good team. A dog constantly distracted by the handler's emotions became fidgety and confused. Dogs had an overwhelming urge to please their people. Too much emotion could trigger false alerts.

"It's not the ruckus," Lucy Coy said.

"What's that?" Creed asked. She interrupted his thoughts so completely he did not know what she was talking about.

Lucy tugged on latex gloves and chin-pointed back over Creed's shoulder toward his Jeep.

"Grace isn't agitated about their shouting," she told him. "She's sniffing in this direction."

Creed turned, his arms still full of rolled tarps and evidence bags. Lucy was right. Grace's nose poked out on the opposite side from where Spencer and his wife were arguing.

"Is it possible she's smelling the contents of the garbage bag?" Even as Lucy asked, they both looked down into the ditch.

"She knew we were finished for the day. But she tends to have a mind of her own."

"I wonder where she gets that?"

He noticed a slight smile and took advantage of it when he asked, "Do you mind if I see if she's alerting to the bag?"

Lucy stepped into the tall grass, moving her gloved hands to separate the blades and get a better look at the ground. Creed could see the black plastic and white fabric flapping in the breeze. He noticed that the air had already chilled as the sun set. The bag was only about six feet away from them.

"Go ahead and bring her," Lucy said. "If something else fell out of that bag, she'll be able to find it in this grass quicker than any of us."

Carefully, he put everything down and went back to the Jeep. He changed out Grace's vest, taking the GPS tracking device from one pocket and tucking it into the pocket of the other. Already she wagged, pleased that he understood exactly what she wanted, as if this was what they had planned all along.

"Grace, you are such a smart girl," he told her.

She licked his chin as he prepared his daypack again, going through all the familiar motions that Grace expected. By the time he put her on the ground and snapped on the leash, she was nose-punching the air. Her feet shuffled impatiently. She was ready to go. He closed the tailgate, and she looked up at him, head cocked to the side as if she couldn't believe how slow he was.

"Okay, Grace. Go find." He used a generic command.

She raced to the ditch, straining at the end of her leash. She didn't stop when she got to the edge. Instead, she zigzagged down, dragging him along. She raced around Lucy and the equipment on the ground.

"Slow down, Grace," Creed told her as the tall grass swallowed her whole and threatened to trip him.

He watched for her to reappear next to the flapping black plastic. He could hear her sniffing and rustling. As he kept up behind her, he held the leash with one hand and parted the grass with his other. She was taking too long.

When he finally pulled back the grass, he could see Grace's tail pointed straight out. She looked up at him and met his eyes. She was about twenty feet away from the garbage bag. But Lucy was right. Grace had found something else.

11

Leaves plastered the surface, but Creed could still recognize what Grace had found. The toes were polished a deep red that blended in with the surrounding grass. Without bending over, he could see a heart-shaped tattoo on the ankle.

He felt Lucy's presence before he turned around and almost bumped into her. He hadn't heard her come up beside him.

"A foot to go along with the hand," she said in a hushed tone. "She's no longer running from or fighting those who hurt her."

She stood completely still and silent now. Instead of a crime scene, this reminded Creed of sacred grounds and paying reverence to the dead. Lucy was unlike any medical examiner he'd met, as much a spiritual leader as a forensic scientist.

"She?" Creed asked. "You think it's a woman because of the nail polish?"

"Good point," she admitted, surprising him. "Not very open-minded of me."

Footsteps rustled in the grass behind them, and Creed glanced around to find Maggie skidding down the incline. It was steeper here. Her hands were gloved and filled with evidence bags.

He made room for her as he pulled Grace's squeaky pink elephant from his daypack. To Creed's relief, Grace was waiting for the toy, wagging, excited, and finished. Or at least Creed hoped she was finished.

He'd seen and dealt with all kinds of crime scenes, but dismemberments were some of the most difficult.

He watched Maggie's reaction. A seasoned investigator, he knew there wasn't much that surprised her anymore. Hadn't she just said that on the short drive? And yet, she winced and shook her head. She crossed her arms over her chest, despite her hands being full. Hands that now fisted around plastic and paper evidence bags.

"Good girl, Grace." Maggie said, remembering to keep her tone upbeat for the dog.

Grace squeaked her elephant and flung her head from side to side to emphasize each bleat of the toy. Usually Creed took her away and let the investigators do their work, but for some reason he hesitated. He couldn't pull his eyes away from those manicured toes. And he hated that Brodie came to mind along with a sudden flood of emotion.

For years, with every search that resulted in the recovery of a young woman's body, Creed had anxiously expected it to be his sister. But he was back here in Nebraska because they had saved her.

Saved her. Not recovered her dead body.

He needed to keep telling himself that instead of remembering how close she had come to being buried in a pasture or flung into a ditch like this woman.

Maybe Hannah was right. Maybe he needed some time off. He only wished he knew what that looked like.

12

Maggie couldn't help thinking how fresh this body must be. The flesh wasn't mottled. There was very little blood. Her mind kept looping over the last two days. Both raids had been clean and uneventful. Almost too clean. Too uneventful.

"We're going to lose sunlight quickly." Lucy brought out a digital camera and began taking photos. "I want to pick up and bag as much as possible. Spencer will need to put someone on duty for the night. Hopefully, we can walk a grid tomorrow."

Then Lucy pointed to Grace, who was happily chomping her toy.

"She seems content now," Lucy said, looking up at Ryder. "Could that possibly mean there are no other pieces in proximity to these two?"

"We'll take a walk on the road," he said to Lucy as much as to Grace.

He looked reluctant to leave. Maggie tried to catch his eyes, but he seemed focused on Grace and what she'd found. As a dog handler, she knew he had trained himself to keep his emotions in check. Sometimes she wished he wasn't so good at it.

"Come on, Grace," he said again, and she bounded up the grassy incline.

When they were out of earshot, Lucy turned to Maggie and asked, "Any chance I can borrow the two of them tomorrow?"

"You'll have to ask Ryder. Pakula won't be doing another raid until we've had a chance to look over what we found today."

Lucy carefully separated the tall blades of grass, gently tamping them down, the long strands bending and laying on top of each other. Then she kneeled down on top of them. Her gloved fingers lifted the detached foot as if it were a fragile porcelain vase. Crumbled bits of leaves and dirt were stuck to the skin. Maggie knew Lucy wouldn't swipe any of it away. Not out here. She'd wait to clean it in her lab where she could examine the foot and the debris attached.

Maggie stepped up alongside her, prepared an evidence bag, then held it open. But Lucy wasn't ready to deposit it just yet.

"Mrs. Spencer may be able to identify this," Lucy said, raising and tilting the foot toward Maggie to catch the fading sunlight. "Or not."

A small heart-shaped tattoo stood out, blood-red against the white skin. It was behind the anklebone, an inch below the dismemberment cut.

"Dark red," Maggie said. "That's not a quick, simple tattoo, even though it's small. Usually, they have to layer it with black ink first, then add different shades of red ink."

Lucy raised one eyebrow at her.

Maggie shrugged and said, "Sometimes all the useless trivia in my head pays off."

Voices above them were getting closer. Spencer's wife was growing impatient.

"I'll head them off," Maggie told Lucy as she helped her with the bag.

She had placed the other collection containers carefully on the grass and added Lucy's case to weigh them down. The breeze continued to grow stronger as clouds roiled in. There was a chill in the air that hadn't been there the last few days.

Before Maggie climbed up the ditch, she said to Lucy, "I just realized that the foot and hand might not belong to the same person."

"Only a serial killer profiler would jump to that conclusion."

"Are you sure?"

Lucy hesitated as she considered it. From where they stood, Maggie knew the other plastic trash bag was close by and to their right. But she only knew this because she had seen it from the road above. It was impossible to see it in the tall grass from this angle.

"Ask her about the tattoo," Lucy suggested. "I'll go check if there's any identifying characteristics on the other piece."

Lucy picked her way through the grass as Maggie climbed up to the road.

They were inside the perimeter Spencer's deputies had created with their vehicles. He was still arguing with his wife. Poor Pakula looked like he was trying to play referee. More deputies had arrived. When Mrs. Spencer saw Maggie, she pushed past her husband and rushed toward Maggie.

"Did you find the rest of the body?" the woman wanted to know.

Maggie put up her hands to stop the woman and stood in front of her so she wouldn't approach the edge of the road overlooking the ditch. "The rest of the body" implied that she knew they had initially found only a piece. She wondered how much the locals already knew.

"Let's go talk over here," Maggie told her and gestured toward Creed's Jeep, the closest vehicle.

She glanced around until she saw Ryder and Grace almost at the intersection. They walked down the middle of the road. Grace wasn't scampering or plowing through the ditches. In fact, the two of them looked like they were simply on a walk.

"They're looking for more pieces," Mrs. Spencer said, watching them now, too.

"Mrs. Spencer, I understand—"

"Call me Nora," she interrupted. "I'm a trauma nurse. You don't need to sugar-coat anything for me."

"Nora, I'm Maggie O'Dell."

"Yes, I know. The FBI agent from Quantico." Even as Nora said this, her eyes were trying to see over Maggie's shoulder.

"What's the name of the young woman staying with you and your husband?"

"Libby. Libby Holmes."

"Does she have any tattoos?"

Her eyes swung back to Maggie's, and her entire face seemed to fall as she said, "Yes. Oh, my God. Yes, she does."

"Can you tell me about them?"

"She has the word, 'breathe.' It's written in script across the back of her hand." Nora brought up her own and pointed to the area.

"Right hand or left?"

Her eyes stayed on Maggie's, the panic growing. She bit her lip as if it would help her remember.

"Right. And she has one on her back shoulder. Left shoulder. It's a flower. The one that's supposed to mean spiritual growth or something like that."

"A lotus flower?"

"Yes," she said it with excitement. Then Maggie saw her realization hit that the reason Maggie might know was because she had seen it.

"No other tattoos?" Maggie asked, trying to keep her tone calm and steady.

She could see Nora was struggling with emotion. She obviously cared very much about this young woman.

"No others," she finally said.

"Could there be any you don't know about?"

"No. Not unless she's gotten one in the last week. We've both been working a lot. Different hours. I haven't seen much of her."

Maggie knew the heart wasn't a recent addition. Skin around a new tattoo usually stayed red and inflamed like a sunburn for days after up to a week. Sometimes the ink oozed.

She searched to locate Lucy without diverting Nora's attention.

"Please, just tell me. Is it her?"

Lucy popped up out of the ditch. Her head swiveled until she found Maggie. She gestured her over.

"Give me just a few more minutes," Maggie told Nora.

"No! You know something. Tell me." She grabbed Maggie's left arm, fingernails digging in.

Calmly, Maggie's right hand shot out around Nora's wrist. A squeeze and a twist made the woman wince and immediately let go, like hitting a switch. The pain wasn't as bad as the surprise.

"Just a few more minutes," Maggie reiterated, her grip easing up, but her fingers still wrapped around the woman's wrist.

She nodded and looked at the ground. Maggie couldn't tell whether she was embarrassed or simply exhausted.

"Please, stay right here," she told her.

As soon as Maggie dropped the woman's wrist, she was rubbing it with her other hand. She kept her eyes on Nora as she walked over to Lucy, who was handing off the evidence bags to a deputy and giving him instructions.

"Is the hand right or left?" Maggie asked before Lucy had a chance to say anything.

"Right."

"Tattoos?"

"It's severed at the radius and ulna, so we have nothing above the hand where you'd normally find a tattoo."

"What about the hand itself?"

"Are you thinking the knuckles? That does seem to be a popular spot."

"No." Maggie heard her own frustration. Nora's impatience and panic were contagious. She turned her back to the road and held her hand up against her chest. Then she pointed to the back of her hand, just like Nora had minutes ago.

"There was nothing there," Lucy told her.

Maggie exhaled a sigh of relief as though she had been holding her breath.

"It's not their missing young woman," she said, and she was anxious to tell Nora. "She has a tattoo on her hand. Nothing on her ankle."

"Okay. At least we know that much," Lucy said, but there was no relief on her face. "Hopefully, we can figure out who this woman is, because one thing seems certain. If the killer didn't want us to know her identity, he wouldn't have left us her fingerprints."

13

Creed was reluctant to come back. The woman in the blue scrubs was waiting for him alongside his Jeep. He knew what she wanted, and he wished he could turn around and walk away.

Pakula had left the scene, headed in the other direction. He'd texted Creed about dinner. Suggesting they all meet for breakfast instead, since it was long after six o'clock. Spencer and his deputies were stringing crime scene tape. Maggie helped Lucy pack up evidence bags and equipment.

None of them seemed to notice Spencer's wife any longer. They had left her to wait for him.

He nodded in her direction but didn't say a word as he raised the Jeep's tailgate. He lifted Grace inside and poured water in her collapsible bowl, then he drank the rest from the plastic bottle.

The woman was tentative now. She certainly hadn't been earlier. He glanced at her through the interior of the Jeep. She was looking over her shoulder. Still waiting. Looking and waiting for Maggie.

Okay, so they hadn't just left her to him. He appreciated that small courtesy and busied himself with routine, off-loading his daypack and removing Grace's vest. Taking his time while Maggie made her way over to them.

He wiped his face with a towel from a separate bag. Drained another bottle of water. Then he pulled out what he needed to fix a meal for Grace.

The whole time he mixed and poured, he pretended it didn't bother him that the women standing alongside his Jeep were waiting.

Creed never worked directly with family members. It was complicated. Too much emotional upheaval. Maggie knew that, and yet, she must have told this woman something else.

Finally, he slid the bowl into position for Grace. But Grace had already felt his tension and watched him rather than eat. He scooted the bowl closer and scratched behind her ears.

"It's okay, girl. Go ahead."

He left the tailgate open for the fresh air. Earlier he'd noticed a chill riding the breeze, but he'd worked up a sweat. It was part of the tension Grace could smell.

When he came around the Jeep to face them, his eyes went to Maggie's. He was almost certain he saw a flicker of discomfort. So she knew he would be upset, and she did it anyway.

"Ryder, this is Sheriff Spencer's wife, Nora."

"I understand your little dog can find missing people, too," Nora said impatiently and not bothering to wait out a formal introduction. "Not just dead people."

"Mr. Creed is here to assist Investigator Pakula's team," Maggie tried to head her off. "As I told you before, your request would need to go through the sheriff's department. It hasn't been established yet that Libby is missing."

Creed was wrong. Maybe Maggie hadn't offered his services. Nora Spencer had only presumed she could appeal to him.

"Oh, I know she didn't just take off," she told Maggie. "Her car's still in the shed. Why would she leave without a vehicle? How would she? And she didn't show up for work. She's never done that."

Creed stayed quiet and studied the woman. Well-earned laugh lines rimmed her mouth and eyes. She talked with her hands. Although she was shorter than Maggie, there was an air of authority. She was used to people paying attention to her. She was used to people listening to her.

"I'm concerned she might hurt herself."

"You didn't mention that earlier," Maggie said. "How old is she?"

"Nineteen or twenty."

"Which? Nineteen or twenty?"

"Does it matter?"

"Yes," Maggie insisted, and Creed could now hear the impatience in her voice. "One is a teenager. The other is not."

"She could be in trouble. Right now!"

"All the more reason you need to be honest with us."

This time, the woman looked as if Maggie had slapped her across the face.

"Are you suggesting I'm lying to you?"

"No, I'm not suggesting it. I'm stating it outright."

Creed had never heard a woman huff and puff quite the way Nora Spencer did. It defied any attempt she had made at being addressed as a victim or a victim's advocate.

"What's going on?" Sheriff Spencer hurried over. Face still beet-red, his eyes pinned down on his wife like he had had enough. "Nora, you need to go on home. Now."

"Ted, this man's dog may be able to track where Libby went."

"That's not for you to decide."

Creed thought it looked like Spencer wanted to take her by the arm and lead her away, but there was a hesitancy that made him realize Spencer didn't dare. Perhaps she was used to getting her way with him, too.

Suddenly, she turned to Creed and took a step forward so they were practically toe to toe. She craned her neck back to look up at him and said, "Libby tried to kill herself six months ago. I'm worried she may have gone off to try it again. Please, it might not be too late."

14

Lincoln, Nebraska

David Ruben liked the way people looked at him when he walked in with two pretty young women. He was used to having three instead of two, but it hardly mattered. He still enjoyed the looks the men gave him. There was a tinge of envy but also admiration. He could almost read their minds: *How did that old guy get two girls?*

Women paid little attention. Maybe they were used to older men with younger women. He knew that some of them assumed he was the girls' dad or uncle. Ruben didn't mind. Nope. Didn't mind at all.

Years ago, just the idea of other men thinking he was screwing these young girls would have been enough to give him a hard-on. These days, it required a more sophisticated blend of ingredients.

Lately, sex didn't even interest him. Controlling these young things gave him a rush more intense than anything he'd experienced with sex. Pushing them to new limits and watching to see what they were capable of doing. That was intoxicating. And he never had to raise his hand or his voice. He just needed to know how to pull their strings, how to goad them, how to unite them, only to turn them against each other. The latter seemed to be the most powerful.

The hostess led them to a booth. Two days ago, they had a table in the corner, but the booth was much cozier. She handed them each a menu, but her eyes stayed with Ruben. She looked older than his girls and a bit worn, but much too young for the name on her hostess badge.

"So Rita, what's your favorite thing on the menu?" he asked her.

"You can never go wrong with one of the burgers, but if it was me, I'd probably order the steak fajitas."

"Ah, spicy. That's right up my alley." He was pleased with the blush the attention produced. He was right. Rita was younger than she looked.

He ignored Vanessa. Her back was to Rita, so she dared to be so bold as to roll her eyes at him. Vanessa had been with him the longest for the last six months. Everyone knew she was his favorite. She could get away with behaviors the others wouldn't think of risking. They thought Vanessa was their confidant, their protector...until she wasn't.

"Dylan will be your server today," Rita told them now while pretending to be distracted by new customers waiting for her back at the hostess stand.

Ruben watched her hurry away. That's when he saw Shelby's eyes darting around. He raised his menu, pretending he didn't notice her flicker of panic. A young waiter approached their booth, and Ruben knew immediately the boy-man was the cause of Shelby's discomfort. The girl was so transparent. She was practically squirming in her seat.

"Hey, I'm Dylan. I'll be your waiter."

Ruben watched for the glint of recognition in Dylan's eyes when he noticed Shelby.

There it was.

He smiled at her a bit too long, although she was trying her best to hide her face in the oversized menu.

"Hello, Dylan," Ruben said. "I think we need a few minutes to decide."

"Oh sure."

"Maybe you could bring us some iced tea."

"Absolutely."

Ruben had to admit Dylan was cute. The head of curly black hair bobbed. He swatted it out of his eyes, but it was obviously his signature feature. It had to be, because he was short and skinny with a flat butt. Other than the hair and a dimpled smile, he seemed quite ordinary. Hardly worth the effort, and certainly not worth the punishment.

"Do you think that was a smart idea?" he asked Shelby with only his eyes flicking over the menu to look at her. He kept his tone calm and casual, as he always did.

"What? It's nothing. We exchanged some chit-chat the other day. It was nothing. Totally nothing."

Too many "nothings," and she wouldn't look at him.

"She gave him her phone number," Vanessa said.

"No, I didn't."

Without putting the menu down, Ruben reached across the tabletop and held his hand open. Shelby knew better than to argue. She folded up her menu and fumbled the cell phone from the back pocket of her blue jeans. At the last minute, she hesitated, then placed it in Ruben's hand.

"I wasn't going to do anything," she said, like a little girl getting caught, but she was saying this to Vanessa, not to him. "We texted a few times. See for yourself. It wasn't like I was interested in meeting up with him."

Ruben scrolled through the texts. Harmless and silly and totally illicit. It broke one of his rules for being in their arrangement. No flirting with boys. When he looked up, he caught the fear in Shelby's eyes before she tucked it away. These girls thought they were so good at pretending.

He liked that. He counted on it.

He handed back the phone, ignoring her sudden relief.

"After he takes our order, text him to see if he wants to party later." He said this while still perusing the entrée section.

Out of the corner of his eye, he could see Shelby's relief transfer into panic. But he also saw Vanessa smile.

15

"I don't trust her," Maggie told Creed on their drive to the Spencer's.

He now realized that Maggie hadn't offered his and Grace's services at all. Nora Spencer had decided on her own to approach and convince him. Nora telling them Libby might hurt herself was all Creed needed to flash back on the many veterans he knew that had offed themselves. Maybe he and Grace could help find this young woman before she hurt herself.

"You didn't have to come along," he reminded her.

Lucy offered Maggie a ride to her hotel when she realized Creed and Maggie didn't agree about this detour.

"She's up to something," Maggie said, referring to Nora Spencer.

"Maybe she's just worried about Libby."

"About hurting herself?"

"Right."

"Don't you find it odd that if she was seriously concerned about Libby hurting herself, why would she jump to the conclusion that a piece of her had been found in a ditch?"

"Did she know it was only a piece?"

"The first thing Nora asked me was if we'd found the rest of the body."

"So she already knew about the dismemberment."

"Exactly," Maggie said. "But I saw the panic in her eyes. She honestly believed it could have been Libby. Getting murdered and dismembered is a far cry from running off and committing suicide."

"You're still thinking all of this has something to do with the traffickers you and Pakula have arrested?"

"Pakula seems to think so, and I can't say that I disagree. He's establishing jurisdiction, so his task force will head the investigation. I think that's really why he called Lucy Coy, instead of letting the county send their coroner."

Creed noticed her quick check of her cell phone.

"You have to admit, it is strange. This Libby suddenly disappears, and a dismembered body appears." Now Maggie stared out the passenger window as the sun started to sink into the cornfield. "And it happens just as these human traffickers seem to be turning on each other. Freddie Mason wasn't even on our list until the car dealer in North Platte gave him up."

"So you're coming along with me to the Spencers' because you're suspicious. Here I was thinking you wanted to protect me."

He watched for her reaction out of the corner of his eye. The smile was slight as she did a quick glance at him. Quick, but he still caught it.

"Hey, I learned my lesson," she said, keeping her focus on the fields. "There's no talking you out of something once you've made your mind up." She waited a beat before adding, "Hard to argue something that I'm guilty of myself."

Now Creed smiled. They understood each other well. And yet, they tiptoed around their feelings.

A V-line of geese honked and crossed above them. Clouds were gathering on the horizon. He liked the wide open spaces out here.

"Actually, I'm glad you came along," he told her. "I've never been comfortable doing a search with the family present, let alone doing one with no law enforcement officials to oversee what we might find."

"You think you'll find something?"

"Libby did leave their house. It'll be difficult to tell whether it was her choice or if someone coerced her. Chances are, Grace leads us to the end of the driveway, where someone either picked her up or put her into a vehicle."

"I never thought about that. Grace will tell us that?"

He glanced in the rearview mirror. At the sound of her name, the little dog raised her head, but she stayed down. They had spent the last two days traveling, and this had been another long day. He hoped it was that simple. If it wasn't, he wouldn't allow her to work after dark.

"The scent trail would end where Libby got inside a vehicle."

"Nora doesn't seem to believe that someone picked her up."

"She missed work," Creed reminded her.

Both Nora and her husband had told them Libby never missed. Even if the schedule didn't work for her, Nora said Libby exchanged with co-workers rather than miss out on the hours.

"Whatever is going on," Maggie said, "this is turning into a strange and wild ride again. I used to expect Nebraska to be peaceful. After all the times I've been here, I'd settle for boring."

16

Maggie was already on edge about Nora Spencer. It didn't help to smell freshly brewed coffee when she and Creed walked into the Spencer house. Nora had made ham and cheese sandwiches for them, stacked carefully on a plate, accompanied by dill pickles and a bowl of tossed salad. Dressed in her work scrubs and sidelined by discarded body parts, the woman still managed to put together a meal for her guests.

Creed was partially right about Maggie's motives for being here. She was suspicious of Nora and wanted to learn more about Libby Holmes. But she also didn't want Creed and Grace out here alone.

Maggie had tried to convince him at the crime scene to wait for morning. As soon as Nora voiced her concern about Libby being suicidal, Maggie knew it would be enough to win Creed over. As a Marine, he knew too many veterans who had succumbed to their PTSD by taking their own lives. But that wasn't all. His father had committed suicide. Eighteen-year-old Creed had been the one to find him.

Maggie couldn't help wondering if somehow Nora Spencer knew she might trigger a soft spot by making the suicide claim. Yes, that sounded like a stretch, and maybe Maggie's skepticism was the reason she'd come along, but she also knew she was overly protective of Creed. Especially since last June.

Four months ago, he'd almost been killed in the middle of Blackwater River State Forest by a serial killer. Even Hannah admitted Creed hadn't fully recovered from his injuries. Ever since he arrived, she thought he looked tired. Of course, that might be only the result of the long drive up from the Florida Panhandle. But there was something else in his eyes that she couldn't quite read. And it bothered her.

"Cup of coffee?" Spencer asked them as he poured what appeared to be a second for himself.

"No thanks," Maggie said.

"Maybe later," Creed told him. "If it's okay with both of you, I'd like to bring Grace inside."

"Oh, right," Spencer said, turning to his wife and adding, "He'll probably need one of Libby's shirts or something."

"Actually, it would help if Grace could go inside her bedroom."

Maggie watched Nora's jaw twitch as she clamped it tight. Spencer had been leaning against the counter and pushed himself away as he realized he'd need to take over from here.

"Go get Grace," he told Creed. "I'll show you the girl's room."

Creed only had to open the back door where they had entered. Grace waited patiently. He picked up her leash and followed Spencer down a hallway. Without a word, Maggie fell in step behind them, expecting to stop Nora from coming along. But the woman stayed planted in her kitchen.

Spencer stopped at the bedroom door, coffee cup still in his hand. With his back facing the kitchen and out of earshot of his wife, he said, "I tried to warn Nora that she can't always fix people. All of us, we realize that in our profession. But as a nurse, it goes against her grain." Before either of them could respond, Spencer started back down the hallway. He glanced over his shoulder and added, "Yell, if you need anything."

Once inside, Maggie closed the door behind them. Creed didn't hesitate. He let Grace off leash and encouraged her to sniff the double bed, lifting and folding back the bedspread. He took one of the pillows and brought it down to Grace, giving her time to run her nose over it.

With only a glance around the room, Maggie knew there would be plenty of Libby Holmes' scent for Grace. Clothes were thrown over the back of a chair. The soles of a pair of shoes peeked out from under the same chair. The closet door was open and displayed an overflowing laundry basket on the floor.

Still, the belongings were sparse. The wall decorations, fixtures, and furniture were basic guestroom accommodations. There were no personal touches, no framed photographs or inspirational plaques. The dresser top was bare except for a makeup mirror and a caddy filled with an assortment of makeup and hair bands.

On the other side of the room was another door.

"We're in luck," Maggie told Creed as she crossed the room and eased open the door. "An en-suite."

"I think we're good," Creed said. He and Grace were inspecting the contents of the laundry basket.

Actually, Maggie was no longer thinking about scents for Grace. Her gut instinct told her she needed to take advantage of this opportunity. Nora Spencer had invited them to help with the disappearance of Libby Holmes. Anything they learned about the girl could help find her.

She shoved her hands deep into her jacket pockets and was pleased to find an extra pair of latex gloves in one pocket and two small plastic evidence bags in the other. Then she stepped into the bathroom. The space was small with a cabinet sink, toilet and shower. She searched for anything that might still have the girl's DNA.

Rather than pluck strands from a hairbrush, she bagged the entire brush. In the trashcan she found a bloodstained band-aid and a used tampon. She put each into a separate bag. She added a couple of other items then realized Creed was standing in the doorway behind her.

"Grace is ready," he said without a single question or accusation about what she was doing.

17

Creed expected this search to be short. It quickly became a reminder of why it was better if handlers knew very little about the victim or the investigation. Human suppositions, preconceived notions and expectations were all too easy to insert and influence a scent dog. Just because Creed knew Libby Holmes had disappeared without a word and without her vehicle, he had already anticipated she had to have left with someone. No way the woman simply walked these gravel roads and expected to get somewhere.

That was what he presumed had happened. But Grace didn't take him down the driveway. She didn't head toward the road at all. Instead, she immediately took off in the opposite direction toward a cornfield. Not just a cornfield, but what looked like miles and miles of field.

Halfway there, she stopped and circled around. Even then, Creed still believed she might simply choose a different path that would lead to the road.

Nope. She poked at the air and waved her nose up and down. She surprised him again and started loping toward the barn. The whole time Creed followed, he avoided looking over his shoulder to locate the gravel road and calculate a route.

Then it occurred to him. Was it possible someone met her out in the barn? Maybe they didn't want to be seen by anyone driving by. They could have pulled their vehicle into the breezeway.

The huge doors were slid open, and Creed could easily see the space was empty now. That could explain why Grace might track Libby to the barn, but not to the driveway. Her scent would have ended as soon as she climbed into a vehicle waiting for her inside the barn.

But Creed was wrong again. Instead of trotting into the breezeway, Grace darted around back and headed behind the barn. She weaved through the opening of a fenced area, the wooden gate left hanging on one hinge. The section, about fifty feet squared, looked like it used to be a vegetable garden, now gone to seed. Dried stocks poked up out of the weeds. Fallen leaves from more than one season stuck to the bottom of the wire fence. In several places, the wire had rusted and come loose from support posts.

A flash of purple caught Creed's eye. He stepped carefully until he was close enough to identify it. A woman's scarf was tied around the top of a post. The soft material waved in the breeze, very much out of place in this deserted garden.

Creed glanced around to find Grace waiting patiently. She stood next to a dip in the soil where the weeds had recently only sprouted again. They grew much shorter than the rest of the area. She looked up at him and met his eyes.

She alerted, but she wasn't alerting to what Creed had asked her to find. There was something else here. Something or someone.

18

Maggie stayed behind with the Spencers after Creed and Grace left out the back door. He'd asked her to keep them from following.

As soon as the door closed, Nora moved to the window above the kitchen sink. She pretended to fuss over the coffeemaker, topping off her cup that Maggie could see was already full to the brim. When she realized her mistake, she set the cup aside and started pulling plates from a cupboard.

"I'm sure you and Mr. Creed must be hungry," she said as she gathered napkins and brought those and the plates to the table. "Ted, watch your manners," she tapped his arm as he reached for a sandwich.

"What? I'm hungry, too."

"Please, go ahead and eat," Maggie told them.

"Shouldn't we wait for Mr. Creed?" Nora asked, glancing back over her shoulder to see out the window again.

"I don't think he'd want you to wait for him."

"You know, I should probably tell him—"

"Nora," Spencer stopped her. "He needs to be alone with the dog. That's how they work together. They can't have you following them around and interrupting."

"Well, I think it would be beneficial if he knew—"

"No. Now sit down and eat."

"I'm not hungry."

"Then drink your coffee. But stay put. You got him over here. Now let him do his job."

Maggie sat at the table and watched their exchange. The Spencers were a study in contrasts, both physically and in personalities. Ted Spencer was a foot taller than his wife, thin, almost scrawny. His silver hair hung shaggy at the end of the day over his collar and stuck out over his ears. His ball cap had left a red line on his forehead that stood out from the other lines on his weathered face. He looked much older than his wife. He talked in a slow and steady manner, with a cadence that matched the way he walked.

Nora was five-two, at best, stocky and solid, with a deep well of energy. Compared to her husband's relaxed gestures and sparse speech, Nora was in constant motion. Even when she wasn't speaking, her facial expressions gave away her thoughts with a subtle eye roll or pursing of her lips.

"Agent O'Dell, can I get you a cup of coffee?" Nora needed something to do with her untapped energy.

"No, thank you."

"If not coffee, I have some ice tea and cold pop."

"Diet Pepsi?"

"Yup. Sure thing. Libby drinks Diet Pepsi," she said happily and headed to the refrigerator, stopping at a cupboard to retrieve a glass.

Maggie almost stopped her, preferring it straight out of the can, but she certainly didn't want to derail the woman from her mission.

"I'd like to ask a few questions about Libby," Maggie said, keeping her tone casual.

Spencer gestured for her to take a seat at the kitchen table as he sat on one on the opposite side. With his wife's back now facing them, he reached over and helped himself to half a sandwich.

The last sunlight was disappearing through the window over the sink, now only a yellow stain on the curtains. The countertop still had streaks of water from a fresh wipe-down. Despite the sandwiches and salad, there were no remnants of their makings. Nora kept a clean and efficient kitchen. But there was a sense of coziness here, too, with pleasant aromas. A cookie jar, breadbox and trivets took their places on the countertops, hinting of a busy but comfortable and content life.

"How long has Libby been living here with you?" Maggie asked, watching Spencer's face even though she expected Nora to answer.

"Oh, let's see. What's it been, Ted? Six months?"

"It was just after Easter," he said around a mouthful of bread and ham.

Nora deposited a glass with ice cubes and the cold can of Diet Pepsi in front of Maggie. She stayed on her feet, grabbing a plate and putting it on the table for her husband, gesturing for him to use it.

"You sure you won't have a sandwich?" Nora asked.

"Sure, if you'll join me," Maggie said, realizing it might be the only way to get the woman to sit down.

She wanted Nora to lower her guard. It was a mistake to have been so confrontational with her back at the crime scene. People skills weren't exactly Maggie's forte. She was more comfortable with dead people and chasing killers. But if she hoped to get any useful information, she'd need to make Nora feel like she was on her side. That she could be a friend, not a foe.

"Where did you meet Libby?"

"I'm a nurse at the hospital. I was on duty when she was brought in after her suicide attempt."

"You invited her to stay in your home?"

"She seemed so lost. She isn't from Nebraska. No family. No relatives."

"How did she end up out here?"

Nora shrugged.

"You didn't ask her?"

"Of course, I asked. She hasn't wanted to share, and I wasn't going to push. The girl just tried to kill herself, for heaven's sake."

"Do you have any idea where she lived before?"

"She has a Virginia driver's license," Spencer offered.

"Do you know how old she is?"

"Driver's license says twenty-one," he said.

"But you don't believe that?"

"Hell if I know. Kids these days all want to be older."

"We did, too, Ted," Nora told him. "You just don't remember."

"Nora, you told me she was nineteen or twenty."

"I didn't know. We had very little information about her when she was admitted to the hospital. And I didn't know Ted snooped out her driver's license." She swatted at his shoulder. "The girl deserves some privacy, Ted."

"You mentioned she has a car?" Maggie stayed on track.

"Not hers. We're loaning it so she can get to work," Spencer said.

"Actually, she's buying it from us."

"Really?" Spencer looked genuinely surprised.

Nora put her hand on her husband's arm. A gesture that sent him back to his sandwich.

"I told you she's paying us a little something every month now that she's working. You just don't remember."

Again, something he didn't remember or a piece of the story they hadn't rehearsed. Maggie wondered if there were other things Nora had kept from him about their houseguest. She waited out the uncomfortable pause between them. Usually people felt compelled to fill a silence. And it didn't take Nora long to do just that.

"She got a job at the Menard's in Hastings. Got it all on her own. She's a smart girl. Hard worker, too." Then to her husband, she added, "She brought home groceries last week. Remember? Even bought that fancy cheese you loved."

Spencer nodded and took another bite.

Maggie tried to put together a narrative that fit Pakula's earlier suspicions. Not being from Nebraska, the attempted suicide, not sharing her age. These were all things that could point to Libby Holmes being a trafficking victim.

"What has she told you about herself?"

"Not much." Spencer chimed in this time.

Nora didn't add anything.

"Have you called her friends? Co-workers?"

"I talked to her supervisor," Nora said. "I only know a couple of her friends. Co-workers really. She doesn't spend time with them outside of work. One said he talked to her over the weekend. I haven't heard from the other. But Libby mostly stays home when she's not working. Goes for long walks along the river." Nora's eyes slid to the window that looked out over the woods behind the house. "She takes pictures on her phone. She has such a good eye."

"How about boyfriends?"

"Oh, no." Her eyes cut back quickly to Maggie. "No boyfriends." Immediately, she seemed to realize she had said it too emphatically. As if to cover or distract, she decided she was hungry now. She pulled a plate off the stack, clanking it clumsily, then filling it with salad. All the while, she kept her hands busy and turned her face away, hiding whatever expression might still be there.

"Any recent arguments with either of you?"

"Arguments?" This time Nora laughed, but the forced sound fell flat. "We all have such different work schedules. We're lucky to sit down together for a meal once a week, let alone argue."

"So you have no idea what or who could have made her leave suddenly without telling you?"

"No."

This time when Maggie tried to wait out the silence, she realized Nora had nothing to add.

"Do you know what she took with her?" Maggie asked.

"Girls these days don't carry purses," Nora said with an attempted smile that didn't stick. "I didn't see her little wallet. She usually puts it in her back pocket of her jeans."

"Cell phone?" Maggie asked.

"No, I haven't seen that either. I can't imagine her going anywhere without it."

Then Nora's eyes widened, and she turned to her husband. "You can track her cell phone, can't you?"

Just at that moment, there was a soft tap at the back door before it opened. Creed stayed in the doorway. His eyes searched out Maggie's then slipped over to Spencer.

"Sheriff, you mind coming with me for a few minutes?"

"You found something!" Nora jumped up, almost knocking her chair over.

"I just need your help for a few minutes," Creed repeated.

"Nora," Maggie attempted to distract the woman. "Do you have any photos of Libby? Perhaps on your phone?"

Spencer had already gotten up from the table and was grabbing his ball cap.

"Stay put, Nora," he told her. "For once, just stay put."

He headed out the door with Creed. When Maggie caught a glimpse of Nora Spencer's eyes, she could see a fresh panic there.

19

"Your dog found something?" Spencer asked as soon as they were outside.

"I'm hoping you can tell me," Creed said.

He led the way, and when Spencer realized they were going toward the barn and not the road, he seemed relieved. That was not the reaction Creed expected, but he took only glances at the man.

"You think she's been hiding out in the barn?" Spencer asked.

Dusk was quickly stealing away the last light of day.

"No. She's not inside the barn."

When the sheriff still headed for the breezeway, Creed veered right and gestured for him to follow.

Grace had stayed outside the gate, waiting for him. She was throwing and catching and gumming her reward toy. Creed guessed the scarf had Libby's scent on it, enough that it distracted Grace. However, Grace didn't alert to the scarf.

Before Creed had gone to get Spencer, Grace tried to lead him back toward the cornfield, her original destination, before the detour to the back of the barn. Creed told her they were finished for the day. No way was he letting her track through rows and rows of corn in the dark. At best, they had a half hour before he needed to bring out a flashlight.

Now standing at the dilapidated gate with Spencer next to him, Creed asked, "What is this place?"

"Nora used to garden out here, but it's been a few years. Too many hours at the hospital. She gets tired."

Creed watched the sheriff. It didn't take long for him to notice the purple scarf flitting around the post like a ghost, the flimsy material matching the color of the sky. Spencer furrowed his brow and stared at it without a word.

"Was this used for anything else?"

Spencer's eyes scanned the area, then came to rest on Grace. She squeaked her pink elephant in rhythm at the honking of geese above.

"This property's been in Nora's family for over a hundred years. Are you telling me your dog may have found human remains?"

"No," Nora said, startling both of them. "That's not what he's saying."

Creed and Spencer spun around. She was out of breath and almost at the gate. Behind her, Maggie jogged toward them. She shot him a look of apology.

"My scarf," Nora gasped suddenly and pointed. "I gave Libby that scarf. She loves it. She never would have…" She hesitated, then said, "His dog found the grave."

"Nora, what the hell are you talking about?" Spencer wanted to know. "What grave? You never told me anybody was buried out here."

"The baby," she said, her eyes glued to the swirling fabric.

"What baby?"

"Libby's baby."

20

It was getting too dark. Soon she wouldn't be able to see even with the enhanced zoom and expanded focus on the binoculars that had cost her almost a week's pay.

Libby swiped over the entire property before settling on the scene behind the barn. They had found the scarf. She had expected to find David Ruben, but the man standing next to Ted was tall, broad-shouldered, with a bristled jaw and a nice butt. He was in his late twenties, maybe thirty, but he was hot even by Libby's standards.

One thing was certain, he wasn't David Ruben. Not even close. Ruben was only a few inches taller than Libby. His pudgy face made him look boyish, but she knew he was like fifty-something. He bragged about having a receding hairline, a bulging waistline and a harem of young girls everywhere he went.

In a crowd, no one noticed him, an ordinary, middle-aged man. Not at all what you expected evil to look like.

When Libby saw the woman running after Nora, she held her breath, thinking Ruben had sent one of his minions. But then she zoomed in on the woman's FBI ball cap. These must be people Ted knew. People he worked with.

Libby swung the binoculars to Nora's face, and her heart skipped a beat. Nora looked tired and worried.

Should she send her a text? What would she say?

Sorry. Thanks for everything. Gotta go.

Nora thought she knew so much about her. How could she tell her she didn't have a clue who she was? That she couldn't imagine what she was capable of doing?

It was better this way. For both of them.

Libby had been preparing for this day ever since she left Virginia. Her employee discount at the hardware store allowed her to stock up on all the essentials. A cute guy in the camping section was the only one who noticed, telling her he liked her idea of fun. That small interaction with a guy set off a signal of fear. It still sent a wave of panic. Still so fresh, she caught herself searching the aisles that day, making sure Ruben wasn't there and hadn't overheard.

She wished she could have taken the car, but she didn't own it yet, and it wouldn't be right to dump it halfway across the country. Because she would need to dump it, sell it, trade it. Otherwise, having the car Nora and Ted let her use would be like leaving bread crumbs leading directly to where she was.

Deep down, she knew she'd never be able to put enough miles between her and Ruben. He always seemed to be in her head. Those thoughts needed to be pushed back and locked up. She could not and would not dwell on them. It was exactly the control he wanted.

Months ago, she tried to convince herself that maybe she could hide in the middle of nowhere. This place was different from anywhere else she had been, and she suspected it was different from any place Ruben would look for her. She also learned some tricks and skills of her own after watching a lot of YouTube videos and listening to Ted talking about tracking cybercriminals. If she could stay off the grid, she might keep herself invisible.

She had been so careful. How in the world had Ruben found her?

Libby pulled her phone out of her back pocket and hesitated, staring at it. Not being on-line, plugged in 24/7, was one of the hardest parts.

She'd gotten sloppy in the last month. This place had a way of lulling her into a false sense of security.

If she sent Nora even a single text, Ted—and definitely Ruben— would know how to track her by using her phone. Seven months ago, Libby taught herself how to disconnect the battery. Ordinarily, the process was tedious, but she'd figured out a way to rig it, so she could reconnect quickly, check her text messages, then shutdown and disconnect in less than a minute. And she did it from a different location each time.

Before darkness swallowed up every last bit of light, she found a safe place. That was another thing she learned about the middle of nowhere. Night was darker. It was over six hours since she last checked. As soon as the phone booted up, the messages started flashing. Thankfully, she'd turned on the silent mode, not that there was anyone close by to hear. But how could she be sure? Even the constant hum of cicadas wouldn't cover an electronic ping. It was so damned quiet out here.

A string of them were from Nora:

ARE YOU OK?

WHERE ARE YOU?

PLEASE LET ME KNOW YOU'RE OK.

And then there were the three lines from the unidentified phone number that had started this panic. Short and simple:

TEXT ME.

WE CAN HELP EACH OTHER.

I'M REALLY SCARED.

21

Creed tried to ignore the exhaustion creeping into his muscles and the fog from invading his brain. He was glad to be back inside his Jeep with Grace resting. Maggie sat beside him, updating Pakula. She told Creed that she had ordered pizza to be delivered to their hotel. But all Creed could think about was getting to his hotel room and lying on the floor to stretch out his aching back, then put some ice on it.

The two-day drive from the Florida Panhandle to the middle of Nebraska—1700 miles in twenty-six hours—should have been a breeze. He'd made longer trips in less time, stopping only to give his dog a break. Usually all he needed was a thermos of coffee and a cooler filled with Hannah's sandwiches. But this was something he had never experienced.

The worst part of this annoying and uncharacteristic fatigue was that Maggie noticed.

Oh sure, they were beyond trying to create or change themselves into date material. By now, they knew each other's vulnerabilities and weaknesses. For some reason, it was difficult to reveal these new limitations to Maggie. Maybe he wasn't ready to accept them himself. They were temporary. They had to be. Dr. Avelyn Parker, who was their K9 CrimeScents' veterinarian, had done his blood labs just last week. The numbers came back great.

In June, a serial killer had shot Creed and left him in a secluded part of Blackwater River State Forest. Then the madman set the forest on fire.

The man had also plastered a half dozen fentanyl patches on Creed's arms. If it hadn't been for Brodie, he would have died from an overdose.

The broken ribs had mended. The scrapes and cuts were gone. But his back was taking longer to heal. Contusion was a fancy way to say he'd bruised his lower back. Not surprising when being dragged through a forest and bouncing over fallen branches, rocks, and tree roots. He knew he was lucky it was only bruised. The lingering brain fog took longer, as did shaking off the effects of the overdose.

Hannah insisted he needed more time off. That he pushed himself too hard.

"Rye, a week is not enough," she'd told him. "You need to take some real time off. Just rest a bit," is how she said it. "Go spend some time with Maggie."

He didn't want to remind Hannah that Maggie hadn't invited him. He'd never been to her home. She had a brother and a best friend she'd never introduced. He hadn't even met her dogs.

Also, Creed couldn't wrap his mind around what taking time off would look like. Work and being around the dogs had always been his escape, his purpose, his sanity.

He glanced at the Jeep's GPS. Eight more miles to the hotel. It was feeling like an eternity. He told Nora Spencer that he would be back in the morning. He'd let Grace lead him into the field. Hopefully, they wouldn't find Libby Holmes had drowned herself in the river.

Creed rubbed his hand over his jaw when he wanted to dig the sandpaper out of his eyes. Then he noticed Maggie watching him. She was pretending to read her phone, but she hadn't tapped or scrolled for a while.

It had been months since they'd seen each other, but it never felt awkward. Until now. It was probably just the fatigue. Maybe he was thinking about it too much. Relationships weren't something he gave much thought to or tried to evaluate. That is until Jason brought it to his attention.

One of his handlers, Jason Seaver, had started a new relationship with a gorgeous nurse. Creed could remember the first time he'd met the veteran. Newly discharged and getting used to half his arm gone below the elbow, Jason had a huge chip on his shoulder. He'd come a long way, and although it was great to see him giddy in love, it was also annoying.

"You doing okay?" Maggie finally asked, interrupting his thoughts.

"Just a little tired," he admitted. It was silly to pretend otherwise, especially with Maggie. She would know. "How does Libby Holmes fit in?" He changed the subject. Besides, it'd do him good to concentrate on something else than where his mind was wandering.

"You mean with the woman in the ditch?"

"With any of it. Pakula's trafficking idea."

"I'm not sure that she does."

"But you suspect she's not who she claims to be, or you wouldn't have taken DNA samples," Creed said, referring to the plastic evidence bags she'd filled with items from Libby's bathroom.

"In some ways, she fits the profile of a trafficking victim. She's here in the middle of a state where she apparently doesn't have friends or family. No one knows much about her. She takes off after another victim's been murdered."

"Wait. You think she knew about it already?"

"I don't know. Libby Holmes' disappearance might have nothing to do with the body in the ditch. Human traffickers rarely kill their product. Some of these guys started out as drug runners or dealers. Then they realized they could only sell drugs once. A person can be sold over and over."

She checked her phone one last time, then slid it into her jacket pocket, crossed her arms over her chest as if bracing for something. The text she had just read left a smile. She said, "Pakula keeps reminding me there's a snowstorm coming. Asking if I have a coat. Did I bring boots? He's like a mother hen sometimes. Did you bring a coat? Boots?"

"I have a jacket and sweatshirt."

Creed had noted the chill in the night air. Usually, he kept his sleeves rolled up and his shirt unbuttoned over his T-shirt, but earlier he had pulled the sleeves down; buttoned the cuffs and the shirt against the cold. And yes, he had packed a jacket, but it was lightweight. Somewhere he had a pair of gloves.

"How bad can it be in October?" he asked.

He'd lived in the south his entire life. He'd never worked a dog in temperatures below freezing. Any snow or ice he'd experienced was short-lived.

"Funny you should ask how bad can it be," Maggie told him. "I remember being in Pensacola once when there was a hurricane coming up the Gulf. I asked how bad can one storm be?"

"Which one was it?"

"Isaac."

"Oh yeah, that was a bad one."

"That's sort of my point," she said with another smile. "Pakula is obviously taking it seriously. I'm joining Lucy early tomorrow morning when she examines the dismembered parts. He's organizing a team to search the roads and fields starting at dawn before the snow covers everything. They'll see how far they can span out from the area where we found the pieces."

"I should have taken Grace a little farther up the road. Does Pakula want us to join him in the morning?"

"I think you can stick to your plan. Maybe Grace can find Libby Holmes before she hurts herself." Maggie looked out the side window into the blur of night, and she absently added, "There's still a chance Libby Holmes might be alive. The woman Pakula's team is looking for is already dead. The dead can usually wait."

22

Clay County, Nebraska

"You girls will thank me tomorrow," Ruben told them as he held the flashlight while they continued to dig. It would take longer with only two. He was really starting to miss not having three. Lately, it seemed like he spent more energy cutting away loose ends than enticing new recruits, but this last time, he had no choice. The girl he had recently cut loose had become a third wheel.

"Don't you want to know why you'll both be thanking me tomorrow?" he asked when he got no response.

Shelby wouldn't look up at him. She wouldn't dare show him the tears he knew she was failing to hold back. Vanessa, however, seemed to relish this task as much as the one that led them to this cornfield in the middle of the night.

She was quickly becoming one of his prized students, not just taking on his assignments, but eager to move on to the next. Up the ante. Show him. Surprise him. Maybe even outdo him, which was flattering though sometimes ridiculous. After all, he thrived on pitting them against each other, pushing them to compete for his attention. Competition quickly sifted the strong from the weak; the loyal from the disloyal. It was a successful process, despite leaving him in a pinch at the moment.

"Isn't this too close to where we ditched the bags?" Vanessa asked, leaning on the shovel and looking up at him.

"That's exactly why we're here. You want to keep them on their toes. Do things nobody expects. Be unpredictable."

"Be unpredictable," she repeated, staring at him. Her face was shadowed, so he couldn't see her eyes, but he knew they were intense when she was thinking and soaking in his lessons.

Just then, he heard something beyond the damned bugs.

"Did you hear that?" he asked.

He shot the stream of light up and behind them, making sure they were alone.

"Probably some animal waiting for us to be finished so he can dig it back up and snack." Vanessa laughed and Shelby cringed.

"Gross. Don't say stuff like that," Shelby told her. It was the first thing she'd said in the last hour.

Ruben kept scanning what he could see beyond the rows of corn. It was too damned quiet out here if you didn't count the cicadas and the rumble of a distant train. When he brought the flashlight back, he swiped across Vanessa's back. The night air had a chill, and yet, she'd taken off her shirt and worked in only a tank top. Ordinarily, Ruben would enjoy the sight of her sweat-drenched body, but he didn't enjoy looking at her most recent tattoo.

Oh, he was all for tattoos. He didn't mind them at all. Quite the opposite, he encouraged them. Even paid for them. But this one bothered him. The black scorpion looked so real, like it was crawling out from under her skin. He wanted to swat it off the back of her shoulder.

"Why?" Vanessa asked, standing straight, stretching her back, then leaning against the shovel handle to take a break. "Why will we be thanking you tomorrow?"

"Oh, right. Because it's supposed to snow tomorrow," Ruben said, keeping his tone casual but his focus pinned on the spot between the tall stalks. He could swear he saw eyes flashing at the end of the row.

"Snow!" Shelby whined. But she didn't look up. "Can we go back to Florida?"

"I don't mind snow," Vanessa said without so much as a look in Shelby's direction. "Extreme temps make you feel more alive."

He couldn't help but smile. The girl was a gifted liar, sometimes saying things to be purposely contrary. She knew how to use her words and actions to please, disguise, or even shock. Of course, the drugs pulsing through her system had something to do with it. But Vanessa was a treasure, and that's why he could forgive her colossal mistake last week. The drugs most likely contributed to that incident as well.

Sometimes the side effects screwed them up. But unlike Shelby, Vanessa quickly claimed responsibility and cleaned up her mess. Still, Ruben realized he needed to be careful with his praise. He needed to rein in Vanessa's ambition. He certainly didn't want her to believe that she could manipulate him, trick him, or worse, believe she was his equal. These girls were his students, not partners.

"As soon as our mission is accomplished here, sweet Shelby, we'll go to Florida," Ruben promised, in a soothing croon he'd practiced over the years. Instantly, he noticed her hunched shoulders ease a bit.

"Somewhere near the ocean?" she asked.

"You got it," he told her, again, making it sound like he'd make it happen just for her when he really wanted to tell her to stop whining and crying. "You'll be able to sit on the beach and sink your toes in the warm sand. I'll even get us some special cocktails to dab."

By cocktails, he meant marijuana derivatives. None of these girls cared much about alcohol these days. A shame, because he missed how slap-happy drunk girls could be. He still enjoyed a good vodka buzz.

Getting stoned, wasted—whatever the new trendy phrase might be—wasn't his thing. And regular, good ole weed wasn't good enough for these young girls. They wanted to dab, and they wanted wax, shatter, crumble. Some of the results were tiresome and unpredictable, especially when the paranoia set in or the anxiety and panic attacks took over.

He didn't really understand why they enjoyed it. Getting loaded was supposed to make you feel good and relieve your stress and tension. Although he had to admit, he liked to watch if any of them experienced hallucinations. And he liked it even more when he could use those against them the following day.

Florida was actually a great idea. Unfortunately, Ruben couldn't say whether rule-breaker, crybaby Shelby would make the trip with them or end up in a nearby cornfield.

23

Maggie was gone when Creed woke up before dawn. Still groggy, he couldn't remember much, except for a long kiss as soon as his hotel room door closed behind them. He wished they hadn't stopped to eat the pizza, because he was pretty sure he'd fallen asleep on her.

He found the leftovers in the mini-frig and a note tacked up against the phone on the desk:

I'll be with Lucy all morning. Be careful at the Spencers'. Remember the SNOW! Let's meet for a real dinner tonight. XO

The *XO* made him smile. Maggie O'Dell was not an *XO* kind of woman. They hadn't used the L-word, and every once in a while he thought he saw signs it was getting harder and harder for her to hold back. He knew Maggie O'Dell well enough to not be the first to say it or she'd run for safe shelter. Whenever they grew closer, she used the comfort and convenience of going back home and letting the months pile up between seeing each other.

But this made him smile. XO. She was running out of casual terminology to tell him how she felt.

He fed Grace and devoured the rest of the cold pizza. Made a thermos of coffee before leaving the hotel. He'd even taken the sweatshirt and jacket. But now, pulling into the Spencers' driveway, the first snowflakes began to fall. Fat, moist splats gathered on the windshield. They were wet, more than icy. Creed already started evaluating how these unfamiliar conditions would affect Grace's tracking. They'd worked in the rain, but never snow and never in subzero temperatures.

Odor molecules clumped closer together in the cold. Moisture made the air heavy and dense, pushing scent to the ground. It would no longer disperse in the air. Instead, it carried with the moisture, sticking to leaves and grass. None of that would be a problem for Grace.

But snow? Creed imagined snow added another layer of cover for Grace to smell through. Even that shouldn't be a problem for Grace. But if the air freezes, the scent would get trapped between the water molecules as they turned to ice. Hopefully, the temperature would stay above freezing and they simply found themselves tracking through the slush.

As soon as he stepped out of his Jeep, those hopes were quickly abandoned. The cold cut through him despite his layers of T-shirt, long-sleeved shirt and hooded sweatshirt. He glanced back at the Jeep's dashboard and saw that the temperature had fallen almost ten degrees just since he'd left the hotel.

"Mr. Creed," Nora Spencer waved to him from the front door. "Would you like to come in for some coffee?"

He had a full thermos, but he nodded and said, "Sure. Is it all right if I bring in Grace?"

"Of course."

Once on the ground, Grace pranced in the snow. She jumped and bit at the falling snowflakes.

"It might look fun now," Creed told her. "But it's already a lot colder than I expected." He swept at the icy moisture gathering inside his collar against his neck.

At least he had warm socks and serious hiking boots. Only ankle-high boots, he realized as he saw the toes being swallowed up by the snow.

"Ted left about an hour ago," Nora told him as Creed stomped off the snow before entering. He started to take one boot off when she stopped him. "Please, don't worry about that. Come on in and get warm."

This morning she greeted Grace, offering out her hand. When she straightened back up, her eyes traveled over Creed.

"You came up from Florida?"

"Yes, ma'am."

"Please, call me Nora. Did you bring a coat?"

"I should be okay," he shrugged, trying to remember if he had another sweatshirt somewhere in his gear to double-up.

"I'll get you one of Ted's," she said and led them toward the kitchen.

"You don't need to do that," Creed said as he glanced at the photos on the mantle as they passed. "Do you have any photos of Libby?"

She stopped in the kitchen doorway and turned, already pointing to the far right corner. "Just the one," she said before noticing the empty space.

She hurried to the spot and found the picture frame facedown. Her fingers grabbed for it, then she flipped it so Creed could see the empty frame.

"She took it with her," Nora said, surprised but obviously pleased. "It was me and her at the farmer's market this summer." She stared off out the window. "We had the best time. Went out for lunch. Came back home. I showed her how to make fresh salsa."

Her eyes came back to Creed. "I wouldn't be so concerned if she had taken the car and left. But it scares me that she just walked away." She glanced back at the frame. "I'm not sure what to make of her taking the photo."

"You said you're worried she might hurt herself," Creed said.

"Yes, of course. I mean, why else would she just walk away?" Her eyes searched his as if she hoped to find an alternate answer. "We confirmed she was pregnant when she was still at the hospital."

He wasn't sure why she was telling him this. He wasn't an investigator. Sometimes it was better to know less about the missing person. Handlers assisted their dogs. Too many preconceived notions, and there was a risk he could influence Grace's search. But he didn't interrupt Nora, recognizing her need to tell him.

"She didn't tell any of us. I figured it might have been the reason she tried to kill herself. She wasn't here a month when she miscarried. It was just her and me. She was so upset. When I told her we could bury him close by, that seemed to comfort her."

Nora blinked away her own emotion, and her eyes darted back to the mantle. She returned the frame to its spot and said, "I have this photo on my phone. I texted it to Agent O'Dell. I'll text you a copy. Let's have some coffee."

He sat at the kitchen table, and Grace leaned against his leg. She was ready to get to work. He needed to rethink safety protocol for her and resort his daypack. Protecting her feet would be an additional challenge if the temperature sank below freezing. Grace didn't like boots. It wasn't that she just disliked them; she refused to move in them.

Nora placed a steaming mug in front of him, then added assorted sugars, cubes, and packets along with a small pitcher of cream. He didn't need any of them. He waited for her to sit and join him, but she was off again, darting down the hallway. She came back carrying a black coat. She wrapped it around the back of a chair, then finally sat.

"Ted's never worn it," she gestured to the coat. "I bought it for his birthday. It's a Columbia Sportswear puffer jacket. I thought it would be snazzier than his old barn jacket. He hasn't a lick of fashion sense."

"This is an expensive jacket. I can't accept it," Creed told her when he really wanted to say that this wasn't his style, either. He'd be more comfortable in one of Spencer's old barn jackets.

"Please, I insist. Trust me, you really can't be out there today with only a sweatshirt or jacket. This is lightweight, but insulated. Believe me, Ted's gonna be wishing he wasn't so stubborn."

By the time Creed left Nora Spencer, he had on thermal socks with an extra pair in his pocket, lined gloves, and a dozen packets of hand warmers. He was most grateful for the hand warmers. He'd used the cold version in the humid, hot temperatures of Florida, so he was familiar with their instant relief. They were small and air activated, making them easy to use. He could even put one inside the pocket of Grace's vest if she got cold.

Nora suggested he park his Jeep in the barn's breezeway. It was a good place for Grace to resume the search, but he quickly saw Nora's reasoning. Just in the short time he'd been inside, several inches of snow had covered his Jeep.

Tucked away now, packed and ready to go, Creed pulled off his sweatshirt and put on Ted's jacket. The instant warmth was amazing. It was tight through the shoulders, but he could zip it up easily. He didn't even mind that the sleeves were two inches too short.

24

"These are clean, sharp cuts," Lucy Coy told Maggie. She ran a gloved finger over the dismembered hand.

As an FBI criminal profiler, Maggie had seen her share of dismembered body parts. Often the method of disposal—Dumpster, take food container, garbage bag—could be as telling as the dismemberment.

"Obviously not his first time," Maggie said. "Are all the pieces this clean?"

"Animals got into one bag, but otherwise, yes." Gently her long fingers picked up and turned the victim's hand so it rested palm up.

They were in the morgue of the local hospital. Lucy had mentioned that she set up arrangements when she became the chief pathologist for the Nebraska State Patrol. Lucy lived outside of North Platte, which was in the western part of the 430-mile wide state. County coroners were usually the county attorneys, so most forensic autopsies were performed in Lincoln in the south-central part of the state. In incidents where time was of the essence, Lucy could use these facilities for preliminary examinations. Or sometimes, when current weather conditions threatened a delay, Lucy could perform the entire autopsy. Especially as Pakula's team expected to gather more body parts.

To Maggie, it made little difference. She was used to windowless basement morgues. This one appeared well equipped.

"There's some bruising," Lucy continued, "around what's left of the wrist. Possible ligature marks, too. It's difficult to tell since he cut just below them. If we find the corresponding piece, it'll be more definitive. However, I did find some tissue under her fingernails."

"She got a piece of *him*?"

"You sound surprised."

"Clean, sharp cuts, but he leaves a possible DNA sample? Seems a bit sloppy. Reckless."

"Or perhaps he knows he's not in the system," Lucy said. "Maybe he enjoys taking risks. He left something else."

She pulled another tray closer and removed the cloth covering the dismembered part. Maggie couldn't immediately identify it, but human teeth unmistakably made the pierced imprint in the flesh.

"I know bite-mark evidence isn't usually conclusive," Lucy said.

"That's how they ended up connecting Ted Bundy to the sorority house murders in Florida."

"I didn't know that."

"He bit one of the victims. From what I remember, his was a distinctive impression because he had a chipped tooth and his incisors were crooked."

"This one's not that remarkable, but it might discount a suspect. It appears to be a rather small mouth."

"So, do all the pieces inside the bag go together?" Maggie asked.

"You're asking if he cut up an arm and put it all in one bag, then moved on to the next? That doesn't appear to be the case. It's more like a jumble of parts."

Maggie waited for more, but Lucy was still focused on showing her the cut marks.

"I believe he used a hacksaw. No surprise there but notice the lack of bone chattering. There aren't any hesitation marks or overlaps. Again, the cuts all appear clean and smooth. In some areas, the skin was snipped before he used the saw."

"Snipped?"

"Possibly tin snips," Lucy said as she showed her, running a gloved finger over a section.

"Not a knife?"

"A knife didn't make these cuts. Some may have been made with a box cutter."

"Hacksaw, tin snips, box cutter," Maggie repeated. "Common tools anyone can pick up in a hardware store."

"I'll submit tissue for DNA and to toxicology. Strangely, there's very little blood. Even at the bottom of the garbage bags."

"He was someplace where he could take his time."

Maggie had investigated murders involving dismemberment, but never one where the killer had taken time to cut the body into so many pieces. Did it mean something? A ritual of some kind? Again, she thought about Pakula's theory, that this victim might be a part of a human trafficking war. Mexican cartels did this sort of thing all the time. They wanted the shock and horror included in their message.

Maggie thought about Freddie Mason. He didn't strike her as smart enough to cut up a body so expertly. She suspected he was a minor cog in a much bigger operation.

She stifled a yawn with the back of her gloved hand. Last night, Ryder had fallen asleep after the pizza and beer. She was worried about him. He didn't seem himself. Grace had helped her make him comfortable, then Maggie left them.

She spent the rest of the evening packaging the samples she'd taken from Libby Holmes' bedroom. She found and drove to an overnight courier just before the last pickup deadline. Then she went over all the information they had on Freddie Mason.

Now she checked her watch. She'd already gotten a text from Agent Alonzo at Quantico. Her team was processing the items.

She wanted to rub her eyes, but that would take stripping off her gloves. Instead, she shoved the plastic goggles to the top of her head and swiped the back of her arm across her face.

"You okay?" Lucy asked.

"Just tired."

"Did you not get any sleep?" Lucy asked with a sly smile caught at the corner of her lips.

Maggie felt a blush rising. She knew exactly what Lucy was implying. The two women had become kindred spirits over the last several years, but she hadn't discussed her feelings for Ryder with Lucy.

"You know I don't sleep much," Maggie said.

"You're right. It's none of my business."

"That's not what I meant." But Maggie stopped short of telling her anything more.

"You realize it's been almost a year since I saw the two of you," Lucy told her. "I thought you should be together back then. What's still stopping you?"

"He's in Florida. I'm in Virginia."

"Right." Lucy turned her attention back to her work.

Maggie allowed a long silence, then released a sigh and said, "Truthfully, I'm not sure what to do about it. My marriage was a huge catastrophe."

"We usually learn a thing or two, even from catastrophes." Lucy looked up at her across the stainless steel table.

"I just remember how relieved I was when the divorce was final."

"Is Ryder Creed anything like your ex-husband?"

"Ryder is nothing like Greg. Ryder is gentle and strong, and compassionate. He's the only man I know who is so comfortable in his own skin that he simply doesn't care what anyone else thinks of him. I really think he'd be happy to live his life surrounded only by his dogs. And yet repeatedly, I've watched him put himself in harm's way to help someone he barely knows."

She realized Lucy was smiling. She crossed her long, lean arms over her chest. Maggie knew she'd shared too much. But if anyone would understand, it would be Lucy Coy. The woman had never married, dedicating her life to what was a male-dominated career when she was getting started in the profession. Maggie knew Lucy was a bit of a recluse, living on an acre with specially constructed outbuildings for the stray dogs she took in and cared for.

"So, you think I'm probably in love with him, right?" Maggie asked.

"The idea of being *in* love makes it sound like a temporary arrangement," Lucy said. "Falling in love presumes you can fall out? Love is never that simple. But it doesn't need to be complicated. You love him. If you believe he loves you, too, that's something precious. It's not something to be taken lightly."

"This really isn't the place to have this conversation."

"What better place than over a life that's been cut short? Pun, not intended." But Lucy draped each cloth back over each tray, signaling her full attention to Maggie. Then she crossed her arms again and said, "The real question," Lucy said, "What are you going to do about it?"

"I have a degree in behavioral psychology," Maggie told her. "So I know why I back away when I get too close. I don't get hurt if I don't care as much."

Maggie shrugged. She'd had this conversation with her friend, Gwen Patterson, who actually was a practicing psychiatrist. Gwen was the only person who knew about the abuse Maggie had endured as a twelve-year-old when her drunken mother would bring home strange men. Just because she knew why she put up barriers to her heart didn't make it any easier to deconstruct them.

"So you keep him at arm's length to protect yourself." Lucy said. "I spent a lifetime alone. Not a choice I made lightly. My only advice, if I may be so bold to offer any, is that you remember it isn't only you who could get hurt."

"I do remember that," Maggie said. "I just suck at relationships."

This made Lucy smile. "From what I understand, it's difficult to get good at a relationship unless you actually allow yourself to be in a relationship."

Maggie nodded. "Point taken. Now, if you don't mind, let's get back on track."

Lucy grabbed a fresh pair of latex gloves.

"Is there anything to show this victim may have been trafficked?" Maggie asked. "I know you have little to go on. Signs of dehydration? Malnutrition? Poor hygiene? You mentioned bruising at the wrist area. Do you believe they're recent?"

"There is one thing that lends doubt to that theory."

"Really?"

Lucy turned to the counter behind her and brought another tray to the stainless steel table. She lifted the cloth cover to reveal the foot. She pointed to the carefully polished toenails.

"I'm no expert in pedicures, but this looks professional. Cuticles are trimmed. Polish is recent. Unless we have a killer with a foot fetish."

The phone rang. Lucy ignored it for the first few rings. Finally, she peeled off her gloves as she walked over and picked up the receiver.

"This is Lucy Coy."

After only a second or two, she grabbed a notepad and started writing. When she was finished, she thanked the caller and hung up.

"I had them run the heart-shaped tattoo we found on the ankle. They got a hit," Lucy told her.

"Wait. Isn't that a popular tattoo and spot?"

"It could be." Lucy glanced at her note. "Nothing conclusive, but a local woman was just reported missing. A twenty-year-old named Kristin Darrow. No one's seen her since her shift ended last Thursday at the Menard's in Hastings. She has a heart tattoo on her ankle."

"A hardware store." That was the first thing that struck Maggie. Then she remembered. Menard's in Hastings?

"I think that's where Nora Spencer said Libby Holmes works."

25

The snow had let up. Creed didn't know much about blizzards, but he suspected this wasn't the end.

It was actually quite pretty. Clumps gathered on the tree branches and stacked on the leaves. It stuck to the cornstalks and filled the ditches between the rows. A fine blanket covered the pastures. The white made the yellow and red grasses even more brilliant. The sun appeared briefly and the entire landscape glittered before more gray clouds rolled in.

The only thing Grace had found so far was the wrapper from a protein bar caught on a barbwire fence. But she wasn't finished. He made her take regular breaks every twenty minutes for water and to check her paws. A scent dog's rapid breathing could cause dehydration, whether in hot or cold weather. Grace didn't appear fazed by the cold or the snow.

On the river's bank, she stopped at a grassy marsh and did a circle as she sniffed snow-coated cattails. She backtracked, this time keeping her nose closer to the ground. But she ended up back at the marsh and the cattails at the river's edge.

The bank wasn't steep. Creed realized Libby could have easily crossed here. Was it possible she had access to a small boat? Or an inflatable raft?

"Wait, Grace."

He stared out across the river. The water ran swift along the bank, not allowing the snow to make a difference. It was murky with debris. He couldn't see the bottom. Ten feet out, a sandbar stretched through the middle, then the river continued along the opposite bank. The other side was thick with woods.

Creed dug in his daypack and pulled out a pair of binoculars. Before he even put them to his eyes, he noticed a glint and movement in the trees. He glanced down. Grace had seen or heard it, too. Her ears pitched forward. Her nose poked the air, and her eyes were glued to the same area. The two of them were so focused, they didn't hear the deer behind them until it darted out of the shrubs. All Creed saw was the white tail racing away.

Grace startled as much as Creed. Then she shot him an accusatory look.

"What? I didn't hear it, either," he told her while he raised the binoculars again. "Hey, at least we don't have to worry about alligators or water moccasins." He could see his own breath. It was getting colder.

He put away the binoculars and brought out a map Nora had sketched for him before he left. She marked where an old one-lane bridge crossed the river. He couldn't see it between the trees.

She also highlighted a couple of paths. One on this side of the river and another on the other side. She called them irrigation dirt roads and suggested Libby could have taken one as a shortcut to get to the nearest highway. Grace didn't even hesitate at the mouth of the first path.

He squatted down and brushed off Grace's vest.

"We need to cross the river, girl."

She wagged and wiggled.

"No, we're not getting in the water."

Creed studied Nora's crude map again and tried to figure out which direction the bridge was. It didn't matter if they crossed exactly where Libby had. Grace could pick up the scent on the opposite side.

His cell phone vibrated in his pocket. He took off his gloves to get at it. It wasn't Maggie, and only then did he realize his pulse had ticked up a few beats.

"Good morning, Hannah."

"I'm watching the weather channel," his partner said. "You didn't take a coat, did you?"

"No. But I have a loaner, and it's quite toasty," he said as he tugged on the sleeves. No amount of effort brought them any closer to his wrists. "And actually we're out in the field right now. The snow is really pretty."

"That's probably what the Donner party said, too, right before they all froze to death. How's Grace doing?"

"She wants to roll in it."

Hannah laughed, and Creed smiled. He loved the melody of her laughter.

"She found several micro cards yesterday in a Shakespeare book and a cell phone in a cereal box."

"Good Lord! There's nothing that girl can't find. Why are you in the field? Electronic devices buried in the ground?"

"No. We're searching for a missing woman."

"Dementia patient?"

"No. A young woman. There's some concern that she may have run off to hurt herself."

"I see."

Both of them had lost someone to suicide. He waited out Hannah's silence. In the distance, a train whistle sounded louder and closer this morning than he remembered yesterday.

"I won't keep you," she finally said. "Just checking in."

"How's Brodie doing?"

"Bored. Yesterday, I took her to Pensacola's downtown library. I wish you could have seen her eyes. She's got her tablet filled with ebooks, but I swear that girl can't get enough."

"I'm glad she's getting braver about leaving our place."

For months after Brodie came to live with them, she hadn't wanted to be around other people. Even the thought of a room full of strangers threatened to bring on a panic attack.

"Rye? Be careful."

"You know I always am."

"I'm serious. You're still healing."

"I'm fine, Hannah." He didn't mind her fussing over him. They had been each other's family for a long time, but he didn't want her to worry. "Grace takes good care of me."

The little dog's ears lifted at the sound of her name.

"I know she does. But Rye, sometimes there isn't a thing you could have done differently."

"You're talking about this missing woman?"

"I'm always saying you have the heart of a rescuer. You've been doing this for a long time. You don't need me to remind you that you *can't* rescue every lost soul."

He knew she was right. He'd been on too many searches that had turned from rescue to recovery missions. But he'd let her say what she needed to say.

"And Rye, some don't *want* to be rescued."

"I know."

The protein bar wrapper Grace had found stuck on a barbed wire fence was a telling sign. It was in the middle of a field. Recent. The paper hadn't had time to weather or get dirty. It hadn't been close to a road or ditch for a driver to discard. If the wrapper was Libby Holmes', he couldn't imagine she'd run off to kill herself, but was still trying to keep her strength up.

"We're getting ready to cross the river," he told Hannah. "We'll take a quick look. If we don't find anything, we'll head back," he promised.

"You're crossing a river in the middle of a snowstorm?"

"There's an old bridge close by."

When she didn't answer immediately, he added, "Hannah, I'm fine. Really. I won't push it. And I'd never let Grace push it either."

"Okay, but call me later."

"I will."

The snow started falling again. He checked his GPS watch. Creed bent down to examine Grace's paws and nose. He readjusted her vest.

"Okay, girl. We're going across the river, but we're not going far. We'll need to head back soon."

He checked his daypack to make sure he'd packed the mesh carrier he sometimes used when it wasn't safe for Grace to be on the ground. He wouldn't make her trudge back in the snow. Right now, there were only a few inches. He figured they could do another hour, then head back. How bad could it get in an hour or two?

26

Creed couldn't imagine a motorized vehicle ever using this bridge. Whatever road or path that led to it was long gone. Grass, shrubs and cattails grew tall enough to hide the entrance. Before he attempted to set foot on it, he tried to examine whether it was sturdy enough to hold him.

He told Grace to "stay," while he ventured down the bank to look under the bridge. The grass was slick and icy with snow. He started to slide and grabbed onto an overhanging branch. The bark was slippery, too, and he almost ended up in the river.

"I'm okay," he told Grace before he glanced up to see her pacing and stretching her neck to keep him in sight.

It wasn't just the safety of the bridge Creed wanted to get a look at. He realized the old wooden structure might provide an opportunity if Libby Holmes had decided to kill herself. He hated to admit that once upon a time he had thought about different methods of suicide, a stockpile, a database readily available. Going off to some isolated location where his body might not be found but simply dissolved back into nature, had been at the top of his list.

But now, he blew out a sigh of relief, the emotion visible in the misty cloud of his breath. There was no one hanging from the galvanized steel guardrails. And no body underneath the bridge, in the water or caught in the debris.

Looking up, however, he was disappointed how much white, snow-clouted sky he could see through the rotten boards that were once a bridge. At least it wasn't a significant fall if he broke through. Maybe twenty feet, at the most.

A chill ran down his back just at the thought of plunging into the ice-cold water. It wouldn't be the first time for him. It was always Grace he worried about. Funny how his vision of dangers now ran through the prism of how they might affect Grace or one of his other scent dogs.

Ice-cold water, snakes, alligators, bears, mudslides? He could handle any of those. But he didn't want his dogs to experience any of them.

Grace's wag accelerated as he climbed back up the embankment. He stomped down a path through the thicket, allowing her to follow him until he reached the edge of the rickety bridge. He briefly considered carrying her. But if she was in his arms and he crashed through, she would go down with him.

He held up his hand and told her, "stay."

The snow was beginning to pile up now, covering the tops of his hiking boots. He couldn't see the boards, let alone the rotted holes he had seen from underneath. None of them had been large enough that he'd fall through, but he wondered how much weight it would take before they'd break.

On closer inspection, the guardrail looked sturdy, the bolts intact though rusty. Creed could see dents along the sides, most likely from bumpers. The rails had held. But they stood about a foot high off the flooring of the bridge and were only about six or seven inches. It would be easy to tumble over the side.

He turned one last time and reminded Grace to stay. Her front paws shuffled in place. Her head bobbed. Her ears stayed forward. She was not happy with his command.

The cold water below made the surface of the bridge slick. The soft layers of snow hid the layer of ice underneath. Creed kept to the middle. If he lost his balance, at least, he wouldn't topple over the ridiculously short guardrails. He stepped tentatively with slow, tight steps. From end to end, he estimated the distance was about fifty feet. Not significant, but under the current weather circumstances, it felt like a long haul.

When he finally reached the opposite side, he turned back to Grace and called out, "Follow!"

She came across, imitating his slow pace and keeping to the path his boots had made. He knew she wanted to run and probably could, but she would do as she was told. Her sixteen pounds wouldn't trigger a crack in the old wood, but she wasn't used to the icy surface either. He crept out onto the bridge, preparing to dash to her if she ran into trouble.

As soon as she was close enough, he swooped her up into his arms. He rubbed her paws with his gloved hands, holding and warming them. She licked at his face and only then did he notice there were tiny flecks of ice clinging to his bristled jaw.

"We check this side," he told Grace. "Then we head back."

The snow was falling so thick now Creed could no longer see the cornfield they had walked through in the distance. There was no wind. No sound. Only white, soft flakes that seemed harmless until he noticed how high it now stacked on the branches.

"We're doing a quick check," he said again as he placed Grace back on the ground. "Then we turn around. Okay?"

She was already poking the air with her nose. A couple of times, she jumped and bit at the snowflakes.

"I'm serious," he said. He waved his arm and told her, "Grace, find Libby."

27

It didn't take long for Grace to pick up the scent again, despite the layers of new snow continuing to pile up. Creed noticed that instead of poking her nose up, Grace sniffed the tips of tall grass and pieces of shrubs that peeked out. She plowed through the snow, keeping her head down and wagging her snout over the patches of landscape.

He didn't like this. The snow kept falling even as the white sky appeared to be getting lighter. It was almost over his ankle-high boots. Grace anxiously bounded through it. Soon it would be up to her chin.

Creed was about to call it quits just as Grace darted around a stand of evergreens. He needed to rein her in. She wouldn't be happy. But when Creed came around, he immediately saw the chain strung across the path. The rusted metal hung from steel posts on each side of what must have been a driveway.

If there had been a road at one time, it was now overgrown and swallowed up. Evergreen branches invaded from both sides, creating a tunnel. Creed had to push through them and duck, releasing patches of snow on top of his head.

"Grace!"

He couldn't see her beyond the scaly, fern-like needles that overlapped. The snow made them heavy. He used his arms to push and shove and weave, the scent of wet cedar overwhelming.

Finally, he fought his way through the last of the tunnel, and Grace was waiting for him. Snow was collecting on her back. He could barely see her vest. As if knowing what he was thinking, she shook herself and tossed her head for him to follow.

The dilapidated shed sat alone in a meadow, hidden by a stand of trees. What Creed noticed first was a set of tire tracks already filling in with fresh snow. The tracks ran from the huge barn door and disappeared in the other direction. Without a word, Creed gestured for Grace to come to him and stay close at his side.

They had either missed someone leaving or arriving.

Creed searched for a worn path that the vehicle had followed. There certainly wasn't a road. As he and Grace approached the shed, he could hear running water. The river was still close by, which meant they were hiking parallel to it.

Grace trotted alongside him. She was impatient. Her nose twitched and her ears pricked forward. Every once in a while, her head swiveled to the trees, but she didn't lead him there. Maybe it was another deer. Creed couldn't see anything. The snow was falling so heavily now it was almost blinding.

He trudged on. It looked like his original theory would prove true. Libby Holmes had someone pick her up. Just not at the Spencers'.

The door squealed on rusted hinges as Creed pulled it open. He stopped short when he saw the silver SUV parked inside. Snow caked its tires and covered the roof.

His eyes darted around the shadows. Space between the worn slats allowed light to filter in. So did the chill. There was no one here, but Grace insisted the scent of Libby remained behind.

Creed placed his hand on the hood. It was still warm. Then he noticed Grace's tail go straight. She was staring up at him and trying to not be distracted.

He turned to find a young woman standing behind him in the open door. Despite the heavy coat and stocking cap, he recognized her face from the photo Nora had shown him on her phone.

"Hey, Libby Holmes," he said. "We've been looking for you."

"You should have gone back when you had the chance."

It wasn't the response Creed had expected, although he suspected she might not want to be found.

Before he could tell her that Nora just wanted to know if she was okay, he felt Grace bump against his leg. When he looked down, he saw that she pointed in the opposite direction, toward the corner of the shed. Her lips pulled back in a snarl.

He glanced at Libby. Her eyes darted over his shoulder. Creed spun around to be met by a blur of blue parka. He barely got a glimpse of the flash of metal. His arm shoved the attacker, avoiding a stab to his gut. But his efforts had only misguided the target, and the knife plunged into his side.

He could hear Grace's growl, her teeth clacking as she snapped at the attacker's ankles. Creed put one hand down to protect her. With the other, he grabbed at the hand still holding the knife shoved inside him. His reflexes moved in slow motion.

He missed.

The attacker was too quick and pulled the blade out. It hurt almost as much as it did going in. All of it happened in seconds.

He found the young woman's face hidden inside the blue hood of the coat. Piercing green eyes, a dazzling white-toothed grin.

Then the pain bloomed inside him, and he dropped to his knees.

"Damn it, Ariel. You may have killed him."

"Don't say my name out loud."

"What the hell were you thinking?"

"I was thinking we need to kill him."

Grace was whining now, and Creed reached out and pulled her tight against him. He kept his head down, watching their feet, hoping they thought he was totally incapacitated.

He pressed his other hand to his side. His fingers immediately became soaked with blood. He needed to pull up the jacket. Get closer to the wound. Apply pressure directly. Maybe the insulated puffer jacket kept the knife from going deep. But right now, it felt like his guts had been pierced by a red-hot poker. He needed to listen and focus.

"You didn't need to do that." Libby's voice.

"Ruben could have sent him. He might be transmitting our location right now."

"Ruben didn't send him. I saw this guy last night with the people I was staying with."

"Maybe they're working with Ruben, too."

"Stop it. We need to think."

"I can finish him. Put him in the back of the car and dump him somewhere miles from here. I don't have a problem doing the dog, too."

Creed cringed at the recklessness of the woman named Ariel. While they argued, he slid his hand down between Grace and his daypack. He tugged at the zipper to an outside pocket where he kept emergency supplies to take care of Grace. He squeezed his eyes shut and let his fingers sort through until he found one of the packs. Somehow, he managed to rip it open without them noticing.

"You can't just dump him," Libby was telling the other woman. "Everyone knows he was looking for me."

Creed stayed hunched over, shielding Grace and his actions. He slipped the hemostatic wound dressing under his jacket and shirt. It was a little tricky. He clamped his jaw tight and shoved his hand under until he found the wound. He let his fingers inspect the damage, stopping short of sticking one in to see how deep the incision was. Right now, he needed to stop the bleeding. He wadded up the gauze and stuck it in, biting back the pain as he applied pressure.

"We can bury him," Ariel said.

"In the snow?"

"Well, I didn't exactly think it through."

"Yeah, I get it. You're not a real big thinker."

"Shut up! I'm here to help you. Remember?"

"Okay, okay. Let's both just calm down."

Still applying pressure with one hand, Creed kept Grace close with his other and hugged her against him, calming her, trying to convince her he was okay. His fingers caressed the tips of her ear. The vibration of her whines told him she didn't buy it. But she licked his hand, and the whine turned into an intermittent cry.

He wished he could tell Grace to run. She'd obey the command. He'd used it once before when he'd gotten into a situation too dangerous to protect both of them. It didn't matter that they were miles away from where they'd started. She could handle that. No problem. But in the snow and the cold? She had already been chest-deep, plowing through it.

No. He couldn't. He wouldn't take the chance that she might get stranded and freeze to death. Even the image made him sick to his stomach, and he was already feeling nauseated. His fingers were sticky with blood, and that was with the jacket absorbing some of it.

"How about dumping him in the river?" Ariel suggested. "The current's pretty strong. Why don't you just let me handle this?"

He knew he could take both these young women. Ariel had blindsided him, but she wouldn't have that advantage a second time. He just needed to tune out the pain. He had to focus, keep his breathing steady, his pulse rate down.

Slowly and quietly, he shuffled his feet, getting them planted while he watched theirs. They were turned toward each other. That was good. They didn't believe he was an immediate threat. He could neutralize them. He didn't need to hurt them.

"Where did you get that gun?" Libby asked the other woman.

A gun?

That changed everything.

Suddenly, Creed's hopes for protecting Grace *and* taking control just fell away.

28

Maggie checked her phone and tamped down her disappointment. She didn't have a text message from Ryder. As she was leaving the morgue, her phone rang, and she scrambled to get it back out of her pocket.

Disappointed, again.

"Hey, Pakula."

"O'Dell. Lucy told me you just left. Are you out in the middle of this?"

"Not yet." The morgue and the hallway that took her to the parking lot didn't have any windows.

"We found three more bags, but the snow is making it impossible to see anything, let alone walk another grid. I'm sending everyone home for the day."

She pushed out the EXIT. A blast of cold air hit her in the face. She felt like she'd stepped into a snow globe.

"How much more of this are they predicting?" she asked, hanging back under a covered portico.

She could barely see the vehicles in the lot through the swirling white.

"Could be through the night."

He didn't sound concerned, only frustrated that they would postpone his original search plans.

"Did Lucy tell you about Kristin Darrow?" she asked him.

"She did. Said you're headed over to Menard's. You know it's still a long shot that these pieces are her."

"I know." Then Maggie realized she probably should have cleared it with Pakula. This was his investigation. "Is that okay with you?" she asked. It wouldn't be the first time she'd overstepped her boundaries with local law enforcement, but she liked and respected Pakula.

"Right now, I'm treating this as part of our investigation. So not a problem. Want me to meet you over there?"

That was Pakula. Always smoothing things over. He was good at it. Sincere. Genuine. She knew that from past experience. Otherwise, she might have thought he was just a control freak.

"I can handle it. Unless you think I'm too much of an outsider."

He laughed. "O'Dell, in case you haven't noticed by now, you and me, we're both outsiders. Sometimes it's not a bad thing."

It was the first time she'd heard Pakula call himself an outsider. There was a reason the man had garnered the position he was in. Pakula had a swagger that made him seem invincible, but at the same time, he had a way of putting everyone around him at ease. He could make you believe he was just one of the guys, one of the working stiffs, no matter who you were. A county sheriff, a lab tech, a waitress at a diner. An outsider? Hardly.

"You check the hardware store," he told her. "I'll see what the local PD has on Darrow. How long has she been missing?"

"Last Thursday. I'm surprised Spencer didn't mention her when we found the first remains yesterday."

"She may have not been reported missing." Pakula suggested. "You think there's a connection between her and the Spencers' house guest?"

"They may have worked at the same store. Don't you think there could be a connection?"

"I don't know," he admitted. "My gut keeps telling me Freddie Mason might know what's going on."

"Maybe we should ask him."

"Not we, O'Dell. The last time you and I interrogated a human trafficker together, he took you and Ryder on a scavenger hunt. Let me know what you find out at the hardware store."

"Will do."

She slipped the phone back into her pocket and searched for her rental. She finally recognized it under several inches of snow, despite being parked next to a huge tree. Fallen leaves plastered the windshield. Clumps of snow weighted the branches. She didn't remember them being so dangerously low over the hood and roof. She slid inside, started the engine, and immediately moved out from underneath.

The SUV's tires dug into the snow without a problem, and Maggie was grateful she'd snagged one of the last 4-wheel drives. She drove to the opposite side of the lot and put it in park, blasting warm air. She needed to call Ryder.

After only a couple rings, it sent her to his voice mailbox.

"It's Maggie. I've been in a basement morgue with Lucy all morning and just came out into the snow. This is crazy! Let me know how you're doing? Maybe we could do an early dinner?"

She sent a text, too.

Then she sat and watched the snow gather on the windshield. She couldn't imagine Ryder and Grace out trudging through this. Her dashboard reported the outside temperature at twenty-eight-degrees Fahrenheit. It was twenty degrees warmer when she parked here earlier in the morning.

She listened to her voicemails to make sure she didn't miss one from Ryder. But there were only two, and both were from Agent Anthony Alonzo back at Quantico.

She scrolled through her contacts and found a number she had added last night. She tapped the call button and almost immediately got an answer.

"Hello?"

"Nora, it's Maggie O'Dell."

"Yes?"

She shouldn't be surprised the woman would be so curt with her. Maggie didn't even disagree that perhaps she deserved it.

"Have you found something?" Nora asked.

"We're still piecing things together." Maggie winced at the unintentional pun. Hopefully, Nora didn't notice. "Have you seen Ryder and Grace?"

"I just got back from the grocery store. His Jeep is still parked in the barn."

After a silence, Nora asked, "He hasn't been in touch with any of you?"

Maggie recognized the uptick of panic creeping back into the woman's voice. This time Maggie was feeling it, too.

29

The woman named Ariel was smarter and more dangerous than Creed initially believed. She knew exactly how to control him. She kept the gun pointed directly at Grace.

Once Libby realized he could stand and walk, she no longer listened to Ariel's suggestions of how to "finish him off." Instead, she insisted they take him along. They needed to get out of the snow and cold and take shelter. But the last thing she said to him convinced Creed she might be just as dangerous as her counterpart.

"You're coming with us," she had said, gritting her teeth to keep them from clacking. "If you do something stupid, it's over." There was a glint in her eyes that hinted of something wild, uncontrolled, and capable of carrying out her threat.

The wind had swept gusts of snow into the open shed. It howled through the rotted slats. Creed could feel and hear the dilapidated building shift and lean in one direction, then settle back.

Ariel insisted they pat him down for weapons. She relinquished the gun to Libby while she did a thorough search, grinning as she squeezed his crouch, then shoved her hands deep in his jean pockets and patted down his butt. She rifled through his daypack, pulling it down to her level with exaggerated force. When he was still too tall, she kicked the back of his knee, sending him down to the ground before he could catch himself.

Nothing in his pack interested her. Last, she grabbed his cell phone and waved it at Libby. "I'll take care of this."

Libby allowed him to clean and dress the wound only after she took Grace's leash and pulled the dog ten feet away. Ariel kept the gun pointed at Grace, too.

Carefully and slowly, he slipped off his daypack and laid it on the dirt floor of the shed. He began pulling out alcohol and more hemostatic gauze from the first aid supplies, all the while keeping an eye on Libby and Grace. Ariel hovered above him, but stayed a safe distance behind. He couldn't see her, but he felt her. And he could hear her raspy breath.

"If you shoot my dog, even by accident," Creed said in a calm voice, "I'll kill you both with my bare hands."

Neither woman said a word. When he unzipped the puffer jacket, Libby gasped before she could stifle it. His shirt and T-shirt were a bloody mess. He caught the anger in Libby's eyes as they flashed up and over his shoulder at Ariel. He tucked away that small piece of information. These two women weren't on the same page. He could use that to his advantage.

As he exposed the wound and poured alcohol into it, he saw Libby wince and turn away. He clamped his jaw tight and allowed a groan this time. He wanted them to believe that it hurt like hell; that maybe it had incapacitated him. But as he continued cleaning the wound, he realized it might be deeper than he thought. Was shock keeping him from feeling the extent of the damage? He did the best he could. There wasn't much more he could do about it out here.

He packed more hemostatic gauze into and onto the incision, then closed it with surgical tape. His T-shirt was soaked with blood and stuck to his skin. He was shivering from the cold by the time he zipped the jacket up.

Before they left the shed, the women were back at it.

"We're leaving my car?" Ariel asked in a whine that sounded more like an annoyed teenager.

"We can't get where we're going by driving."

Libby gathered up a backpack that Creed hadn't noticed before. She led the way, and they marched out into the blinding snowstorm. It was impossible to see farther than ten feet. He took some pleasure in Ariel's exasperated sigh. She clearly hadn't signed up for this part.

Creed tucked Grace under his arm on the opposite side of his wound. Snow caked his boots and felt like wet cement. He shielded Grace as he ducked under low-hanging branches, heavy with snow. In some places, even the women had to bend and weave between trees and shrubs. Not a single piece of green or yellow was left. A thick blanket of white covered the entire landscape.

Creed could still hear the river. In the distance, a train whistle sounded closer.

Libby stayed in the front. Ariel followed Creed, but he heard her stumble and fall back twice. He told himself he could wait this out. He was a Marine, being forced to walk single-file between his two captors in snow up to his knees. But he could wait. The fire burning in his side insisted he wait.

Several times, a crack then crash stopped them. At a glance, they could see branches snapping under the weight of the snow. In the complete silence, the sounds were amplified and dangerously close.

It was no longer just snow that was falling. Some of the precipitation had turned to ice. Tiny needles pelted Creed's face. He hugged Grace close to his body now, using both arms to protect her and keep her warm. Holding her tight meant not being able to apply pressure to his wound. All he cared about right now was getting out of this freezing cold. That was the best thing he could do for Grace and for himself.

30

The drive from Grand Island to Hastings was only twenty-six miles. What should have been a thirty-minute trip had taken Maggie an hour. Billows of snow blew across the road and up over the vehicles. Her fingers clenched the steering wheel. By the time she arrived at the hardware store, her back and shoulders ached from the tension.

Judging by the parking lot, a little snow didn't stop the locals. She stepped out of her rental and her hiking boot disappeared into what had to be a half foot of snow.

She checked her phone. No messages. She tried not to worry. Ryder would be the first to remind her he was perfectly capable of taking care of himself and Grace. But when was the last time he'd experienced snow like this?

She asked at the front of the store to speak with the manager and pretended to not be surprised when a young man who looked fresh out of high school appeared before her.

"Hi, I'm Kevin," he said, his eyes summing her up, ready to take her complaint.

She showed him her badge as she introduced herself, ignoring his eyes going wide as he repeated, "FBI? Is this about Kristin? I already told the police everything I know."

"Is there some place we can talk?"

He gestured for her to follow him and took her to the back of the store. The empty break room smelled of stale coffee.

"I don't know what else I can tell you," Kevin started before she asked a question. "She wasn't even on the schedule to work Thursday. She was filling in for another worker. You know, what's weird about that is I didn't notice because they look so much alike."

Kevin was a chatterbox. Maggie simply nodded and let him continue.

"Half way through the shift, I realized Kristin didn't have her own name badge on. She constantly forgets it. We can't just make new ones every time someone forgets. So I noticed she has Libby's on, and she tells me it was on her smock in her locker so she just put it on. Customers wouldn't notice. They look so much alike. It's just funny how—"

"Wait a minute." Maggie held up her hand. "Libby? Are you talking about Libby Holmes?"

"Yeah. She was supposed to work, but she traded with Kristin. They're not supposed to do that. They need to call me, but I—"

"Kristin and Libby look alike?"

"Oh yeah. They could be sisters."

"Kevin, I'm going to need to see your security camera files for Thursday."

"Security cameras?"

"The in-store, as well as the ones in the parking lot."

"I'm not sure how to do that."

"You're the manager, Kevin. I'm sure you'll figure it out, or you know who to call. I'll need to look at the receipts for the last ten days."

"You need to see how much money?"

"Items bought and time stamps. You probably have a digital way we can look at it. I'll have Agent Anthony Alonzo call you from Quantico. He'll give you instructions."

"Quantico?"

She could see Kevin was already in over his head. She wrote her name and phone number on a card and handed it to him just as her phone started to ring.

"I don't know how soon I can do any of this."

"I'll check back with you in an hour," she said as she left the room, digging her phone out of her coat pocket and trying to find a quiet corner.

A quick glance told her it wasn't Ryder. It was Agent Alonzo.

"Hey, Anthony. I was just talking about you."

"Stop. You'll make me blush."

"I have another assignment for you."

"Well, this was quite a mishmash you already sent me," he told her.

"Mishmash? Is that your word of the day?"

"Very funny," he said.

A fashionable computer nerd, he never seemed to mind a good ribbing. Besides, she had usually plied him with enough designer coffees that automatically moved her requests to the top of his busy list.

"It's such a gorgeous fall day, I'll let you have that one," he said.

"Oh, please don't tell me it's sunny and sixty degrees."

"Seventy-two degrees," he bragged.

"We're in the middle of a blizzard here."

"That doesn't surprise me," Alonzo told her, and she could practically hear him grinning. "Haven't you noticed, O'Dell, that severe weather seems to find you? Seriously, you need to start wearing some crystals or carrying sage."

"I don't believe in good luck," Maggie said.

"I'm not talking about a lucky charm. You need something stronger to ward off all that evil crap that seems to follow you."

She wished there was such a thing, but right now, she knew he had information for her. "What have you found in the mishmash?"

"Ganza's still working on the blood samples, but he pulled some decent fingerprints off the hairbrush. Let me get this straight. This woman is missing, not dead. Correct?"

"She's missing right now." Maggie unzipped her coat and found a secluded corner at the back of the store. Prints and DNA wouldn't mean a thing if neither was entered into one of their databases. "I'm guessing she's been missing from somewhere else for longer. That's why I suggested you check CODIS."

CODIS, the Combined DNA Index System for missing persons, was specifically designed to collect and assemble data, not only from the missing but also from unidentified human remains. Sometimes family members submitted their own DNA in the hopes it would help find their loved one. Maggie and Pakula had used it before to identify children who had been trafficked. Last year, they'd found two little girls, so damaged they couldn't tell their rescuers who they were.

"She's not in CODIS," Alonzo said.

"I figured it was a long shot."

"But I did find her."

"If you don't have her DNA, and she's not in the database, how did you find her?"

"She was arrested for shoplifting last January. Charges were dropped. But it was enough to put her fingerprints into the system. And her fingerprints showed up at a crime scene back in February. No charges, but she's considered a person of interest. How sure are you that this hairbrush belonged to your missing person?"

"I took it from her personal bathroom."

"The prints we pulled belong to someone named Emma Hobbs. Not Libby Holmes. She's seventeen years old. Lived in Richmond, Virginia, until about eight months ago. I'm still gathering information and checking records.

"Police weren't able to question her. She sort of just disappeared. No new charges on her credit card. Nothing on her Venmo, which had been active. Parents are divorced. Neither filed a missing person's report. I haven't had time to explore the intricacies of her dysfunctional family. Weirdest thing is, she graduated from high school early. With honors. Sounds like a smart kid."

"What was the crime scene?" Maggie asked.

"Oh yeah. That part is even more interesting. She and another girl were persons of interest in a murder."

"Murder?"

"There was never enough evidence for arrests. Sounded brutal. Police report suspected the victim was abducted from a local Walmart, drugged and beaten to death. Get this…with a hammer."

31

Creed wondered if he would have seen the old trailer even if they weren't in the middle of a snowstorm. Hidden inside a grove of trees, vines had grown up the sides and over the top. Plastered with snow and ice, the structure blended into the landscape.

Sagging branches creaked with new frozen weight. They hung so low, Creed had to bend and crab-walk under them. Grace smelled the blood and sensed his discomfort. She wiggled impatiently, wanting to walk on her own. He held her tight.

In places, the snow had already drifted. Instead of letting the pain in his side slow him down, he took pleasure in watching Ariel struggle to keep up behind him.

It should have reinforced his confidence knowing that he could escape at anytime, but he remembered how reckless both women appeared to be. The way Ariel came at him with no hesitancy; the fact that she stabbed him despite his attempt to block her suggested she had done this sort of thing before.

These two were running, hiding. From someone named Ruben. Libby Holmes didn't want to be found. She swept a booted foot to clear the snow and revealed two steps up into the trailer. She left the door hanging open for Creed, but barely glanced back at him, more concerned with getting out of the cold.

There was a welcoming blast of warm air. Even Grace lifted her nose from under his arm. The space was cramped. Creed's head almost brushed the ceiling.

A quick look around, and he realized Libby must have been preparing this place for weeks. Maybe months. It was clean. He could smell a hint of cinnamon and chicken noodle soup when he expected mold and dust. The wind gusted and ice pelted the metal roof. The trailer swayed a bit, but he didn't feel a single draft.

In the back, a sleeping bag spread out over the small bed. A miniature refrigerator hummed. An empty pot sat on the two-burner stove. The cabinets all had shiny new hinges. A corner of the countertop was chipped, but sanded down. The surface looked worn but clean. Plastic jugs of water lined up against the back. In the small stainless steel sink, a plastic bowl was soaking. If Creed listened closely, he could hear the low rumble of a generator at the back of the trailer.

"Bitchin' nice place," Ariel said as she slammed the thin door shut and stomped her boots. She heeled her feet out of them and left the boots by the door.

"The owner passed away a few years ago," Libby told them. "I guess he used it for fishing. You can't see it right now, but we're close to the riverbank."

"So nobody else uses it?" Ariel asked.

"I'm not sure anyone remembers it's here. It's really off the beaten path. That shed where you parked your car is his, too, but there's no house. I asked around. I guess he lived in town. He must have had this little piece of property to get away, go fishing. When I got the generator working, I decided to fix it up."

"You did a good job," Creed said.

He could see the beginning of a blush from the compliment, but she shrugged and turned away to peel off her coat, gloves and stocking cap.

"I work at a hardware store," she said. "I like learning new stuff. And we get a really good employee discount."

Two benches and a table were across from the counter. Creed sat down on the closest one, trying to make himself smaller and hoping to keep his claustrophobia at bay. A couple of years ago, he got buried in a mudslide. Outside the trailer windows, all he could see was a blur of white. It certainly wasn't mud, but it had the same effect of making him feel closed in. Buried.

Right now, he needed to concentrate on fitting in. The less threatening they perceived him, the better his chances of not getting shot. Although, he quickly noticed that Ariel must have tucked the gun away. It was no longer in her hand. She was moving around the trailer, opening cabinets and drawers, "oohing" and "aahing" her surprise.

"There's even a bathroom!" she yelled from behind a door. "Perfect, because I've had to pee for the last hour." She slammed the narrow door behind her.

He felt Libby's eyes as she pulled out a small coffeemaker and began spooning grounds into the filter. Grace poked her head up and licked his chin.

"Would it be okay if I gave Grace some water?" he asked.

She didn't answer. Instead, she reached to a cabinet above her and pulled out a bowl, then poured water from one of the jugs. She handed it to him and went back to making the coffee.

"Thanks."

Without looking at him, she asked, "Did Nora send you?"

"Yes." He placed Grace at his feet with the bowl. He had a collapsible one along with water in his daypack, but he used what Libby had given him. "She's pretty worried about you."

"She doesn't need to be. I can take care of myself."

"How the hell did you get water all the way out here?" Ariel was back.

"You can't drink what comes out of the faucets," Libby told her as she filled the coffeemaker from the jug she had used for Grace. "For the toilet, I pumped water in from the river. It just took a long hose and a little electric pump that hooked up to the generator. I filled the tank enough so I could at least go to the bathroom out here."

"Wow! This is really amazing. Ruben would never think of looking for you out here. You know how much he hates being in the woods. And the dirt path through the pasture? I drove by it like three times before I realized it was the one you said to take. Nobody'll find that after all this snow."

Ariel dropped onto the opposite bench and slid all the way over so she could lean her back against the wall. She must have taken off her coat in the bathroom. Now she propped up her stocking feet on the end of the bench. As if she just remembered Creed, she stared at him, eyes narrowed and darting down to include Grace.

"As soon as the snow lets up, I'll go dump his phone," she said to Libby. "I can dump him, too, you know. And his little dog."

Libby kept her back to the two of them. She pulled out coffee mugs from the cabinet. Creed noticed she had three of them.

He ignored Ariel and tugged off his gloves. Then he unzipped his coat and was immediately disappointed to find his side wet and sticky again with fresh blood.

32

Maggie was back in her rental, warm air blasting, windshield defrost on high and wipers still having a problem keeping up. She stayed in the parking lot, trying to decide what her next move should be.

She had reduced the young, easy-going manager to a fidgety mess. She already knew he couldn't meet her demands as quickly as she'd like. Alonzo had taken over. All the way from Quantico, he could be more charming and convincing than Maggie. Besides, he had access to cyber channels that she didn't want to know about.

So here she sat, staring at her cell phone and out at the snow. Every once in a while, the wind gusts were strong enough to rock the SUV. Her mind should have been working on the puzzle pieces. Kristin Darrow had substituted for Libby Holmes. There had to be a connection. Kristen fills in for Libby and vanishes. Then days later, Libby goes missing.

On line, Maggie found a photo of Kristin that her family had given to the local police. She compared it to the one Nora had shared with her of Libby. The two women looked very much alike. Maybe enough alike that a killer could mistake one for the other.

Alonzo said Libby Holmes had changed her name and lied about her age. She was seventeen-year-old Emma Hobbs, a suspect in a murder investigation. No, not a suspect. A person of interest.

Was it possible that the Spencers—a trauma nurse and a county sheriff—could be fooled so easily?

Did Libby/Emma go off to hurt herself again, like Nora feared? Was she taken? Or did she have something to do with Kristin Darrow's murder? How dangerous was this woman? And Ryder and Grace had risked their lives for her, walking into a blinding snowstorm.

This was all spinning into something bigger. And the worst part? She still hadn't heard from Ryder.

She tapped her phone and checked her voice and text messages.

Nothing.

She brought up his contact page on her phone, trying to decide whether to call again or text. As her finger hovered, she stared at his photo. She'd caught him with a rare smile, one corner of his lips upturned, a dimple barely visible under his carefully manicured stubble beard. He smiled more with his eyes than his mouth.

"Where are you, Ryder Creed?" she asked out loud.

She didn't care if he thought she was being overprotective. She sent him another text.

WHERE ARE YOU?

I'M STARTING TO WORRY!

Starting to worry?

She forced a laugh at that. She was beyond "starting."

The gauge on the dashboard showed the outside temperature at twenty-six degrees.

There was one thing she knew that gave her comfort. Ryder would take care of Grace. He might push himself, but he'd never jeopardize the little dog's health and safety.

Okay, so maybe his cell phone battery had died. He could have found some place to take shelter. There were other farms. It wasn't like this part of Nebraska was a vast wilderness.

Although, looking out at the ice pelting her windshield now, she realized this storm could make it feel like a vast wilderness. She couldn't even try to find Ryder and Grace without getting lost.

She scrolled and found Pakula's number. He picked up on the second ring.

"Hey, O'Dell. You find anything?"

"Quite a bit, actually. Right now, I'm worried about Ryder and Grace."

"You haven't heard from him?"

"No. And Nora said his Jeep is still where he parked it this morning."

"I'll talk to Spencer. See if there's a way we can check on him. Call a few neighbors. I'm sure he's probably just hunkered down somewhere to get out of the cold."

"I hope that's the case. But there's something else, Pakula. Something I just learned about Libby Holmes. She's not who she said she was. We all thought she was a victim. She might actually be dangerous."

33

Libby Holmes hated having her safe place invaded, although she had to admit, she did like having her hard work recognized. Nora had been generous in giving her a room in her home. She made sure Libby felt welcome, stocking particular foods after discovering they were Libby's favorites. Allowing her to borrow one of their cars.

Ted, on the other hand, pretended to be indifferent, all the while hiding his suspicions.

From the beginning, Libby knew her time with the Spencers would be limited. She figured she'd move on after a few months. But it had been easy to settle in, and suddenly two months turned into six.

She placed the steaming mugs of coffee in front of her intruders. The little dog had fallen asleep at the man's feet. He kept one hand down close to her, as if he wanted to be ready to snatch her up and protect her again.

Libby admired and resented him at the same time. She admired that he cared enough about the dog that he'd shield it with his own body. Yet she resented his audacious bravery. He didn't think she or Ariel were worthy adversaries, even after Ariel had almost killed him.

Libby was still trying to figure out how Ariel had gotten her gun, and so quickly. Actually, Ted's gun. She knew where he hid his backup. He probably wouldn't notice it missing unless his clean T-shirt supply dwindled. Libby thought she was good at stealing, with no one noticing, but Ariel was better. Ariel had barely arrived. They had only just met each other. Libby hadn't left her backpack for more than a minute to use her binoculars and survey the man tracking her.

It bothered her, but she was impressed that Ariel was fast and cunning. It reassured Libby that maybe the woman could really help her escape. Maybe a part of her wished Ariel had been successful in killing the man. It would have made things easier.

Just because it's easy doesn't make it right. She used to know these things. She used to care about doing the right thing. Now all she wanted was to leave as soon as the snow stopped and the roads cleared.

Nora had sent him. She was still trying to save her. Nora had saved her before when no one else gave a damn. She kept Libby's secrets, even from her husband. She'd taken risks to protect Libby. Just like this man with his little dog.

There was so much Libby had not shared with Nora. She didn't dare tell her about David Ruben. How could she? Nora believed she was lost and frightened. She did not know what Libby was actually capable of doing. Poor Nora. She still believed she could save Libby. But the truth was, Libby was more like Ariel than she would ever be like Nora.

"We came looking for you to help you," the man said.

When she looked up at him, he added, "My name's Ryder. Her name's Grace."

"Ryder," Ariel smirked. "That's a stupid name."

"My grandmother chose it. It comes from the Old English word meant to ride, of course, but referred to a horse-mounted warrior or a knight."

"Good for you. Your name is so special."

"Isn't that why you chose Ariel? You wanted to be special?"

"You think you're so smart? You have no idea."

Libby ignored their exchange. She stared at the dog the whole time and caught herself wishing she was special enough to someone who'd want to be her warrior.

The dog woke and looked up at all of them. She licked his hand and put her head down again.

"Oh, isn't that precious," Ariel crooned unnecessarily snide. "You couldn't afford a full-sized search dog?"

Libby knew it was the type of comment Ruben would have rewarded with a smile or a laugh. In that brief moment, she recognized she had changed. Ariel was still too close, newly running from him and the arrangement. His influence was too recent. Libby had learned how to survive without him. How to escape from him. Or so she believed until yesterday.

No, deep down Libby still feared she would never be free of David Ruben. Otherwise, why had she prepared this safe place in the woods? She had escaped before. With Ariel's help, she could do it again. She had to, because if he caught her, he would definitely kill her.

Kill or be killed.

She sipped her coffee and watched the man sip his. She watched and wondered how long it would take for the drug she'd slipped in his to take effect.

34

This time it took Maggie over an hour to drive the twenty-five miles back to Grand Island. She seriously thought about finding a hotel in Hastings to avoid the return trip, but she was anxious to get back to some normalcy, a hotel room with her meager travel items. And she found herself eager for the companionship of Pakula and Lucy Coy. The three of them were the only out-of-town team members who wouldn't be able to be home with their families.

Though the snow had let up, the wind had not. Traffic had been a crawl in a swirl of white, interrupted only by the red taillights to follow.

With dusk came a new dread. Branches heavy with snow and ice began to break, taking electrical lines down with them. By the time Maggie pulled onto the last street, she released a huge sigh of relief to find the surrounding businesses and her hotel with the lights still on.

She waited patiently as two pickups with front blades pushed snow across the hotel's parking lot and entrance. They were remarkably fast and efficient, shoving and adding to an already tall ridge at the end of the lot. The wind continued to blow and drift snow back over their fresh paths.

Maggie barely parked and her phone began ringing.

Please let it be Ryder.

Her stomach flipped as soon as she saw the caller I.D. It was Hannah Washington, Ryder's business partner. The exhaustion of the day threatened to dismantle Maggie's resolve. How in the world could she explain Ryder's disappearance? Then it occurred to her. Maybe Hannah had heard from him.

"Hey Hannah."

"I hope I'm not catching you at a bad time. It looks like y'all are in the middle of a blizzard."

"It's a lot of snow in October."

"Is Rye there with you? He hasn't been answering his phone."

"Actually, I've been trying to get ahold of him, too"

"I hope he and Grace aren't still out looking for that poor young woman."

Maggie leaned back in the seat and closed her eyes. Her nerves felt like they were tangled together in a knot between her shoulder blades.

"Maggie?"

"I'm sorry, Hannah." She swallowed hard. She didn't know what else to say.

"You don't know where they are, do you?"

"I've been leaving messages for him all day. His phone battery may have died. You know Ryder better than anyone, Hannah. He must be taking shelter somewhere. He has to be." She bit her lower lip before she added all the other possibilities her FBI profiler mind could imagine. "He has to be, right?"

"When I talked to him late this morning, he told me they were going to search a little more then head back."

"Did he mention where he was or if he was having any problems? With his phone? The snow? Getting lost?"

"Rye getting lost? I can't imagine that. He did say they were getting ready to cross the river. I remember that."

"The river?"

"I asked how they were going to cross the river in the middle of a snowstorm. He said there was an old bridge."

Maggie tried to conjure up an image of the Spencers' property. There were cornfields and woods, but she couldn't remember seeing a river or going over a bridge.

"Maggie?"

Hannah's voice had taken on a solemn tone that Maggie hadn't heard before.

"Rye wouldn't appreciate me telling you this, but under the circumstances…"

"What is it, Hannah?"

"Last June, the incident in Blackwater River State Forest. I know you didn't see him much over the rest of the summer."

"We cancelled on each other a couple of times."

Maggie couldn't remember the excuses now. She was under pressure to form a special crime unit at Quantico. The new director had given her free rein on her selections, but he also wanted it done and ready to go as soon as possible. She should have pushed for some time off.

"Rye was injured more than he let on."

"I wondered about that," Maggie said.

But she didn't dare ask during their phone calls. Hearing it, confirming it, only made her sick to her stomach. She shouldn't have asked him to take part in the trafficking project. Ryder had a strong sense of duty and obligation. Last year, this task force had given him his sister back. How did she not realize he was still hurting?

"He had what they called a lower back contusion. Rye said it was a fancy way of saying it was bruised. But it was bad enough to form a hematoma. That, with the broken ribs and the drug overdose…"

"Are you worried that he might be incapacitated?"

Maggie remembered how tired he was last night. She thought the two-day drive and the long day of searching were enough to cause his exhaustion. She suspected there might be a lingering injury. And now, how could she tell Hannah the woman Ryder and Grace were searching for might be dangerous?

Hannah was taking too long to answer.

"I know this," Hannah finally said. "He'd never put Grace in harm's way. When I talked to him, there was nothing in his voice to suggest he was in distress. If something happened, it came shortly after I talked to him. Otherwise, he was all set to head back."

Maggie stared out the windshield. She could barely see the entrance to the hotel less than thirty feet away through the blinding snow. And yet, all she wanted to do right now was drive out to the Spencers and figure out a way to find the path Ryder had taken.

She needed to talk to Pakula and the sheriff.

Then she thought of something. If Ryder called Hannah, they might be able to track his phone and find a location.

"Hannah, we've got to believe he's okay. I'm going to check on something. Let's keep in touch, okay?"

As soon as she ended the call, Maggie called Agent Alonzo.

"You're getting impatient," he said, in place of a greeting. "That's not a good sign."

"Sorry, I know it's late. I need a big favor."

35

K9 CrimeScents
Florida Panhandle

Jason Seaver finished the last kennel chores early. He had Brodie to thank for lightening his load. Weeks ago, Hannah insisted Ryder treat her like a full-time employee. Brodie was a hard worker and a fast learner. But she'd taken on Ryder's bad habit of not knowing when to quit. As Jason walked to the house, he could see her at the clinic, helping Dr. Avelyn.

He'd have plenty of time to clean up and get to Pensacola Beach for a late dinner with Taylor. They hadn't seen each other for over a week. He missed her. Of course, he'd never admit that to his buddies, who were already hell-bent on endlessly teasing him. Calling him "lover boy" and "Romeo." Those were the two nicer terms.

Truth was, he didn't really mind. Jason had never had an actual girlfriend before. Sure, he'd dated in high school, but his best friend, Tony, was a stud and usually the catalyst. Women flocked around Tony. Then they both joined the Army and went off to Afghanistan.

Ironically, they'd both survived war only to come home broken. It was over a year ago that he lost his friend. He missed him. Sometimes he still had conversations with him in his head.

Jason caught himself balling up the fingers on his artificial hand. The new lining looked more like skin, but it was a little weird getting used to it. In the span of two years, he'd gone from an empty shirt sleeve to a robotic contraption and now fingers with sensors.

As an Army nurse, Taylor was fascinated with the continuing process. Jason couldn't hold back a smile, remembering how she asked him to try out the new sensors on her body. He shook his head. Sometimes he still couldn't believe his luck. A gorgeous, smart girlfriend. A job he loved. And a home and family.

He felt a nudge on his leg, as if the black Labrador walking alongside him wanted to be included. Jason stopped to pat Scout's head.

"You're at the top of the list, buddy," he told the dog.

If it wasn't for Scout, Jason wouldn't be here. And *here* was home.

Sometimes, this place amazed Jason. Hannah and Ryder had built an incredible business. Tucked into the trees at the edge of Blackwater River State Forest, their fifty-acre property housed and trained dozens of dogs they'd rescued. The huge colonial house had been renovated to be their office and home for Hannah, her boys and now Brodie.

Hannah's kitchen was the central meeting place. The kennel, however, was the focal point of the business. A warehouse-sized building with large plate-glass windows and surrounded by fenced yards, it included a commercial kitchen, sleeping crates, beds and a couple of sofas. Upstairs was a loft apartment for Ryder.

The property also included a field house with an Olympic-sized swimming pool for water training. The veterinary clinic was stocked with the latest and best equipment. It included a surgical suite and a veterinarian—Dr. Avelyn Parker—on retainer.

Jason and Scout lived in a cozy doublewide trailer just steps away from the kennel.

This place was more than a job and free housing for Jason. It had been his salvation. And now it was his home and family. So when he came in the back door and into Hannah's kitchen, he knew immediately that something was wrong.

Hannah Washington was a pillar of strength and wise beyond her years, with advice you could take to the bank. She had tough standards. Jason and Ryder weren't allowed to bring women home to spend the night. She didn't want her boys asking questions. Said it was hard enough raising them without their daddy who had died in Iraq. But Jason had come to depend on Hannah's moral compass. Ryder had confessed once that Hannah made him a better man, and Jason hoped that was true for him, too.

She paced the kitchen with her cell phone in her hand. Maybe she was expecting a call. He barely garnered a nod, acknowledging his presence. He made his way to the coffeemaker and poured himself a mug. Scout greeted Lady and Hunter. Even Hannah's two dogs seemed tense and stressed by her motions.

Jason had planned on just checking in. He wasn't much of a coffee drinker, but he knew it was the acceptable social protocol and seemed to spur on conversation. Besides, Hannah usually had something delicious coming out of the oven.

He couldn't figure out if she was expecting a phone call or deciding on making one. Hannah looked distressed. Jason took a place at the kitchen table and waited.

She stopped at the island and put her phone on the countertop. Her hand stayed close by, fingers drumming. She glanced over at him then back down at the phone.

"What's going on, Hannah? Is everything okay?"

"Might just be a bad feeling." She shook her head. "Rye's not answering his phone. Nobody's heard from him. I was the last one who talked to him this morning."

"His battery might have died. Was he and Grace still doing the ESD search?"

If Hannah didn't look so distressed, Jason would have mentioned the irony—leave it to Ryder to let his phone battery run down in the middle of searching for a bunch of electronic devices. He knew Ryder had a love/hate relationship with his cell phone. He knew it was necessary to be in touch, but unlike most people, Ryder didn't use it quite like everyone else.

The guy was a wiz with gadgets. The kennel and training facilities had the most advanced security cameras, digital monitors and alarms. Ryder could check in 24/7 with a touch of an app. He could change temperatures and turn lights on or off.

"A young woman went missing." Hannah interrupted his thoughts. "They were out searching for her."

"When was the last time you talked to him?"

"Before noon. It was just starting to snow."

"Snow in October?"

"It's a full-blown blizzard now."

Jason looked at the wall clock. It was after five. That was a long time, even for Ryder. If Grace had gotten hurt, Ryder would still carry her all the way back, no matter how cold or how much snow there was.

Hannah's eyes met his, and the coffee kicked up acid in his stomach.

"I've got this bad feeling he's hurt," she said.

Jason didn't want to say it out loud, but he had the same feeling.

"Have they gone to look for him?"

"I don't think they know where to start. He left his Jeep at the farm where the woman disappeared. He told me they were getting ready to cross a river. It sounded like they'd been walking for hours. And now with the snow..."

"Don't they have, like snowmobiles or something?"

"I was trying to watch some news. They were showing fields still with cornstalks. Branches full of leaves breaking, taking down electrical lines." Then her hands flew to her mouth. "Oh Lord, what if some electrical lines came down on him and he can't get out from under?"

"Ryder's been in Afghanistan. He and Rufus led Marines through mine fields. I think he can handle just about anything."

"I know you're probably right. I just have this awful feeling that he's hurt." She steadied her hands by wringing them together. "They said the temperature is in the twenties. Good Lord, that's cold, even for a stubborn Marine."

36

Jason hated seeing Hannah like this.

"Rye said they were worried this young woman had run off to hurt herself," Hannah told him.

He could feel her eyes searching his face. She knew he had veteran buddies who had offed themselves. Jason didn't think she knew about his own attempt at suicide. It felt like a lifetime ago. He was an entirely different person back then, but he still preferred Hannah didn't know how close he'd come. Only Ryder and Scout knew.

"Ryder might have found her," Jason said. "Maybe she's hurt, and he can't move her?"

"It's possible." She didn't look convinced. She looked worried. Worried like he'd never seen Hannah before. "It does no good for us to sit around and imagine."

The back door opened, startling both of them. Brodie and Hank came in. The American Staffordshire terrier went everywhere with her. The two were inseparable. But it was a good thing. Jason swore he'd seen a change in Brodie's confidence level since the big dog adopted her as his new owner.

Within seconds, the tiny cat she'd named Kitten shot out from another room and weaved around all the dog legs to greet Brodie. All this was a welcome break. It even made Hannah smile.

"Dr. Avelyn said Hank's shoulder looks good," Brodie told them.

Ryder had found the dog at the edge of Coldwater Creek back in June. Someone had shot the dog and left him to die. Jason thought Hank was probably the scariest dog he'd ever seen—lean and muscular, with a massive head and jaw. Turned out, he was affectionate and friendly with people, but a little shy and cautious around the other dogs. He also had soulful eyes. He could roll those up at anyone, and it was hard not to like him.

Brodie looked up from the dogs. She looked at Jason, then Hannah, and within seconds, asked, "What's wrong?"

"Are we that transparent, Sweet Pea?" Hannah smiled again, but this one was forced.

"Did I do something wrong?" Brodie asked.

"Oh sweetie, of course, you didn't do anything wrong."

"Then what is it?"

Jason couldn't help thinking Brodie sounded more like a teenager than a twenty-seven-year-old woman. When she first came to live here eight months ago, Hannah explained to Jason that living in captivity had stunted Brodie's emotional growth.

He knew the malnutrition—from the starvation and drugs Iris Malone had subjected her to—had played havoc with Brodie's physical well-being, too. Tall and willowy, she had the straight hips and small breasts of a teenager.

Her years of confinement had robbed her of too many things, but she had grown in other ways. She was smart, perceptive, and fearless. And she insisted on the truth, always. That's why Jason left this for Hannah to tell. Because he already knew from previous experience that Brodie would immediately know if he lied.

"We're a little worried about Ryder."

"Has something happened?"

Jason could hear a subtle panic in her voice, but she stood perfectly still, long arms at her side. Hank brushed up against her leg, already alert to her discomfort. Even Scout scooted so close to Jason that part of his butt was on Jason's foot.

"We don't know. No one's heard from him since this morning."

"Well, if he and Grace are on a search, he probably lost track of time. Just because he doesn't call anybody doesn't mean something's wrong. Does it?"

A logical notion. Jason knew Brodie hated carrying a phone. Hannah had gotten her one, and most of the time Brodie forgot it somewhere. She spent more time trying to find it than she did using it.

"It's a little different," Hannah told her. "There's a snowstorm going on. And it's very cold."

Silence and tension filled the kitchen.

Jason tried to imagine if the roles were reversed. What would Ryder do if he was the one sitting here and Jason was the one a thousand miles away, possibly hurt and not responding? He didn't need to think about it for long. He knew the answer.

"How many hours is it from here?" he asked Hannah.

"To Nebraska?"

"Eighteen to twenty? Isn't it?"

Jason was already calculating it in his head. He brought out his phone and tapped in Milton, Florida, to Omaha, Nebraska, bringing up a suggested route. 1110 miles. Seventeen hours and eight minutes.

"What are you thinking?" Hannah asked.

Before Jason could answer, Brodie said, "I'm going with you."

37

Grand Island, Nebraska

Maggie met Lucy down in the hotel's bar. The place was crowded and noisy. Most likely, the hotel had filled up with stranded motorists. She was grateful that Lucy commandeered a corner booth.

The scent of French fries and burgers on the grill reminded her she hadn't eaten lunch. She slid in on the opposite side of the table, noticing Lucy's drink. Usually, the medical examiner had a glass of wine. Tonight, a rocks glass sat in front of her with amber liquid.

"Have you eaten yet?" Maggie asked. The aromas tempted her, despite the knot twisting in her stomach.

Lucy shook her head. Her short black hair looked more tousled than usual, the white feathered streak more prominent.

"This is all I want right now," she said, wrapping her fingers around the glass but not taking a drink.

"Are you okay?"

"Pakula brought me more pieces." She swirled the amber liquid. When her dark eyes came back to Maggie's, she said, "I haven't found a single organ yet. I'm having a more difficult time with this than I thought I would. What kind of evil reduces a living person to mere pieces?"

A waitress appeared, asking Maggie, "What can I get you, hon?"

"I'll have one of those," she pointed at Lucy's glass.

"Scotch, no rocks. Got it."

"And a cheeseburger with a side salad."

"You want the works on that burger, hon?"

"Sure."

"Anything else for you, ma'am?" she asked Lucy before she left.

Lucy shook her head again.

When the waitress was gone, Lucy said, "You get 'hon.' Old lady me gets 'ma'am.'"

"Actually, I would prefer ma'am. Strangers calling me 'hon' makes me want to slap them."

Lucy laughed, a full-throated laugh that made Maggie smile.

"This has been one helluva a day," Maggie said, running her fingers through her hair. It was still damp from her quick shower. "I saw Pakula's SUV. Have you heard from him?"

"He had some phone calls to make." Lucy sat back now taking a long look at Maggie. "He told me about Ryder going off the grid. How are you doing?"

"Me? I'm fine." But Maggie could hear the false bravado in her voice.

The waitress brought Maggie's drink, and both women went silent. Maggie took one sip and forced herself to set it down on the table when she wanted to knock it all back and enjoy the burning sting.

She had hoped the hot shower would relieve the tension in her shoulders and back. The tight-fisted drive in a slick snow tunnel should have taken her mind off of Ryder. Instead, it kicked up a gnawing panic in the pit of her stomach. Maybe food would help. It might improve her focus. She needed to concentrate on what she'd learned at the hardware store.

She glanced around the dark room. There was a steady hum of conversation, a constant click and clack of silverware on plates. Maggie leaned forward, elbows on the table, fists holding up her chin.

"This missing woman who Ryder and Grace are searching for? Libby Holmes? She's not some lost soul attempting to hurt herself."

"No?"

Maggie kept her voice low. "And if you confirm that we've found Kristin Darrow, then all of this just got more complicated."

"What makes you say that?"

"Kristen wasn't supposed to work the night she disappeared. She was filling in for Libby."

Maggie brought out her cell phone, took a few minutes and pulled up the photos side by side. She set the phone on the table and slid it over to Lucy.

The medical examiner glanced at the photos. Her eyes widened and slid up to meet Maggie's.

"I know," Maggie said. "They could be sisters, they look so much alike. The manager told me Kristen was wearing Libby's name badge because she forgot hers."

"Coincidence?"

"You know what I think about coincidences. I'm wondering if the killer made a mistake. Maybe it was Libby he wanted. She could have found out and disappeared. Or, and I hate to think about this possibility, maybe Libby played a part. She could have set Kristen up."

Lucy put the phone against her chest and sat back suddenly. She nodded at Maggie to do the same. The waitress appeared and placed a platter with a cheeseburger and fries, along with a bowl of salad, in front of Maggie.

"Anything else for you gals, right now?"

"No, this is great," Maggie told her. "Thanks."

As the waitress left, Lucy's eyes darted up and behind Maggie again. This time, she simply slid over. Pakula took the place next to her. Before he settled in, he was already searching for the waitress. Maggie shoved her platter of food to the center with the fries facing him.

"She just left. Go ahead," she told him. They had shared enough meals over the course of the week that they'd gotten into a routine like an old married couple.

"Thanks. I'm starving."

As he grabbed a couple of fries, Lucy showed him the photos on Maggie's cell phone.

"Who am I looking at?" he asked as he grabbed a pair of reading glasses from his jacket pocket.

Maggie glanced around to make sure no one was paying attention to them. Then she said, "On your left is Kristen Darrow. She's the hardware store worker who disappeared last Thursday."

"The one we might have found," Pakula added.

"On your right is Libby Holmes. Both women work at the same store. The manager told me Kristen was actually filling in for Libby on Thursday. She was even wearing Libby's name badge because she forgot her own."

Pakula looked up over the frame of his glasses to meet Maggie's eyes. He handed her phone back to her over the table. Folded up his glasses and tucked them into his jacket. All the while, his eyes never left hers.

"Okay, before you ask me why Spencer didn't know about her yesterday," Pakula said. "The family only reported her missing this morning. She lived alone in an apartment in Hastings. Her family lives on a farm about fifty miles away, but she was usually in touch with them a couple of times a week. When they didn't hear from her, and she didn't answer her phone, they started getting worried. Her father drove in. Checked her apartment. Found her cat all alone and hungry. Last night, they found her car still parked in the Menard's parking lot."

"Does Spencer know now?" Maggie asked.

"Not yet. I haven't shared with anyone except present company. As far as I know, we don't have a confirmed ID," he glanced at Lucy. "Is that still true?"

She nodded.

"Spencer is Clay County. Hastings is in Adams County. Plus, Hastings has its own police department, so they're investigating her disappearance. Nothing suspicious here, O'Dell. Really, I think it all just happened quickly. Spencer's a part of my task force, so his guys have been working with us for the last several days."

"Does the Darrow family know anything about what we've found?" Lucy asked.

"I'm told they're asking questions. Officially, we're the only three who know. The heart hasn't been found yet." He paused and glanced at Lucy again. Waited for her confirmation, then continued, "I've been granted temporary jurisdiction until that happens. Of course, with the assistance of local law enforcement and the State Patrol."

The waitress appeared again.

"What can I get for you, sir?"

Maggie and Lucy exchanged a look. Pakula was "sir."

"My wife will kill me if she finds out how much red meat I've been eating."

"Not to mention fries," Maggie added.

"People seem to really like our buffalo chicken sandwich," the waitress offered.

"Deal. Add a salad with that, so I can tell the wife had veggies."

"And what would you like to drink?"

He glanced at Maggie's and Lucy's glasses. "I'll have what the ladies are drinking."

Maggie waited for the waitress to be swallowed up in the crowd before she asked, "So, are you still thinking this is related to human trafficking?"

Pakula shrugged as he added ketchup to the corner of Maggie's plate. Then he dipped the fries in, two at a time. "I'd like to believe it was that easy."

Maggie felt her cell phone vibrate in her pocket. She plucked it out quickly. She didn't bother to constrain her sigh of disappointment.

Still not Ryder. A text from Agent Alonzo. He'd arranged for her to look at the Menard's security video tomorrow morning.

"Everything okay?" Lucy asked.

"I keep hoping to hear from Ryder."

"About that," Pakula said, wiping his mouth with a napkin. "I guess Nora has been contacting neighbors, asking if anyone's seen Ryder or Libby. Having them check their outbuildings. Ted tried to get down an old irrigation road, but he said it's already drifted over."

Maggie had only taken one bite of her burger and didn't want any more. She grabbed for the whisky instead and took another sip.

"This doesn't feel right," she told them. "Last night when Ryder and I were at the Spencers', I bagged some items from Libby Holmes' bathroom." She paused to see if either of them would question her tactics. I overnighted them to my team at Quantico."

Lucy leaned in closer, interested. "Is that how you know she isn't who she claims to be? Isn't that what you said earlier?"

Maggie nodded. "They were able to pull prints and got a match from a shoplifting charge. She's a seventeen-year-old from Virginia. Her name's Emma Hobbs. She's wanted for questioning as a person of interest in a murder investigation."

"You're kidding. Murder?" Pakula asked.

"Her fingerprints were found at the crime scene."

"How sure are they that this is the same person?" Lucy asked.

"Photos match. Fingerprints match."

"That's why you think she's involved in this murder?" Pakula asked.

Maggie nodded. "Alonzo is still getting me details about the case in Virginia, but he said it was brutal. Two teenaged girls drugged another, then beat her to death with a hammer."

"Whoa!" Pakula leaned in. "You said this Libby was only a suspect. She wasn't arrested?"

"Right. And she disappeared before they could question her."

"The Spencers must not know about this," Pakula said.

"I'm not so sure Nora doesn't," Maggie told him. "Last night, when Ryder and Grace started their search, they found a grave behind the barn. Nora admitted Libby miscarried when she first arrived. Ted knew nothing about it."

"And you're worried Ryder and Grace are searching for someone who may be dangerous?" Lucy asked.

"Or she's led him to someone who is," Maggie suggested.

38

Hastings, Nebraska

David Ruben hated the cold. And snow pissed him off.

He texted Vanessa to let her know he and Shelby were stuck in Hastings for the night. He decided he would not drive in this crap. The expense of another hotel room in a different city was simply an inconvenience. Money was never a problem. His parents had left him plenty after their tragic accident, an accident he orchestrated. It was one of his first successful experiments and probably his most brilliant.

The snow was a reminder of things he couldn't control. They needed to finish up business and hit the road for some place warmer. Shelby's idea of Florida sounded better and better.

Vanessa didn't answer as quickly as he would have liked. She was probably still tired. She did the bulk of the digging last night. Or it peeved her that Shelby got to spend the night alone with him.

He couldn't be upset if that was the case. After all, he'd worked hard to create that exact atmosphere. He wanted his girls jealous of each other and vying for his attention. Part of his strategy was built on that motivational premise.

Shelby came back to the room, beaming. She presented a tray full of goodies.

"They have free popcorn and Coke in the lobby. I brought you some, too."

She had such a radiant smile when she was happy. He rewarded her with one of his own and gestured for her to put his can of cola on the nearby night table. He sat on the edge of one of the queen-sized beds and channel-surfed. Shelby took the chair by the window, watching the snow and gobbling popcorn.

Before they left the Walmart, Ruben suggested they buy whatever they needed for their sleepover. Shelby did love a shopping spree. It put her in an absolutely effervescent mood. Or maybe it was the drugs. She was like a shaken champagne bottle waiting to blow her cork.

He stopped and considered the opportunity for only a second or two. Did he want to waste his time teasing her? She was certainly primed for sex. Sometimes he missed the days when he screwed his girls all night long. He did still enjoy watching. He just couldn't participate anymore. Not to his satisfaction. He'd rather stick to other ways of controlling them. Seeing him vulnerable or weak was not an option.

Also, he'd discovered being a father figure was much more powerful. Young women learned too quickly how to use sex to manipulate men. The fact that it didn't work with him contributed to his all-powerful image. And his influence.

So he ignored Shelby and continued looking for local news. He wanted to see if there was anything about the missing hardware store worker. It was probably too early for information on the boy waiter.

Out of the corner of his eye, he saw Shelby on her phone, texting someone. He pretended not to notice. It couldn't be another boy. She had to have learned her lesson. But when she smiled, he felt the low boil at the back of his skull. Already his teeth started to clench.

She looked up at him. The smile was more radiant than before as she said, "Got it! We finally have directions and an address for Emma Hobbs. She's living in a place in the country not far from here."

He was impressed. Shelby and Vanessa were working together as a team. Since last week's mishap, the two had been determined to use their social media connections and on-line skills.

Shelby tapped something back, then looked up again and asked, "Should we start calling her Libby Holmes?"

39

Florida Panhandle

Brodie was packed and ready to go before Jason could change his mind. It was a given that Hank would go along, but she needed to figure out a way to sneak Kitten with her. They had been inseparable for almost a year. She couldn't leave the cat behind.

She just couldn't.

Hannah prepared food in two travel coolers, enough for three or four days. Brodie knew that was Hannah's way of compensating for not being able to join them.

A streak of guilt almost kept Brodie from going when she realized Hannah might have to handle all the kennel chores. Then she overheard Jason arranging to have his veteran buddies come help. She accidentally overheard part of his phone call with Taylor, too. He sounded so disappointed that he wouldn't be able to see her.

Secretly, Brodie didn't like Taylor Donahue. She wasn't sure why, she just didn't. It was bad enough that Hank recognized her, got excited and wagged at her, but then to listen to Jason's lovey-dovey talk was a bit too much. The woman was too pretty, her body too perfect. She couldn't walk into a room without every man gawking at her. None of that was Taylor's fault, but Brodie could tell that Taylor liked it. Liked it a lot. Used it to her advantage.

And why did Taylor still care about what other men thought when she already had Jason? He should be enough for her. Jason was more than she deserved.

Taylor got her last boyfriend, John Lockett, killed. Lockett had been Hank's owner. When it came right down to it, Brodie figured it was Taylor's fault that Hank had gotten shot, too.

No, Brodie didn't much like Taylor.

So why, when they were only a few miles across the Alabama border, did she bring up the woman? It sort of fell out of her mouth.

"Is Taylor mad at you for leaving?"

"I wouldn't say mad, but I think she's disappointed."

"Hannah looked sad."

"Hannah's really worried."

Jason's cell phone pinged. He had it in a holder facing him so he could glance at the incoming messages without touching it. Brodie watched his eyes read the message then dart to the rearview mirror.

"You brought Kitten with you?" he asked.

Busted.

"He's never been away from me. And he gets along just fine with Hank and Scout. I promise you won't even know he's here." She avoided looking down at her feet because out of the corner of her eye she could see his little head poking out of the duffle bag.

"You better tell Hannah. She's been looking all over for him."

"Okay."

"You did remember your phone, right?"

"Of course." She was pretty sure it was still on her bedroom dresser. "It's somewhere in my bag. Can I just use yours to text Hannah?"

"Sure."

She twisted the phone around to face her and tapped in the message. It was tempting to get a peek at the messages he and Taylor had exchanged. Instead, Brodie adjusted the holder back in place.

She knew Jason and Hannah were really worried about Ryder. Just because he didn't call or text or answer his phone didn't mean he was in trouble. Cell phones gave people a false sense of security. Having one in her pocket never made her feel safe. She tried to explain that to everyone, then finally gave up and let Hannah get her one. They all seemed to feel better knowing she had it, but she hardly remembered to take it with her. Unlike her canister of bear spray, which actually could protect her.

She pulled her leg up under her and took a look into the back of the SUV. Both Scout and Hank were in their soft-shell crates, pretending to sleep. Well, Scout was actually sleeping. Hank always seemed to keep a half-open eye on Brodie.

The sun started to sink behind the trees. Brodie sat back. She turned so she could look out the side window and tried to tamp down a sick feeling as she watched the landscape glide by. She hadn't been away from Ryder and Hannah's property for more than several hours. And when she was, it would usually be less than twenty or thirty miles. The last time she was on a road trip was when Ryder brought her to Florida from Nebraska. Now she was making the same trip in the opposite direction.

Her stomach churned, remembering. Back then, she was still so scared. So weak. Her therapist, Dr. Rockwood, insisted Brodie replace those memories with good ones.

"It's okay to pull them out. Examine them, then tuck them away and think of something good in your life."

The exercise was supposed to stave off a full-blown panic attack. She hadn't experienced one in months. And now as she watched everything familiar slide past her window, Brodie felt the tingle in her nerve-endings. She tasted the bile threatening to back up. She needed to breathe.

"Hey, Brodie," Jason's voice startled her. "Are you hungry? You mind handing me one of those sandwiches Hannah packed?"

She swallowed hard. Gulped in a breath. Blinked her eyes.

Maybe her going along was a bad idea.

40

In his fever dream, Creed walked through a forest. Grace was at his feet, though he could barely see her. She whimpered, and he jolted, reaching for her, but she wasn't there. The grass grew as tall as his knees. It was blood red.

He tried to call for Grace, but his mouth didn't work. He was dreaming. Somehow, he knew that. He was on the edge of consciousness. He could hear Libby and Ariel talking. They were close by, but he couldn't see them either. His eyelids were too heavy, and he couldn't leave the forest.

"When was the last time you saw Ruben?" It was Ariel, but he knew she wasn't talking to him.

"It's been a while," Libby said.

"Was he using the fake walking cane back then?"

"I don't remember."

"He's so lame sometimes. Lame. Did you hear that? I made a joke and didn't even know. Hey, you want a few of these gummies?"

"No. Thanks."

"One time—this is so funny. He sent us in to a convenience store and we were supposed to see how many items we could lift while he talked to the clerk and bought cigarettes from behind the counter. We like literally had about two minutes. Did he ever have you do that?"

"No."

"Did he ever take you to Walmart or Target," Ariel's voice had changed to a low growl, "And in the middle of, you know, like the shampoo aisle or someplace, did he have you pick out a customer for you to kill?"

The wind howled through the trees, but Creed thought he heard Libby say, "Yes."

Branches rattled above him, some cracked and started raining down. Dirt came with it. Earth falling from the sky. He looked for Grace and missed part of the mumbled conversation. He picked only words and phrases out of each gust: "torture," "cut the heart out," and "leave him in a ditch."

He wasn't sure if they were talking about him. Would he be able to feel the knife again, way out here in the middle of the forest with all the red grass?

"Well, did he make you choose an undercover name?" They were back to Ruben and Ariel's sing-song continued, "You know, like for when you had to get a hotel room. He always had one of us girls go in and get the room. Pay cash. But you have to give them a name. What name did you choose?"

"I didn't do that. It must be something new."

"Are you sure you didn't? Or you just don't want to share it with me. I mean, I get it. You still don't trust me."

"I didn't say that."

Creed could hardly hear Libby. Her voice came from behind the trees. Ariel's fell from the sky.

"No, that's okay. Trust should be earned."

"Let me guess," Libby said. "You chose Ariel."

"It's beautiful, isn't it?"

From Shakespeare, Creed thought. *The Tempest.* A spirit obligated to serve a magician. Where had he just seen Shakespeare? All he could see were tiny little cards falling like rain from the pages.

"What did he do?" Libby asked.

Creed tried to find her. It sounded like she was behind him now. He'd need to backtrack, but there was no way to turn around.

"What do you mean?"

"What did he do to make you run?"

The silence lasted long enough, Creed thought he and Grace were alone. When Ariel's voice came again, it sounded stripped of all the joy and carefree spirit that had lifted it to the clouds. Now it seemed to grumble up from the ground, boiling through the dark red grass.

"I don't want to talk about it," she said. "Look, are we gonna do this or not? He wasn't part of the plan. We need to get rid of him."

Creed realized the grass was dripping wet and rubbing against his pant legs. It painted the fabric with streaks of red. He wiped at the mess with the palm of his hand, only to discover the grass wasn't actually red.

It was drenched in blood.

And it was at that moment Creed knew the blood was his.

41

Maggie stood at her fourth-floor hotel room window. She couldn't sleep. Every time she tried, she thought about Ryder and Grace. She'd gone down to his hotel room to make sure all his things were safe and untouched. They'd given each other keycards to their rooms. Maggie's idea of intimacy.

She was ridiculous. Immature. She was so lame at relationships.

Why did she continue to put up boundaries? She cared about this man. Deep down, she knew she loved him. And yet, she kept him at arm's length every chance she got.

She had no clue what a relationship with him looked like. What kind of promises could they make to each other when their individual lives kept them a thousand miles apart? She would never ask him to give up his home. And she knew he would never ask that of her.

So what did that mean?

To her, the questions were rhetorical. As long as she kept thinking of them in that way, she never had to find an answer.

There was one thing she was certain of, however. She wanted Ryder Creed in her life. No, it was more than that. She couldn't imagine a life without him in it.

"Ryder, where are you?" she asked out loud as she stared into the white blur of night. "You have to be safe."

The parking lot down below looked like mounds of snow. There was nothing to distinguish the vehicles buried underneath except their basic shapes.

Her phone pinged behind her. It was tethered to the desk as it charged. She left her perch to check the incoming message. Her adrenaline was gone. Exhaustion had settled in. The sound had generated only a slight uptick of her pulse, whereas earlier, every nerve-ending had alerted to any possible communication from Ryder.

It was Agent Alonzo. He was letting her know he'd sent her an email.

She glanced at the digital clock on the nightstand—half past midnight. She shook her head and smiled. When constructing a crime unit, she unintentionally surrounded herself with members as driven as she was.

She logged into her account. His email included several attachments. The first one included a news article from a local publication. The headline read: Sterling, Virginia All-American Athlete is Suspect in Murder Case.

Emma Hobbs, an honor student and star soccer player at Dominion High School, has been named a person of interest in the murder of a Richmond woman. Gina Franklin had been missing for two weeks before hikers found her body near Abington, Virginia. Hobbs, who graduated early from high school as a National Merit Scholar, was expected to begin college in August at the University of Florida on a soccer scholarship.

Maggie remembered Nora saying that Libby Holmes was smart. Turns out she was an All-American athlete, too. And yet, somehow, she got mixed up in a murder.

She pulled up Nora's photo of Libby and compared it to the high school graduation photo the news article had included of Emma Hobbs. Despite knowing both photos were of the same teenager, Maggie had to look for the resemblance. Emma's smile appeared careless and confident, a high school graduate ready to take on the world. Libby looked so much older and hardened. Both smiles were genuine, but a spark was missing from Libby's eyes, replaced by something flat and cynical.

Emma graduated last December. The Spencers said she came to live with them just after Easter. Maggie searched the news article. The body of Gina Franklin was found on February 25. In less than ten months, Emma was suspected of murder, got pregnant, changed her name, traveled 1300 miles, then tried to commit suicide.

And now she may have gotten another woman murdered.

Maggie opened the other attachments Alonzo had sent. One was a police report. The other was a copy of the autopsy report for Gina Franklin.

Autopsy report.

Alonzo had told her the murder was brutal. Maybe she could find some answers in the report. But her eyes were tired. She saved and closed everything, deciding to pull out her laptop.

As she walked by the window, she noticed the snow had stopped falling and was mostly just blowing. Through the swirl, she couldn't see much. While her laptop powered up, she used her cell phone to tap out one last text message.

RYDER, I'M THINKING ABOUT YOU. HOPE YOU AND GRACE ARE SAFE. AND WARM.

She needed to keep her mind busy. She clicked on the attachment and scrolled through the scanned pages of the autopsy report. Halfway down the third page, she stopped.

Alonzo had told her the victim had been beaten to death with a hammer. He did not, however, mention that the body had been dismembered.

42

Jason had been driving for over eight hours. It was long after midnight. He'd been up since 5:00 a.m. chores. Hannah's goodies and even the Red Bull weren't working. And Brodie had gone uncharacteristically quiet. She was probably tired, too. Once in a while, he glanced over. In the blue dashboard lights, he could see her eyes were closed. He didn't think she was sleeping, though he'd told her it was okay.

Hannah had texted him when she found Brodie's cell phone on her bedroom dresser. He wondered if she didn't know she'd forgotten it, or if it was another thing she didn't want to tell him?

His GPS showed a Drury Inn coming up in Hayti, Missouri. They'd just crossed from Tennessee through a corner of Arkansas and over the border into Missouri. Another twenty minutes, and he figured they could get a couple rooms, grab some sleep and free breakfast, then get back on the road by seven.

He was cocky to think he could drive straight through. If he didn't have Brodie along, he would have pulled off at a rest stop, reclined the seat, and got a few hours of sleep that way. So far, he'd purposely avoided rest stops. He wasn't sure if they'd trigger a panic attack for Brodie, but he certainly didn't want to find out. When they filled up the gas tank, he looked for other open spaces for the dogs and chose fast-food places for him and Brodie to use the restrooms.

As soon as he slowed down to take the exit for Hayti and Caruthersville, Brodie jerked up to face the windshield.

"What's wrong?" She wanted to know.

"Nothing. Everything's fine. I'm a little tired," Jason explained. "I thought we could get a couple of rooms and grab a few hours of sleep."

"We'd have separate rooms?"

"Yeah, is that okay?"

When she didn't answer, he glanced over. Her fingers were wringing the hem of her T-shirt.

"I'll see if they have any connecting rooms," he suggested. He wasn't sure which part was making her uncomfortable?

Finally, she said, "Okay. Hank can still be with me?"

"Yeah, of course." He paused, then added, "And Kitten, too."

Her eyes checked the backpack at her feet. "Are you mad I brought him?"

"No, not at all. I wish you trusted me enough to tell me." He took a left turn into the hotel's parking lot.

"I trust you."

"Then why didn't you tell me?"

"I didn't think you'd let me bring him."

"We could have at least talked about it," Jason told her. "I would have brought a crate for him."

"Oh, that's okay. He likes being close to me." She checked on him now, caressing his head. His two front paws stretched out and started kneading, but his eyes stayed shut.

"I'll check us in and pull around to the back. We'll take him out and walk him with Scout and Hank before we go to our rooms."

Kitten had grown up surrounded by dogs. Jason thought it was silly that Brodie trained the cat on a leash and harness. Now he was grateful. And the cat obviously didn't mind riding in a vehicle.

He got their room keycards. The hotel had adjoining rooms on the first floor near the exit. The outside area for pets was decent grass. The entire place was nice and quiet, with few vehicles in the parking lot.

The guy at the front desk told Jason breakfast started serving at 6:00 a.m. A hot breakfast with sausage, biscuits, gravy, scrambled eggs—the works. The rooms were clean and comfortable with mini frigs, microwaves and plenty of space to prepare the dogs' meals. Brodie even approved of the arrangement, asking if they could keep the door between the rooms open.

Despite it being after midnight, Jason texted Hannah to let her know they were okay and settling down for a few hours of sleep. He thought about texting Taylor, but stopped. They were nowhere near a relationship that accepted or expected texts at two o'clock in the morning.

Dogs, cat and Brodie were all settled down. Everything seemed good until Jason woke up to Scout nosing him. He could hear a low whine, and immediately he worried the dog was sick.

But the whine wasn't Scout. It was coming from the next room.

43

"Brodie?" Jason tapped on the open door before sticking his head around the doorjamb.

Scout wasn't as polite. He rushed into the room like he had been going back and forth for a while. He was panting when he looked up over his shoulder at Jason, as if wondering why Jason wasn't following him.

The bedcovers were all mussed up. A corner lamp was on, but Jason couldn't see Brodie in the bed or anywhere in the room. He thought she might be in the bathroom. Then he heard the low-pitched whimper, and he realized it was coming from the floor on the other side of the bed.

"Brodie, are you okay?"

He had pulled on jeans over his boxers, but he was barefooted and bare-chested. He stepped slowly across the room. Hank's big head poked out from around the bed. Scout nuzzled him, then looked back at Jason.

As soon as he could see her, his stomach dropped. Brodie sat in the corner, her back against the wall, her knees up against her chest with Kitten snuggled tightly in-between.

At first, Jason thought something was wrong with the cat. Maybe she'd left him in the backpack for too long during the drive. But even Kitten was looking at him, imploring him to do something. The whimper wasn't coming from the cat either. It was coming from Brodie as she rocked back and forth.

He'd never seen her like this. Nothing even close.

"Brodie, what's wrong?"

He eased himself down to his knees, ignoring Hank's slobbers and Scout head-butting him. It was as if both dogs were prodding him to do something to make this better. Obviously, they had been trying for a while with no success.

"Is Kitten hurt?"

She wouldn't look at him. Her chin tucked into her chest. But she managed to shake her head.

"Are you hurt?"

Another shake. Her tousled hair spiked up, but the bangs were plastered to the sweat on her forehead.

"Bad dream?" He took a guess.

This time, she nodded.

"It scared you?"

Another nod.

He glanced at both dogs, one on each side of him, each watching Brodie now. She was still whimpering, and Hank cocked his head from side to side.

"Want me to stay with you for a while?"

A vigorous nod.

"Would it be okay if I put my arm around you?"

She hesitated now, and he remained still. Both dogs were waiting, too. Finally, there was a subtle shrug followed by a nod.

He was careful, slow, deliberate and yet a little awkward. Stupid as it sounded, Jason had only learned recently how to deliver a comforting hug. When he was a teenager, he was too immature. After he lost his arm, he was too angry.

Now, he crawled up beside her and gently looped his left arm up behind and around her thin, shuddering shoulders. He let her ease herself against him. Before either of them had a chance to get comfortable, Hank and Scout pushed into them. Jason's first impulse was to make the dogs back off, but immediately Brodie reached for them, letting Kitten settle in her lap as she wrapped an arm around each dog and buried her face in Hank's side.

Jason leaned his back against the wall. His arm was still around Brodie, but Scout was sitting in his lap, all seventy pounds of him. He felt Brodie shudder against his side, and he thought she was crying harder now.

He was so not good at this. He wasn't sure what else to do.

She gulped for air and tears streamed down her face. Hank turned his head so he could lick her face. Brodie gulped again and hiccupped. This time, Jason realized she was half crying and half laughing at the two big dogs trying so hard to be in their owners' laps.

44

Grand Island, Nebraska

Maggie's phone woke her up. She was still in her clothes from the night before. She didn't remember curling up on top of the bed and falling asleep. In three quick moves, she grabbed the phone off the desk.

"Alonzo," she said, in place of a greeting. "Don't you ever sleep?"

"Actually, I find I only need about four or five hours."

Her twenty-something team members had a way of making her feel old, and she wasn't more than a decade ahead of them.

When she waited too long to respond, Alonzo said, "Oh gosh, did I wake you up? I thought you never slept."

"It's okay. You've got something."

"Yes. You asked me to track Ryder Creed's phone."

Maggie dropped to the edge of the bed as her pulse ticked up.

"Did you find it?"

"Got a couple pings. One was just before noon yesterday. The cell tower isn't far from where you're staying. About twenty miles."

"That must have been when Hannah called him."

"The other ping was earlier this morning. Around five-thirty."

She glanced at her watch. She hadn't realized it was after six.

"Was it the same location?" she asked.

"Different tower. Which is good. Multiple towers allow us to track the location of the phone by measuring the time delay. You know, the time delay that a signal takes to return to the tower from the phone."

"Right." She left those things to the experts.

"The problem is the second tower is almost thirty miles away from the first. And the antenna that's picking it up is clear in the opposite direction. I'm checking other towers," he told her.

"Wait. That was this morning?"

"Yup. About five-thirty."

"Can you tell if it was a phone call?"

"Registered activity. It was brief."

"What about in-between Hannah's call and the five-thirty activity?"

"Nothing. It went dark shortly after the first phone call. Right now we're trying to triangulate the information from the towers."

Maggie stood straight up and began pacing. It could mean Ryder had simply found shelter some place after he talked to Hannah. But why so far away? He and Grace wouldn't have walked that far in the snow. Immediately, her mind conjured up scenarios of them being thrown into the trunk of a car and whisked off.

And why hadn't he contacted her? Or even Hannah? If he had enough battery power at five-thirty, he could have at least sent a text. The panic gnawed at her. Of course he didn't text. Because he couldn't.

"You can still track it even if it's shut off, right?" she asked.

"When you turn off your phone, it usually stops communicating with nearby cell towers."

"Don't give me that 'usual' crap, Alonzo." She let him hear her frustration. "You can still track it if it's off. Please tell me you know where it is."

"I can give you the longitude and latitude using the information we have, but with only those two intercepts, it's still going to be about a two-mile square area."

"You're still tracking it, though, right?" Maggie asked again.

"No. We can't. Not after the second intercept. It's not just powered off. My guess is the battery's been pulled."

"You mean the battery's gone dead?"

"No, pulled. Removed. Disconnected. Usually if a battery dies, there's still enough juice. If the battery's been pulled, this is the best we've got."

She asked him for the coordinates and jotted them down while she told herself this was more than they had yesterday. At the same time, Maggie tried not to think about what it meant if Ryder's battery had been disconnected. He wouldn't have done it. And once again, it pointed to someone else controlling his phone.

Controlling him.

As soon as she finished with Alonzo, she called Tommy Pakula. He answered on the second ring and sounded like he had been awake for hours. She told him what Alonzo had discovered. He listened without interrupting. When she finished, she paused long enough for him to ask questions.

"You realize that's still a lot of ground to cover," he told her. "And speaking of ground, that might be exactly where the phone is. On the ground and covered by eight inches of snow."

"If it was used at five-thirty, I'm hoping that means it's someplace above the snow."

She stood at the window. The trucks with blades were working the parking lot. Snow was in the air, but it was difficult to tell if it was new stuff falling or old stuff blowing around. Besides, she had to believe that Ryder was still with the phone. Grace, too. She tried to envision them in an old shed in a pasture.

When Pakula didn't respond immediately, Maggie tamped down the anger circling around her panic, threatening to replace it.

"Look, Pakula, I know you have your hands full. If you don't want to help, just say so. I'll go on my own."

"Hold on. That's not anywhere close to what I was thinking. Some of these back roads aren't plowed yet. Our 4-wheel SUVs won't cut it. We need more ground clearance. Give me a few minutes. Let me see if I can borrow someone's pickup. I'll call you back."

Maggie sat down on the edge of the bed, holding her phone. And for once, she did the only thing she could at the moment. The one thing she hated to do. The one thing she knew she was terrible at doing.

She waited.

45

Maggie insisted Pakula take the passenger seat up front next to Sheriff Spencer in the extended cab of his Dodge Ram 2500 with a front plow. Climbing up into the monster truck required the running board. She remembered her drive back last night from Hastings to Grand Island, and how it felt like she was skating with the wind shoving her along. This ride felt solid. She could hear the tires gripping the road, and she liked the high vantage point.

"Nora's been calling folks practically all night," Spencer told them. "She's concerned about Libby, but she's worried sick about your guy and his dog. Feels guilty for sending them out in a storm."

Maggie wanted to tell Spencer Nora should feel responsible. She wanted to ask if his wife made a habit of lying to him. Except it didn't matter. No amount of guilt or remorse would help them find Ryder.

"I'm glad your people tracked his phone," Spencer said. "We've been trying to track Libby's since yesterday."

Maggie hadn't thought about that, and she wanted to kick herself. Instead, she asked, "Did you get anything?"

"Nothing. And that girl used her phone like it was an extension of her hand."

"They think her battery's been disconnected," Pakula told Maggie. "Same as Ryder's."

"I don't even know how to get to my battery," Spencer said. "Is it possible to damage the battery if you drop your phone?"

Maggie and Pakula looked at Spencer at the same time. Neither had thought of that scenario. Of course, Maggie's mind added other situations that included the phone getting crushed or smashed by someone else. Again, she reminded herself that Ryder could take care of himself. But maybe not if someone had blindsided him.

She raked her fingers through her hair, trying to settle her nerves. She'd left most of her meal last night. The result was extra space for the acid to churn.

"Those coordinates," Maggie told the sheriff, trying to steer all of them back to the task at hand. "Do you recognize where that is?"

"Fields and pastures, mostly. I haven't lived out here all that long. Nora inherited the farm a few years ago and convinced me to move out of town. But I can tell you, the roads within that radius will all be gravel or dirt."

"What about other structures?" she asked. "Are there old sheds or barns on some of these properties?"

"Sure."

His nod was exaggerated enough that Maggie suspected he was placating her.

"We had neighbors checking their outbuildings, at least the ones they could get to," he added with a glance in the rearview to catch her eyes. When he didn't see what he hoped to see, he added, "Like I said, Nora is really worried."

Maggie wasn't impressed. She still didn't trust the woman and didn't care if he saw it. She wanted to ask if he was surprised by how many things his wife had not told him about Libby. The baby and the miscarriage? She doubted those were Nora's only two lies of omission.

"Her name isn't Libby Holmes," Maggie said, and watched for his reaction.

"What's that?" Only a glance in the rearview mirror.

"And she's only seventeen."

This time, he twisted in his seat to look back at her. His bushy eyebrows furrowed into a V.

"Seventeen?" he asked. "How do you know that?"

Pakula kept his eyes ahead, watching the endless obstacles. Some streets were blocked with downed trees. Power lines dangled in places. It was taking forever just to get out of the city.

Maggie needed to be careful with what she told Spencer. She wasn't sure if Pakula had told him that the dismembered body might be Kristin Darrow, Libby's co-worker.

"I sent something to my team that had her fingerprints."

"You took something from her room?"

"That's what bothers you?" Maggie asked. "It doesn't bother you that this girl lied to you? That your wife may have lied to you?"

"Nora doesn't know that she's seventeen. Or that she lied about her name. She hasn't told us anything about her past."

Maggie stared out the side window. She could feel the sheriff's eyes on her in the mirror. Pakula didn't say a word. It was one of the things she liked about the man. He was good at playing the role of the neutral observer.

It was a long shot, but Maggie figured she had to take it. She turned back so she could see his reaction as she added, "Her fingerprints are on file because she's a suspect in a murder."

"Murder? What are you talking about? That's crazy. That girl failed at killing herself. I can't imagine her trying to kill someone."

More than anything else, Maggie hoped he was right.

46

This was going to be impossible.

Maggie stared out at the windswept field. Cornstalks bended over under the weight of the snow. Cattle huddled together. Miles of white ran all the way to the horizon.

On the interstate, semi-trailers barreled along. Traffic hadn't slowed. But out here, the roads were deserted. Gusts of blowing snow caused whiteout conditions. It swirled all around the vehicle. Sometimes it felt like they were driving in a tunnel. Maggie couldn't see, no matter which window she looked out. She wasn't sure how Spencer knew he was on the road.

What was she thinking? That they'd drive around until they magically found the discarded cell phone? And somehow, Creed and Grace would be there with it?

Pakula was probably right when he said the phone could be on the ground and covered with drifts of snow. Creed could have dropped it without knowing after he talked to Hannah. According to Alonzo, the phone had gone dark after that call.

Now, if the phone glowed red or emitted an audible ping, it would be too difficult to see or hear it in these miles of white covered landscape.

Except that Alonzo had intercepted activity at five-thirty this morning. A lost phone didn't send a signal without being powered back on. And then miraculously go dark again.

"We're about a mile away," Pakula told Spencer. He was watching a GPS device that he'd placed on the dashboard of the pickup. Supposedly, it was more sophisticated and accurate than the vehicle's built-in device.

Maggie watched the pops of color crawl on the screen and intersect different colored lines. She was too wired to focus on it. She'd leave it to Pakula. Instead, her eyes stayed on the ditches and fields, searching for anything that didn't belong.

"It wasn't snowing hard at five-thirty," Pakula said. "Did Agent Alonzo say the activity that registered would need to be user initiated?"

"Yes," Maggie answered without taking her eyes off the landscape. "Sheriff, can you slow down?"

Spencer tapped the brake so hard the motion jerked all of them forward. The tires slid a bit before gaining traction.

"Sorry," he mumbled.

She hadn't seen a single shed or building that wasn't a part of a farm. Only fields and pastures. Even the cattle had nowhere to go.

When did her heart start pounding in her ears? Her palms were sweaty, and a knot began forming in the pit of her stomach.

Last March she had gotten caught in a restaurant when a tornado hit. She and others were trapped in the basement for hours while debris rained down, threatening to bury them alive. All the while, storms continued to rage above. But during that time, she didn't feel as helpless as she did right now. There was always one more thing to try. She knew then that she needed to just hang on until someone came to the rescue.

Now here she was: the rescuer. She felt more powerless than when she was in that basement. The only thing similar was the panic gnawing at her. A time bomb clicked in her head with the rhythm of her heart. There was a dread building that she didn't want to confront. The longer she didn't hear from Ryder, the more she believed something terrible had happened to him.

"How far could he and that little dog have gotten?" Spencer asked. "It was already snowing yesterday morning,"

"Someone may have given him a ride," Pakula offered.

"Or forced him inside their vehicle." Maggie only said what Pakula was tiptoeing around. "And they would have made him throw out his cell phone."

"We're not going to see a thing from the road." Spencer leaned forward as he turned up the defrost. The windshield wipers couldn't keep up with the blowing snow that crystalized and fogged up the edges of the glass.

"Let's go ahead and get as close as we can to what Agent Alonzo gave us," Pakula insisted.

"Sheriff, how far away is your property?" Maggie asked. She wanted to calculate how many miles Ryder and Grace could have actually walked. "Are we close?"

"We're clear on the other side of the river," Spencer said, waving his arm at pastures that stretched far into the distance until a line of trees and shrubs met them.

"The river." Maggie remembered Hannah mentioning that Ryder was looking to cross over the river. "It's on the other side of the trees?"

"Yeah, it curves along here."

"What is it?" Pakula was looking over his shoulder at her. He could sense she was on to something.

"When Hannah talked to Ryder, she said he was looking for an old bridge."

"He went all the way over the river?" Spencer snorted and shook his head. "They got farther than I thought."

"Grace might have led him to the river," Pakula said.

She wondered if he was thinking what she was. Did Libby go looking to drown herself? Hide? Or did the killer dump her body in the river?

"It'll be near impossible to find that rickety bridge under the snow. But there's a pasture road or an irrigation path." Spencer leaned over the steering wheel as if that would give him a clearer view. Then he said, "What am I talking about? It'll be impossible to find those old two-tracks with the snow drifted over."

From the road, Maggie could see the wind and heavy snow had ravaged the trees out here, too.

"We're almost right on top of it," Pakula pointed at the GPS device. "Let's stop. Take a look on foot."

Maggie zipped her coat and pulled up the collar. She tucked the bottoms of her jeans into the tops of her boots and yanked on her gloves. When she opened the door, she still wasn't prepared for the frigid blast that hit her in the face.

Out in the open, the wind whipped at anything that wasn't tacked down. Her hair flew around her face. Pakula lost his ball cap, catching it in mid-air. He threw it back inside the cab and lifted the hood of his coat over his shaved head.

She couldn't imagine how they were going to look for a cell phone. It would literally be like searching for a needle in a haystack, unless it was attached to Ryder.

Pakula suggested they go in different directions. Maggie was already plowing knee-deep through the ditch and headed for the trees along the river. She didn't look back to see which way the men went. The snow had drifted high enough that it made it easy to climb over the barbed-wire fence.

She hadn't noticed the cattle until they were only twenty feet away. White faced and with their brown backs blanketed with snow, they blended into the landscape. They watched her, curious but more interested in huddling together against the wind.

At first, when she saw the black bag partially covered and down by their legs, Maggie dismissed it. She had seen salt blocks in pastures.

Maybe they came wrapped. Farmers delivered hay. Was black paper involved in that process? She knew very little about agriculture and taking care of livestock.

Trudging passed, she concentrated instead on the effort of lifting each foot up out of the snow and placing it down. Then the realization hit her, and she jolted to a halt.

Black plastic bags.

How could she have forgotten? There were still pieces of Kristin Darrow to be found.

She spun around and looked for Pakula. He was too far away for her to wave to him. Her voice would get lost in the wind. She wrestled her phone out of her coat pocket and pulled off her glove to text a message.

FOUND A BLACK BAG.

She waited and watched. It took too long. Finally, he stopped. One glance at his phone, and he reeled around looking for her. She waved her arm clear above her head.

Spencer saw Pakula tromping through the ditch and followed.

By the time they joined her, Maggie had edged closer to the cattle. She kept her movements slow and natural. Did cattle spook easily?

"It's practically on top of the snow," Pakula said as he came up beside her.

"It's possible the cows uprooted it," Spencer said. "Course, it could just be garbage."

Maggie kept glancing around. She was impatient, and she hated to admit that. As important as it was to discover more body parts, that's not what they were searching for.

"Do you mind if I move on?" she asked Pakula.

"You two go ahead," he said. "I'll take care of this. I'm going to take a look. Just to make sure." He secured his hood as the wind ripped at it.

Maggie started out again before he even reached for the bag. The trees and the river were an impossible distance away. A black and white wall rose out of the landscape. It felt like walking in quicksand. How could something as light as snow be so impenetrable?

"O'Dell!" Pakula yelled.

She turned. She was still close enough to see the look on his face. It made her heart bang against her chest. Her feet were blocks of concrete finding their way back. She was breathing hard, leaving a visible trail behind when she finally reached him.

The wind tore at the plastic as Pakula struggled to keep it open. The bottom part of the bag had frozen to the ground. Pakula kneeled in order to secure it and look inside. Spencer stood beside him. His expression was equally troubling.

And suddenly, Maggie didn't want to see what they'd found. She didn't want to know. Paralyzed, she stayed ten feet away.

In the last decade, she had seen how many bodies? Not just bodies. Intestines strung across tree branches. Dismembered organs in takeout containers. But she knew absolutely none of that would prepare her to find a body of someone she loved.

Pakula locked eyes with her, then held up a cell phone in one of his gloved hands. He gestured for Spencer to grab the edges of the bag while he dug out something else. It was stiff when he tried to unfurl it. But before he did, she recognized the long-sleeved shirt. Horizontal stripes, light and dark blue. She remembered thinking the colors brought out the indigo in Ryder's eyes.

Now there was a large, oblong stain. Deep red, it stretched across one side of the shirt.

Blood. Lots of it.

47

Interstate 55

Brodie appreciated that Jason let them pretend nothing weird had happened. She was relieved that he didn't make her talk about it. She wasn't good at reading people's emotions, one of the consequences of being held in captivity for so many years. Honestly, she could barely understand her own emotions. But from what she could tell, Jason seemed okay this morning.

They woke up to his wristwatch's alarm. Brodie had fallen asleep. From the jerk of his body against her, she knew he had fallen asleep, too. His left arm was wrapped around her shoulders, and she had cradled herself into his chest and lap. Kitten was still in her arms. Hank and Scout had sprawled out on the floor close enough to touch each other. Hank's chin weighted down Brodie's left thigh. One of Scout's paws poked her in the ribs.

"You doing okay?" was all Jason asked.

Now back on the road, Brodie's panic attack simply felt like one of her nightmares. It was over and hopefully gone, at least for a while. She should have seen it coming. That whisper in the back of her mind as they drove farther and farther away from the only place where she felt safe.

The rush of adrenaline had drained her, left her completely exhausted. The shower hadn't rejuvenated her in the way water usually did. She was glad all she had to do for the next several hours was sit, watch the landscape glide by and make conversation that would help keep Jason awake. It should be that easy. Except it wasn't easy at all.

Earlier, Jason had brought breakfast to their rooms, two trays stacked with an assortment of hot and cold foods. It fascinated her to watch him eat. Despite the fully functioning new mechanical hand, he obviously had adjusted to not having it. Instead of using it, he still relied on his left hand and had developed interesting habits to compensate for the missing limb.

Expertly, he speared scrambled eggs, sausage and potatoes onto the fork, layering and loading up each time, not wanting to waste a single motion. And he figured out how to pick up toast or his glass of milk without putting down the fork.

Brodie had learned to observe carefully out of the corner of her eye, because she didn't want him to know she was watching. She had her own weird habits, like using her fingers instead of utensils. A fork and knife sometimes felt as foreign to her as if she were trying to eat with chopsticks.

The dogs and Kitten didn't care about any of these things. Scout and Hank had finished their prepared meals and asked for nothing more. Yes, they also watched, but only because they were hoping a stray morsel might fall their way.

It was during breakfast that Jason called Hannah and did something with his phone so both of them could hear her and talk to her at the same time. Hearing Hannah's voice made Brodie's chest ache all over again.

In the last several months, Hannah had become Brodie's friend, confidant, and mental healthcare provider. Hannah was more of a mother to Brodie than Brodie's own mother, who lived in Atlanta and seemed content to visit only twice since Brodie's arrival. Of course, she called and texted. Why did people believe a few words on a phone screen were "keeping in touch?"

Ryder had tried to explain that their mother had gone on to create a life of her own to fill the void of not having them. At the time, it was the only way she knew how to survive. Brodie didn't understand, but she was okay with it. At least, that's what she told everyone.

Now, sitting in the Jeep and traveling even farther away, Brodie tried to prevent the ache from growing. Did it have anything to do with returning to Nebraska? She'd spent sixteen years there without knowing where she was. Seasons changed according to how hot the shed was that Iris had locked her in, or how damp and cold the concrete floor was in the basement.

In the first year, before Iris started locking Brodie in a room, a closet, or one of the various outbuildings—before the basement became her more permanent cell—Brodie was allowed to see the outside and even allowed to go along on car rides.

She remembered rolling hills, meadows with purple and yellow flowers, rows of cornfields and cows. Lots of cows. The wide-open sky seemed bigger and bluer than any other she'd seen. And she liked how it spread all the way to the horizon. At one point when Iris chose darkness as Brodie's punishment of the week, Brodie remembered wishing that Iris or her son, Aaron, would dump her in a ditch or leave her in a field, just so she could see the sky again. She didn't care if it was night and dark outside, because at least she'd have the stars.

Brodie finally felt safe living in Hannah's house. The fifty-acre property was isolated by forestland and protected by security cameras and alarms. She knew it wasn't failsafe. Several months ago, an intruder had proven that. But it was more than that. It felt like a home. She was part of a family again.

Suddenly, she wanted to go back. She wanted to be in her room, listening to the familiar sounds of birds outside her window, of Hannah clanging pots and pans down in the kitchen. She wanted to do her morning routine of chores.

She started worrying about the dogs in the kennel. Who would make sure that Molly wasn't scared if there was thunder? Would anyone notice if Knight was stiff and needed a massage where his amputated leg was set inside his prosthetic? Would Jason's friends realize Chance wasn't mean at all? He just needed a reassuring voice to tell him he was a good boy.

How many miles had they gone? Was it too late to turn around?

Of course, it was too late. She needed to breathe. She needed to concentrate on Ryder and Grace. All those years he searched for her. What did a few uncomfortable days matter?

She could do this. She had to do this.

48

Jason knew Brodie wasn't fine. He tried not to ask her too often. He knew she hated it but would politely answer each time that she was fine.

He weighed his options as he stole a glance now and then from behind his sunglasses. Gut instinct told him to call Hannah, but that felt like a betrayal. Loyalty, trust... Jason understood how precious both were. He was still trying to earn Brodie's trust. Show her she could lean on him. She didn't have to go through PTSD all alone.

He had to admit, Brodie was a pretty good pretender. He figured he should know, since he had spent a good deal of time pretending he was fine when he came back from Afghanistan. Back then, after all the surgeries and rehab, the only thing that got him through the week was daydreaming about and perfecting his Plan B.

When doctors loaded him up on prescriptions for painkillers, anti-anxiety and sleeping pills, Jason stashed them away. He noted each pill's purpose and cataloged them by color and size. He knew by heart which one he'd need to take first, second and last for the ultimate result. If living got too hard, dying would be easier by implementing his Plan B. It became his escape, his trapdoor.

Brodie didn't have a Plan B. How could she? During those sixteen years, she fought starvation and all kinds of punishment, from isolation and darkness to being drugged and wounded. It pissed off Jason every time he tried to think about what she'd been through. Afghanistan and that IED he'd encountered seemed like a cakewalk compared to what she'd been through.

She'd survived all of that, only to have the residual fear and anxiety derail her from enjoying her newfound freedom. PTSD was a bitch. In some ways, it was worse than the actual event, because the actual event eventually ended. The PTSD reared its ugly head repeatedly, and always when you least expected it. It grabbed you by the throat and you had no idea if it would strangle you for two minutes or two days.

They'd left the hotel only an hour ago, and Jason took the first major exit at Sikeston, Missouri.

"What's wrong?" Brodie asked, jerking straight up in her seat and looking around.

He held back a grimace. He hated that her default was to assume something was wrong.

"Nothing's wrong. There's a McDonald's. I thought I'd get some coffee. You need anything?"

"No, I'm fine."

This time, he rubbed at his jaw to catch himself.

"Are you feeling sleepy?" she asked.

"No. I'm wide awake."

"Then why are you getting coffee? You don't even like it."

"What makes you think I don't like coffee?"

She went quiet for a minute, like maybe she'd revealed something she shouldn't have. The truth was Jason didn't much like it. He pulled into the McDonald's parking lot but found a shaded slot instead of going around to the drive-thru lane.

"Well," she explained. "You always have a cup, but you sit with your hand wrapped around it. You don't bother to put anything in it."

"Ryder drinks his coffee black," he challenged her.

"Yes, but he drinks it. Hannah puts cream and a teaspoon of sugar. No more. No less. She stirs it then blows on it before her first sip. And she looks like she enjoys it. You just sort of let it sit. You only take a few sips. And you always have a lot to pour down the drain."

"Okay, you're right. I'm not a fan," Jason said. "When people ask if you want a cup of coffee, it's not usually because they want to drink coffee with you. Most of the time, they just want to talk."

"So it's a prop."

"Sometimes. Not always."

"So, what do you want to talk to me about?"

This time he smiled at her and said, "I guess I'm busted."

"Last night?"

"No," he said, and immediately regretted his bumbling. "Not unless you want to talk. I just wanted to ask you…"

Her expression reminded him of a wounded animal. One glance in the rearview mirror, and he saw Hank looking up and watching, ready to console.

"Do you want to go back?" Jason blurted out. It was silly to sugar-coat anything with Brodie. "Because we absolutely can do that."

"But what about Ryder?"

"We'll figure out something else."

She sat quietly again, chin down, eyes out the window, hands wringing the hem of her shirt. Kitten stretched out in her lap, and Brodie's fingers left the twisted fabric to pet the cat.

"I don't understand why I feel like this," she said.

"Like you're swimming away from the edge, and you can't feel the bottom anymore."

Her eyes flew up to meet his, and he could see her contemplating the idea. She was an excellent swimmer. Ryder trusted her to do the water training for their scent dogs.

"You finally found a comfortable spot," he continued. "Why leave that and move into deeper waters?" Now he was sounding lame even to himself. He needed to stop while he was ahead. What would Hannah say?

She was so much better at this. Maybe it was best if he stuck to what he knew.

"When I got back from Afghanistan, I felt like everyone was staring at my empty sleeve. My family didn't have a clue how to deal with what happened to me. I felt like I might drown in their pity."

She was listening, eyes wide and intent. That was something he noticed about Brodie. She gave him her full attention, as if she wanted to hear every single word. Sometimes he felt like his buddies listened only until they found a break to interrupt and get their chance to talk.

"But Hannah and Ryder," Jason said, "they didn't see what I couldn't do. They saw past my amputated arm and looked at all the things I could do."

He shrugged, uncomfortable that he was making this about himself and not Brodie.

Still, he continued, "The thing is, I've got a new home and a new family, and it's great. But feeling safe and secure..." he struggled to find the words. "I don't think it's necessarily about a single physical place. This sounds corny, but I think it's a feeling deep down inside you. Something you take with you, no matter where you go."

Her forehead scrunched, but her face remained blank. She was good at hiding her feelings. That was partly why last night had taken him off guard.

Jason wanted to tell her she didn't have to do this. That it was okay if she wasn't ready to venture out beyond her comfort zone. After what she'd gone through, she deserved some leeway. She didn't have to be brave 24/7.

He wanted to remind her that Ryder wouldn't want her to jeopardize all the progress she'd made just to go looking for him. Actually, Ryder would be upset with Jason for allowing her to come along. He'd be worried that something like last night would happen.

"I want to help find Ryder," she said. "I don't want you to think I'm a big baby and so messed up that I'll be in the way."

"I would never think that at all. We're in this together."

"Are you going to tell Hannah and Ryder about last night?"

"Last night?" He pretended to play dumb. "We got rooms at the Drury Inn. Got some sleep and had a darn good free breakfast."

She offered a slight smile, but a hint of embarrassment flitted across her face before she knew how to hide it.

"And I won't tell Hannah how much you liked their biscuits," she said with a bigger smile.

"That's a deal."

49

Along the Platte River, Nebraska

In the dark early hours of the morning, Ariel had started to drive Libby crazy. She paced the cramped quarters of the trailer like a caged animal, either too high on whatever she was taking or having withdraws, to even consider sleep. She was anxious to get out, and Libby was anxious to get rid of her.

It didn't help that the dog wouldn't stop growling at Ariel with every pass. Ariel kicking it had only made matters worse. Libby knew if Ariel thought she could pick it up without getting bit, she'd have thrown it out into the snow hours ago.

When Ariel suggested dumping the guy's phone, Libby didn't argue. She dug up a pair of knee-high snow boots and handed them to Ariel.

The boots fit perfectly. Libby wasn't surprised. Ruben had a type and that included physical traits: lean, athletic, but small-framed. He wanted them strong enough to handle his dirty work, but small enough that he could still overpower them. He liked them cynical, with equal parts of self-doubt and self-assurance. It seemed like a contradiction, but he had a wicked way of bringing out both and capitalizing on the result.

She saw so much of herself in Ariel. The parts she didn't like, some of them she'd tried to get rid of. Even the fact that Ariel wouldn't share what the final straw was that made her flee. Libby had never shared her turning point either, not with Nora, not with a single soul. To speak it out loud would make the horror too real. It prevented her from commiserating with guilt and regret that she hadn't left Ruben's arrangement sooner.

He warned them in the beginning, like he was doing them a favor by telling them ahead of time. Once they accepted the terms of the arrangement, they could never leave. Of course, he told them this right after he outlined all the perks: weekly cash allowance, car payments, rent, beach vacations, etc. It didn't take Libby long to notice he customized the list to entice each recruit. And he was good at his word.

There were times when he'd ask a girl point-blank if she wanted to leave. He'd ask in front of the others—always in front of the others. Three. He liked having three of them.

Behind the vulnerable one's back, he'd tell the other two that he was afraid she was going to blow it for all of them. He had a skilled way of doing it, so that by the end of the conversation, he remained cool, calm and collected while the other girls were a raging pack of wild animals, feeling betrayed and offering to get rid of the traitor by any means possible.

Libby was kidding herself if she believed for one minute that she had escaped. Maybe it was impossible to think she could do it a second time.

So in the dark of early morning, Libby led Ariel through the blowing snow. She guided her through the maze, some of which were now tunnels because of fallen tree limbs. She took Ariel about halfway back to the shed that housed her vehicle. The snow had let up; the wind had not.

"Text me when you're finished," she told Ariel. "I'll meet you."

As Libby trudged back, she noticed their footsteps were already starting to fill in with the blowing and drifting snow. She doubted Ariel could find her way to the shed. The SUV wouldn't be able to plow through the snow. She told Ariel this and worried she wouldn't listen, even after Libby explained that if the vehicle got stuck in a snowbank, they wouldn't have any mode of escape when the melting began.

Ariel assured her she wasn't going to take the vehicle. She simply wanted to walk far enough in the opposite direction to throw away the dog handler's phone. Libby had already dismantled the battery yesterday, but Ariel insisted she show her how to connect it. Before she threw it in a ditch, Ariel said she wanted to turn it on just long enough to redirect anyone who might look for the man. Make them look somewhere else.

Libby actually thought it was a good plan. If nothing else, it would buy her a little more time. Plus, she got rid of Ariel for a few hours.

Libby suspected Ariel really wanted to get back to her vehicle to replenish her drug supply. The gummies she'd offered Libby were not the only source of her continuous high, but she had to be running low.

The drugs would be a problem. She didn't like Ariel being high. She didn't trust it. Drugs could make Ariel unpredictable and vulnerable. They obviously made her fidgety and impulsive. Maybe she only counted on them to make her brave, but yesterday, they had made her reckless. Stabbing the dog handler was stupid and yes, now she understood it was also cruel.

The drugs weren't entirely to blame for the sparkle in Ariel's eyes when she talked about "finishing" the man and dumping his body. As Libby left her in the early morning dark, Ariel was still mumbling about coming back and cutting him into pieces. Ruben had a way of bringing out the savage in all of them. He rewarded the behavior until it was ingrained in them and became almost instinctual. He once bragged about having his own army of homegrown killers.

Despite all of Ariel's bravado, Libby wouldn't be surprised if she ended up lost in the dark. She claimed to have a "stellar" sense of direction. An odd word, but that was what she said. And Libby had to admit, Ariel didn't appear frightened of anything. Her mannerisms certainly didn't match that of the panic-stricken voice on the phone, the one telling Libby to get out of the house. When they were away from the safe glow of the trailer and heard a coyote howl, the sound freaked the hell out of Libby. Ariel didn't even flinch.

None of it mattered. Ariel didn't matter. Libby wasn't looking for a new best friend. She didn't need anyone. She just needed a means of escape.

She took her time going back to the trailer. A broken branch with leaves still attached worked like a broom. She dragged it behind her, helping the wind cover her tracks. So what if it made it difficult for Ariel to find her way back? She hadn't come this far to leave tracks for Ruben.

Survival of the fittest.

Another lesson of Ruben's.

The drugs were an unpleasant reminder of Ruben and how much he liked his girls addicted to more than just his cash handouts, spa days, the expensive iPhones and other gifts. Libby still felt the sting of his anger when she turned down the assortment of drugs he provided. To make up for it, she surprised him with her first tattoo. That was when she was still flying on a natural high of rebellion.

She knew he was dangerous. They all did. It was part of his attraction. The adventure, the reckless abandon of their past goody-two-shoe lives brought excitement even if it came laced with a bit of terror. Then came the actual tests. His voice came to her

What are you willing to do?

What are you capable of doing?

How far are you willing to go to find out?

She shook her head, not wanting to remember that part. A chill tingled at the back of her neck. She pulled up her collar and yanked the stocking cap down further. It didn't help. She knew dislodging this chill had nothing to do with the snow or the cold.

Libby shook her head again, disappointed how much Ruben still influenced her.

50

Creed slipped in and out of consciousness. He heard Grace whimper. This time when he jolted, the pain in his side brought him to the surface. His eyes flew open, struggling to focus. Something warm and wet on his arm.

Grace!

Finally, he could see her in the dim light. He tried to touch her, only to find his hands couldn't move. A zip-tie bound his wrists together. Grace scampered around, paws batting at him, excited licks finding his face. That's when he realized he was on the floor, twisted into a fetal position, wedged into a corner of the trailer.

He saw the table and bench where he'd been sitting. It was diagonal from him now about five feet away. He pushed himself up and against the wall, despite the red-hot poker in his side. The door to the trailer was directly across from him, and he couldn't help wondering if they were getting ready to drag him out.

The wind still howled. The generator hummed. But Creed couldn't hear anyone else inside the trailer.

Was it possible they left him?

He looked at Grace and watched her. She panted, obviously stressed, but she also wagged and nudged him in between licks. Her ears were back, humbled and excited to see him awake. But she wasn't listening or alerting to any other noises or anyone's presence inside or outside the trailer.

A single light above the sink made the space glow yellow. The windows showed darkness, with a white flurry brushing against the glass. He wasn't going to wait another minute. He relaxed his balled up fists, rotated side-by-side wrists to face each other, loosening the zip-ties enough that in seconds he was able to free himself.

They had thrown his daypack underneath him. Or maybe that's how he landed when they shoved him into the corner. Either way, it was his advantage. His cell phone was gone.

No. They had taken that before they'd drugged him.

The coffee. How stupid of him to be tricked so easily by a couple of girls.

Nothing seemed to be missing from his pack. Creed pulled out the emergency kit he had for Grace. He shoved his hand deeper and came back with an assortment of candy in colorful wrappers. *Brodie.* He smiled and plunged his hand back in until he found a water bottle.

Grace's collapsible bowl was in a side pocket. As Creed started filling the bowl, Grace leaned in, lapping at the falling water, not able to wait for him to put the bowl down. He petted her while she drank, talking to her in a quiet tone, and telling her what a good girl she was. He brushed his hand against her side, and she winced in pain.

He remembered her whimper. Somewhere in his muddled mind, he had heard one of the women say, "Hey, stop kicking the dog."

He shook the fogginess from his mind and let anger replace it as he dug out a canine energy bar from a Ziplock bag. Hannah had made them from scratch, formulating them especially for the dogs. He broke off a piece and offered it to Grace. She noticed him watching the door. He watched as she listened. After a few seconds, she took the piece of bar and chewed. He broke off another piece and popped it into his mouth. They took turns until it was gone.

In Grace's first aid kit, he found a blister pack of Clavamox, an antibiotic. He fingered it open and swallowed it down with a sip from water in the bottle, forcing himself to leave just a little. He pulled out the container of pain meds, but immediately stopped. Was Tramadol was an opioid? The overdose last June felt too recent.

Grace was watching him. Paying attention only to him. No other sounds. No one approaching the trailer.

He ran his fingers gently over her side again, and she flinched.

He twisted off the pain med's protective cap and poured one tablet into the palm of his hand. Also in the kit was a small container of peanut butter. Before he had the lid off, Grace was drooling. He coated the pill with peanut butter and gave it to her.

"One for you," he said as he palmed another pill into his hand. "And one for me." He popped it into his mouth and drained the rest of the water.

He continued to watch Grace for any signals. Her nose lifted, sampling the air, but her ears didn't pitch forward. He figured he had a few more minutes. With the first aid kit opened and ready, it was time to check his wound. It didn't surprise him, but he was disappointed to see that it was a bloody mess again.

51

"This doesn't mean he's dead," Pakula said.

Maggie wanted him to shut up. His good intentions were only making her slide further off the imaginary ledge she was already on. She felt like she was hanging onto it by her fingertips. One wrong move and she might fall into the abyss. Her nerves were scraped raw. Her mind was a blur. And she couldn't stop seeing that bloody shirt—Ryder's shirt.

Pakula had found something else inside the black garbage bag that seemed to convince him Ryder's disappearance might be connected to the murder of Kristin Darrow. He told her he'd explain later.

All the way back, Pakula was on his phone, and Spencer was on his radio. Both men ordering and putting into play the necessary procedures for reporting, alerting and searching for a missing, wounded dog handler.

One thing Maggie noticed through the haze of her panic, Pakula called Ryder, an official member of his human trafficking task force. Ryder wasn't law enforcement, but Pakula had just put him on the level of one. It would elevate his search.

"A sock," Maggie said to Pakula when it was safe for her to discuss it without wanting to scream. One black crew sock, stiff with blood. Too small to be Ryder's.

Spencer had dropped them back off at the hotel. It was snowing again. The sheriff needed to respond to some emergency storm related calls.

Pakula gestured to the hotel's restaurant.

"I can't eat," Maggie told him.

"We can find a quiet booth to talk. You don't mind if I eat, do you? I haven't had breakfast."

"Tommy, I'm serious."

She placed a hand on his arm, and he stopped to look at her. To the left was the bank of elevators. To their right was the hallway to the restaurant. Only now did she notice the stubble on his face. He hadn't shaved yet. Her phone call must have woken him despite his "ready-to-go" voice.

"I just…" She didn't want to tell him she was on the verge of breaking apart. Dread and urgency pranced through her veins, causing her pulse to race. Her palms felt clammy. Her knees threatened to buckle without warning.

"Look, Maggie." Pakula's voice was low and gentle, but not condescending. She suspected it was the same tone he used with his wife and daughters. "I have an idea what you're feeling. What you're going through. Believe me, you don't want to curl up and dwell on it. The best thing you can do for yourself and for Ryder right now is continue to put the puzzle pieces together."

When she didn't respond, he put a hand on her shoulder and told her, "We'll find him. That's what we do."

Suddenly, her cell phone started pinging messages, one after another.

"Sometimes there's a delay," Pakula explained. "Who knows why? I hate these things. Come on. Join me for a few minutes. I'll tell you about the sock."

As Pakula ordered breakfast, Maggie brought up the text messages she'd missed. She didn't stop him when she heard him order an extra order of wheat toast, bacon, and Diet Pepsi.

Three of the messages were from Agent Alonzo. The first simply told her he had gained access to the security camera's digital files for the hardware store in Hastings. So she didn't have to go there. The second said he was reviewing them. The third told her he was emailing her some of the more "interesting" ones.

There was also a message from Hannah asking her to call when she got a chance. Maggie's stomach slipped to her knees. How was she going to tell Hannah about the cell phone and the bloody shirt? However, a second message from Hannah made her sit up. Her movement even grabbed Pakula's attention.

"What is it?" he asked.

She reread the message before she looked up across the table at him.

"One of Ryder's dog handlers, Jason Seaver, is driving up with his search dog to help look for Ryder."

"That's actually not a bad idea," he told her. "So, what's the problem?"

"Brodie is coming with him."

52

"Tell me about the socks," Maggie told Pakula.

She had spent the last several minutes explaining about the security camera files from the hardware store. At first, she believed it was a long shot. The idea of the killer buying his dismemberment tools at the place where his victim worked seemed far-fetched, but Maggie had known killers who were bold and often cocky. The bigger the risk, the greater the gratification.

Agent Alonzo had already pinpointed footage he wanted her to review, and she was impatient to get up to her room and her laptop to get started. But first, she wanted to hear about the socks found in the garbage bag with Ryder's phone and shirt.

"In one bag we found yesterday, Lucy said there was a small, black sock. The sole was soaked in blood."

"How do you know it wasn't the victim's?" Maggie asked.

"It's all together possible," he admitted. "But what are the odds that we find another one that looks like its match with Ryder's stuff? If not a match, another that looks like the same brand or make. It reminds me of the crew socks you buy in a pack of six."

That clammy feeling was back. She remembered the autopsy records she'd poured over last night.

"So what are you thinking?" she asked him.

"Cutting up a body is messy work." He must have noticed the panic flit across her face because he put up a hand as if to stop it. "I'm not saying they did the same to Ryder. The shirt and phone wouldn't be the only things left if that were the case." He paused. Her face must have started to show her nausea.

"Just stay with me for a minute," Pakula said. "Someone who's done this before doesn't want to ruin a pair of shoes. Plus, shoes leave footprints that can be traced. But socks? You take off the shoes and leave the socks on. Walk through the mess and toss them with the body. No way we can trace socks, right? Or at least, that's what he's thinking."

"Why only throw away one?"

"It wouldn't surprise me if we find the other one when we find more of Darrow. And I'm not saying the sock we found yesterday is identical to the pair we found today. I'm saying it could be a part of his M.O. A habit he's developed."

"You're saying the person who killed Darrow may have hurt Ryder?"

His response looked like equal parts of reluctance and clarification.

He put his hands on the table, one on each side of his plate. Turned them palms up. "Isn't that what you're already thinking?" he asked her.

Why fool herself? It was exactly what she was avoiding. She still did not want to believe that Ryder had been blindsided and injured. But if he had, she held out hope that he and Grace had escaped and were hiding somewhere. If he lost his phone in the attack, that would explain why he couldn't call or text for help.

With her elbows already planted on the table, Maggie leaned in. The restaurant was empty, in between the breakfast crowd and lunch. Still, she kept her voice low and asked, "What about Libby Holmes?"

"What about her?"

Pakula was cleaning his plate with a wedge of toast, sopping the remains of his over-easy eggs. Maggie couldn't watch. She'd barely gotten her toast and bacon down.

"The murder back in Virginia," she refreshed his memory.

"I thought she was just a suspect. There was no arrest, right?"

"Doesn't mean she wasn't involved." She sipped her Diet Pepsi, hoping to wash away the nausea. "I read the autopsy report last night. The body was dismembered."

Pakula stopped mid-sop and stared at her. "Now why the hell didn't you tell me that?"

"I am telling you. So, you think it could be connected?"

"That's one hell of a coincidence if it's not connected."

"If Lucy can confirm Darrow's identity, then we have to consider Libby is involved in her murder somehow. She may have run away because she's a part of it. For all we know, she's holding up somewhere with the killer and simply waiting for the snow to stop, so they can make a run for it."

She watched him. He wasn't dismissing her theory, or he would have already said it.

"And you think they have Ryder? Or they may have hurt him?" he asked.

She hated looping this idea in her mind. And she still didn't want to say it out loud. Afraid her voice might show too much emotion, she nodded.

"But why dump Darrow's body and stick around? We started finding it before the snow started. She disappeared last week. They had plenty of time to take care of business and beat it out of town. Out of the state." He shook his head, then gestured at her leftover bacon. "Are you going to finish that?"

"No. Go ahead."

She waited as he chewed. Perhaps it helped him think.

"We should go with your first gut reaction," he finally said.

Maggie couldn't remember what it was. Evidently, her expression told him that.

"Remember, the two women look like they could be sisters. What if the killer meant to get Libby? Didn't realize his mistake until it was too late."

"It doesn't explain how or why she was involved in the Virginia case."

"We both know how easily young girls can be manipulated. Even by guys like Freddie Mason."

"What about Mason?" Maggie asked, suddenly reminded of the trafficker. Was it only two days ago they believed this could be some sick revenge war between human traffickers?"

"I'm trying to talk to him. He's already lawyered-up. Some young hotshot from Lincoln who informed me he needed to be alerted forty-eight hours in advance, so that he could be present during any questioning of his client." Pakula dragged a palm over his shaved head.

Maggie pretended not to notice that the stubble on his jaw was more pronounced than on his head.

"Whatever's going on," she said, "I think we agree that Ryder and Grace have been taken."

"An injured."

"You're not making this any better."

"I said injured, not dead. And he could be hiding somewhere."

"What about Nora Spencer? Maybe there's more she's not telling us."

"Look, O'Dell, I know you've got a problem with the woman, but—"

"She lied about the baby. She even lied to her husband. You don't think she knows more than she's told us?"

"Not everyone has evil intentions. I think she tried to do a good thing, and got in over her head."

"You believe that?" Maggie asked.

"Yes, I have quite a few years under my belt dealing with liars and criminals. You're not the only one, O'Dell, who has experience in profiling scumbags."

She sat back, kept her hands on the table, folding her paper napkin into an accordion. "You're right. I'm sorry."

"If you're not satisfied with what Nora's told us, call her up. Go talk to her again." He scrubbed a hand over his jaw as if weighing what he wanted to say next. "Look, I know it's tough when you're personally involved in a case. I understand. I get that. How long have you and Ryder been together?"

Her eyes swung up to meet his, and the flush started at the back of her neck.

"Is it that obvious?" she asked.

He granted her a smile, then added, "What's not obvious is why you're hell-bent on hiding it?"

53

By the time the trailer door opened, Creed was sitting at the table. Grace sat on the bench between him and the wall, protected by his body. He had prepared coffee. Three mugs.

The shock on Libby's face was worth the pain and effort.

"Ariel's right behind me," she said a bit too quickly. "She still has the gun."

"Coffee?" he asked. "I made it this time without any drugs."

"Look, as soon as the snow lets up, I'm out of here and you can go back to your nice world with your little dog."

She whipped off her stocking cap. The static electricity left her short hair sticking straight up. She heel-toed off her boots, letting them fall by the door. That's when she noticed Creed's boots already there, still dripping with clumps of snow.

He sipped coffee and watched as she realized he'd already been outside. Not only had he been outside but he'd decided to come back. Was she wondering how she missed his footprints in the snow? He'd taken Grace out and boot-swept an area for her to do her business.

She processed all this without changing her expression as she hung her coat next to Creed's on the far wall. Was she really going to pretend they were just two people waiting out the storm? Was she going to pretend she and her friend hadn't stabbed him, slipped him some drugs, then shoved him in the corner with his hands zip-tied?

He glanced out the window and noticed Libby didn't. In fact, it didn't look like she was waiting or watching for Ariel. Maybe he had a few minutes to divide and conquer.

"Which one of you kicked, Grace?"

"What?" She feigned surprise. Finally, something she was bad at.

"If either of you do it again, I will hurt you."

"Yeah right, Mr. tough guy." But when her eyes met his, the smirk slid off her face. She had to look away. "You're awfully protective of a stupid little dog."

"This little dog was smart enough to find your baby's grave."

Now came the genuine surprise, but it arrived with a tinge of anger. "What are you talking about?"

"I asked her to find you, and she took a detour behind the barn."

The ruddy color from the wind and cold seeped away. Her face went white. A hand shot out and grabbed the counter. The other hand swept the unruly hair out of her face.

Her eyes met his again, and he wouldn't let her look away this time. She stuttered-stepped to the opposite bench and dropped onto it. He saw the emotion behind her eyes, moist and raw, before she blinked it away.

She reached for one of the mugs and wrapped her fingers around it, leaned over the steam.

"Did you leave the scarf for the baby or for Nora?" he asked.

This time, she looked at Grace.

"So she found my scent from the scarf?" she asked.

"She's also a cadaver dog."

The wince was real, a fresh sting like reopening a gaping wound.

He gave her a reprieve from his scrutiny and looked out the window. Downed tree branches made it impossible to see very far. Anything that was green twenty-four hours ago was now covered. The wind swirled so much it was difficult to tell if it was new snow falling or the old stuff still blowing around. It wouldn't be easy to navigate out there. He wondered what was keeping Ariel. Maybe she'd gotten lost.

After a few minutes, he said, "Nora was worried you ran off to hurt yourself again."

"Yeah, well, Nora worries too much."

When she took off her coat, she pushed her sweater sleeves up. With only a glance, Creed could see where the skin still puckered on her wrists. She saw him notice. Her fingers left the mug and tugged the cuffs down, then returned to the mug, all in two quick, simple motions that seemed familiar to her.

"I'm sure Nora and Ted have the entire county sheriff's department out looking for me," Libby said.

"No, just me and Grace. "

She studied his face as if checking for sarcasm. She still hadn't taken a sip of her coffee. Maybe she didn't trust that he'd do the same to her as she had done to him.

"Everyone else was out searching the ditches," Creed told her, pausing so he could study her reaction. Then he added, "They're looking for more black garbage bags with body parts."

"Right. Very funny."

"A young woman was murdered and cut up into pieces."

Now she stared at him, genuinely surprised.

Surprised, but not shocked.

"You wouldn't happen to know anything about that?" he asked.

54

"Why would I know anything about it?" Libby countered.

She tried to keep the shock from her voice, but she knew her face had already given her away. Soon the man would be able to hear the hammering of her heart against her ribcage.

He was lying. He was clearly playing with her, and she didn't appreciate it, even if she deserved it. He just wanted to get back at her for drugging him. Tying him up.

Truthfully, she probably didn't need to drug him. The knife wound had to be painful. Between that and the storm, he had already been incapacitated. But if she didn't knock him out of the picture, Ariel would have done something worse. Something irreversible. Libby could see it in her fiery green eyes.

But this guy wasn't messing around about the body parts. A young woman, cut into pieces? In the back of her mind, Libby immediately thought about Ruben.

"Nora thought it was me?" she asked.

"At first, yes."

He was watching her again. There was something about this guy that unnerved her. It wasn't like he was judging her or anything like that. And he certainly didn't waste time with bullshit. He was straight in your face. Nothing held back. In the past, she'd wished more people would be upfront and honest. He was doing exactly that, and she didn't like it.

But it was more than his boldness. It felt like those blue eyes could see deeper than she wanted him to see.

"Why did you run?" he asked. "If you weren't going off to hurt yourself?"

"You don't know anything about me." It was a ridiculous thing to say. And useless. Even she could hear herself unraveling around the edges. But she was good at distracting and deflecting, so why not continue to counterpunch?

"Everybody seems to think attempted suicide is a terminal illness," she told him. "Or it's like if you didn't get it right the first time, of course you'll try again."

He sipped his coffee as if he didn't care. "My dad shot himself in the head. Got it right on the first try."

She stopped her jaw before it dropped completely open. Most people wouldn't have noticed. This guy did, though. She stared at him, waiting for details until she realized he wasn't offering anything more. So that's how he wanted to play this. He'd make her ask. Want her to give up details in exchange.

She couldn't figure him out, and yes, it bothered the hell out of her. It didn't help that he was handsome for an old guy. He had to be thirty.

"I was the one who found him," he said, with no prompting.

For once, his eyes weren't on her. He was looking out the window. Maybe he was thinking about his father. Maybe he was bullshitting her until Ariel got back.

"He was watching football," he continued. "At first, I thought he was asleep on the sofa. He looked peaceful. Surprisingly, it wasn't even all that messy."

His eyes swung back to hers as if he needed their effect to deliver his next blow. "Vertical wrist cuts," he said with a glance at her hands. "Now that had to be messy."

She wasn't used to anyone talking about suicide like this. Usually people tiptoed around it. Thought they were being polite. Libby figured they really didn't want to know the details. Even Nora hadn't asked any questions.

Libby held his eyes. What game was he playing? She wondered if he was just pissed about getting stabbed and trussed up by a couple of girls. Guys like him probably weren't used to being overpowered so easily.

He was over six feet tall, broad-shouldered, lean and muscular. Ariel made a big deal about his abs when she was taking off his shirt. She wanted to take the T-shirt off, too, just to look at his body, but the T-shirt was too bloody. Ariel was already disgusted that she had walked in the trail of blood he'd left on the trailer floor. It had soiled her only pair of socks. She stole a pair from his backpack, then bragged about how warm they were.

Now, pretending to get bored with him, Libby shrugged, following his casual lead. "Sure. It's a helluva mess. That's the point. To bleed out quickly. And if you do it right, you're not supposed to be around to care much about whether or not you stained the bathroom tiles."

He nodded. Listened. Nothing to add. Those blue eyes searching to understand.

The dog snuggled up against him, readjusting and shooting a look at Libby before she ducked her head and laid it on his lap. His right hand petted her, then rested on her back. In that brief second or two, Libby caught him grimace.

The dog's bump, even as gentle as it was, caused him pain. He was hurting. Must be bad if a nudge had broken his carefully curated blank expression. How much leverage had he given up in that brief glimpse?

Yes, that was exactly how little she trusted anyone these days. Before she realized it, her mind was already spinning and concocting ways to use his pain against him. Another lesson she'd learned from Ruben. If you know a person's weakness, you can turn it into your greatest weapon against them.

"So what made you run?" he asked, interrupting her thoughts.

"Excuse me?"

"You said you didn't go off to hurt yourself. But you did run away."

"Maybe I just wanted to be left alone for a while."

"And you couldn't just tell Nora that?"

"I don't owe her anything. She doesn't care about me. To her, I'm just some mixed up girl that triggered her martyr syndrome."

"Really?"

"Look, you think you know me, because what? Your daddy killed himself and oh, by the way, I tried to do the same thing, so you think we have something in common. You don't have a clue who I am or what I'm capable of doing."

He wasn't impressed, and even Libby had to admit her rant sounded like a stupid teenager. Where the hell was Ariel? Maybe she didn't want to wait for the snow to stop. Maybe she was halfway to Lincoln by now. Or stuck in a snowbank.

"Nora cares about you," he said, his tone still composed and all matter-of-fact. "You should have seen how panicked she was when she thought those body parts were yours."

"How did she know it wasn't me?"

Libby figured he was making it up about the body parts to scare her. To goad her. Rile her up. Make her reveal something. She could play this game, too. Call his bluff. Whatever the hell he was doing. There was no way he could possibly know about Ruben. Or about what happened in Virginia?

"We found a tattoo on the foot," he said. "Nora said it wasn't yours."

It didn't matter. It barely registered until he dropped a bomb by adding, "A small, dark red heart on the outside of the ankle."

Libby let out a small gasp before she could catch it. An intake of breath. That was all. She swallowed hard to cover it up. But suddenly the trailer seemed to tilt to one side.

No, it wasn't possible. That tattoo had to be popular.

And yet, she knew it was possible, because she knew exactly who had a tattoo like that on her ankle. Someone Libby hadn't heard from since last week. Someone who had done her a favor and taken her place.

55

Maggie was relieved to be back in her room. Pakula was right. She needed to work. Keep her mind occupied. However, twenty minutes later, she was fidgety. Couldn't sit still. Couldn't sit at all. She paced a trail from the desk to the window and circled the room, always checking outside on every loop.

Agent Alonzo had zipped and dropped the digital security files from the hardware store into three separate emails. He would preview others, search and scan using his sophisticated equipment back at Quantico's FBI crime lab. Then he'd send them along, digitally earmarking particular segments after he matched receipts and timeframes.

But the first three files were taking forever to download.

Maggie hated waiting.

She slid her cell phone into the back pocket of her jeans so she could feel its vibration. She didn't want to miss a call or text. Still, she yanked it out to double check when it was quiet for too long.

Less than an hour later, the restlessness was overwhelming. She packed up what she needed, grabbed the spare keycard and moved to Ryder and Grace's room.

Nothing had changed from when she had checked it last night. Ryder had left his travel duffle on the valet in the corner. A couple of T-shirts, still folded, were left on the bed with the long-sleeved shirt he had worn the day before. The bed was made, perfect folds and tucks as if housekeeping had taken care of it, but Maggie knew from previous morning-afters that Creed had, in fact, made his own bed.

On the desk were some of Grace's items: an extra pink elephant in case (heaven forbid) her original went missing; a collapsible water bowl and a spare leash.

She opened the curtains wider, allowing the white gray of the sky to lighten the room. She set up her laptop on the desk, but did so without moving a single one of Grace's items.

After only minutes of settling down to work, she was back on her feet, still restless. At the end of the bed, she stood looking over Ryder's things. She picked up the long-sleeved shirt, its cuffs still rolled up, then put it on, slipping in one arm, then the other. The shirttails almost hung to her knees. She wrapped the shirt around her body like a familiar old cardigan. She breathed in Ryder's scent. Shoved the rolled sleeves up over her elbows and sat back down.

Now she was ready to work. Per Alonzo's instructions, she put in her earbud and called him as she opened the first digital file. The quality of the security camera footage was better than she expected. It would make a tedious job easier.

"You all set?" Alonzo said in place of a greeting.

"Brief me on what we're looking at."

"Your friends at the hardware store were very cooperative. Especially when Kevin learned that a second of his employees—Libby Holmes—was now also missing. I checked out the receipts for the last day Kristin Darrow worked. The day she substituted for Libby. I expected to work my way backwards for up to a week if necessary. I don't think it will be necessary."

"You think you found something already? Did you see her leave with someone?"

"Inside cameras are above average quality. Outside cameras, not so much. So I spent some time looking for Darrow while she worked. Fire up the first video."

Maggie hit PLAY while Alonzo was talking. She recognized Darrow with a customer at the end of an aisle. It looked like she was answering the man's questions and pointing to products on the shelf. The guy was tall, older, with a dark ponytail, long sideburns. He wore a polo shirt and khakis. He seemed interested in the items on the shelf. Not in Darrow.

"I can't tell what the products are," she told Alonzo, expecting to see saws or utility knives."

"Forget the shelves. Forget the gentleman she's talking to. Take a look behind her in the middle of the aisle. The short, pudgy guy in the dark T-shirt."

Maggie stopped and backed up the file. She waited until the man was in view, then she froze the frame. She tapped PLAY and kept her eyes on him. Darrow had her back to him as she helped the other customer. This guy took a box off the shelf and stole glances at Darrow.

"Maybe he's waiting for her to finish so he can ask a question," she suggested.

"Keep watching."

The customer in khakis grabbed what he needed, thanked Darrow and left. Darrow went around the end of the aisle and disappeared from view. The man who had been watching hurried to the end of the aisle, stopped and peered around the corner where Darrow had disappeared. He glanced in the other direction before he turned and followed Darrow.

"I found him watching her from afar a couple more times," Alonzo said.

"What did he end up buying?"

"That's the thing. All he bought was a bottle of soda from the end cap frig."

"That's it?"

"That's it. I tried to find him in the days before. Nothing."

"Is he the only guy you found suspicious?"

"Well, wait a couple of minutes. I'm not finished with him."

Maggie heard the agent slurp and reached for her can of Diet Pepsi to do the same. Her stomach had settled a bit, but she felt like she had a time-bomb ticking inside her chest, seconds running down with each click.

"Open the next file. I isolated some other views that the guy appears in. Forward to 05:37. This is from a camera with a front view of that aisle. It's a little farther away, but it gives an interesting take." He waited for Maggie to catch up before he started narrating.

"Okay," she told him. "I see Darrow just walked away and headed to the right."

She watched the young woman pass by three aisles before she turned and went up the fourth. The short man in the T-shirt peered around the end of his aisle, then glanced in the other direction. Maggie didn't need Alonzo to narrate what she saw. The guy looked at another young woman walking toward him. A customer. She nodded at him, but stopped and waited as he turned to follow Darrow.

She had blond hair piled up on top of her head. She was tall and lean, showing off well-shaped arms in a tank top. A tattoo peeked out, but Maggie couldn't make out the design. After she nodded at him, she returned to her shopping cart, where another young woman stood waiting. The other one was a bit shorter and wore blue jeans with a white, lightweight jacket.

"Are you able to determine if either of these two women is Libby Holmes?"

"We get a closer look at them when they're checking out," Alonzo said. "I ran facial recognition software. Neither is Holmes. But think about it. If Holmes is involved, she's not going into the store with them. She was supposed to be working."

"You're right. It'd make sense that she stayed in the vehicle. She's already told them to look for the woman with her name badge. What do they buy?"

"Pull up the third file. I'll give you a minute to catch up before I start reading off the receipt."

She found them in the checkout lane. The shorter woman with brown hair handed each item to the clerk to scan, while the blond pretended to be interested in the impulse items. At one point, her head pivoted to watch Darrow walk by. Then she dug out her cell phone and started tapping her thumbs.

"Ready for the list?" Alonzo asked.

"Go ahead," Maggie told him as she watched the clerk scan the UPC code on a hacksaw.

"First off, they buy drop cloths and plastic sheets," he said, "but no paint or stain. It's like they don't even bother pretending. The list reads like the ultimate dismemberment tool kit."

She steeled herself as he continued.

"Assorted black cable ties. They chose the pack of 600 for seven dollars and ninety-nine cents."

She wasn't in the mood for his attempt at humor, but sometimes it was the only way to get through this stuff. Electrician cables were better known as zip-ties. But 600? Other than hands and feet, what else did they need to tie down?

"Three rolls of duct tape," he continued. "One Gerber folding knife, three gallons of Clorox, a thirty-two ounce Pro-strength Drano, two utility knives with replacement blades, two boxes of black garbage bags, one—"

"That's good," she interrupted him. "I don't need to hear the rest." The nausea returned. "Are you able to see them get into a vehicle?"

"No. I watched them leave the store. The guy met them right before walking out. They're smart enough to park away from the outside cameras. But the blond came back about an hour later."

"I'm afraid to ask what they forgot."

"She went directly to the end cap frig. Bought two Pepsis and get this—a Yoohoo."

"Yoohoo?"

"It's a delicious chocolate drink. I didn't realize they carried them in hardware stores."

Again, Maggie wanted to shut down Alonzo's attempt at humor. Then she understood the point he was making.

"They must have gotten thirsty," she said, "while they waited for her shift to be over."

56

This gas station was bigger and busier than any of the others, and immediately Brodie felt her entire body go into alert mode. She enjoyed watching people from the safety of Jason's Jeep, but she had to pee.

She'd need to wait for Jason to come back. He'd already pumped the gas but went inside to buy her a phone, despite her telling him she didn't need one. "When we start looking for Ryder and Grace, we'll need to communicate with each other," he'd told her.

"I won't wander off," she promised.

"I don't expect you to wander off. Look Brodie, if we're working as partners, we have to stay in touch even if we get separated."

She was used to all of them being overprotective of her. It became instinct for her to bristle at their attempts, but she realized Jason had a good point. Plus, she liked that he said they were partners.

"Do you really think Ryder got lost?" she'd asked him just before he left for the convenience store.

"No." He hadn't taken time to consider his answer.

"But if he's not lost—"

She didn't finish, and Jason let her question drop. All he said was, "We'll find him. And Grace."

An old man with feathery gray hair parked his SUV at the pumps in front of them. He'd backed in so close there was little room between the bumpers. And his vehicle was so close to the pumps that he practically had to squeeze out of his door. He limped, holding onto the side of the SUV as he pumped the gas.

The place was crazy busy. She hoped Jason would be back soon so she could pee and they could leave.

That's when she noticed Hank panting. He was watching the chaos, too, his head wagging side to side, ducking and stretching to follow certain customers. Hank didn't trust too many people, either. Brodie figured they were both works in progress.

But now she realized he might still be thirsty. They had taken both dogs for a short walk along a sad patch of grass at the far end of the gas station lot. Jason suggested leaving them out of their crates to stretch and cool off. The air was warm and muggy, and Brodie couldn't imagine a snowstorm going on less than 500 miles away.

"Hang on," she told Hank and Scout. "I'll get you two some more water."

She reached under her seat for a bottle of water, careful not to disturb Kitten. He'd curled up into a soft sweatshirt she'd placed on the floorboard between her feet.

Instead of turning around in her seat, she decided it was easier to get out and open the door to fill their water bowl. She couldn't reach it from the passenger side, so she went around and opened the other back door. She'd barely tucked herself inside the door well when Hank began to growl.

Brodie glanced up to see the old man climbing back into his vehicle, but that wasn't what agitated Hank. His head twisted to look out the back of their Jeep. Brodie didn't notice the man with the gray hooded sweatshirt until he rounded the Jeep's back bumper.

"Get out of my way, bitch," he muttered, shoving her to get to the old man's SUV.

Her forehead bounced off the top of the door well, and she grabbed hold of the driver's seat headrest to keep from losing her balance. The rest was a blur. As soon as the guy pushed Brodie, Hank was on his feet.

The intruder grabbed the door handle to the SUV, banging the door open against the pumps. The old man let out a startled yelp just as he was being dragged out from his seat.

Before Brodie could react, Hank jumped out. In seconds he plowed into the car thief, and the man went down. Hard. Knees and elbows hit the pavement, only to be flattened when Hank's front paws came to rest on the small of the man's back.

The old man had tumbled out but leaned against the gas pumps to stop from falling. Blood dripped down his temple. That's when Brodie touched her forehead. Bruised. No blood.

Others had come to see the ruckus, but no one attempted to help. Brodie made Scout stay as she grabbed a towel and the water bottle, then closed the door.

"What the hell's going on?" Jason yelled, racing around the vehicles. "Oh, my God. What happened? Brodie, are you okay?"

"I'm fine," she told him as she handed the old man the towel she had dampened. Her heart pounded. Her pulse raced, and her eyes never left the man squirming underneath Hank's weight.

"Get this frickin' dog off of me," the guy screamed.

He looked small, especially with the hood of his sweatshirt now tumbled off and exposing his face.

"What's going on here?" A man in a uniform weaved his way between the onlookers and the vehicles.

"A pit bull attacked someone," a woman said from the group of bystanders.

"No, no." The old man shook his head and waved his hands. "This guy yanked me out and tried to steal my car. The dog stopped him. This dog saved me." He looked at Brodie with glassy eyes, still shocked by what had happened. "Is that your dog?"

Brodie thought it was pretty obvious. Even as Hank pressed his full seventy-five pounds down on the man's back, he was looking up at her, waiting for her signal. And she swore he was smiling.

57

"He made the mistake of shoving me," Brodie told Jason later when they were back on the road. "When he tried to sneak past."

"We haven't trained him to do that," Jason said.

"Protective instinct."

Jason nodded. They both knew Hank had taken a bullet meant for his first owner. He hadn't been able to save John Lockett, but the dog almost died trying.

"I'm glad he didn't try to take the Jeep," Jason said. "Why did you get out?"

Brodie hadn't considered that the guy could have easily opened the Jeep's door and climbed into the driver's seat. Jason had left it running to keep her and the dogs cool. She hadn't bothered to lock the doors when he left to go inside the store.

She studied his face, looking for disappointment or anger. She saw neither. Expecting punishment was still one of her instinctive reactions.

"Hank was unsettled and panting," she tried to explain. "I was getting him a drink of water. I didn't want to climb over the console." Although she'd climbed over it before on other stops. Did it sound like a lame excuse?

Brodie promised herself to be more careful, more aware. But she didn't say it out loud.

She couldn't be more proud of Hank. Ryder had offered her first choice of any dog in their kennel. She had chosen Hank because he looked sad and handsome and ferocious all at the same time. And he enjoyed it when she read to him. He cocked his head when she did different voices for each of the fictional characters, so lately she read novels that were dialogue heavy. He seemed to like rom-coms the best.

"How's your head?" Jason asked.

She'd already forgotten about it. Her fingers skimmed over the area. It hurt, but she said, "It's okay." She had worse.

"Did he scare you?"

She hadn't given the car thief much consideration. She hadn't even seen his face.

"I didn't have time to be scared. It happened so fast."

"Next time—and I'm not saying there will be a next time—but don't hesitate to use your bear spray," he told her.

When they were ready to leave the hotel, Jason noticed that Brodie attached the holster to her waistband. By now, it was a habit, a part of her daily ritual when she got dressed for the day. She hadn't needed to use it yet, but just having the canister close gave her a sense of security. She didn't need bear spray as long as she had Hank.

"Hank isn't in trouble, is he?" she asked, only now realizing that might be a part of what the officer wanted to talk to Jason about.

"No, he's not."

"That woman thought Hank attacked the guy."

"People think all bully terriers are aggressive and have violent tendencies."

Brodie turned and glanced at Hank. Back in his crate, she could see his big chest rising and falling. She could hear the low, familiar hum of his snoring.

"Let's talk about something else," Jason suggested. "Are you hungry?"

Brodie laughed.

"What?"

"Do you ever stop thinking about food?"

"Yes, I have other things on my mind."

"Like Taylor?" she asked, watching for his reaction.

She liked when Jason smiled, but she didn't like that Taylor was the reason for it.

"Yeah, I guess." His voice sounded shy, but his grin widened.

"Are you in love with her?"

"I really don't know. I've never been in love before, so I'm not sure what it's supposed to feel like?"

"Is it because she's a bit of a slut?"

"What?"

The Jeep actually jerked with his reaction, and Brodie braced against the dashboard.

"Who said that?" He wanted to know as he straightened out the steering wheel and stayed in his lane.

"Taylor. She said she was a bit of a slut."

"She was joking around."

"But you like having sex with her, right?"

"Geez, Brodie! That's kind of personal." The smile slid off his face. "I don't think this is something we should discuss"

"The sex you're having with Taylor, or sex in general?"

"Either. Both." The subject tongue-tied him.

"But how will I learn about all this stuff if no one will talk to me about it? Romance novels are full of the female perspective. Maybe it would be good to get the male perspective."

"Well, the male perspective is, guys don't talk about it."

She stared out the side window and allowed a smile. She'd learned two things from their exchange. First one: he didn't know if he was in love with Taylor. The second: they were definitely having sex.

Was it jealousy she was feeling?

Brodie didn't understand how she felt about Jason. He'd said on more than one occasion that she and Ryder and Hannah and the dogs were his family. She certainly didn't think of him as a brother. She glanced over at him and realized she'd probably only succeeded in making him think of Taylor.

She stayed quiet. He needed to concentrate on driving. The traffic continued to clog both lanes of the interstate. It hadn't let up for the last several hours. They were pointed west now, but thick gray clouds blocked out the sun. This could be part of the storm front.

She wasn't good at conversation. She'd just proven that. Too blunt. No filter. Was it wrong to be straightforward? As her mind tried to wind up another subject, Jason startled her, breaking the silence.

"You can ask me anything, Brodie. Maybe just not about sex."

"And you can ask me anything, too," she said. "If you want."

"Let's start with simpler stuff. Like, what's your favorite color?"

"That's easy. Yellow."

"Yellow? You never wear yellow."

"No, but I enjoy looking at it. Anything that's yellow is usually cheerful. Daffodils, baby ducks, the sun. It's hard to see yellow and not smile."

He looked over at her and went quiet again, but now he was smiling. It was a real smile that took over his whole face, including his eyes. She liked making him smile.

58

Along the Platte River, Nebraska

Grace jolted in Creed's arms. The hair on the back of her neck stood up. Immediately, he knew two things. Ariel was close by. And it was Ariel who had kicked Grace.

He stopped himself from sneaking a peek out the window. He didn't want Libby to know right away that Ariel was headed back. He wanted to keep working on her. Making her more comfortable with him. Okay, comfortable wasn't the correct word. He was wearing her down. She was tired. He was the only one of them who had gotten any sleep, although it felt more like a drug-induced nightmare than sleep. But now, she was upset. So much so, she couldn't pretend.

"How do you know her?" Creed asked. She'd gasped when he told her about the dead woman's heart tattoo.

"It's probably not who I thought it might be." She shrugged like it didn't matter, but she wrapped her arms tight across her chest. "I mean, how many women get hearts tattooed on their ankles? It's probably like the number one thing."

"Nora was frantic it was you. Why didn't you at least leave her a note or text her that you were okay?"

Another shoulder shrug. She was good at them. Somewhere she'd learned a shrug would be accepted as a sufficient response.

"She took you in," Creed pressed on. "Helped you."

She watched him so intently, Creed felt like he was trapped in close quarters with an unpredictable, wild animal. Libby wasn't the one who'd attacked and stabbed him, but there was something in her eyes that made him believe she was capable of doing the same, especially if it meant surviving. After all, she had drugged him. For all he knew, she was the one who zip-tied his wrists, then rolled and kicked him into the corner.

"She said I didn't owe her anything."

The pronouncement made her sound childish. However, her eyes continued to bore into him, daring him to challenge her. The Tramadol reduced his pain to a dull roar. He was ready to put aside any hesitation he had earlier about using his strength against either of these two women. No one would kick Grace again. He'd make sure of that.

"Nora must have helped you with your miscarriage," he said.

A flicker of emotion crossed her face, but her eyes remained hard and steady.

"She kept your secret," he continued. "Even from her husband."

"I didn't ask her to do that."

"It's actually above and beyond what friends do for each other."

"Nora's not my friend."

"Really? What is she then?"

"She's a nurse. They feel compelled to save their patients."

"Sure. But I doubt they feel obligated to invite them into their home and offer their guest bedroom."

"I didn't ask her to do any of that."

"Did she know you were running away from this Ruben guy?"

Her eyes fixed on his, but he couldn't decipher whether it was anger or fear. The pain made his brain a bit slow.

When it was obvious she wasn't going to tell him about Ruben, he pressed on. "How do you and Ariel know each other?"

"What?"

She wasn't ready for the switch, her mind still occupied by the man named Ruben.

"Ariel. How do you two know each other?"

"Actually, we just met for the first time before you showed up."

She smiled at his surprise.

"But we're alike more than we're not," she added.

It was a strange thing to say, and Creed waited for her to explain. She didn't.

"It's none of your concern," she said instead.

"What does it matter what you tell me?" Creed asked. "It's not as if I'm going to tell anyone. Besides, you intend to kill me."

"What? No, I'm not. That's not part of the plan."

"It's part of Ariel's plan."

She met his eyes again, but the weight of his stare made her look away.

"This has gotten so crazy," she said, standing up and pacing the small area.

"So make it stop."

"I thought I did," she yelled at him, for the first time raising her voice. "It obviously didn't work. Okay?"

"So, what do you plan to do? Run and hide again?"

It stopped her in her tracks. When she raked her fingers through her hair, her hand was shaking.

"Maybe you should trust me instead of Ariel," he told her.

"Maybe I should let her kill you like she wants, so you'll finally shut up."

As if on cue, the trailer door swung open, bringing a blast of cold air along with a snow-caked Ariel. She looked at them, eyes darting back and forth. Before she said a word, Creed knew she was flying high.

59

Ruben hated waiting almost as much as he hated the cold. He stood at the hotel room window, staring out at the blinding white.

Traffic slowly resumed as trucks plowed roadways and dispersed sand with salt. It was a tedious way to live. A wasted portion of life consumed with shoveling, pushing, and piling small mountains of ice chunks, only to have it all melt away in the next several days. He couldn't leave this part of the country soon enough.

He glanced at his phone. Nothing. He had told Vanessa not to leave Lincoln until he gave her the go ahead. The last thing they needed was for her to end up sliding into a ditch or being in a pileup on the interstate. He knew she was just as anxious as he was for this to be over. She wanted to meet them at the address, and she wanted to do it now. But being in a hurry had landed them in the mess they were in. They needed to get it right this time.

Parked in the far corner of the lot below, Ruben watched three white utility vehicles with a logo for the local public power district. Three uniformed men—one for each vehicle and all wearing matching blue coats—talked and gestured to each other. Then two of them got in their vans and left. The other pulled out a duffle bag and shuffled through the snow to the hotel's entrance. The bag looked like an overnight case and not a tool bag. Perhaps he was finished for the day. It was clear the hotel still had electricity.

In fact, Shelby was binge watching sappy Hallmark Channel movies. Love and happily ever-after endings with perfect men and pretty but stupid women. Why did all women, regardless of age, find those themes enticing?

Actually, he was relieved that Shelby had found something to occupy her time, so he didn't have to talk to her. Another reason he preferred three girls around him at all times. They kept each other entertained with their discussions of silly and pointless subjects. And when they grew tired of each other, it didn't take much to pit them against one another. Having just two was easier, but three made everything so much more interesting.

If only Emma Hobbs hadn't slipped through his fingers. How did he not see that she'd be a problem? A good girl trying to be a bad girl but failing miserably.

He had set his sights on her long before she knew him. He saw her at a high school soccer game. The field was one of his recruiting grounds. Outdoor events gave him viewing access without questions. He was free to walk around, learn valuable information and follow them to waiting cars that provided a license plate and then an identity.

The recruits didn't need to be rebels. Good girls often wanted to know what it felt like to be bad girls. But athletes, he'd found, were especially interesting because they were competitive. He liked that. He liked to use that particular skill to his advantage.

These were the things he counted on each and every time. But Emma, now Libby, had tricked him. She'd bailed on him. Managed to escape and ultimately knew enough to destroy him. Obviously, if she had spoken to anyone about what she'd seen or experienced, no one believed her. But he couldn't rely on that. As long as she was alive, Ruben was in jeopardy. It took seven months to find her. He would not let her get away again.

Finding her took longer than he expected. But he knew the good girl in her would eventually tell him exactly where she was hiding, and he was right. As much as she claimed to hate her mother, she couldn't stand not letting the woman know that she was okay.

It all came down to natural instinct. Years ago, Ruben read an article about social media sites becoming one of the biggest threats to blowing the cover of hundreds of witnesses kept in secret protection around the country. All Ruben had to do was stick with it and monitor the mother's Facebook page. Emma would never expect him to still be searching for her half a year later, let alone on social media. He'd made it clear he didn't use the sites and didn't want his girls to use them either. She certainly wouldn't have expected him to do something like befriend her mother and be accepted.

Eventually, his patience was rewarded. Wading through recipes and boring day-to-day drivel finally paid off. The message he'd been waiting for came in a post on the mother's Facebook page.

ALL'S GOOD. HAVE A JOB AT MENARD'S.

OMG!! WHERE ARE YOU?

CAN'T TELL. #3233. DOING GREAT! I'LL BE IN TOUCH SOON. LOVE YOU!

At first glance, he'd missed the significance of #3233. For all he knew, Emma and her mother had some silly code. She came to him with a laundry list of uptight rules. He should have known how much trouble she'd be when he discovered she didn't have a single tattoo.

"My mom would kill me if I got a tattoo," she'd whined until he'd convinced her that alone was the best reason to get several.

Rebels without causes. Those were the girls he looked for and found easily. Until Emma Hobbs. She was too smart. Too rigid. Athletics had pounded too much discipline into her. Her working-class, single mother had weighed her down with a conscious.

Ruben was the one who gave her street creds. He was the one who taught her how to shoplift *without* getting caught. How to change her name and create a whole new persona. Never once did he have one of his girls use his lessons against him.

Never. Until Emma.

Of course, to be fair, he usually got rid of them before they thought about leaving the arrangement. He could get a whiff of their discontent before they even considered it.

There was one thing Emma Hobbs might not have realized—despite her somewhat admirable attempt. She did not know what great lengths David Ruben was willing to go to hunt her down. If she'd been watching her mother's Facebook posts, she must have believed it was finally safe to make contact.

The smart, scholarship girl had no clue that Ruben had been watching and reading all of her mother's vapid posts. When he finally hit pay dirt, he was not about to let her slip through his fingers a second time. He was determined to break their code. Could it be that Emma was telling her mother where she was?

It turned out to be fairly simple. He realized that each individual store had an identifying number. Sure enough, all he had to do was google Menards and store #3233, and he found where she was just like that. Hastings, Nebraska.

He had to hand it to her. He didn't know where the hell Nebraska was. A small Midwest town was the last place he'd look for her, let alone a hardware store. The good girl was still wickedly clever. And that made him more determined than ever.

The name change was trickier. But knowing where she worked made it a slam-dunk. Or it should have. Having three girls would have helped. Three pairs of extra eyes to search from the photo he provided. Problem number one: he was down a girl. But that was a separate project that would need to wait to be remedied.

Problem number two: how could he possibly have prepared for Emma to have a doppelgänger? And at the same place where she worked. The resemblance was uncanny. She was even wearing Emma's, aka Libby's, name badge.

Vanessa said the girl had whined some excuse for it. By then, it was too late. She couldn't possibly be allowed to live after what they had already done to her. What else could he do, but chalk it up as another lesson, and use it to motivate the girls to correct their mistake. Give them a chance to make up for disappointing him.

Evidently, it worked, because the two of them had put their heads together and figured it out. Although he knew it was probably Vanessa more than Shelby. He glanced at the girl stretched on her double bed, texting and plotting, but still absorbed in the television screen and the sappy movie.

Never mind, he told himself. They had searched and found an address. They had found Emma's hidey-hole. As soon as this blasted snow stopped, they would finish up their business and head to Florida. Who knows? If they did a good job, maybe he'd feel generous enough to let Shelby come along.

60

As soon as Ariel rushed into the trailer, Libby knew she was high. Her eyes were too wide and bright. She reeked of weed. The musky odor rode the fresh, cold air that blew in around her. With only a glimpse, she saw the dogman noticed, too.

"Hey, why the hell did you let him loose?" Ariel shouted. Her voice was too loud for the small space, and she managed to turn "loose" into a hissing sound.

"He let himself loose while we were gone," Libby told her. "I guess you didn't tie him up tight enough."

"Damn! I should have hog-tied his wrists and feet together. That stupid dog kept snapping at me. Help me. We can do him again."

She talked about him as if he were still unconscious. Libby didn't move. The guy didn't either. They watched Ariel peel off layers of outerwear, swinging her arms too much as she pulled them out of the sleeves. She yanked off her gloves using her teeth, pausing in between to point her finger gun at him.

Libby stayed at the counter where she continued to stir soup on the stovetop. She stopped from rolling her eyes. The dogman stayed at the table. She could see him reach over to reassure the little dog by putting his hand on her. The gesture did little to stifle the dog's snarl. Her lips were pulled back, baring teeth. For a fleeting moment, Libby wondered what it would be like to be loved and protected by this man.

"Seriously, we need to get rid of this guy," Ariel said, as she attempted to kick out of the boots Libby had given her. In almost the same rushed breath, she added, "What smells so bitchin' good?"

Libby shook her head and ignored her.

The boots were caked with snow. Ariel hadn't bothered to stomp any of it off before she barged back into the trailer. They would leave a puddle. Struggling to keep her balance, Ariel finally plopped on the floor and started tugging. Watching how clumsy, yet aggressive she was, Libby felt a pang of regret. She shouldn't have called her. She was so immature, and the drugs not only triggered her impulses, but heightened her urgency to act on them.

Over the phone, Libby had heard the fear and panic in Ariel's voice. It reminded her so much of herself. Last winter, when she fled from Ruben, she had no one to turn to. No one she could trust. Would her kindness be her downfall? And did she really believe this strung-out, reckless girl could help her? Or had she allowed herself to be sucked into the vortex of Ariel's desperation?

All Libby needed was an escape vehicle. Now she started worrying about the price she'd pay for that one simple thing.

She'd let herself get out of practice, out of the routine of being careful. Staying with Nora and Ted made her slip into a false sense of security. She'd become too comfortable. Too complacent. How silly of her to think she might actually live a normal life?

Ariel was a startling reminder of what she'd left behind. Of what she had escaped. How close had Libby come to being Ariel? She'd been so disciplined all her school years. When her father left, Libby honestly believed it was her fault, despite what her mother told her. Then, if it wasn't Libby's fault, it had to be her mom's, right?

So many stupid head games. She let out her frustration on the soccer field. She buckled down and worked hard to get good grades. The good athlete, the good girl. Good enough to win her father's praise.

Then he married someone else. He got too busy to come to her soccer games. He started having kids with his new wife. It was stupid. She was a teenager. Too old to be jealous of little kids, but she was. Because her mother had told her he didn't want to be tied down. Obviously, that wasn't true. He just didn't want to be tied down to Libby and her mom.

She became what she loathed: a whiny rebel without a cause, immersed in her own pity party. Her mom told her she had too much time on her hands. Libby had graduated in December and wouldn't leave for college until summer. She suggested Libby get a job.

That's when her mom became a part of the problem, too.

Then, in three short months of childish rebellion, Libby took all her hard work and accomplishments and turned it all into crap. She accepted invitations to the drunken house parties she'd stayed away from throughout high school. Suddenly, she enjoyed the release and reckless abandon the alcohol helped her feel.

The first time she lied to her mother was easier than she expected. The downhill spiral happened so quickly. One day she was partying with a bunch of lame college-bound teenagers like herself. Then next, she was contemplating joining Ruben's arrangement.

She had seen things she couldn't unsee. Done things she couldn't undo. All that blood streamed out into the bath water, sloshing over the rim and pooling on the floor. She didn't stick around to see how Ruben and the others had gotten the stains out.

She could still conjure up the fear that had overwhelmed her in the days that followed. It shook her to her core, set her teeth chattering and her bones aching. Ruben would kill her.

She hid in her father's backyard, up in the elaborate treehouse he'd built for his new kids. The cold rain kept them in the house for two days. None of them ventured out to the backyard.

Eventually, they all left for a few hours. She saw a slice of the luxury SUV driving away with four bobbing heads. She had been to her father's house enough times to know where he kept a spare key. Knew him well enough to find the wad of cash he hid from his new wife. She told herself he owed her, but she had no justification for the clothes she stole from her stepmom. She wondered if the woman even noticed the few missing items from the bulging drawers and tightly packed closet.

She knew without a doubt that her life would never be the same. Forget the same. It would never be normal ever again. There was no going back.

"We could poison him," Ariel's voice brought Libby back to the trailer. Her idiotic proposal only proved Libby's point. This was her life now where poisoning someone was discussed as an option for survival.

"He's sitting right there," Libby said without turning from the stove. Instead, she leaned into the steam of the chicken noodle soup. She was sacrificing two cans of her emergency stash to feed these two.

She reached up and brought down a bag of hard rolls, giving them a good look for any green. Satisfied, she pulled down a container of peanut butter. What she wouldn't do to make everyone go away and leave her to her little trailer in the woods.

She could be happy here. Okay, maybe not happy, but content.

This place had become her peace and quiet, her refuge. Yes, she had a very nice room at Nora's house. But here, she could relax without being under anyone's scrutiny. She had cleaned and repaired and stocked it, little by little. This felt like home. There had been times at work that she caught herself longing for just a few hours here, an afternoon.

She had grown accustomed to the songbirds calling to each other throughout the treetops. On a clear day, she could hear train whistles in the distance. The rush of the river's current sloshed along the bank, not more than a hundred feet away. Twice when she'd delivered supplies after dark, she'd heard a coyote howl. Maybe it was the same one she and Ariel had heard that morning. There was something primitive and unsettling about that sound.

Libby had spent all summer coming and going, but she'd never stayed overnight until now. Instead of feeling safe and isolated, she'd spent the dark hours listening for Ruben and jumping at every sound.

"Seriously," Ariel said, startling Libby, appearing right next to her. Ariel kept her back to the table and attempted—without succeeding—to lower her voice for conspiratorial effect. "I mean, like really, how are we gonna get rid of him?"

61

Creed pinched one of the pills he'd stuffed inside his pockets. While the girls conspired with their backs turned to him, he could finally allow a grimace from the pain. He needed another Tramadol, but now he couldn't remember if the pain med or the antibiotic was in his right or left pocket.

The side of his clean T-shirt was already damp despite the fresh dressing he'd applied just hours ago. Was it only hours ago or longer? The loss of blood made him slightly dizzy and disoriented. The smell of the soup triggered nausea.

He identified the pill as a painkiller and sneaked it into his mouth, casually washing it down with the lukewarm coffee. Just as casually, he moved his fingers to the bandaged wound and pressed against it, biting down so hard he thought for sure he'd crack a molar.

The girls didn't notice. But Grace did. She was panting, standing on the bench beside him and tapping her nose against his arm. She could sense his pain, and the smell of his blood upset her.

He wasn't sure how much blood he'd lost, but he knew the risks of not stopping it. After a certain percentage, his body would start to compensate by constricting the blood vessels in his limbs as his heart lowered the amount it pumped outside the center of his body. Would it affect walking? Probably. Maybe even standing up. He noticed his breathing had already become more labored. Weakness and fatigue would set in, and there was a chance he'd go into shock.

He couldn't afford to lose consciousness. Who knew what these two wolves, particularly Ariel, would do to him? Best-case scenario, they'd leave him to die. Worse case, Ariel would finish him. He didn't mind that so much, except for Grace. He hated seeing her like this. She was panicked and hurting from her own injury. She wouldn't leave his side even if they killed him.

He checked his watch. Damn! Why hadn't he set an alarm for her next dose of pain meds? He'd take his chances with his own, but not hers.

Already his mind struggled to figure out the timeframe. How long it had been since Ariel stabbed him? Twenty-four hours? Longer? How much longer?

Grace pushed her nose against his arm again, and he released his fingers from his side so he could pet her until he saw they were bloody. Grace nudged his arm aside, then tucked her nose between his arm and the back of the bench. When she saw she had his attention, she sat down and stared up into his eyes.

The girls were still whispering at the counter. Ariel was trying to whisper. Libby seemed to realize how ridiculous the gesture was with Creed sitting less than fifteen feet away. He had been able to mask the pain before, but now the simple movement of reaching behind his back sent a fire through his belly.

Creed clenched his jaw and slowly moved his clean hand along the back cushion without leaning into the table too much. He didn't want them to hear or see what he was doing. He scooted his butt forward a few inches for his hand to squeeze into the crack where the seat cushion met the back cushion.

He looked at Grace out of the corner of his eye. She was watching, no longer panting. All of her attention focused on his search. His fingers found something hard and about a quarter inch thick. He slid a finger down until he felt an edge, then a square corner. The table hid his hands, but not his movements. Slowly, he dislodged the object. When he could finally get a grip on it, he brought it to his lap.

Grace relaxed and wagged, satisfied that he had retrieved what she had alerted to. He stole a quick look. He shouldn't have been surprised. The girl was still working, sniffing out the newest scent in her repertoire. The item, now safely tucked between his legs, was a cell phone.

62

Grand Island, Nebraska

"Are any of these images good enough for facial recognition?" Maggie asked Alonzo.

"I'm one step ahead of you, boss."

She hated when he called her boss. Technically, she was.

"Have you gotten anything?"

"The guy took extra precautions. He never looks at a camera, but he appears to know where all the cameras are. The bill of his cap is pulled down. Those chunky, black-framed glasses cover a good portion of his face.

"But I grabbed some decent screen shots of the women. Right now I'm running them against socials. It'll take a while. I'm betting the old dude doesn't have a Facebook or Instagram account. But if I can find just one of the women, there's a chance she's taken pictures—even selfies—that capture the guy."

"That's a lot of betting and maybes, Antonio. I don't have a lot of time here."

"You think these three have Ryder?"

"Don't you?"

"I guess we need to consider it."

"Libby Holmes, aka Emma Hobbs, is involved," Maggie said. "She's obviously a part of this."

"If she helped snatch and murder Kristen Darrow, why wait until almost a week later to run?"

Maggie didn't have the answer. All the killer profiles she'd constructed in the last ten years didn't seem to apply to Libby. And yet, how does a teenager end up a suspect in one murder investigation and, seven months later, become a part of another without being involved in the actual murder?

Unless she was manipulated or coerced.

Maggie had worked on human trafficking cases where victims had helped their captors recruit or kidnap other victims. Sometimes the victims had been imprisoned, isolated and abused for so long they simply remained silent and agreeable to avoid further punishment.

She thought about Brodie Creed and all those years her captors had drugged and starved her. Self preservation made people do strange things. Fight or flight was a natural instinct, but when you couldn't do either? What were the options? Give up or get along?

Maggie stared at the computer screen as she played the last video file again. These young women, possibly teenagers, looked healthy and fit. The video's quality was good enough to tell they weren't emaciated or jittery. They both looked calm and confident. As the blond turned to watch Kristen walk by, there were no jerks, no darts, not a single uncomfortable gesture. Both women had complete and steady control over their body language. From this point of view, they certainly didn't look cowed or bullied into taking part in this shopping spree.

And yet, Maggie couldn't help wondering what hold this man might have over them.

"Maggie?"

She startled at Alonzo's voice. She'd forgotten they were still connected.

"How did they end up paying?" she asked.

"A VISA gift card."

"That has a serial number, right? Can you track how it was purchased?"

"Probably. Don't be surprised if they paid with cash," he told her. "Gift cards are easier to travel with than a money roll. You can get them almost anywhere: gas stations, grocery stores, Walmart. I believe you can purchase up to $500 on one card. Now, I will be able to tell you where the card was purchased, but again, if it was bought with cash, that might not help us."

"My gut tells me these three are still here. Get some screen grabs of their faces to distribute to local law enforcement. We have enough for them to put out APBs. We find these three, we find Ryder and Grace. I think Libby must be with them. Does she have any social media accounts?" Maggie asked.

"Libby does not. But Emma did. Not much help there, either. Posts stopped around the end of February."

"Photos?" Maggie asked.

"I'll check again, but I didn't see anyone who might fit this guy's description."

"Send me the links. Wait a minute." Why hadn't she thought of this sooner? "Can you access Libby's cell phone?" Spencer said his people had tried, but maybe Alonzo had more access.

"I already checked. There aren't any accounts with her name. No cell phone. No credit card. No driver's license."

"Spencer said she had a driver's license."

"It must be a counterfeit."

"So good that a county sheriff couldn't tell the difference?" But even as Maggie asked this, she suspected Spencer had sneaked a quick peek, hoping only for more information about the girl.

"Hey, there are plenty of young women named Libby Holmes, but no facial recognition matches the photo you sent me. When I put in Emma Hobbs, I got an immediate match."

"Okay, getting back to the cell phone," she said. "Nora was certain Libby's was not left behind. Spencer told us he tried to track it. So she obviously had a phone. If the Spencers put a third person on their account, would that person be listed separately?"

"The phone's activity would be. Do you know the number?"

"No, but I'll text you Nora's and Ted's. If you get into their account, we could see if Nora is still in touch with Libby."

"Didn't you just say this guy is a county sheriff?"

"He is," Maggie said without preamble. She knew what Alonzo was asking. And she knew very well what she was asking of him. "Ryder was still a part of our task force when he disappeared looking for this girl. Nora Spencer hasn't been entirely honest with us from the start." Maggie didn't bother hiding her frustration, but she hated that her voice sounded a bit desperate. She caught a glimpse of her reflection in the hotel room's mirror, and she was glad Alonzo couldn't see it. "I'll deal with rules later. Can you get into the account or not?"

"Already on it. So you think Libby might still be texting Nora Spencer?"

"I think it's possible. Actually, I hope she is."

"But she wouldn't tell her husband?" Alonzo asked.

"She didn't tell her husband the girl was pregnant."

"Point taken."

"Were you able to find out anything more about the Virginia case?" she asked. "Was there any mention or innuendo that it could have been related to human trafficking?"

"Human trafficking?"

"Maybe I'm grasping at straws," Maggie tried to explain. "A middle-aged man accompanied by young women who could be teenagers. In this security footage, they're buying dismemberment tools as calmly and casually as if this stuff is for a home improvement project. They've done this before."

"I can check databases."

"But we already have similarities with the Virginia case."

"Except no mention of a middle-aged man. Only the two teenagers," Alonzo told her. "And lots of dead ends. No one else was charged."

"What about the other girl? The other suspect?"

"Lara White. Eighteen. Richmond, Virginia."

"Maybe we could talk to her."

"Not possible. She died in a car accident."

"You're kidding?"

"I wish I was. I'm still waiting for details about the accident."

"When did it happen?" Maggie asked.

"February. Right about the time Emma Hobbs disappeared."

"I don't like this," Maggie said. "I don't like this at all."

63

Interstate 80

Jason noticed that Brodie had gotten quieter some time after they crossed the border from Missouri into Nebraska. She asked fewer questions and stared out her side window for longer periods. Jason glanced into the rearview mirror at Hank and realized he had started using the big dog to determine Brodie's emotional state. She could hide her eyes and her feelings from Jason, but she couldn't do the same with Hank.

They were on the west side of Omaha and still hadn't run into snow, but it was definitely colder. Since Kansas City, he watched the temperature go down. The sun dipped behind clouds on the lower horizon, painting the sky with streams of orange and purple.

He couldn't remember the last time he'd used the Jeep's heater. Brodie had taken off her shoes and tucked her stocking feet up underneath her. He thought maybe she'd fallen asleep. Neither of them had gotten much last night. He was doing okay, but ready to get settled, stretch and let the dogs do the same.

Hannah had reserved rooms for them—adjoining rooms, per Jason's instructions—at the hotel where Ryder was supposed to be staying. Hannah suggested he keep in touch with Maggie, but so far, Jason put off calling her, choosing instead to text a few times to let her know their status. Her responses were brief: a thumbs up or a simple "OK." He wasn't sure if she appreciated them coming to help, or if she thought they'd be in the way.

Hannah mentioned that he should be careful of not stepping on the toes of local law enforcement, to respect their boundaries. As far as Jason was concerned, they already had their chance, and they botched it. They still hadn't found Ryder and Grace. Maybe they needed to step aside and let Jason and Scout do their search.

Brodie stirred, then bolted upright, readjusting herself. She sat straight up as if something had stung her.

"What is it?" he asked.

"Familiar territory," she said with a shrug, as if it was no big deal, but her eyes darted over the fields like she was looking for something in particular. Her body pressed back into the seat and her arms wrapped around her chest.

"Do you want me to stop?" he asked.

"No, it's okay. Just keep going. You can't see any of it from the interstate."

By "any of it," he figured she meant Iris Malone's property.

"Nebraska brings bad memories," he said.

"It's not Nebraska's fault."

He glanced over and felt a clammy sweat come over the back of his neck. The tension in her rigid body telegraphed a dread and anxiety that was palpable. He didn't need to look at Hank. In fact, he avoided looking back at the dog this time.

"We'll be passed it soon," Brodie said, reassuring herself as much as Jason.

He wondered how she knew. Could she sense it? Did the road signs tell her? Was there a landmark?

She hadn't shared any details with him about the farm or the place called "The Christmas House," where they had found her. He never asked.

All the shrinks he'd seen wanted him to talk about "the event," like reliving the moments of that IED going off would somehow make him whole again. All it did was get him to think about it until he couldn't make the images go away. He hated that might be happening to Brodie right now. That this landscape may have triggered all the pain she had endured.

Once again, she surprised him when she asked, "Did you ever kill anybody? I mean in Afghanistan?"

Without even hesitating, he said, "Yes."

"Do you ever feel bad?"

"No." Again, without hesitation, but his fingers tightened on the steering wheel, because he knew her line of questions wasn't about him. "I was a sniper. If I didn't kill them, they would kill many others."

She nodded, but her head swiveled back towards the side window as she said, "I guess war is different. You weren't killing innocents."

"Aaron Malone wasn't innocent, Brodie."

"But he wasn't like Iris. I think he was afraid of her, too. He wasn't much older than me."

"At some point, he was a grown man who knew right from wrong." He glanced over at her, wishing she'd look his way. "And it wasn't right what they were doing to you."

"When he left me at the Christmas House, he left bags full of food. I know he did that without Iris knowing." She reached down between her feet and pulled Kitten up into her lap. "I know he put Kitten inside to keep me company."

Jason remembered Ryder saying the Christmas House was where Iris exiled her rejects. She left them there—or had Aaron leave them—until her brother Eli could pick them up. The only reason Eli got delayed was because he was showing Ryder and Maggie where he'd buried other girls his sister had discarded. Those were the ones he'd killed. Some, he claimed to have sold to human traffickers.

The task force knew there were at least six girls from the photos Iris had kept on her mantle. But they believed there could be more. Aaron had to know what his uncle did with the girls and young women Aaron left for him at the Christmas House. At any given time, he could have said "no," instead of hauling and locking Brodie in yet another closet or shed or the basement.

He didn't know what to say. The brewing anger he felt surprised him, so he stayed quiet and listened.

"I tricked him," Brodie said. "The others left letters and messages behind, so I knew Iris was getting rid of me for good. I just didn't know what came next. The food Aaron left made me stronger, think clearer. And Kitten…" The cat rose as if on cue and rubbed against Brodie's neck. "Kitten gave me a reason to want to escape. Aaron probably saved my life."

She stared out the windshield. The look on her face lacked emotion even as she added, "He saved mine, and I ended his."

Before Jason could find a response, she switched gears on him again and said, "I can't possibly have survived only to get my life back but lose Ryder and Grace. They're okay. They have to be."

64

Grand Island, Nebraska

Maggie went over the security footage outtakes several times, stopping and starting and making notes. On the third run-through of watching the items slide by, one by one on the checkout's conveyor belt, something else caught her eye. The girl handling the items wore a lightweight jacket. It was white on the black and white video. It triggered her memory of another white jacket.

She fumbled with the computer application's basic tools. It took her a couple of tries, but finally she figured out how to zoom in on the jacket's logo on the upper left side. She took a screenshot.

The image was blurred, but she could make out the shape of the letters. She isolated the shot in the corner of her computer screen, then did a quick Google search of images. She was looking for women's lightweight jackets made by Columbia sportswear. In less than a minute she found a matching logo, and quite possibly she'd found the exact jacket.

She grabbed her phone and called Lucy Coy. Her back was stiff, and as she stretched, she glanced to see what time it was. She had been at this all afternoon. Just when she expected the voice mail prompt, Lucy answered.

"Hi Maggie. You must have heard the news."

"News? No, I've been holed up in my hotel room." Technically, Ryder's room, but no one needed to know that. "What news?"

"A farmer found two garbage bags when he was plowing through his pasture to check on his cattle."

"So you have more to process."

Maggie thought about the bag they'd found earlier in a pasture. She didn't want to think about how many pieces Kristin Darrow had been reduced to. She couldn't calculate without imagining the same could happen to Ryder.

Before Lucy started filling her in on the details of the new find, Maggie said, "Actually, I had a question about the jacket we found in one of the first bags. Do you have a minute?"

"Oh, sure. Okay. You know I still haven't found a single organ."

A cold, clammy sweat started at the back of Maggie's neck. Nausea threatened to send up the contents of her stomach. Instead of sitting down, she paced. She and Lucy had shared details like this before. Treating them casually with each other prevented the gruesome reality from working on your mental state. Unfortunately, Maggie knew her mental state was beyond treating any of this as casual. But Pakula was right. She needed to keep her mind working on the puzzle pieces.

"Alonzo sent me a copy of the Virginia victim's autopsy report. I'd like to send it to you. Do you mind taking a look at it for similarities?"

"Of course, I can do that. Now, what did you want to know about the jacket?"

"Do you remember seeing a brand name logo?" she asked.

"Let me get my photos."

Pacing only made things worse. She sat on the edge of the bed. She grabbed a water bottle from the nightstand and guzzled half of it.

"Looks to be Columbia," Lucy said. "I've had a chance to examine it. I don't believe it was the victim's. The blood spatter indicates the person wearing it was facing the victim when the trauma happened. All the blood is on the outside. There isn't any soaked from the inside."

It was more information than Maggie needed right now. Much more than she wanted.

"So one of the perpetrators was wearing the jacket? Someone who participated?" Maggie asked.

"That's my theory. Of course, a blood spatter expert could give you more exact details. Maggie, it's a woman's jacket."

"I know. I spent most of the day looking at the young woman who was wearing it."

"What are you talking about?"

"We've been reviewing the video from the hardware store's security cameras. On the day Darrow disappeared from work, there was a middle-aged man with two young women inside the store. It looks like they bought everything they needed to kill her."

"From the store where she worked?"

"Yes. While she was still working. I just watched the man follow her and point her out to his accomplices. One of the women was wearing that white jacket."

Lucy went quiet. Maggie waited.

Several years ago, she had stayed at Lucy's home outside of North Platte. She watched her one morning in her meditation stance: eyes closed, body completely still. She was used to the woman's calm demeanor, her ability to spiritualize the madness and violence. Dismemberment was especially difficult for most seasoned forensic investigators. Yesterday, Lucy admitted that even she had a difficult time with the brutality of this murder.

Finally, Maggie heard the hiss of a long drawn-out sigh, then Lucy said, "Well, I suppose that might explain the bite mark. I thought it was much too small to be a man's."

Maggie ran her fingers through her hair and resumed pacing. She avoided looking over at Ryder's belongings. Finally, she said, "This is turning into something much stranger and complicated than any of us expected. I'm not sure if the young women are willing accomplices or if they're abused and manipulated captives."

She paused at the window again, the images from the video surveillance still played in her mind. "They look like teenagers. Libby Holmes is only seventeen, and they don't look much older."

"You're thinking they may have been coerced to participate?"

"It wouldn't be the first time," Maggie said. "Some version of Stockholm syndrome. Young victims can easily be manipulated. There's a trauma bond that forms, and a captive starts to identify with the captor, even complying with the captor's demands and his agenda."

"You're thinking like an FBI profiler."

"I am an FBI profiler."

"But perhaps it's simpler than that."

"What do you mean?"

"Humor me for a minute," Lucy said. "For the last several days, you and Pakula have focused on human trafficking. The things you've seen and experienced have changed your perceptions. Which was absolutely necessary for many of us in law enforcement. A decade ago, kidnapped and runaway teenaged girls were being arrested for prostitution instead of the men selling and buying them. No one realized the magnitude of what was going on. In some ways, it was beyond our imaginations and comprehensions.

"But at the same time, perhaps we shouldn't be so quick to relieve every teenage girl of responsibility for a crime just because we aren't able to conceive that a young girl would be capable of such a heinous crime. There are still people here in Nebraska who debate whether Caril Ann Fugate was Charlie Starkweather's partner or an innocent fourteen-year-old girlfriend forced to go along on his killing spree."

Maggie had little experience with killer couples, let alone a group of three. The dynamics of peer pressure, competition, or simply pleasing one another could all play roles in how far things could go. It made the situation more incendiary.

One vicious killer was dangerous. But three working together? Perhaps that explained their boldness. They were brazen enough to buy their murder instruments at the victim's place of employment then wait for her to get off work. They even came back in to buy soft drinks while they waited.

"I haven't dismissed the idea that they're willing accomplices," Maggie said. "I just watched them buy gallons of bleach, drop cloths, a hacksaw and box cutters like they were preparing for a DIY home project.

"I have to tell you, Lucy, all my experience and research of criminal behavior doesn't help explain the psychology or mindset it takes for what looks like two ordinary young women to plan and take part in methodically killing then dismembering another young woman."

"We don't know the facts yet," Lucy told her. "And you might be right. This man could have control over them. But I will tell you this: the bite mark is post mortem. There are many things one person can coerce another person to do, but whether forced or agreeing to bite the flesh of a corpse, seems beyond the pale."

"In other words, don't underestimate these girls."

"That would be my best advice."

"It makes me more concerned about Ryder and Grace."

"Pakula brought me his shirt."

Maggie stopped mid-pace. She crossed her arms around herself. The panic had settled too close to the surface and threatened to suck her breath away.

"Is there a chance it's not Ryder's blood?" Maggie asked, thinking about the white jacket.

"I suppose it's possible."

The silence that followed revealed Lucy believed it was his.

"The wound," Maggie finally managed to say. "It's bad, isn't it?"

"Abdominal wounds can be tricky. They tend to bleed profusely."

Abdominal wound.

Maggie closed her eyes and swallowed her emotion. Would she have preferred the medical examiner not to share her expertise? Would she prefer she lied and said it didn't look bad?

"How are you holding up?" Lucy asked.

It would be ridiculous to claim she was fine when, in fact, she was far from fine. Instead, she told the truth. "Lucy, I'm terrified we'll be too late."

65

Maggie's second phone call picked up after only two rings.

"Hello?"

"Mrs. Hobbs?"

"Yes?"

"My name's Maggie O'Dell. I'm a special agent with the FBI."

"Oh my God! Emma. Have you found her?"

"I'm sorry, that's not why I'm calling." Maggie winced at the woman's anticipation.

She expected as much, but it didn't make things easier. And although she'd gone over in her mind what she'd say, it already sounded hollow and insincere. Like it or not, there was no way she could tell her Emma might be safe and okay in Nebraska when she had no clue whether that was true.

"Actually, I have some questions," Maggie said.

"More questions? I told the police there's no way my daughter would hurt another person, unless it was in self defense."

"You're referring to Gina Franklin's murder?"

"Yes. Isn't that what this is about? That's all you people seem to care about."

By "you people" Maggie knew she meant law enforcement. She didn't mind being clumped together, but technically, she spent most of her time investigating and not enforcing. The distinction didn't matter to families hoping for any news about their loved ones.

"My questions are about Emma," she told Mrs. Hobbs. When she remained quiet, Maggie couldn't move forward without asking, "Why haven't you filed a missing person report?"

Alonzo said Emma Hobbs was seventeen. Her mother's address was listed as her home when she disappeared.

"They told me it was a waste of time. She obviously ran away because she was guilty."

"Someone in law enforcement told you that?"

"In so many words."

Her anger suggested an exaggeration of the truth. Maggie wasn't sure if Mrs. Hobbs' frustration was with the local police because they hadn't found her daughter, or if it was with herself for not searching harder.

"Was Emma seeing anyone or involved with someone before she disappeared?"

"I don't know. She was partying a lot. Which is something she rarely did throughout high school. I figured she should be allowed, right? She's a good kid. She's always been a good kid. She's worked really hard to get a scholarship to play college soccer. That's what she's always wanted. What she's always loved. I thought maybe the partying was something she just needed to get out of her system before she left for college."

"She wasn't spending a lot of time with any one person?"

"She became very secretive. I don't think she was hanging out with any of her regular friends. They're all athletes like Emma. I know they drank alcohol sometimes, but they wouldn't use drugs. Suddenly Emma was coming home late at night, drunk. Maybe even stoned. I was upset. I told her I was disappointed." There was emotion attached to the word. "I still can't believe I told her that."

The hitch in her voice made Maggie uncomfortable. She'd always lacked the patience for interviews with victims' loved ones. Put her in a room with a criminal, and she could find a way to trick and outmaneuver the information she needed. But interviews with a victim's family member required too much handholding and head nodding. She simply wanted to push on to the details that would find the middle-aged man who may have orchestrated two brutal murders.

"Did she ever mention a friend named Lara White?" Maggie asked as she readjusted her earbud and stopped at the desk where she'd left a notepad and pen. Supposedly, Lara White was a person of interest in Franklin's death, too. That is, until her unfortunate automobile accident.

"No, that name doesn't ring any bells."

"Did Emma know Gina Franklin?"

"The woman who was murdered?"

"Yes."

"No, of course not. I told you, that was all a misunderstanding. There's no way Emma was involved."

"What did Emma say about it?"

Mrs. Hobbs went quiet. Maggie waited.

"By the time the cops came knocking on my door, Emma was gone. She was supposed to be staying at her father's. I didn't realize she wasn't there."

"She just disappeared without letting you know where she was?"

"The divorce was not amicable. We split up three years ago. I don't want to sound like one of those ex-wives who blames everything on her ex-husband, but he went from being at Emma's soccer games and spending weekends with her, to hardly having any time for her, because he and his new wife were starting a new family."

These were exactly the things Maggie didn't have the patience to wade through. She put down the pen and resumed her pacing, stopping to glance out the window. Families of victims looked for reassurance that they weren't to blame. They second-guessed decisions that often had nothing to do with why or how the victim was targeted or attacked.

"He hasn't heard from her either?"

"He claims she wasn't even supposed to stay with him the whole week. That's where I thought she was."

"She didn't usually check in with you?"

"She used to. But she was spreading her wings. Cutting loose. Whatever they call it these days. She wanted me to cut her some slack. I thought I'd give her some space, you know?" The emotion hitched, again, at the end of the question. "And I honestly thought she was with her father."

"I know this is difficult for you," Maggie said, "But I need to ask, again, why didn't either of you file a missing person report?"

"By then, the cops told us she was a murder suspect. No, not a suspect. A person of interest. And yes, they laughed at me when I suggested filing a missing person report. I think they still believe we know where she is and we're helping her hide."

"What about her cell phone?"

"They said she must have ditched it. Somehow, they seemed to know she didn't just turn it off. They accused us of helping her disappear. They threatened to charge us as accessories for the murder. It was all so crazy."

Maggie had hoped this conversation would lead to the man in the video feed or some facsimile of him appearing in Libby/Emma's life before she left Virginia. She kept telling herself the cases were too similar to not be connected. She needed a better description than the brief digital caricature they had of a short, frumpy man with a saggy middle wearing a Husker ball cap and thick black-framed glasses to disguise his face. Alonzo had suggested the guy was middle-aged, but there was no way to be certain of that. She had hoped to get a name.

"Murder is a serious allegation," Maggie told Mrs. Hobbs. "They must have evidence that suggests your daughter was involved somehow. You can't think of anyone she may have met, perhaps at one of the parties?"

"Unfortunately, I never met any of them. You have to understand, Emma has always been so very responsible and conscientious. She's never lied to us, let alone just taking off and disappear. I've been worried sick about her. I thought she left me a message on my Facebook page three weeks ago, but my ex-husband said it was probably someone playing a cruel joke on me."

"What was the message?"

"It was just a few lines. The week of her eighteenth birthday. It said that all was good. That she had a job at Menards. When I asked how she was, she said she was doing great and that she'd be in touch soon. That she loved me."

Maggie fought the urge to tell her Emma was safe. But honestly, she had no clue if that was true. And if Emma was eighteen now, she could legally be on her own. If that's what she wanted.

"Why did your ex-husband think it was a joke?" Maggie asked.

"He thought it was ridiculous that Emma would get a job at a hardware store, of all places."

66

Creed conjured up enough energy to slide out of the booth-style dining table. Both women turned from their respective places in the trailer to stare at him. He raised his hands in a gesture of surrender.

"I need to take Grace outside, then I need to feed her."

"Permission denied," Ariel said. She had her drug paraphernalia spread out on the counter. "You both can stay sitting there in your urine and feces."

"Don't be stupid," Libby told her. "He can go outside. And you're not toking in here."

"It's freezing outside," Ariel whined.

"Then maybe you should stop using."

"Come on. I bet you've never tried shatter. I have a whole sheet here." She pointed to the thin, amber-colored wafer that looked like glass. "It's ten times stronger than marijuana." She tapped it with a small mallet and it broke into tiny pieces, just like glass. "You put a few pieces into a joint. Believe me, it makes everything better, and I have plenty to share."

While Ariel pleaded her case, Creed stood up. In the tight confines, he was only three feet away from her. Libby was on the small bed at the back of the trailer, less than ten feet. He kept his back to both of them, hoping neither would see that he grabbed the end of the table and needed to lean on it, just to stay upright.

"I know what shatter is," Libby told Ariel. "It's the crack of cannabis. It's also ten times more addictive and can make you paranoid, cause hallucinations and affect your memory. I like to keep my mind sharp."

"Wow, what a good girl you are! Keep your mind sharp." Ariel's snort pretty much said she didn't care what Libby thought. "Suit yourself," she added as she shoved her cell phone out of the way to give herself more room.

Creed could see that small motion was enough to trigger a glance from Libby.

"Ariel, you never told me. How did you get my phone number?" she asked. "How did you know Ruben was coming for me?"

Creed only half listened to them by now. Thankfully, they had forgotten about him for the moment. He motioned to Grace, lifting and cradling her close to his body. Her sixteen pounds felt like he'd hoisted a crankcase. The pain in his side made him forget the bruised back muscles, but now every part of him screamed, the pain punching at him from all sides.

"I told you about that, didn't I?" Ariel didn't raise her head from the task of sprinkling pieces of shatter into the joint she was about to roll.

Creed braced against the wall close to the door, trying to figure out how to bend over to put on his boots. Grace sat, ears pinned back and her eyes focused on the bloody T-shirt.

"No, you didn't tell me," Libby said. "Remember, sharp mind." Her index finger tapped her right temple to emphasize her point, which was lost on Ariel, who still didn't look up.

Across the length of the trailer, Libby's eyes found Creed's. Even at fifteen feet, he could see that she knew he was hurting. Her face remained expressionless as she lounged with a pillow between her back and the wall. Was she distracting Ariel to take the attention off of him and Grace? He couldn't tell.

"So how did you know?" she asked, prodding Ariel.

"Just because I left doesn't mean I don't have connections."

"You stayed friends after you left?"

"I wouldn't say friends. More like adversaries with something in common. Something we can't share with anyone else except each other. Because truthfully, all the stuff Ruben had us do, who would believe us, right?"

Ariel rolled the joint like an expert, but she wasn't finished with her explanation. "It's kinda nice to keep in touch. Most of us don't have friends or family anymore. Ruben made sure of that. You know how good he is at alienating us from every single person who might have liked or loved us. Of course you do. You're here in the middle of nowhere because you don't have anywhere to go either."

Her fingers stopped, and she stopped. Creed even halted his efforts to pull on boots. But it wasn't him and Grace that made Arial hesitate.

Her face scrunched up like she smelled something bad, then she continued, "He shamed us into hating whatever friends and family we had. Convinced us how corrosive they made our lives. *Corrosive.* I wasn't even sure what that word meant. By the time we leave the arrangement, there's no one left for us to go to."

She looked over at Libby when she said, "Isn't that what happened to you? No friends or family left? He's done that to all of us. I don't have anywhere to go. There's nobody looking for me."

Ariel shrugged her shoulders as though it were no big deal, then added, "Except it's different with you. Ruben really wants to kill you. It's like he's obsessed with you. He has a hard-on to see you tortured and dead. That is, if Ruben could get a hard-on." Ariel snickered under her breath.

Creed listened, but kept his head down. Had Libby noticed that Ariel didn't really answer her original question? How did she get Libby's phone number?

He tried to ignore that his boots were still soggy inside. Immediately, his socks grew wet and his feet got cold before he left the warmth of the trailer.

Gritting his teeth, he slipped Ted Spencer's jacket on and slow-zipped it as far up his neck as it would go. He pulled on gloves, then picked up Grace, tucking her close on his other side. A gust helped open the door and shot him with a blast of cold air that Creed found refreshing even if it made his eyes water and his chest hurt.

He took slow, careful steps and still slipped on the last step. Catching his balance required gripping Grace and another stab of pain, but he was grateful to leave the tension that filled the trailer.

Grace licked at the snow as soon as he put her down. The wind had created a crust on the drifts, and the small dog was light enough to walk on top.

For Creed, it wasn't as easy. Instead of plowing through snow, his boots had to crunch through, then pick up and pull out his foot with each step. If he didn't raise his leg high enough, the toe of his boot caught on the upper crust. It tripped him once. He stumbled down to one knee, catching himself against a tree before he lost balance entirely and ended up facedown.

The pain shot across his abdomen, liquid fire searing his insides. He closed his eyes to a full constellation of stars, though it was too cloudy for actual stars. When he opened his eyes, he saw drops of red on the snow even in the fading light.

Once again he wondered, how much blood had he lost? How much more could he afford to lose? Did he even care anymore? He was almost too exhausted to care.

Then Grace nosed his arm and stared up at him. She was waiting for a sign that he was okay. He brushed snow off her back and patted her head.

"I'm fine," he told her, but Grace's eyes didn't leave his. She wasn't convinced. The dog knew him too well. Better than Hannah. Better than Maggie.

He rubbed Grace's head, dislodging more snow, then used the tree to stand back up. He remembered the look of concern Maggie had given him in the hotel room. She was worried about him. Leaning against the tree, he grated the side of his boot to cover up the blood in the snow. It was an empty gesture. Snow dusted the surface. In a minute or two, the sweep of his boot would be completely gone.

White crystals blowing off the treetops coated his hair and eyelashes. Creed made his way around the back of the trailer, trying to get out of sight. There were no windows here, and he wanted to check out the phone Grace had found between the cushions. He'd slid it into the side pocket of her vest.

He waited for Grace to do her business and allowed her to shoulder-skid through the snow. It made him smile watching her. Hopefully, it meant she hadn't sustained any lasting injury from Ariel's kick.

Just as he squatted down to unzip the pocket on Grace's vest, he heard the door slam against the side of the trailer. His gloved fingers left the zipper, and he pretended to be brushing snow off Grace when Ariel bounded up behind them. She had a small bag strapped across her parka like she expected to be outside for a while. She didn't look happy about it.

"She seriously won't let me smoke in the frickin' trailer," she said, then stood over them, watching him and Grace as she lit up.

Creed got the feeling Ariel considered him a major obstacle in the way of her plans. He wasn't sure if it was the drugs dictating the intensity. Didn't Libby just say that they could cause paranoia? He wondered if Ariel's plans were even the same as Libby's.

Without a word, Creed kept his pain and disappointment in check as he led Grace back inside the trailer. He'd need to be patient a little longer.

67

Interstate 80

The snow was beautiful, falling glitter gathering in the corners of the windshield. Brodie watched out the windows of the Jeep and thought it looked like a soft, fluffy quilt spread out over the pastures.

"It's been a long time since I've driven in this stuff," Jason said.

She glanced at him and noticed his jaw clenched. Both his left hand and his mechanical right hand were grasping the steering wheel. They passed by vehicles that had skidded off the interstate and had been abandoned; the snow covering them so completely Brodie hardly recognized the white hump underneath. But traffic hadn't slowed down despite the thin layer of white slicking the surface and the continuous bursts of snow dust blowing across.

A couple of times, she felt the Jeep slide unexpectedly, but Jason seemed to know how to respond. She couldn't imagine there was anything Jason didn't know or couldn't figure out how to do.

"You're doing a good job," she said, for lack of knowing exactly what was appropriate.

"Thanks." His jaw relaxed enough to allow a smile. "Not much longer." He chin-pointed to the dashboard's GPS. "Only fifty more miles to our exit."

In the last few minutes the sun started breaking through the clouds, an orange disc sinking into the quilted cornfields. The clouds seemed to be catching on fire with streamers of red, pink and yellow.

On the radio, the weather forecaster said tomorrow would be sunny, with temperatures near forty degrees. A slow meltdown was expected.

The first winter Brodie spent with Iris Malone and her son, Aaron, was sad, but not frightening. By then, Iris was calling Brodie Charlotte because she reminded her of her daughter, who had died years before. At first, Iris was good to her, dressing her in Charlotte's clothes, letting her sleep in Charlotte's bedroom and allowing her to play with Charlotte's toys.

The woman had convinced Brodie that her parents were upset with her. Brodie understood. In the beginning, she didn't blame them. She had disobeyed and disappointed them. She was a bad girl. A naughty girl. Brodie had never heard her parents actually say any of those words. She believed Iris because she knew she had misbehaved. She had broken rules her parents had taught her.

At a rest stop bathroom, the little girl had asked Brodie if she wanted to come see her new puppy. Brodie should have asked her father if it was okay. Instead, she followed the girl, thinking she'd simply get a quick peek. But then she became mesmerized by the RV.

The girl had taken Brodie's hand and invited her to come up into the vehicle for a tour. It was a house on wheels with a kitchen, bedroom, and even a bathroom. Brodie had never seen anything like it before. Iris asked if she'd like a ride, and Brodie was already seated at the table enjoying a milk shake.

It wasn't until years later that Brodie realized the milk shake must have had a drug to make her sleep. Iris seemed to have access to an endless supply. By the time Brodie woke up, they were miles away from that rest stop. Iris was on her phone talking to Brodie's parents, who were furious with her. At least that's what Iris said, and she was very persuasive.

She said she tried to explain to them, but they were so upset they didn't want her back right now. Brodie had never had an adult lie to her before. To her eleven-year-old brain, it seemed more believable that her parents were upset with her than to imagine a strange woman she'd just met would make it all up.

That first Christmas was tough. She'd begged Iris to let her call her family, and Iris did. Holding the phone out of earshot, Iris pretended to talk to Brodie's mother. She remembered the sinking feeling as she watched Iris shake her head.

There was fresh snow. Christmas snow! Not the slush or ice that she and Ryder had experienced, but real snow. Aaron was only a few years older than Brodie. He taught her how to make snow angels. They took turns riding a sled down a small hill in the pasture. For a few minutes, she didn't miss Ryder and Gram and her mom and dad.

That evening, they opened presents in front of the fireplace. There was even a stocking for Brodie, except that it had Charlotte's name on it. Brodie really wanted a new book for Christmas, but Charlotte got another doll to add to her collection.

She remembered wondering what happened to the little girl who had asked if she wanted to see her new puppy. The one who had brought her, hand-in-hand, to the RV. She wasn't there to celebrate Christmas with them, and even at eleven, Brodie knew not to ask about her.

There were nights when she could hear a child crying in the middle of the night. Once she even ventured out into the dark hallway, following the sound. Iris met her at the staircase, told her she was only dreaming. The next night, her bedroom door was locked. From the outside.

She still wondered about the other Charlottes. There had been many times Brodie had heard whispers pleading for help. It sounded like the voices were coming from inside the walls of the big two-story farmhouse. The ceiling creaked with footsteps in the attic. Doors rattled against locks. Not all of these things happened at night. It seemed impossible there might be other children locked away. Until it didn't seem impossible at all.

Brodie's own locked door quickly taught her she shouldn't mention these incidents. When Iris started drugging Brodie's food, it became difficult to separate out which sounds and sights were real and which were simply drug induced.

Despite the drugs, Brodie knew she was right about there being others. She had found some of their messages scribbled inside a torn corner of wallpaper, a note written in a dusty manual next to the hot water heater, and a letter tucked inside a decade old magazine.

They found no other girls or women imprisoned in the big house when Brodie was rescued a few miles away at the Christmas House. But there was evidence that others had been there.

No one seemed to know how many little girls Iris—with the help of Aaron and her brother, Eli—had taken using the same ruse they'd used with Brodie. They had found the RV in an old shed. Ryder had told her that investigators also found a hidden box with personal items from the victims. Brodie's book, "Harriet the Spy," a gift from her grandmother, was found inside. The special inscription Gram had written, along with a Polaroid of Brodie and Ryder, were the clues that helped to lead them to her.

But what happened to all the others?

The Charlottes still came to Brodie in her nightmares. The first time it happened in Hannah's house, it was so real Brodie wondered how they had traveled all those miles. Last night, she almost expected to see them standing in the corner of the dark hotel room. There didn't seem to be anywhere she could go that they didn't follow.

The Jeep was slowing down, and Brodie saw their exit in the headlights.

When had the sun gone down?

The clouds had also broken up, revealing the first stars of twilight. The purple horizon met the white covered landscape. Behind them, the moonlight made the snow glitter. Even the lights of the city seemed to twinkle.

She wanted to remember this view of Nebraska, and not the one from slits in a boarded up basement window.

Brodie hoped Ryder was looking up at this same sky. Hang on, she told him in her mind.

68

It didn't surprise Creed that Libby was still wide awake when he and Grace returned to the trailer. She stared at him the whole time he fixed Grace's meal, using the last bottle of water to rehydrate her food. He could do it by rote, but his fingers fumbled trying to open the bottle.

Libby noticed. "It's the blood loss."

"What's that?"

"Fogs the mind. The simplest things feel like an obstacle. I just thought after a certain point I'd fall unconscious." She saw his confusion and added, "Who knew you could lose so much blood and still be alive?"

Then he realized she was comparing his wound to her, slitting her wrists. He wanted to laugh. Tell her that her self-inflicted wound wasn't even close to the same thing. He left it alone. He didn't have the energy to waste, because "fog the mind" was putting it mildly.

Digging through his daypack, he found a couple of protein bars at the bottom. Human ones he'd forgotten about. He pulled both of them out, waved them at Libby.

"Would you like one of these?"

She looked surprised.

"They taste like cardboard," Creed told her, "but they're pretty good nutrition-wise."

"Okay."

He stayed at the counter and tossed one over to her. She caught it in one hand, but was still watching him. He stirred Grace's food and put the collapsible bowl down for her before he started to unwrap his protein bar. Libby was still staring at him.

"Why would you do that?" she finally asked.

"Do what?" He took a bite but kept his eyes on the trailer door and Grace.

"Give me one of your last bits of food?"

"You shared your soup with me."

She shook her head like she still couldn't quite believe him, then she peeled back the wrapper.

"There's a first aid kit under the sink," she told him. "Nothing fancy, but it has alcohol, bandages, and some Tylenol."

"Tylenol."

"Pain, fever," she said. "You're kinda sweaty, and it's not hot in here."

He stayed leaning against the counter, suddenly afraid he'd lose his balance. Ever since he'd stood up from his place at the table, he could feel the floor tilting. He thought it might actually be the wind rocking the trailer. But once outside, he noticed the wind had died down considerably and the snow-covered ground made him dizzy.

"Here," she said, getting up. "Lay down. I'll get it. Looks like you need to clean it again."

"How do you know all this stuff?"

"Living with a nurse for six months, I suppose."

Before he could move, she squeezed in next to him to retrieve the kit from the cabinet. Grace looked up, hesitating at her bowl, only half of the food eaten.

"Go ahead and finish, girl."

"You really love that dog," Libby said, handing him the kit, then sitting at the table to get out of his way.

"Her previous owner dumped her at the end of my driveway. She was skin and bones, but I could tell she'd recently delivered a litter of puppies."

"They took her away from her puppies?"

Creed noticed a flicker of emotion.

"Puppies are cute," he said. "Some people keep them or give them away. Or tie them up in a burlap bag and dump them in the river."

Her eyes went wide before she caught herself and said, "Now you're just trying to shock me."

"I wish it weren't true." He didn't like to think about it, but that was exactly where he'd found Jason's dog, Scout—in a burlap bag with his siblings. Instead, he told her, "I rescued her, and she's rescued me over and over again. Grace and I have been through a lot together."

"Really? While finding missing people?"

"Let's see. Last spring, a tornado picked up our Jeep and flung it a few miles."

"I didn't realize search and rescue could be dangerous."

"You mean other than getting stabbed?"

This time, she looked a bit embarrassed.

"So who is this guy, Ruben?" Creed wasn't sure how to broach the subject, other than being straightforward. He needed to wait for Grace to finish before he moved to the proffered bed in the back.

"Just some guy."

"What did you do that made him want to kill you?"

Libby did a quick glance out the window. It was dark now. The downed branches cut out any fading light.

"It's a long story," she finally said.

"It's your lucky day. I just happen to have quite a bit of time on my hands."

He made her smile. Again, before she realized and stopped it.

"I wouldn't want to shock you and your little dog."

"I was a Marine dog handler in Afghanistan. I can't imagine there's anything you could have done that would shock me. And as for Grace? A couple of days ago she found a human trafficker's catalog on a microSD card stuffed inside a book of Shakespeare."

She furrowed her brow. "A memory card? She could smell that?"

"Electronic devices, cocaine hidden in peanut butter jars. She even found some kids stowed in the hull of a fishing boat. They were under piles of Mahi."

He waited in case she decided to tell him about Ruben on her own. Of course, she remained silent.

"Is Ruben the father of your baby?"

"God, no!"

She said it like the very thought was repulsive. It was the most emotion Creed had seen from her.

"He's like fifty-something. He's older than my dad," Libby said.

"Does the father know about the baby?"

"I didn't even know. Don't get me wrong. It's not like I was some kind of virgin. I've messed around before, but I was always careful. I was focused on soccer and college."

"So, you were in college?"

Another shrug combined with a shake of her head and a slight smile. She was trying to decide whether to tell him the truth, but perhaps not the whole truth.

"It wasn't a big deal. I worked hard, followed all the rules, did everything I was supposed to do. I just wanted to cut loose, you know? So I met this guy at a party. I didn't even know his last name. I barely remember what he looked like. I honestly thought we were too drunk for anything to have happened."

She made it sound like it didn't matter, like it was as casual and inconsequential as she pretended it was. Then she looked up at Creed. In that brief moment, he saw a vulnerable young woman who had no clue how she had gotten to where she was right now.

He knew what it felt like to lose your way, to maybe even lose yourself. Brodie disappearing. His father's suicide. Both of those tragedies had turned his world so far upside down, he didn't believe he'd ever be able to course-correct his life.

"I found out about a month later when I was in the hospital," Libby interrupted his thoughts. "After I tried to off myself. Nora came to talk to me about it. She thought the baby was the reason I did it."

"But it was Ruben."

Her eyes confirmed it as they darted away. He noticed tears welling up and figured that was the end of the conversation.

"I was so tired of running," she told him. Even her voice now sounded tired. "No matter how far away I got, I was still looking over my shoulder. Finding out about the baby gave me a reason to stop."

She paused, then in almost a whisper, she added, "I should have known I could never escape from him."

"There are people who want to help."

"People?" She glanced back and forced a laugh. "Nobody can help."

"Nora, Ted…me."

The last one stopped her, but when her eyes met his, they looked sad. She looked resolved to her fate when she said, "He'd destroy us all."

Creed was so focused on Libby he didn't notice Grace. Her ears pinned back, her tail tucked. Only now did he hear the low-pitched snarl.

As if on cue, the trailer door whipped open, bringing in Ariel with a howling gust of wind. Her eyes were on fire. Her face was white but pinched with anger. She slammed the door shut, and that's when Creed noticed she had the gun again. Her index finger curled over the trigger. She poked at him with it as if the gun were simply an extension of her hand.

"That son of a bitch stole my phone."

69

Libby stayed planted sitting at the table. She crossed her arms and rolled her eyes when Ariel glanced over, letting out a long sigh. She pretended she didn't have time for this nonsense when, in reality, her heart hammered against her ribcage. Her palms were slick with sweat, and she already felt her hair sticking to her forehead.

"I told you we couldn't trust him," Ariel said, bobbing her hand and the gun with every animated gesture.

Libby had stolen Ted's gun, never once imagining how easily it could be taken from her. Despite all her recently earned street creds, she really wasn't good at this. Maybe she and Ariel weren't as much alike as Libby thought. Killing seemed to be a natural instinct for Ariel.

No, it was the drugs. They could make you do things you'd never believe you could do.

"We can't just let him walk around here," Ariel insisted. "The minute we turn our backs, he's stealing stuff."

At least, she was deferring to Libby like she needed permission. But she was so unpredictable. More and more, Libby was seeing her as a liability instead of an asset.

To his credit, the dogman stood perfectly still. She noticed he'd somehow eased himself in front of his dog. While Ariel pleaded her case, she didn't see his finger tap the side of his leg, signaling for Grace to quietly scoot behind his legs and edge against the lower cabinets.

Libby tried to catch a glimpse of his eyes. She didn't expect to see fear, but could she tell if there was any truth to Ariel's accusation? A flinch? A tell? Anything? She thought she was pretty good at keeping her emotions in check, but this guy had her beat.

That's when she saw it.

The cell phone was exactly where Ariel had left it while she smashed and mixed her designer drugs. It was the drugs that were now making her hallucinate, triggering paranoia and igniting her anger. The sight of the phone eased the tension from Libby's shoulders.

"Your cell phone is on the counter," Libby told her, pointing to it.

Chaotic situation diverted. Now she could tell her to put away the gun.

Ariel's eyes flicked to the counter and just as quickly darted over to the dogman. The accusation was still there. Was she using the phone as an excuse to get rid of him, and now she was angry because Libby blew her ploy up?

Whatever was going on in her drug-addled mind, Ariel's intensity did not diminish, nor did her firm grip on the gun.

"He wasn't a part of the plan," she whined, keeping her eyes on him. "He's going to ruin everything."

"He didn't come here to hurt us."

"But just his being here will end up hurting us. Don't you get that?"

"So what? Your solution is to kill him?"

Ariel hesitated. Maybe she was reconsidering. Then she smiled.

"I could just shoot his little dog." And this time, she shifted the gun's aim to his feet.

"You'll have to kill me first," he finally spoke, but didn't budge.

"Oh, so brave," Ariel cooed in mock admiration. "Taking a bullet for your sweet little dog. She bites, by the way. Not so sweet." Her face scrunched in a scowl, then gave way to another smile. "How about I give you both half a chance?"

"Cut it out, Ariel," Libby told her, but she could tell Ariel wasn't listening to her any longer.

She lifted the revolver and with the expertise of someone familiar with guns; she unlatched the cylinder, tilted it and clicked until bullets started filling her palm. Three of them went into her pocket. Then she showed the dogman the other three and, with animated motion, slid each bullet back into the chamber. She slammed the cylinder back and spun it before clicking it in place.

Ariel pointed the gun again at the man's legs. Without hesitation, she pulled the trigger.

70

Ariel was out of his reach. Instead of diving for the gun, Creed dropped to his knees, putting his body—center mass—directly in front of Grace.

The click echoed off the walls almost as loud as a gunshot.

Creed looked down at his chest, expecting to see a wound he didn't feel. He did this before realizing his good fortune. The chamber was empty. He stayed down in case she fired a second shot.

Then, true to her character, Ariel did something else he didn't expect. She laughed. She laughed hard, relaxing her grip on the gun so she could hold her middle.

"You're such a dumbass," she said. "I wish you could have seen your face."

"Stop it, Ariel." Libby told her. "We're supposed to be helping each other." Then she marched across the trailer, holding out her hand. "I want my gun back. Now!'

"No way." Ariel's nostrils flared. She tucked the weapon into the waistband at the small of her back like an experienced gangster. "I'm obviously the only one willing to use it. It stays with me."

She pushed passed Libby, brushed passed Creed and Grace to grab her cell phone off the counter. She glared down at him as she tucked the phone inside a pocket. He could easily read that glare. She was telling him she knew he had taken her *other* phone.

But Creed knew something too, and he held her eyes to convey his own message: *Yes, I have it, and now I know you want to keep it a secret.*

71

Grand Island, Nebraska

Jason left Scout and Hank with Brodie and Maggie in the hotel's half empty pub. He insisted on unpacking the Jeep by himself, and for once, Brodie didn't argue. She was eager to find out any new information Maggie might have about Ryder. Also, Maggie was one of the few people Brodie felt comfortable with. Last June, they had bonded over decomposing bodies left deep inside Blackwater River State Forest.

It took three trips to unload, partly because Jason wasn't used to the snow. He was finding it difficult to maneuver in the boots Hannah had sent with him. They felt big and awkward, like clown shoes on feet that were already oversized. The snow had stopped falling, but it was a challenge lumbering through the drifts, then reckoning with icy surfaces where snowplows had gone over.

Finally finished, he checked the time while he slow-walked back down the hall to the elevators. Was it too late to call Taylor? He hesitated. He hadn't talked to her in two days, only sending text messages while on the road. But even they were short, casual updates:

STOPPING FOR GAS IN MEMPHIS

JUST CROSSED THE MISSOURI/NEBRASKA BORDER

SNOW!!

He was careful—maybe too careful—to leave out words that were inappropriate. Words or phrases that might spook her like, "missing you." Taylor had made it clear she didn't want anything serious after everything she'd just been through. In the last year she'd dealt with two obsessed suitors: one willing to die for her; the other willing to kill.

It sounded crazy. If Jason hadn't been a part of the actual drama, he might wonder if it was an exaggeration. But he knew what she'd gone through. It made him care about her more. She'd been to Afghanistan as an army surgical nurse and survived. It would take time, but she'd survive what she was going through now, too, trying to regain custody of her son and convince the boy's grandparents that she was worthy. Jason didn't mind being along for that journey.

Before he reached the bank of the elevators, he turned around and headed back to the adjoining rooms where he'd dropped off his and Brodie's stuff. He'd transferred perishables from their coolers to the mini-frigs, but hadn't unpacked anything else. He'd left the door between the two rooms open, like they'd done at their hotel last night.

He pulled out his phone. One more glance at the time, and he hit the call button before he changed his mind.

Three rings then, "Hey!"

A single word spoken with excitement. That's all it took, and he felt the tension slide away. How was it possible for the sound of one person's voice to make him feel so good?

"I forgot how cold snow could be," Jason told her, keeping himself from blurting out what he really wanted to say, that he missed her.

She laughed. "It was sunny and eighty-five here today. So, are you finally there?"

"Yeah, I just brought up all our stuff to our rooms."

"Rooms? You and Scout need more than one room?"

"No, Brodie and Hank are with us."

"Brodie went with you?"

He wasn't sure why that would be a problem, but the change in her tone said otherwise. Was she concerned he'd have to take care of Brodie when he already had his hands full, searching for Ryder and Grace?

"She's really worried about Ryder," he explained. "And she really can take care of herself."

"Oh, I know she can."

He thought he heard an edge attached to the comment. Almost a snide that he'd never heard before. Maybe he was just tired. They hadn't gotten much sleep last night. Taylor was actually agreeing with him that Brodie could take care of herself, but the silence that followed suddenly felt uncomfortable.

"Scout's never experienced snow before," he said, pretending he didn't notice. "I'm not sure he'll be able to track in this stuff. It's deep and heavy. Any of Ryder's scent will be buried underneath."

He didn't mean to get so serious, but the realization had come to him while he unpacked the Jeep. The weight of the task ahead was starting to settle in. Somewhere between the clown boots and slipping on the shoveled but icy sidewalks, he realized he might be in over his head. And he couldn't count on his usual failsafe to help bail him out, because that failsafe was Ryder.

What the hell was he thinking? Picking up and driving a thousand miles like he was some superhero riding in to save the day. And Scout was barely two-years-old, still a newbie to scent training. Sometimes the dog was wild and goofy, head-butting Jason when he knew he'd earned his reward toy. What Jason called playful, most handlers would probably call undisciplined.

"He'll do fine," Taylor interrupted his thoughts, her voice back to a reassuring tone.

This was what he loved about her, how perceptive she was, that she understood exactly why he was worried without him needing to explain.

Then she added, "He'll do great, because he has you to guide him."

72

Maggie couldn't believe how good it was to see Brodie and Jason and the dogs. Especially the dogs. She hugged them too long, and they let her, wagging hard against her with their whole bodies. These days she found herself missing her boys, Harvey and Jake so much more. Those two could make her smile during the darkest of times. Their previous owners had abandoned them before they came into Maggie's life. But they were safe and happy now, and they loved her brother, Patrick, who doted on them when she was away.

Funny, she used to believe she didn't need anyone or anything. She used to be an expert at compartmentalizing feelings. Her best friend, Dr. Gwen Patterson, would call it progress, that she missed her dogs, that she cared so much about Ryder.

To Maggie, it felt like the unraveling of her emotional defense system. In the past, caring about people and getting too close only resulted in pain. There was still a trigger in her psyche that wouldn't let her forget that.

But then Jason and Brodie along with Scout and Hank showed up, and suddenly, all she could think about was how much they felt like family, like a support system that she needed. *Needed.* All it took was one look at them, and Maggie could see her own concerns about Ryder and Grace mirrored on their faces.

Brodie wanted to know everything with pointed and direct questions. Usually, Maggie appreciated being able to be straightforward without picking and choosing her words to soften or cushion what was really happening. But she hesitated with Brodie. Ryder was protective of his sister, who was still feeling her way around the real world.

Brodie was strong. Maggie had seen the proof for herself. But she also knew how fragile someone with PTSD could be. She'd spent the day pacing Ryder's hotel room wearing one of his shirts as if it were a security blanket. Her own mind felt like it was spiraling out of control.

How would Brodie react to hearing her brother might be injured? That he might be... No, Maggie refused to even entertain the other options right now. She had given some basics and the timeline, but she waited for Jason to join them for the rest.

They huddled in a corner booth of the hotel's pub. The dogs lay tucked under the table at their feet. When Jason arrived, Brodie scooted over, and he took the place beside her. Maggie noticed how comfortable the two were with each other. Twenty hours in a vehicle could do that.

She waited while he ordered a burger and asked if Brodie wanted one, then he ordered hers, knowing without asking what she wanted on it and with it. Maggie hadn't thought about food, and only now realized the two were probably starving. When the waitress paused for Maggie, she gave in and decided on the soup of the day. Maybe it would warm her from the inside out. She'd been chilled ever since the morning trek through the snow. Which was probably a good place to start.

When the waitress left, she told Jason and Brodie that they found Ryder's cell phone.

"So he lost it?" Brodie asked.

Maggie watched her eyes. They were difficult to read. She gave a slight shake of her head, her eyes never leaving Brodie's. "No, I think someone took it from him." She paused to let that sink in as she glanced at Jason.

She tried to explain. "We tracked his phone by using cell towers in the area. What we discovered was that it went dark just after his call from Hannah."

"He could have shut it off to save the battery, right?" Jason asked.

"Or the battery ran out," Brodie said. "That's why I hate these things. We treat them like they can't fail."

"You still need to carry one," Jason told her. "Sometimes it's the only way to get in touch with somebody when you're in trouble."

"It obviously didn't help Ryder, and he's in trouble."

Maggie sat quietly until they finished, guessing this wasn't the first time they'd discussed the matter.

"Where did you find it?" Jason asked.

"In a pasture. It was in a black plastic garbage bag tossed on top of the snow."

"Why would Ryder do that?" Brodie asked, then seconds later, her eyes blinked wide. "Oh, right. You said someone took it from him."

"His shirt was in the bag, too." She paused, hating to deliver the next piece of information. "There was a bloodstain on the shirt."

She searched their faces and waited. Jason looked like he expected something like this. Brodie just stared somewhere over Maggie's shoulder.

"There was nothing else in the bag?" Jason asked.

"No." She couldn't tell them about the sock without getting into Kristen Darrow and didn't want to do that right now.

"If they thought law enforcement was tracking the phone," Jason said, "which you were, it would make sense to ditch it, right?"

"I believe so. They pulled the battery out."

"Wait a minute," Jason's eyes lit up. "Do you know if Ryder had Grace's vest on her?"

"I didn't see them leave," Maggie said. The regret surprised her with yet another sinking feeling in her gut. "I know she had it on the day before when they did the electronic device search."

"I can't believe I didn't think of this. Sometimes Ryder puts a tracking device in Grace's vest pocket in case they get separated. It might not be easy to track if there's no cell service, but it could be worth a try."

Maggie was already sliding out of the booth and pulling out her cell phone to call Alonzo. "I'm going to check on that. I'll be right back." She headed for the hotel lobby, where she knew she could get a better cell phone connection.

On the way out, she glanced at one of the televisions hung strategically throughout the pub for sports fans. It wasn't a game that caught her eye, but a red banner with LOCAL BREAKING NEWS. She recognized the enhanced screen shot from the surveillance video. The audio was turned down, but the captions gave a phone number to call with information. Right now they were labeling the three suspects, "persons of interest." Despite the latest and best technology, the zoomed screen-grabs were grainy. Still, maybe someone would recognize one of the women.

Maggie was impressed. Alonzo was fast. Pakula must have used every bit of his authority and persuasive talents with the local media.

With any luck, someone would recognize one of the trio.

Now, if Grace had a tracking device, Alonzo could locate it.

This was all good. So why did that lump in the pit of her stomach continue to linger? She could feel the rhythm of her heartbeat pounding in her chest, drumming at her temple, like a ticking bomb telling her there wasn't much time left.

This was the part when she hated everything she knew. She hated how much experience she had delving into the minds of killers. What they were capable of doing. They had no limits. Felt no remorse.

Her mind was trained to play out their sick games. Anticipate, predict and maybe, if she was lucky, trick them. Once or twice she'd won, but how many times had she lost? And at what cost? Those losses had stripped her of feelings, shredded her beliefs in a greater power who should be able to contain such evil. She'd learned enough lessons to last her a lifetime.

But this time was different. This time wasn't some game. It wasn't about saving the next victim. It was Ryder and Grace. She could not lose him. Not now.

Over the past twenty-four hours she caught herself running a mantra in her head, a thrum of beats and words—okay, maybe it was even a prayer—hoping that Ryder and Grace were okay. That they were still alive.

She told herself it was a good thing that Alonzo and Pakula had acted quickly. And at the same time, she couldn't stop wondering if these three killers had indeed taken Ryder and Grace, what would they do when they saw this breaking news?

The lump in her stomach didn't just linger. Now it churned and started to twist into knots.

73

Friday, October 8
Hastings, Nebraska

Ruben didn't sleep. He didn't need much. Three or four hours max. It was something that happened in his forties. As if an electrical switch had been flipped inside his mind. He used the dark hours to feed his imagination.

Even as a teenager, his imagination tilted to the wild side. While other boys his age dreamed of sexual conquests, Ruben was more fascinated with how to make girls scream. Yes, pleasure could sometimes accomplish that, but Ruben found fear a more satisfying medium.

At some point, fear became less intriguing. Human behavior became a driving force. What were people capable of doing? What could they be manipulated into doing? Along the way, he developed a curiosity about human anatomy. Most recently, he obsessed with witnessing a person's last breath.

Simply put, he was a lifelong student, learning by a hands-on approach.

Right now, that made him smile as he walked down the quiet hotel hallway. He'd left Shelby to sleep. She'd need her rest to help Vanessa with their next project. They couldn't afford to botch a second effort. Besides, Ruben could handle this current job all by himself. He expected little resistance and there was no need for ritual or ceremony. This was a utilitarian mission.

His ordinary looks, with his receding hairline and middle-aged, short, stocky body, provided him with a sort of power. Add a sweater vest and walking stick, and he practically became invisible. He knew how to be friendly enough without being memorable. People treated him like he was no threat. That's if they noticed him at all.

Earlier Ruben had taken his walking stick and gone down to the lobby, telling Shelby he was going to grab a few more free refreshments. He preferred a walking stick to a walking cane, though both seemed to telegraph handicapped. The stick was more of a fashion statement, almost useless for taking weight if leaned on. However, it turned into a nifty weapon if used correctly.

Ruben lingered and strolled along the periphery, watching the guests enjoy their complementary beverages. He drank a cup of coffee. Made chitchat when appropriate, but mostly he watched and waited without anyone noticing that he was watching and waiting.

When the man appeared, Ruben knew him immediately. He hadn't changed out of his uniform. Hadn't even taken off his nametag. Larry grabbed himself a Coke and a bag of popcorn, then headed back to the elevator. Ruben let him enter before he stepped in alongside the man. He leaned over to tap a button, then stopped himself like he noticed the one he wanted was already lit, already headed for his same floor.

On the fourth floor, Ruben let the man get off first. He trailed him at a safe distance, pretending to busy himself with finding which pocket he'd slipped his keycard into. Larry stopped at room 425, and Ruben passed by him like his room was just down the hall.

Now, with everyone fast asleep in the early morning hours, Ruben counted on Larry being sleepy-eyed and a bit annoyed by the knock on his door. He counted on Larry looking out the peephole and seeing a plain man with a friendly face that seemed familiar. And Ruben counted on Larry opening the door.

Ruben stood in front of room 425. He dug his hand deep into his trouser pocket and wrapped his fingers around the handle of the switchblade knife. With his left hand, he knocked on the door. Two taps followed by one word said casually, without a threat, but with authority: "Manager."

Sure enough, Larry paused at the peephole, then opened the door. He listened to Ruben's explanation while trying to wipe the sleep from his eyes.

After mere seconds, Larry stepped aside and let Ruben into his room for the hotel manager to check and see that the overflowing toilet above Larry's room had not leaked into his ceiling.

Again, Ruben smiled to himself. Not only had he gained access, but he would lead the unsuspecting guest into the only space that wouldn't leave a stain on the carpet.

The man stood beside him, still rubbing at his half-awake eyes and trying to stare up into the corner over the bathtub where Ruben pointed out. Poor exhausted Larry, the electrical utility worker, didn't even notice the knife.

74

Libby jerked awake. She had fallen asleep with her head on the table. In the dim light of the trailer, it took her a second to remember where she was. Her pulse raced. She heard panting and looked for the dog. It stared at her from its spot alongside its sleeping owner. They were still curled up on the bed.

The panting continued, and only then did Libby realize it was her. She sucked in air and almost choked. Her eyes darted around. From the corner of her eye, she saw movement outside the window. Ariel's blue coat stood out against the early morning gray.

The nightmare always derailed her physically and mentally. But every time she woke up, she was grateful to see there was no bathtub full of blood. Still, she checked her hands. It had taken her days before she felt like she had gotten all the blood out from under her fingernails.

With time, the dream only grew more vivid. Details she had forgotten or tucked away while awake rammed themselves to the forefront of her sleeping mind. She'd never be rid of the memories, no matter how far she ran away. They were embedded inside her like some disease, reminding her of what she had become.

That was exactly what David Ruben hoped to accomplish. Libby understood that better now after meeting Ariel. He liked to take regular teenage girls, manipulate their confidence, make them feel isolated from any other support system, then pit them against each other to compete for his rewards of praise, money and drugs. He made them feel like they were a family. Told them they needed to watch out for each other. Only Ruben's "watching out" for each other encouraged tattling and tracking their cell phones.

He spoiled them with manicures, tickets to sold-out events and parties in luxurious hotel suites. But at the end of an evening with invited guests, Ruben wanted to know which guest they'd most like to watch die. He seemed to be obsessed with experiencing what it felt like to take someone's last breath.

At first, Libby shrugged it off as part of a drug-laced, alcohol-induced fantasy game. A sort of dungeons and dragons.

But then there were the favors. One girl's mother nagged her constantly. Ruben took care of it. Gave the mother something else to worry about. That's how he said it. Libby was never sure what he'd done. Sometimes his resolutions were subtle. Most of the time, they were not. She remembered another girl whose ex-boyfriend kept stalking her. Ruben promised to put an end to it. A week later, the guy was injured in a hit-and-run accident.

His favor to Libby fell under the subtle type. In her rebellious phase to teach her father a lesson and gain his attention, she started shoplifting. Minor items at first: lipstick, sunglasses. Then she moved on to dressing room swipes: T-shirts that fit under her sweater. She got caught last January. The mall cop even had her arrested, handcuffed, fingerprinted.

That got her father's attention. Mostly, it just made things worse between him and her mother.

Back then, Libby liked that he got in trouble. And she actually liked the adrenaline rush the shoplifting gave her. But the next time there was no mall cop. The next time there was David Ruben.

He knew right away that she wasn't stealing just for the stuff. It was like he understood her. And for some stupid reason, it made an impression with Libby. Here was someone who didn't mind her experimenting on the wild side. Someone who actually encouraged it.

This friendly faced, middle-aged man. What harm could there be in hooking up with him?

He made it clear from the beginning that he wasn't interested in sex. He was just some old guy with a lot of money who enjoyed pulling a fast one on people, having a good time, pushing the envelope.

Plus, he didn't turn her in when he saw her shoplift that expensive handbag from a ritzy retailer that probably would have pressed charges, not like the other place where her father had managed to get the charges dropped.

She could continue her rebellious stint. Except she had no clue what Ruben expected in return. Libby shook her head. The image of that poor woman in the bathtub. Eyes dead but wide open. Her body submerged, blood coloring the bath water as Ruben and the others cut into her flesh. Her skin was so pale against the blood-red water.

She had stayed back. She couldn't believe what was happening. The rest of them were high, but Libby had only pretended. She was expected to participate. Ruben handed her a bright yellow utility knife, but she slipped into a puddle. Banged her knee. Her palms were immediately stained.

While the others hovered over the bathtub, Ruben glanced back, not paying her much attention but instructing her to get more towels. When they first checked in, he swiped extra from a housekeeping cart in the hallway. He'd piled them on the bed. Libby wondered why they needed so many. A swim party? How naïve she'd been.

When she left the bathroom, she walked right past the towels and tiptoed to the door. Somehow, she managed to sneak out. They were all too absorbed in the task at hand. It was simply dumb luck that no one noticed her slip away. They didn't even hear her stumble. Her knees had refused to keep her upright. She remembered crawling out of the hotel suite, keenly aware that she needed to hold the door so it wouldn't make a sound.

She took the stairs. She could barely breathe. She missed steps and clung to the railing so she wouldn't fall headfirst. Outside, it was cold and raining, but she didn't care that she wasn't wearing a coat or shoes.

None of that mattered.

A pitter-patter on the trailer roof made her sit up straight. She glanced around, trying to catch her breath. She needed to let the memories fuel her, not paralyze her. She tried to concentrate on the new sound, though it was barely audible over the hum of the generator. Her eyes darted out the window. Streaks of water etched the glass.

Meltdown. That's what she was hearing. The snow on the branches above was starting to melt. The realization quickened her pulse. There was little time left.

Run or be found.

Beyond the streaks, she saw Ariel leaning against a tree, staring down at her hand. From twenty feet away, Libby could see the light of the cell phone. During the storm, Libby's own phone had little to no cellular reception. Out here, it was sporadic even on a clear day.

But Ariel's phone appeared to be working. Then Libby saw her pull off her glove and tap the screen.

She was messaging someone.

75

Something was bothering Jason. He was too quiet. Last night, Brodie thought he was just tired from the two-day drive. She wondered if he might be concerned about their sleeping arrangements, but she discarded that as soon as they went up to their rooms. He'd already created a comfortable area on the floor of Brodie's room for all of them to be together, if that's what she chose.

She was grateful Jason understood, though she wasn't sure she did. Why was she still having panic attacks? She had learned to deal with so much when she had no choice but to survive. She remembered when Iris punished her with darkness by taking the only light bulb from the already dark basement. Brodie had learned how to go deep inside her mind, closing her eyes, because despite the black surrounding her, that simple gesture helped calm her. She still kept her eyes shut in the middle of the night when she felt the panic creeping back into her mind.

But she was safe now. No one would hurt her again as long as she was strong. As long as she had Hank and Jason and Scout. And of course, Kitten. She had smiled about that last night as she watched Jason feed the dogs and cat. Then, without even discussing it, they all settled down to sleep like it was part of their normal routine. With their bellies full, the dogs crashed and sprawled. They enjoyed the extra space after being confined to the Jeep for too many hours.

And they all slept. No nightmares. No Charlottes.

Brodie's mind had been preoccupied with Ryder and Grace, but she found comfort in the exhausted bodies surrounding her and in the sounds of their breathing, even a few snores. Hank looked up once to make sure she was okay. Jason stirred a few times, then readjusted. Almost instinctively, all of them touched each other throughout the night in the subtlest of ways.

This morning her mind picked up where it left off, going over the things Maggie had told them about Ryder's disappearance. Brodie sorted through the details and tried to fill in the gaps Maggie had left out. And now she was convinced the FBI profiler had left out what she didn't want them to know.

To be fair, Brodie knew Maggie probably didn't think she had lied to them. Brodie, unfortunately, had developed an innate lie detector. She had to in order to survive Iris Malone's constant lies. The woman had used them to control Brodie. Withholding the truth turned out to be a crueler punishment than kidnapping her.

Lies of omission were trickier. Brodie understood that. She'd even used the tactic herself. Hannah said some lies didn't count as much as others. And there were a lot of different kinds besides lies of omission.

There were little white lies and bold-faced lies along with lies people told themselves. Of course, they could just be stretching the truth or pulling your leg or yanking your chain. Brodie read a lot, so she recognized these. She didn't always understand the reasons people lied, but she knew when someone wasn't telling her the truth. She had asked Ryder to always tell her the truth, no matter the cost.

It wasn't a request she could make of Maggie O'Dell, and so Brodie's mind continued to imagine what Maggie knew that was too uncomfortable to tell. What was too terrible she felt she had to keep it from them?

The fact that Jason didn't notice meant something else preoccupied him. Although Brodie was good at detecting lies, emotions were an entirely different subject. She couldn't figure out her own emotions. How could she possibly figure out someone else's?

But this morning Brodie realized Jason was worried about something. He hardly commented on breakfast. He loved breakfast. And the biscuits were better than the ones they'd had yesterday. She watched him load his daypack, sorting items, packing and unpacking them like he couldn't decide what he and Scout would need. She'd never seen him so unsure.

Perhaps he simply wasn't prepared for the temperature change. She casually recommended layers, and he seemed grateful for the tip. Yet it didn't solve his hesitancy.

Maybe it was the snow that threw him off. When they walked from the hotel to the Jeep, his shoulders hunched together, and he lifted his feet too high like the snow might trip him.

Over the past several months, Brodie had spent a lot of time observing Jason. She found him fascinating in a way she couldn't quite explain. Sometimes he hummed when he worked. She'd caught him singing once, and instead of being embarrassed he added gestures like he was playing a guitar, performing for her like a rockstar, just to make her laugh. It worked.

When she first arrived in Florida, she was still frightened of dogs. Iris had sent one of hers to attack Brodie once during an attempted escape. The scar on her ankle still displayed the indentions where the dog's teeth had sunk down to the bone. In those first weeks, when Jason learned Brodie shared his love of reading, he took time to tell Brodie stories about each of the dogs in Ryder's kennel. All of them were rescues that had been abandoned. Each had an incredible story, and Jason narrated them like fictional tales. Somehow he knew Brodie would relate to their plights and maybe not be as frightened of them. Again, it worked.

She felt close to Jason, but not like she did with Hannah or Ryder. So why couldn't she read his emotions?

She helped him rearrange the dogs' crates so they could restore a seat in the back for Maggie. Scout and Hank were excited this morning with pent up energy. They had walked them as best they could, but Scout almost pulled Jason off his feet, wanting to run in the deep snow.

Now they waited for Maggie while the Jeep filled with warm air and the dogs settled into their spaces. Kitten crawled up to take a look out of the window. But Jason still fidgeted with the heating controls, the windshield wipers, the GPS. Brodie glanced around. No signs of Maggie yet. She decided she needed to ask him what was wrong.

"Something's bothering you," she said and left it for him to fill in the blanks or shrug it off.

He hesitated. She hoped it had nothing to do with her.

"I'm worried Scout won't be able to track in the snow," Jason finally said.

She gave him her full attention, turning her body to face him. From his backseat crate, Scout raised his head and listened after hearing his name.

"Why do you think that?" Brodie asked.

"Ryder and Grace disappeared while it was still snowing. All of their scent will be buried underneath."

"But the scent is still there?"

"Oh sure. Cold is good at preserving."

"Dogs can track scents that are underground. Isn't dirt heavier than snow?"

"It's not about heavier. When it's wet and below freezing, the ice encapsulates the scent molecules."

"But when it starts to melt, it'll release the scent, right?"

"I suppose so," he admitted.

She pointed out the windshield.

Along the hotel's entrance, a carport protected guests from the elements while they unpacked their vehicles. A steady drip streamed from the roofline.

"It's warming up," she told him.

His eyes darted to the dashboard to check the digital display for the outside temperature.

"Thirty-nine degrees," he said. He pulled out his cell phone, slid his finger over the screen, and tapped. "The high today for Grand Island, Nebraska, is going to be forty-five. I never even considered it might get warm enough to melt with all this snow on the ground."

"Nebraska weather," Brodie shrugged. The temperature going up and down was one thing she, unfortunately, remembered well.

"Thanks," Jason said, then he surprised her when he added, "I'm really glad you're here."

76

Maggie texted Jason to let him know she'd be just a few more minutes. She needed to make her phone calls from the hotel lobby. Once they were on the back roads plowing through the snow, cellular service would be unpredictable.

Alonzo had already given her the bad news. So far, none of the facial recognition programs had found serious matches for their suspects. Alonzo supposed none of them had been arrested, which made his task more difficult. And to make matters worse, without consistent cellular service to connect to and gather location information, they had no way of accessing Grace's GPS tracker.

She leaned against a wall in the far corner of the lobby. She was physically spent from a night of pacing interspersed with an hour or two of tossing and turning. She ran fingers through her damp hair from a shower that relieved none of the tension in her shoulders. She was exhausted, and the day was only beginning.

Pakula had no good news either. The tip line brought in sightings of the hardware store trio, but as he warned her, the reliability of those tips was questionable. One or all three were allegedly spotted in a Lincoln restaurant, a truck stop outside of St. Louis, a Denver bookstore and even a Gap store at Mall of America.

Pakula said it would take more manpower than he had available to even sift through for promising clues. He also told her Spencer and his deputies were out dealing with storm related issues, including domestic disputes and traffic accidents. But he added they would be available to her at a moment's notice. And so would he.

Maggie appreciated their offers, but the fact was, they weren't any closer to knowing what had happened to Ryder and Grace.

"The good news," Pakula told her when she went quiet, "the snow has stopped. The plows are out in full force, and it's warming up."

When she still didn't respond, he added, "We've been passing along Ryder's photo to law enforcement across the state. We'll find him, Maggie. I promise."

"Thanks," she managed.

The last phone call she made went unanswered, and Maggie couldn't help wondering if Nora Spencer was simply ignoring her.

She climbed into the backseat of Jason's Jeep and filled them in on everything she had learned. She ended by saying, "Nora's not answering her phone."

"Tell me again who Nora is?" Jason asked.

"Nora Spencer." Maggie turned to greet the wagging dogs. Though they were in their crates, she pressed her hand against the soft mesh, her fingers meeting their wet noses.

"Nora is the county sheriff's wife. She's the one who asked Ryder to find the young woman who was staying with them."

"Libby Holmes," Brodie said. "But her real name is Emma."

"Right. Nora and I clashed a bit when we met. I didn't like the way she convinced Ryder to search for Libby. She lied about some things. I guess I don't trust her, and she knows that."

Maggie felt Brodie's eyes on her now, watching, waiting, expecting more. If something horrible had happened to Ryder, his sister was going to find out soon enough.

"It's not just that Libby Holmes changed her name," Maggie said. "She's a person of interest in a murder in Virginia from last February.

Pieces of a body were found in a ditch not far from here. It hasn't been confirmed, but we think it's someone who worked with Libby. I don't have this figured out, but one thing I know for sure, Libby Holmes is connected to her co-worker's murder."

"You think she helped?" Brodie asked.

"I honestly don't know. It's possible that the three people who took Kristen Darrow meant to take Libby. They look alike. Darrow was working Libby's shift. She was even wearing Libby's name tag. Her family didn't report her missing until the morning before we started finding pieces of her."

"So that could have been why Libby took off." Jason said.

"She didn't take her car. The Spencers' property is out in the middle of nowhere. It's not like anyone would just run away on foot. Ryder thought Grace would simply take him to the road or the barn, where someone picked her up or coerced her into a vehicle."

"But that wasn't the case," Brodie said. "Ryder and Grace found a longer trail of scent."

"Yes, but I'm not sure that trail didn't lead to the killers."

Brodie was watching her, then finally said, "That's what you couldn't tell us last night."

Maggie was too exhausted to explain. It was a combination of wanting to protect Brodie and not divulge evidence. Instead, she simply nodded. Then she said, "Jason, do we need to begin where Ryder and Grace did, or can we start in the middle?"

"How do you know where the middle is?"

"Hannah mentioned Ryder was looking for an old bridge to get across the river. Sheriff Spencer pointed out an old irrigation road that would take us close to where that is. It's also not far from where we found his phone."

"Sure. We can start there. Worse case scenario, Scout doesn't pick up a scent and we go back to where they started. Did you bring something for Scout?"

Maggie didn't want to admit that she had worn Ryder's shirt for a couple of days. The dog might smell her scent more than Ryder's.

"I brought a T-shirt and the socks he wore the first day," she told him as she lifted the plastic bag with the two items. "Will that work?"

She saw Jason and Brodie exchange a look before Jason said, "Let's hope so."

"I remembered Grace's sleeping blanket, too."

"Why would we need something from Grace?" Brodie asked, but she was looking at Jason, not Maggie.

"In case they got separated," he said and left it at that, busying himself now with getting the Jeep in motion and avoiding Brodie's eyes that still hadn't left him.

Despite their earlier exchange, Maggie realized Jason was trying to protect Brodie, too. Last night, when he asked Maggie for the items, he admitted that Ryder and Grace might no longer be together. It was a hard admission, part of it getting stuck in his throat. Maggie had been grateful it was over the phone and not in person, but it had left tears welling in her eyes.

She hated this. It was time to go find them.

77

Ruben had already cleaned out their vehicle, wiping down surfaces and eliminating the smallest pieces of trash that might lead to their identity. He'd gotten good at it. Kept individually wrapped Clorox and alcohol wipes in his pockets just for this.

He packed their belongings and loaded the van before sunrise wearing Larry's coveralls, leather driving gloves, and coat. Even the dead man's boots fit perfectly.

Somehow Shelby had slept through the packing and his comings and goings. Or so he thought. When he finally finished and came back to the room, she was dressed. She had fetched quite the spread from the free breakfast bar, remembering that he liked Fruit Loops and leaving a tray on his bed. Maybe she was learning.

He rewarded her with a smile and a thumbs-up, then checked his cell phone. There was a new text from Vanessa:

ON MY WAY. MEET YOU THERE IN AN HOUR.

Vanessa had told Shelby last night that she had stolen a "sweet ride" with four-wheel drive from Lincoln Airport's long-term parking.

Ruben was pleased. These girls were working hard to redeem themselves and make up for their colossal mistake. The lessons he'd taught them were finally sinking in. He was glad they'd have a new vehicle for their quick getaway. They could ditch it for another as soon as they reached Omaha. From there, they'd head south.

As crazy as the blizzard had been, this morning the snow had started melting. Trucks with plows on the front and sand drizzling out the back were returning the roadways back to asphalt. But as soon as they left the major highways, Ruben realized the utility van could easily get stuck on the back roads. The melting sludge pulled at the wheels and sent them swerving. By the time Shelby pointed out the farm that was their destination, Ruben was grinding his teeth and clenching his fists around the steering wheel.

Then he reminded himself that Emma would pay for all these inconveniences. That made him feel better. He'd prepared the back of the utility van with drop cloths, but after zigzagging through the snow, he knew they wouldn't be able to take their time with her.

There were no vehicles in front of the house. Only one set of tire-tracks were left in the snow, and it was easy to see the vehicle had driven out the driveway.

Ruben parked close enough that he didn't have to walk far, but kept the windshield facing away from the house.

"How close is Vanessa?" he asked. He knew Shelby had been texting her.

"About ten minutes away."

"Tell her to park on the road somewhere safe and walk over. We don't want anyone seeing her vehicle. You wait here," he told her. She was already sitting in the windowless back. "I'll be right back in ten."

He slipped his switchblade into the coat pocket. Made sure he had enough zip-ties and duct tape in the other pocket. He pulled on gloves and a stocking cap he'd found on the driver's seat, then pushed up the bridge of the thick-framed glasses. He marched his way to the front door, grateful Larry's boots were so warm.

He barely knocked before it opened. The woman was short and a little overweight. She wore blue scrubs, and her hair was pulled back into a ponytail, accentuating the lines at the corners of her eyes and mouth.

"Our electricity seems to be fine," she told him.

"You or your husband didn't call in that it was out?"

"No."

She wasn't making this easy. He fished a piece of paper out of his pocket, almost bringing out a zip-tie. He pretended to read the paper, then looked at her again. "This is the Spencer place, right?"

"Yes, but I didn't call in a power outage."

"Maybe your husband did."

"He's been gone a few hours."

"Well, my supervisor's gonna be upset if I don't check. You mind if I come in and take a look at your breaker box?"

Ruben wasn't sure that was a real thing. Nora Spencer hesitated for a second or two, then gestured for him to come in.

78

Scout was anxious to get to work. Jason would need to settle him down before he snapped the leash to his working vest. The big dog had already recognized the preparations for a search. Back at the hotel, Jason had watched a custodial worker toss scoops of salt and chemicals onto the sidewalks. It was yet another thing he hadn't thought about.

A handler's number one priority was to guide and protect his dog. Equip and prepare for conditions and obstacles. Scout's success depended on Jason's preparation and awareness.

Would the dog need protection from the temperatures, the humidity, or the terrain? In this case, it was snow and ice, along with the chemicals on the sidewalks and roadways. Jason had applied wax to Hank's and Scout's paws while they were still in the hotel, triggering Scout's excitement. He was glad he caught this obstacle but wondered what other dangers these weather conditions would bring.

The irrigation road was little more than a dirt path, not a road. The Jeep bumped over the ruts and pushed through the drifts, kicking up the melting sludge. In the city, he had to maneuver around downed branches and dangling electrical lines. Out here, the destruction wasn't as obvious. Trees were mostly clumped around farms. Otherwise, the landscape was barren pastures or cornfields buried under snow.

Maggie insisted this road was on the other side of the old wood bridge that Ryder and Grace would have crossed. The bridge would be impossible to find in the snow. This way, they could avoid that search. She pointed to the treeline at the edge of what looked like a wind-swept meadow. Beyond the trees, she promised, was the river.

Jason couldn't see it. But then he couldn't see a single building, let alone a farm. They had driven by some. And while the snow was melting, the blanketed landscape—thick with layers—would require more than one forty-degree day before it'd reveal whole pieces of the ground underneath.

He was used to having shrubs for scent to cling to and patches of grass where it could sink between the blades. This white-duned prairie simply baffled him. But he knew one thing for sure. He could not let Scout know that. He couldn't let Scout get a whiff of his misgivings.

Scout had impressed him before. He needed to remember how awesome his dog was. After all, Scout had found a dead body in an old chest freezer. Of course, Jason didn't believe him at the time. He thought his dog, a notorious chow-hound, only wanted to get at the tasty frozen food inside.

Trust your dog!

It was something Ryder constantly drilled into him.

And despite Jason's doubts right now, despite hating this cold, unfamiliar territory, he needed to show only enthusiasm. He had to be mindful that he didn't translate any of these feelings to Scout.

Be excited. Let Scout believe this was one big, fun adventure. A game of search and find.

Why kid himself? The hardest part would be staying optimistic. This was the third day since Ryder and Grace had disappeared. During their road trip, Jason tried to imagine the pair had simply hunkered down in an old shed. As a Marine, Ryder would surely find a way to keep them warm, even if he was injured.

Now that he stood here feeling the bite of cold stinging his face and listening to the distant sound of a train, Jason realized how rare a piece of shelter might be. Hope drained from him like grains of sand slipping through an hourglass. Urgency nagged at him.

He glanced over at Maggie. She'd climbed up onto the tailgate with binoculars. At the other end of the Jeep, Brodie had snuggled down Kitten in the front seat with a fleece throw. She wrapped a scarf around her neck and pulled up the hood of her coat while talking in a low voice to Hank, as if giving him a rundown. She talked to the dogs and cat a lot. He liked that. Sometimes he found himself wanting in on their conversation. The animals always looked so content, so attentive and comforted by her voice.

She offered both dogs some water then snapped the collapsible bowl to the canteen and looped the strap around her neck and shoulder. She looked ready and prepared, but Jason knew there was nothing that prepared you for finding the body of someone you knew. Someone you loved.

He had seen things in Afghanistan. He'd lost friends there and here, too many by their own hands. But Ryder... He'd never met a stronger mind, a stronger will. The guy was a survivor. He was a rescuer at heart. Hell, he'd rescued Jason.

Whatever had happened out here, he had to believe Ryder wouldn't give up. And he wouldn't let a bunch of snow defeat him.

79

Creed heard the tap-tap of water. He wiped a hand over his sweat-drenched forehead. His palm came away damp and red.

He looked up and saw the branches dripping with blood. No sky though light filtered down. Raindrops fell, but the pitter-patter sounded far away, taking extra seconds before he felt it.

The fever had taken him back to the blood forest. His mind seemed to know this, though his body couldn't respond. Eyelids fluttered but refused to open. His breathing was slow and labored.

He reached for Grace, comforted to find her warm body beside him. Relief swept over him. She was still with him, even if he couldn't see her. He kept a hand on her back, not taking a risk of losing her, because in the nightmare Grace hid somewhere in the tall grass.

His other hand swept around him, fingers searching the air for the coveted cell phone he'd found. Ariel's phone. The one she didn't want anyone to know she had.

It didn't matter. It didn't work. Maybe it was out of juice or paid minutes. He'd secretly tapped quick, illicit texts to the only phone numbers his failing mind could remember. Each time, the same message flashed on the screen: UNDELIVERABLE. TRY AGAIN LATER.

He didn't have "later." He wanted to throw the worthless phone against the wall, but it would have taken too much energy. Still, he wasn't sure where it had gone. Had it slipped from his fingers? If so, it was probably back in Ariel's pocket.

A faint voice came from a distance. He strained to make out the words that mingled with a constant buzz and competed with the rhythm of the rain.

It was Ariel. She was giving instructions or excuses. He couldn't distinguish between the two. Ariel…from Shakespeare. Prospero's Ariel. The old man had sent the sprite to cast spells and leave his enemies in a dreamlike state. That must be what was happening. Ariel had sent him out of the way.

He squinted. Tried to blink. Neither attempt opened his eyes, but he could see her down deep beneath the branches. A black spider crawled over her shoulder as if emerging from underneath the surface of her skin.

She wasn't who she claimed to be. He needed to wake up. He needed to tell someone. Anyone. But somehow, he knew it was already too late.

80

Libby couldn't believe how clear-eyed and energetic Ariel was this morning. She didn't think she had gotten any sleep. The drugs seemed to fuel her. Every time Libby woke up, Ariel was pacing the narrow aisle of the trailer, crouching to look out the windows as if she expected a creature to emerge from the dark. A creature in the form of David Ruben.

What did Ariel know that she wasn't sharing? Was her so-called contact letting her know that Ruben was close? And why wasn't she telling Libby? Was she afraid Libby would simply take off without her?

Now as they trudged through the snow, Libby measured Ariel's breathing by the raspy sound following her closely, walking in her footsteps like the indented snow would reduce her effort. She was breathing too hard. Was it the drugs? Or fear?

This started out as Ariel coming to Libby's rescue, providing her an escape vehicle. And that was exactly the way Libby viewed her, simply as a means to get her away from here. She figured as soon as they were far enough away, she'd ditch Ariel, then disappear.

That was then. Now that she recognized the damage Ruben had inflicted, Libby felt a nagging obligation to help Ariel escape, too. Whoever she texted last night seemed to send Ariel into the paranoid frenzy of pacing the trailer like a caged animal. Now, she tagged along behind Libby as if she was afraid to lose sight of her.

When they finally arrived at the shed, Libby noticed her own wave of relief wasn't shared by Ariel. The tension continued to hunch the blue parka around Ariel's shoulders like she was bracing against the cold wind. But the wind wasn't all that cold this morning. The sunlight streaked down through the broken branches, and it felt warm and wonderful.

In fact, Libby felt buoyed by the dripping snow. The crunch underfoot turned to a slush. All good signs that the melting would aid their escape.

Still, Ariel jerked at sounds behind them. Her head pivoted, watching and examining the trees surrounding them.

Libby asked for the keys and Ariel dug deep into her pocket before relinquishing the key fob. Libby climbed in behind the wheel and started the SUV while Ariel slid in on the other side. The air vents blasted on high, and Libby tapped down the cold. They could afford a few minutes to wait for the heater.

This was it. Finally!

Then, as she adjusted the seat and mirrors, her eyes skimmed across the dashboard and her heart skipped a beat. The fuel gauge was on empty.

"There's no gas!" She shifted to face Ariel.

"What?"

"How can the tank be almost empty?"

Ariel's eyes darted away, and she stared out the windshield. In a matter-of-fact casual tone, she said, "I guess it might have run down when I was out here."

"You ran it when you came to get your drugs?"

"For a while, yeah, I guess. It was frickin' cold. Can't we just drive someplace and get more?"

"I don't think we have enough to get anywhere."

Libby pushed the seat back and punched the engine off. She sat quietly, trying to keep the anger from turning into panic.

"I know where we can get some," Libby finally said. "But we'll have to walk to get it. Ted keeps extra containers in the barn."

"The people you stayed with?" Ariel's eyes were wide with disbelief. "We can't go back there."

"It doesn't matter if he's watching the house. We can slip through the trees and get in through the back door. No one will see us."

Libby's own suggestion made her sick to her stomach, but there was no other way. She couldn't have come this far, to only come this far. The snow might have slowed him down, but eventually, Ruben wouldn't sit and wait and watch. Eventually, he'd come looking for them. Their window for escape was closing quickly with every drip of melting snow.

81

Jason let Scout run and weave. He shoveled snow with his nose, biting at it, then shaking his entire head, spraying all of them. He leaped into drifts and sent snowbanks crumbling behind him. Hank only watched, staying by Brodie's side, apparently not interested in his buddy's wild antics.

Just when Jason thought the dog was ready to get serious, Scout launched himself into another pile of snow, bounding and plowing then galloping through melted stretches of meadow. His undercarriage was soaked and dripping in between strands of icicles.

Jason glanced back and saw Brodie stooped over something in the sludge. Maggie was at her side.

"Scout, come," Jason called as he circled back to the two women. The dog head-bumped his leg. A sign he wasn't ready to stop. But he didn't argue. He trotted beside his handler, coming to a halt when Jason did and staying put except to nudge a greeting at Hank.

"What is it?" Jason asked.

Brodie fished a small, bright yellow piece of cellophane out of the ice melt.

"It's a butterscotch candy wrapper." She held it up. "I put some in Ryder's daypack. Our grandmother used to have candy dishes filled with our favorites every time we visited. Ryder would crunch these." She smiled at the memory, then looked up, her face serious. "You're supposed to suck on them."

Jason sneaked a quick glance down at Scout. Should he be concerned his dog missed this? How much scent would be left on something Ryder unwrapped? And maybe unwrapped with gloves on.

Maggie squatted down about twenty feet away from where Brodie found the wrapper. She, however, didn't attempt to poke at whatever caught her attention. When she looked up, her eyes searched for Jason's. He didn't like what he saw.

He approached slowly, stepping carefully with eyes down. The snow had melted but left a thin glass layer of ice. More snow covered the smashed down blades of tall grass. He searched the spot where Maggie now pointed, and Jason could barely see the tiny drops of what looked like blood. Before he could say anything, Brodie was standing next to him.

No one said a word.

Scout barreled over and instead of stopping him, they all instinctively stepped back, letting the big dog investigate. In seconds, his whiskers twitched, his nose snorted over the area. He pawed the ice, breaking up the scent to get a better sniff.

Without paying attention to any of them, the dog circled with his head down, muzzle bobbing. Then he took off, slowly at first. He tested the air, then the ground. His walk turned into a trot, and Jason kept up with him. He didn't bother checking on the others. He didn't want to lose sight of Scout.

It didn't take long, and the dog skittered to a halt, nails clacking on the ice. He reared his head, nostrils flaring, his snout seesawing from side to side. He swooped down, grazing the ground. At one point, he poked his nose into a drift, snorting before pulling it out and shaking his head.

Jason stood back. With only a quick glance, he could see Maggie, Brodie and Hank kept their distance, but they were watching closely. When Scout looked up at him, Jason remained stock-still. Despite the chill in the air, his palms were sweaty. His pulse raced. There was nothing he could do about either, but he tried to keep a blank expression on his face.

Scout hesitated. He skimmed the ground again with his nose. Turned and sampled the air to his left. He stood and stared out at the vast stretch of the snow-covered cornfield in front of them. The stalks hadn't been harvested yet. The wind and snow had pushed them onto their sides, like fallen dominos. Instead of rows of corn with ditches between the rows, there were rolling humps of snow. It would be an obstacle course to trudge through the field now.

Jason's eyes searched for footprints, or maybe a path carved out before the heavier snow had fallen. He looked back to the treeline in the opposite direction. Maggie seemed convinced that the dense camouflage along the river might be where Ryder had holed up during the storm. Scout had been heading in that direction until they found the wrapper. And the blood.

With his head swinging back and forth, Scout headed out into the field. The melting snow snarled the cornstalks, some broken, most of them twisted and frozen. In places, Scout could walk on top of the ice-crusted drifts, but every once in a while, his leg poked down. For Jason, it was a matter of stomping his feet and lifting them back up. Slow but steady. He didn't want to doubt his dog, but he couldn't believe that Ryder would have chosen to come this way.

Then Jason remembered. Ryder and Grace were tracking Libby Holmes, someone who might not have wanted to be found. Ryder didn't choose. He followed his dog. Like Jason was doing right now. So, if Scout took him through this snow-crusted cornfield, that's where the trail was leading Scout.

Jason pulled up his collar and increased his pace to keep up with his dog. There were no trees to block the warm sunshine, but there was also nothing to stop the wind, which had kicked up. Just as he convinced himself that it would be a long slog, Scout stopped suddenly.

The dog circled, nose twitching, ears peeled back, gait ready and alert. Jason couldn't help thinking his dog had found something Jason hadn't asked him to find. Scout turned to look at him, waiting and watching while he circled the spot. He didn't take his eyes off his handler. When Jason drew close, he could see that the ground had been leveled here and appeared sunken. Cornstalks had been cleared in an area about ten feet squared. Just enough room to bury a body.

Then he heard the low-pitched whine. It was coming from his dog, and Jason's stomach did a freefall to his knees.

82

Ruben hadn't intended to cut the woman, but clearly she deserved it. He'd barely turned his back, and she raced to a bedroom down a long hall. She slammed the door in his face. Locked it. The door was solid, but Ruben had learned a long time ago how to kick out a doorknob lock. They were pathetic contraptions.

Nora Spencer was elbow-deep in one of the dresser drawers when he broke through. She wasn't able to find the weapon she or her husband kept underneath the folded T-shirts. Even as he rushed her, she continued to search. It wasn't until he slashed her arm that she stopped. That gave her a surprise, but instead of cowering, she grabbed one of the shirts and wrapped it tight around her arm. She was totally unprepared for his second slash that caught her shoulder and neck.

"Where's Libby?" he demanded.

Her eyes darted around him, but he was pleased to finally see shock and panic. She retreated to a corner. He watched as her body slid down the wall and crumbled into an uncomfortable sitting position.

"She's not here. She hasn't been here for days," she managed, pressing on the wound on her neck.

He shook his head.

Not possible. She had to be here. She was lying.

His time was up, and he was pleased when Shelby appeared in the doorway. He needed the interruption. They couldn't afford another mistake, and yet, here he was ready to gut the only person who might tell them where the hell Libby Holmes was.

"Tie her up," he told Shelby.

"Really? She's bleeding all over the place."

The woman was scrambling to wrap her wounds, a frenzy of fingers snatching and grabbing. Probably a worthless endeavor. There really was a lot of blood.

One thing she didn't do. Nora Spencer didn't ask who he was. She didn't ask why he was here or what he wanted with Libby. He stared at her for a moment. It was almost as if she had been expecting something like this. Or someone like him.

His cell phone pinged. He dug it out of the uniform's deep pocket.

A text message. Vanessa.

JUST SAW LH SNEAK IN THE BACK OF THE BARN.

He smiled. Grabbed one of the T-shirts from the drawer and wiped the knife blade. He handed Shelby a roll of duct tape and told her again to tie up the woman. "Or wait until she bleeds out. In the meantime, make sure she doesn't call anyone."

"What if she doesn't die?" Shelby asked.

"Then make sure she does. You know how to do that."

83

From the trees about half a mile away, Libby scanned the roads leading to the Spencers' property with her binoculars. There was rarely traffic, so a passing vehicle would stand out. When she saw the electric company's van in front of the house, she immediately felt a wave of relief. They could use the distraction to sneak in and out.

Finally, a break. She was still frustrated. It was already mid-morning, and they had left the trailer just as the sun was coming up. Drifts of snow and broken branches made her regular path an obstacle course. It didn't help matters that Ariel kept droning on about leaving the dog and handler behind without tying them up or locking them in.

"We could brace the door and burn the whole place down," Ariel had suggested.

Libby had stopped in her tracks to stare at her. "People would see the flames. The tank would explode."

"That would be so cool. No way he could survive."

"Did you hear me say that people would see the flames? They would send the fire department and cops."

"Oh yeah. But we'd be gone by then."

Libby had simply shaken her head and went back to high-stepping over the snow-covered debris. She tried to ignore Ariel muttering behind her about how they could have at least tied the guy up.

Fact was, Libby hated thinking about Ryder and his dog, Grace. They didn't deserve any of this. They were only trying to help. The guy didn't look good this morning. He'd been mumbling in his sleep, his body twitching and sweat dripping off his forehead. The little dog appeared inconsolable as she lay by his side. Every once in a while, she'd get up and sniff him especially under his nose as if checking for his breath.

Once when Ariel was outside, Libby thought she heard the dog crying. She looked up to find Grace staring at her. Something unexpected tugged at her, and she found herself trying to explain to the little dog, even saying out loud, "I didn't ask for either of you to come find me."

It was too late to do anything for him. Maybe the dog understood that part, because she cuddled back down closer to him, almost on top of him. He didn't move. Didn't shift or stir.

When they were on the road, Libby would call and tell someone. But she knew it was an empty offer. The guy might be dead by then.

Kill or be killed. Survival of the fittest.

She hated that Ruben's mantra still droned in her head. Time was slipping away even before the delay at the shed. And the delay was made longer by Ariel, who refused to leave the SUV. It was like talking a scared cat out of a tree. How did Ariel not see that running out of gas on a country road in the middle of the wide-open prairie would reduce them to sitting ducks?

Not for the first time, Libby wondered just how old Ariel really was. Sometimes she acted like a stubborn fifteen-year-old. Every teenager wanted to be older. They all fudged their ages, but Ariel had presented herself as older and more competent. She had the SUV. All the drugs. Everything implied she knew her way around.

Yet, whenever Libby caught a glimpse of Ariel's vulnerability, she suspected they were about the same age. The months had matured Libby beyond her eighteen years. But Ariel?

It didn't matter. They were both in the same boat now. They had a shared experience that changed them forever. The shared experience of David Ruben. And he would certainly kill them both if he caught them. They were stronger together.

At least that's what Libby kept telling herself until she had to talk Ariel out of the SUV. Of course, she could have left Ariel and went to collect the gasoline on her own, but she didn't trust that Ariel wouldn't drive off without her, only to get stranded and blow the one chance Libby had to escape. Besides, they needed more than one container of gasoline. If they were in this together, Ariel needed to get her act together and help.

Now, as Libby struggled with the old barn door, Ariel still didn't help. Libby put her shoulder to it and pulled with her whole body, hoping the rusted hinges didn't squeak. She opened it just enough for the two of them to squeeze through. Only then did she notice Ariel had the gun in her hand. She stopped from saying anything. She wouldn't risk the sound of their voices traveling in the cold air.

The scent of hay always amazed her. The Spencers hadn't had animals inside this old barn for years, and yet, the place still held those smells as if they were woven into the wooden walls and the dirt floor.

She could see through to the breezeway and noticed the black SUV parked there. The dog handler's. She'd seen him getting out of it how many evenings ago?

Her car was parked in the shed across the property. She was so stupid. If she had simply taken it, she could be hundreds of miles away. That's what caring about people got you. She didn't want to steal from Nora and look where it got her. Right back here, stealing containers of gasoline.

"The containers are back here," she whispered to Ariel as she circled around into one of the empty stables. "If we can grab three, that should be enough."

When she didn't respond, Libby turned to look over her shoulder. Ariel was staring at something outside the stable, but she held the gun down at her side.

"What is it?" Libby hissed. Her pulse kicked up. Her palms were sweaty as she grabbed the handles of the containers. She realized they were heavier than she expected. It wouldn't be easy to run with them.

Ariel hadn't moved.

Footsteps.

Libby's heart stopped. She held her breath. She wanted to gesture to Ariel to get down and move farther into the stable, but Ariel just stood there. She made no attempt to hide.

A bulky figure dressed in a navy blue coat and matching cap walked into view without hesitating or asking a single question. Libby's eyes darted back and forth, then she saw Ariel smile, and her heart stopped.

David Ruben removed the cap and smiled back. He glanced at Libby, but to Ariel he said, "Good work, Vanessa."

84

It was easy to follow the trail Libby and Ariel had left. In the sunshine, their deep footprints stood out in the otherwise pristine snow. Creed had swallowed a handful of Tylenol and pain pills. Maybe they were working, because he no longer felt the fire in his side. Mostly, he felt numb. His breathing was a bit ragged, and Grace kept popping her head out of the mesh carrier to check on him.

He was surprised to find the SUV still in the shed. More surprised to see both sets of footprints leading all the way back to the Spencers'. This time, Libby had taken a shortcut instead of the long winding maze she must have deliberately trekked that first day to make it difficult if anyone went looking for her.

Whatever the reason, Creed was grateful for the shortcut, despite it taking them through more trees, which meant more broken branches and debris to climb over.

At one point, he could see the two women ahead. He watched them sneak across a meadow and through the graveyard where the purple scarf still twirled in the wind. He saw them squeeze through the door at the back of the barn. Seconds later, he saw a man leave Nora's house, stop at the electrical company van parked in front, then casually walk all the way to the barn.

The Spencers didn't have livestock. Creed wondered if they'd care whether the electricity was on out there.

Creed slipped around to the front of the barn. Muffled voices came from deep in the back. He stopped at his Jeep, keeping the vehicle between him and the voices. As quietly as possible, he eased the back door open and slipped off the mesh carrier, releasing Grace into the cold Jeep. He put an index finger to his lips. Grace wasn't happy but wagged and settled down.

He reached under the driver's seat from the back and pulled a small revolver from its holster. The Ruger LCR fit nicely in the palm of his hand. He wasn't in the habit of carrying a weapon but brought it along on road trips. Finished, he gently closed the door, cringing at the click.

Now, he could feel the stitch in his side as he crouched down, listening for footsteps. A sudden wave of nausea sent him to the ground. He waited it out, leaning against the Jeep. When the feeling didn't totally recede, he decided on the ground would be a better approach. Slowly, he crawled on hands and knees toward the voices.

"Your name's Vanessa?" It was Libby.

"I told you Ariel was something I made up. Hey, you wanted to believe what you wanted to believe."

"I thought you were helping me. I thought you wanted to get away from him, too."

He could see a sliver of Libby's face. Ariel and the man had their backs to him. But Ariel was pointing the gun at Libby. He shook his head. He was right about her.

He pulled himself closer, using two wooden troughs to hide. About five feet stood between him and the man. The guy was shorter than Creed, but carried some bulk. Taking him down in his current condition would not be easy. He figured he had one try.

He carefully slipped the revolver into his right hand. He'd need his left hand to pull himself back up to his feet. Somehow he managed it, but not without notice. Libby saw him. He froze.

"Ariel, it's not too late," Libby said, keeping her eyes away from him. She was giving cover. "We can still escape."

Three quick steps and Creed grabbed the man he figured was Ruben. He wrapped his arm around the guy's thick neck and brought the revolver to his temple.

Ariel turned and jerked backward, almost losing her balance.

"What the hell?" Ruben sputtered, and Creed knew his grip was tight enough. But how long could he hold it?

"I told you we should have killed him," Ariel said to Libby like they were still in this together.

"Shoot him, Vanessa," Ruben spit out the command before Creed lifted and tightened his arm. "Do it now," he grunted.

"Drop the gun, Ariel," Creed told her. "You don't need this guy. You're strong without him. You kicked my ass all by yourself."

She squinted at him like she was trying to figure out if he was playing with her. Either that or she was taking aim.

If the man simply dropped his legs out from under him, Creed wouldn't be able to hold him up. He wasn't sure he could hold his grip much longer.

Ariel pointed the gun. Creed held her eyes. There was no passion in them. Not like when she tried to shoot Grace. Now she looked tired. Spent. Her eyes blank.

"Shoot him!" Ruben yelled at her.

Ariel shrugged, pointed the gun, and pulled the trigger.

Creed felt the man's head jerk, then a sting skidded over his shoulder. The man's body went limp against Creed's chest. He'd been holding him around the neck when the bullet hit Ruben in the forehead and blew a burning path across Creed's shoulder.

"Oh my God!" Libby said.

Creed couldn't hold the guy up any longer. Both of them slid to the ground. He pushed him off and staggered back to his feet.

"Is he dead?" Libby said, staring at Ruben's body, wide-eyed, with a trembling hand over her mouth.

Creed glanced back down at the man, then looked at Libby. He couldn't help thinking she expected him to get back up.

"You killed him," Libby said. "I can't believe you killed him."

"So are you coming with me?" Ariel asked.

"No, it's over," Libby told her.

"Don't fool yourself. It'll never be over."

"Listen, Ariel... Or Vanessa. We don't need to escape now."

"Okay. Suit yourself," Ariel told her. "There's only one real escape left." She pressed the barrel of the gun to her own temple.

"No, stop!" Libby yelled.

Creed moved in front of Ariel, trying to distract her with his hands up in surrender. His revolver dangled from his finger to show he wouldn't use it. "You don't need to do this."

In the back of his mind, he tried to remember her game of Russian roulette. She'd missed shooting Grace. An empty chamber. How many bullets had she put into the gun? Did she add more since then?

"Maybe you can finally be free," Ariel told Libby. "That's what I'm planning."

And she squeezed the trigger.

85

Maggie was on her cell phone with Pakula when she heard what sounded like a gunshot.

Jason and Brodie were packing up the Jeep. All of them were on edge since Scout's discovery. She might have dismissed the sound except both dogs jerked their heads in the direction it had come from. Out here, with nothing to compete with it and few buildings or trees to absorb it, the sound pierced through the cold air.

"Was that what I think it was?" Maggie looked at Jason.

"What's going on?" Pakula wanted to know.

She called him even as her hands were still shaking. She knew immediately what Scout had found. It was a grave in the middle of the cornfield. A fresh grave. The fact that it wasn't far from where they'd found Ryder's cell phone kicked up a renewed panic.

"I think we just heard a gunshot."

"Someone's shooting at you?"

"No, it's too far away."

"It might be a hunter," Pakula said, but she could tell from his tone that his own suggestion didn't convince him.

"It came from the direction of the Spencer place. It's less than a mile from here."

"Out in the country, it could be anything. Look, Maggie, you found something. It pushed your stress level to the brink, but there are all kinds of explanations."

The second gunshot made her jump. She saw it startled Jason and Brodie, who were putting the dogs up into the Jeep and securing them in their crates.

"I hope you're right," Maggie told Pakula while her gut said he was totally wrong. "Send an ambulance, too," Maggie added. "Just in case."

"Okay. But stay put. We'll be there in fifteen minutes."

"Pakula, I'm not staying put. Meet me at the Spencers." She hung up before he could argue. She tapped Nora's phone number, listened to the volley of unanswered rings, then kicked at the snow when the voice messaging prompt came on.

"Nora, it's Maggie O'Dell. Call me back. It's urgent."

She headed to the Jeep just as Jason looked over his shoulder and waved to her. He was ready to go. Seemed they all had the same idea.

As soon as they came around the curve and passed the last stand of trees, Maggie could see the Spencers' property. She pointed it out, but Jason had already noticed. He'd been careful on the snow-packed roads but speeded up at the sight of the farmhouse. The Jeep fishtailed, slinging them against their seatbelts. He slowed down, maneuvered back to the middle of the road. Frustrated, he slapped the steering wheel with his mechanical hand.

"You're doing a good job," Brodie said without a glance.

Maggie stared at her from the backseat. She couldn't believe how calm Brodie appeared. Back at the grave in the cornfield, Maggie expected Brodie to be upset. But true to her nature, she showed little emotion. A grimace. Her brow furrowed. The only thing she said was, "It's not Ryder."

Her denial sounded so certain it sparked hope in Maggie, until Maggie reminded herself that this young woman had survived for sixteen years by denying her reality. Was it only a coping mechanism?

The only vehicle parked outside of the house was a utility van. There was nothing else different. And yet, Maggie was unsnapping her holster and reaching for her weapon.

Before Jason put the Jeep in PARK, Maggie had her door open. She restrained herself from running to the house. The sunshine had transformed snow into icy sludge. There were two sets of footprints. The larger set had trudged from the van to the house and back. The smaller set hadn't left the house.

Jason and Brodie were behind her. She shook her head at them and put up a hand for them to stay back. She should have taken a minute to devise and share a plan. Instead, she gestured at the footprints, and Jason nodded. Then he turned around and headed to the van taking Brodie with him.

That's when Maggie noticed Brodie's gloved hand gripped around something. She recognized it was one of the canisters of bear spray Ryder often kept in a holster on his belt. Maggie felt an unexpected wave of relief. She didn't need to worry about these two. They weren't just tag-a-longs. Both of them could take care of themselves.

Maggie didn't knock on the door. She suspected it was unlocked. She gripped the doorknob in one hand and her service revolver in the other. One last glance over her shoulder, and she saw Jason and Brodie heading to the barn. It looked like they were following a set of footprints.

Maggie eased the front door open, then pushed it wide as she stayed back behind the doorjamb. A scuffling sound came from down the hallway. Just before she entered the house, she heard sirens in the distance.

The scuffling noise continued, and Maggie followed, keeping close to the walls. It was coming from the last door on the left. It was already open a crack. She kicked it to swing in and led with her weapon.

"Nora!"

The woman was soaked in blood. What looked like her own. Bloody fabric was tied around her neck and arm. She sat on the bed with a landline phone next to her. Across the room, a young woman was tied to a straight-back chair with duct tape.

"A man. He's in the barn," Nora told her. "Go. Please. I heard gunshots."

Maggie's pulse had already been racing. Now her heartbeat threatened to gallop out of her chest. She ran down the steps and got to the utility van when she skidded to a halt.

Jason was coming out of the barn's breezeway, his arm wrapped around and holding up Ryder. Brodie had Grace in her arms. Another young woman was close behind. When she saw Maggie, she trotted toward her, gesturing to the house.

"Nora?" she called out. "Is she okay?"

Maggie nodded. She didn't trust her voice. And now that Ryder had seen her and caught her eyes, she didn't want to take hers off of him.

The sirens were louder. Close.

The woman ran around Maggie and into the house. Maggie started across the yard, knees wobbling, pulse still racing. He was alive! Grace, too.

Finally, she stood in front of him, and despite the grimace of obvious pain, he smiled at her. His arm was looped around Jason's neck, and she knew he couldn't stand on his own.

She ruffled her hand over Grace's head. Then carefully she came in close on Ryder's other side. She tried not to think of the massive blood stained on his coat. One on his side. Another on his shoulder where a patch of the coat was gone.

Without a word, he raised his arm as much as possible, and she slipped underneath so he could drape it over her shoulder. She could hear his breathing and hated how labored it sounded. She looked up and his face was close enough that his bristled jaw brushed against her forehead.

A Clay County sheriff's SUV trailed Ted Spencer's truck. Behind was a rescue squad vehicle, a State Patrol vehicle and an unmarked SUV. Pakula had brought the cavalry with him.

86

Creed woke to an unfamiliar sound. Dim light cast shadows. He expected to see the cramped quarters of the trailer. His hand searched for Grace and found only bedsheets. Someone stirred, and his eyes darted to the silhouette sitting next to his bed.

"Brodie?"

"Grace is okay," his sister told him, scooting the chair closer. Of course, she knew Grace would be the first thing on his mind. "She's with Hank and Scout. Can I get you anything?"

He glanced around the hospital room, reacquainting himself with the space. He pointed to the tray on the other side of the bed. "Some water." His throat felt like sandpaper.

She didn't hesitate, moving with purpose as though she'd done this a few times. She handed him the oversized plastic jug, then she pulled the tray within reach.

He sipped while is other hand dropped to his side. The bandage was dry, no blood seeped through the thin hospital gown. He still wanted to peel it up. Take a look. Instead, he asked, "What day is it?"

"Monday. How do you feel?"

He thought about it before he answered. "Tired."

They asked him that too often. Although, he didn't really remember much. Snippets. Enough to know they were taking turns in the chair next to his bed. Brodie, Jason and Maggie. Hannah? No. If he'd seen Hannah, he would have known he was in terrible shape.

He tried to sit up, and a sting in his shoulder stopped him. Brodie pulled a remote from the side of the mattress. She pushed buttons and his bed started to move, adjusting. His fingers found another bandage.

"The bullet grazed you."

"Right."

This wasn't the first time they had to remind him. As foggy as his mind was, he wished he could forget Ariel pulling the trigger. And now he remembered Libby. She had visited him, too. Sat quietly beside the bed when he was mostly unconscious. But he could hear her. He could hear most of them. He just couldn't respond. It took too much effort.

He had listened to her confess. Apologize. And even cry.

"It's not your fault," he tried to tell her, but the words stayed in his head no matter how hard he tried to say them out loud. It was too hard to open his eyes.

The same thing had happened when Maggie sat beside him. It must have been the first night he was here. He could hear her talking to him. She was upset and worried. He wanted to tell her he was okay, but he was still in the barn. Visions of Ariel and Ruben imprinted on his mind. A movie reel played over those last moments. Ariel's eyes. The spark gone, replaced by a cold resolve. He should have grabbed the gun. He could have saved her.

Sometimes they don't want to be rescued.

Hannah's words.

Beside him, he heard Maggie apologizing that she had waited too long. He wanted to tell her he could take care of himself. But that wasn't what she was talking about. He tried to listen.

"I should have said it sooner. I love you, Ryder Creed."

The movie reel began again, a gunshot. Ruben's body jerking, but Creed grabbed onto her words and tried to hold on. He heard her laugh to herself, then tell him, "Real brave, huh? Finally professing my love when you're unconscious?"

The reel took over. Ariel's eyes, no longer fiery green. A second gunshot.

Later, when he did wake up, Maggie was gone. Jason had taken her place. This, Creed remembered because his young handler was quite blunt in his greeting: "You scared the hell out of us."

Now here with Brodie, he realized how lucky he was to have so many people who cared about him.

"When can I get out of here?" he asked.

"Well, since I'm your next of kin," Brodie said this with an exaggerated pronouncement of pride, "the doctor has been talking to me."

He smiled. "So, when can you bust me out of here?"

"You know you lost a lot of blood?"

He remembered the bags hanging alongside him and glanced up. They were clear now. "I can rest at home," he told her.

"But you know you won't."

"Seriously, when?" He met her eyes. Almost exactly a year ago, they were on opposite sides of a hospital bed back here in Nebraska.

"Jason's out making arrangements for us to trailer your Jeep, so we can all ride back together."

An unexpected wave of relief swept over him.

"Don't get so excited," Brodie noticed. "Hannah has already given us all kinds of instructions and limitations."

There was a knock on the door. Before either of them said anything, Maggie peeked in. "You're awake!"

"And he must feel better," Brodie told her. "He's asking when he can go home." She stood and gestured for Maggie to take her place. "The doctor usually does his rounds this time of morning. I'll see what he thinks."

"Because she's my next of kin," Creed said to Maggie.

Brodie rolled her eyes at him before she left. That was more in tune with the little sister he knew. But it impressed him. She was taking charge. She and Jason seemed to have everything under control. So why did Maggie still look so worried?

She touched his arm before she sat down.

"You look better," she said.

"And you're a sight for sore eyes." Other than the worry, she looked good. Really good. She wore a black turtleneck sweater and blue jeans. Her auburn hair was loose, wisps under her chin and almost to her shoulders. No ponytail and ball cap. No FBI gear.

He scratched at his bristled jaw and watched her. Sitting up in the bed made it easier to focus. "What a mess, huh?"

"It was definitely more than you bargained for."

"What happens now? I mean to Libby?"

"Pakula and I spent most of Saturday interviewing her and another girl who was with David Ruben." She sat back and released a long sigh. "Their stories are very similar and very strange."

"This guy Ruben wanted to kill Libby. She never told me why." He closed his eyes for a moment, tried to remember. "When I told her about the body pieces we found, it looked like she knew the victim."

"She did. Lucy just confirmed the identity. Kristen Darrow was Libby's co-worker at a hardware store. She was filling in for Libby when Ruben, Vanessa and Shelby came to kill her. Shelby said they made a mistake. They thought Kristen was Libby. They also murdered a waiter from a restaurant in Lincoln. Scout found his body in a shallow grave. It was in the middle of a cornfield not far from where Vanessa dumped your phone."

"Vanessa. She told us her name was Ariel," Creed said. It was a lot to take in. "She tricked Libby. Told her she was running away from Ruben, too."

"She was texting Ruben and Shelby the entire time she was with you two at the trailer. But they thought she was back in Lincoln waiting for them. Libby seems to think Vanessa had changed her mind and wanted to escape from Ruben, too. She said when they were in the SUV and realized they needed gasoline, Vanessa didn't want to go to the Spencers'. Libby claims she had to talk Vanessa into it."

Creed shook his head. Would he ever get that image out of his mind? The resolve in her eyes. Like she had no other choice.

"Ruben's done this before. Libby bailed on him when he killed a young woman in Virginia. He expected her to help cut up the body. She said she sneaked out. Disappeared. Ran and covered her tracks. Stopped when she got to Nebraska. Now that we have David Ruben's name and fingerprints, we might be able to see just how many times he's done this before."

"So, what happens to Libby?"

"She has a lot of questions to answer in Virginia. Pakula told her she can't leave Nebraska. He wants to charge her with abduction and assault of a member of his task force."

"That's not right. It was Ariel who stabbed me. Libby helped Grace and me find shelter. She's just a mixed-up kid."

"Well, this isn't something we can figure out over a couple of days. This is way bigger than any of us imagined. Lots more information to gather, jurisdictions to be considered. For instance, her name isn't Libby. Did you even know that?"

"No. I didn't." But he wasn't surprised.

Maggie leaned in, reached over, and took his hand. She smiled when she said, "Sometimes you drive me crazy. You want to rescue everyone."

"But you love me, anyway."

She cocked her head and raised her eyebrows.

"I heard what you said the other night."

Now she couldn't hide the blush that crawled up her neck, and he held her hand tight so she couldn't take it back.

"I love you, too."

Author's Note

Warning! There may be spoilers.

Readers often ask where I get my ideas. Sometimes I don't need to look further than my own backyard. When I say backyard, I mean my home state of Nebraska or my adopted state of Florida.

In April 2018, I was invited to speak at Hastings College Perkins Library in Hastings, Nebraska. This part of Nebraska is close to where I grew up. It's fertile river valley with cornfields and pastures where migrating Sandhill cranes stop to feed every spring and fall. The Platte River, Interstate 80 and the railroad tracks cut through here, almost parallel to each other, running from one end of the 430-mile-wide state to the other end. This area holds a special place in my heart and in my mind, so although I enjoy taking readers there, it's unsettling to use it to drop dead bodies even if it's based on real life.

Getting back to April 2018 and that invitation. I remember how warm and gorgeous that spring day was. I remember because after my talk, I stayed overnight and drove back to Omaha the next day...*in a snowstorm*. Yes, that's Nebraska weather.

At a reception before my talk, I had the opportunity to visit with Susan Franklin who is the director of the library, along with others. As with many receptions or dinners I attend, the subject turned to murder.

Susan's husband is the Clay County Sheriff. No, not Ted Spencer. The *real Clay County Sheriff,* Jeff Franklin. Six months earlier, Sheriff Franklin was part of a search party that found the remains of a missing Lincoln woman. Remains that were found in black plastic garbage bags dumped in roadside ditches and cornfields. Twenty-four-year-old Sydney Loofe had been murdered and dismembered.

At that time, many details of the case were still unknown. But what we did know was shocking and unsettling.

In June 2021, fifty-four-year-old Aubrey Trail was sentenced to death for the murder and dismemberment of Sydney Loofe. In November, his twenty-seven-year-old accomplice, Bailey Boswell, was sentenced to life.

Fallen Creed is not a true crime rendition of that case, but I do use some facsimile of the details, as I have done in many of my novels. What you might find unreal is probably real, because truth is always stranger than anything I can make up.

Once again, I want to thank all of you for welcoming these characters into your reading life. And I want you to know I'm already researching and working on *Midnight Creed*.

The biggest compliment a reader can give an author is to tell a friend. If you've enjoyed this book, please share it with a book lover. And thank you for reading my books.

Acknowledgments

As always, a big thank you to my friends: Sharon Car, Marlene Haney, Sharon Kator, Amee Rief, Leigh Ann Retelsdorf, Pat Heng, Doug and Linda Buck, Martin and Patti Bremmer, Dan Macke, Erica Spindler, Dr. Elvira Rios, Maricela and Jose Barajas, Luann Causey, and Christy Cotton.

Special Thanks to:

My publishing team: Deb Carlin, Linda and Doug Buck, and Joshua Mackey.

Dr. Enita Larson of Tender Care Animal Hospital in Gretna, Nebraska, for her veterinary expertise in helping me figure out injuries, drugs and all things dog. Enita has also generously allowed me to use a combination of her children's names for the character, Dr. Avelyn Parker.

My adopted Hastings family: Anne and Keith Brown and Ed Rief.

And Susan Franklin, Director of the Library at Hastings College Perkins Library for igniting a spark.

Thank you to all the librarians, book clubs, book bloggers and booksellers for mentioning and recommending my novels.

An extra special thanks to all my readers, VIR Club members, and Facebook friends. With so many wonderful novels available, I continue to be humbled and honored that you choose mine. Without you, I wouldn't have the opportunity to share my twisted tales.

Last, a huge thank you to my pack: Deb, Maggie, Huck and Finn. Duncan and Boomer, *we miss you two tremendously!*

CPSIA information can be obtained
at www.ICGtesting.com
Printed in the USA
LVHW031921230222
711734LV00001B/1/J